WITH ALL DESPATCH

This Richard Bolitho adventure follows in sequence PASSAGE TO MUTINY and immediately precedes FORM LINE OF BATTLE. It is spring 1792, and England is enjoying a troubled peace, but as the clouds of war begin to rise Richard Bolitho has no choice but to accept an appointment to the Nore, and the thankless task of recruiting for the fleet. In the process he comes up against a ruthless gang of smugglers. Treason is never far distant, murder commonplace, and when a king's ransom is in peril Bolitho is ordered to proceed "with all despatch" to recover it.

Books by Alexander Kent
in the Charnwood Library Series:

COLOURS ALOFT!
SLOOP OF WAR
TO GLORY WE STEER
COMMAND A KING'S SHIP
WITH ALL DESPATCH

ALEXANDER KENT

WITH ALL DESPATCH

Complete and Unabridged

CHARNWOOD
Leicester

First published in Great Britain in 1988 by
William Heinemann Ltd.,
London

First Charnwood Edition
published December 1989
by arrangement with
William Heinemann Ltd.,
London
and
G. P. Putnam's Sons,
New York

British Library CIP Data

Kent, Alexander, *1924–*
  With all despatch.—Large print ed.—
Charnwood library series
Rn: Douglas Reeman I. Title
823'.914[F]

ISBN 0-7089-8530-0

Published by
F. A. Thorpe (Publishing) Ltd.
Anstey, Leicestershire
Set by Rowland Phototypesetting Ltd.
Bury St. Edmunds, Suffolk
Printed and bound in Great Britain by
T. J. Press (Padstow) Ltd., Padstow, Cornwall

For my Dormouse,
with all my love

Therefore with courage bold, boys, let us
    venture;
Like noble hearts of gold now freely enter
Your names on board the fleet, all friends
    forsaking,
That we may soon complete this
    undertaking.

Anon

1

A King's Officer

REAR-ADMIRAL SIR MARCUS DREW stood to one side of a window and idly watched the comings and goings of people and carriages outside the Admiralty. Like the other windows in his spacious room it was tall and broad and enabled him to distinguish the passers-by from the more regular visitors who daily, hourly even, thronged the Admiralty corridors in search of employment. Captains, young and not so young, some of whose exploits had once brought pride and hope to an England at war. Seeing the most persistent applicants, and having his subordinates turn the majority away, took much of the admiral's time. He studied some puddles in the road left by a sudden shower. Now they shone like pale blue silk, reflecting the April sky while the clouds receded across London.

For this was spring 1792, another year of uncertainty and threats of danger from across the Channel. But you would not think as much to watch the ladies in their frivolous gowns and bright colours, with their carefree, posturing escorts.

Two years back, when news of the bloody revolution in France had hit London like a broadside, many had feared that the butchering, the murderous mobs and their guillotines would somehow spread their horror across the Straits of Dover. Others, naturally enough perhaps, had found comfort in their old enemy's terrible change of circumstances.

It might have been better if England had put aside the rules of war for once and attacked the French when they were caught in their own turmoil. But that had not even been considered.

Drew turned away, his day, and the thought of dining later on in St. James's with some whist afterwards, turned sour.

Their lordships of Admiralty expected miracles if they imagined that the fleet, left to rot in harbours and estuaries for most of the ten years since the American Revolution, could suddenly be rebuilt to anything approaching its old strength. Thousands of seamen and marines had been thrown on the beach, unwanted by a nation for which so many had died or been maimed in the King's name. Officers, too, left on half-pay if they were lucky, begging for berths in the merchant service, trying to return to the sea which had been their chosen life.

Rear-Admiral Drew was nevertheless content with his own lot. There was even the promise of a mistress on a permanent basis now that he had managed to obtain an appointment for her husband, a young captain, in the East Indies.

He stared hard at a huge painting on the opposite wall. It depicted Admiral Vernon's seventy-gun flagship *Burford* with all flags flying, her broadside battering a Spanish fortress, "The Iron Castle" at Porto Bello, at almost point-blank range. It was how the public, the romantics, liked to imagine a sea-fight, he thought. No blood, no terror of a surgeon's blade, just the majesty of battle.

He permitted himself a small smile. Vernon's fight

2

had been some half-century ago, but the ships had changed hardly at all since then. No, he decided, his appointment here at the Admiralty was better than any quarterdeck. He would have his mistress, and his elegant London rooms; he would, of course, need to be seen on Sundays in the family pew on his Hampshire estate, with his wife and children.

He returned to the ornate table and sat down without enthusiasm. His clerk had placed his papers in order. The clerk's duty was to interrupt him after a pre-arranged time during each interview. It never stopped.

Soon the French would declare war. One could hardly describe this uneasy pause on the fringe of the Terror as little better anyway. As always England would be unprepared. Ships and men. Ships and men.

His gaze fell on the name on the uppermost sheet. *Richard Bolitho Esquire*. It looked much-handled, and Drew wished that someone else could take his place today. Richard Bolitho, who had distinguished himself in the American Revolution, and a man luckier than most, had held two highly successful commands since, the last being the frigate *Tempest* in the Great South Sea. His final battle with the frigate *Narval* and supporting schooners had been legendary. The French *Narval* had been seized by the notorious pirate Tuke after an uprising within her own company. The *Bounty* mutiny, then the horrendous news from Paris had given Tuke mastery of the barely defended islands. Only Bolitho's command had stood between him and total control of the rich trade routes from the Indies.

And now Bolitho was here. He had, to all accounts, visited the Admiralty daily for several weeks. Like

3

most professional sea-officers Drew knew a great deal about Bolitho. About his old Cornish background, and his fight against the shame which had cost his family dearly. His only brother Hugh had deserted from the navy after killing a fellow officer in a duel, and had then gone to seek his fortune in America; even worse, as a lieutenant, then the captain of a Revolutionary prize frigate.

No amount of courage and honour could completely wipe that stain away. And he had paid his debt in full, Drew thought as he turned over the papers. Wounded to the point of death; and then after the fight with Tuke's *Narval* Bolitho had been struck down by fever. He had not been employed for two years and, if half of what Drew had heard in the elegant rooms around St. James's was true, he had nearly died many times during his fight to live.

Their lordships must have a reason for their change of heart, the admiral decided—although on the face of it, it would seem better if Bolitho turned down this appointment, and be damned to the consequences.

Drew's eyes sharpened as he recalled the rumour about Bolitho's attachment for a government official's lovely wife. She had died of fever and exposure after some desperate journey in an open boat. Drew covered the papers with a leather folder. *An official's lovely wife.* That would make a change from some of the dull, earnest faces he had seen across this table, with their high-sounding requests in the name of duty or the King, as the fancy took them.

He picked up a small brass bell and shook it impatiently. *Get it over with.* In the event of another war against France, without the standards of monarchy to guide the old enemy, there might be no

4

room for yesterday's heroes. Admiralty agents in Paris had reported seeing whole families of alleged gentle-folk being dragged through the streets to lie beneath the blade of Madame Guillotine: even the children were not spared.

Drew thought of his serene estate in Hampshire and suppressed a shudder. It could not, must not happen here.

The clerk opened the door, his eyes downcast like a well-rehearsed player.

"Captain Richard Bolitho, Sir Marcus!"

Drew gestured expressionlessly to a chair which faced the table. As a captain he had taught himself the art of inscrutability, just as he had learned the skill of missing nothing.

Richard Bolitho was thirty-five but looked younger. He was tall and of slim build, and Drew observed that his white-lapelled coat with the buttons and gold lace of a post-captain hung just a bit too loosely on his frame. As he sat in the chair, Drew could sense his tension in spite of his efforts to conceal it. A shaft of sunlight played across his face and hair, a loose lock above the right eye barely hiding the great scar received when he had been hacked down as a youthful lieutenant in charge of a watering party on some island or other. The hair was black, like a raven's wing, and the eyes which watched him steadily were grey, and reminded Drew of the Western Ocean.

Drew came straight to the point. "I am pleased to see you, Bolitho. You are something of an enigma, as well as one of England's heroes." The grey eyes did not blink and Drew felt off-balance. Irritated, too, that he and not Bolitho had been suddenly put on the defensive. After all, Bolitho was the one who had been begging for a ship—*any* ship.

He began again. "Are you feeling returned to fair health?"

"Well enough, Sir Marcus."

Drew relaxed again. He was in command. He had seen the sudden anxiety which even Bolitho's impassive gravity could not contain.

Drew continued, "You will know this tale of old, Bolitho. Too many captains, and not yet enough vessels to receive them. There are fleet transports and supply vessels, of course, but—"

Bolitho's eyes flashed. "I am a frigate captain, Sir Marcus—"

The admiral raised one hand so that the frilled lace spilled over his cuff.

He corrected, "*Were* a frigate captain, Bolitho." He saw the pain cross his face, the deeper lines which seemed to sharpen his cheekbones. The fever might still lurk there. He said smoothly, "And a fine one to all accounts."

Bolitho leaned forward, one hand grasping the hilt of his old sword so tightly that the knuckles were as white as bones.

"I am recovered, Sir Marcus. In God's name, I thought when I was admitted—"

Drew stood up and crossed to the window again. He had no sense of command or victory now. If anything he felt ashamed.

He said, "We need men, Bolitho. *Seamen*, those who can reef and steer, fight if need be."

He turned briefly and saw Bolitho staring down at the old sword. Another part of the story, he thought. It had been in the family for generations. Had been

6

intended for Bolitho's brother. His disgrace and treachery had killed their father as surely as any pistol ball.

"You are being appointed to the Nore. As captain-in-charge of some small craft." He waved his hand vaguely. "We have had many deserters from the Nore —they see smuggling as a more profitable profession. Some have even decamped to the Honourable East India Company, although I—"

Bolitho remarked coldly, "John Company has a record of treating its people like *men*, Sir Marcus, not as some will use them."

Drew turned and said sharply, "It is all I can offer. Their lordships believe you to be suitable for it. However—"

Bolitho stood up and held his sword tightly against his hip.

"I apologise, Sir Marcus. It is not of your doing."

Drew swallowed hard. "I *do* understand." He tried to change the subject. "You will have none of your past company with you from *Tempest*, of course. She came home well before you and is now in service with the Channel Fleet. *Tempest*, and before that the— *Unicorn*, I believe?"

Bolitho watched him in despair. *Doing his best.* He heard himself reply, "*Undine*, sir."

"Well, in any case—" It was almost over.

Bolitho said quietly, "I shall have my coxswain. He is enough."

Drew saw one of the gilt door-handles drop; the clerk was right on cue.

Bolitho added, "It is history now, maybe forgotten entirely. But one ship, *my* ship, was all His Britannic Majesty's navy had in the whole ocean to meet with and destroy Tuke." He turned and appeared to be studying the great painting, hearing perhaps the true sounds of war, feeling the pain of a ship under fire. He continued, "I fell that day. It was then that the fever rendered me helpless." He faced Drew again and smiled. The smile did not touch his grey eyes. "My coxswain killed Tuke. So you could say that he saved the islands all on his own—eh, Sir Marcus?"

Drew held out his hand. "I wish you well. My clerk will attend your orders. Be patient, Bolitho—England will need all her sailors soon." He frowned. "Does that amuse you, sir?"

Bolitho took his cocked hat from the hovering clerk.

"I was thinking of my late father, Captain James as he was to all who knew him. He once said much the same words to me."

"Oh, when was that?"

Bolitho withdrew, his mind already grappling with the brief outline of his commission.

"Before we lost America, sir."

Drew stared at the closed door, first with fury and then unwillingly, with a slow grin.

So it was true after all. The man and the legend were one.

Captain Richard Bolitho opened his eyes with a start of alarm, surprise too, that he had fallen into a doze as the carriage rolled steadily along a deeply rutted track.

He looked through a side window and saw the various shades of green, bushes and trees, all glistening and heavy from another rainfall. Springtime

8

in Kent, the Garden of England as it was called, but there seemed precious little sign of it.

He glanced at his companion, who was slumped awkwardly on the opposite seat. Bryan Ferguson, his steward, who did more than anyone to direct the affairs of the house and estate in Falmouth. He had lost an arm at the Battle of the Saintes. Like Allday, he had been a pressed man aboard Bolitho's ship *Phalarope*, and yet the events then had joined them together. Something unbreakable. He gave a sad smile. Few would guess that Ferguson had only one arm as he usually concealed the fact with his loose-fitting green coat. From one outthrust boot Bolitho saw the gleam of brass and guessed that Ferguson was carrying his favourite carriage pistol. *To be on the safe side*, as he put it.

God alone knew, the Kentish roads were deserted enough, perhaps too much so for highwaymen, foot-pads and the like.

Bolitho stretched and felt the ache in his bones. It was his constant dread that the fever might somehow return despite all that the surgeons had told him. He thought of the two years it had taken him to fight his way back to health, and finding the strength to relive it once again. Faces swam in misty memory, his sister Nancy, even her pompous husband the squire, "The King of Cornwall" as he had been dubbed locally.

And Ferguson's wife who was the housekeeper in the great grey home below Pendennis Castle where so many Bolithos had begun life, and had left to follow the sea. Some had never returned. But above all Bolitho remembered his coxswain, Allday. He had never seemed to sleep, had been constantly close by, to help in the struggle against fever, to fetch and

9

carry, and too often, Bolitho suspected, to accept his delirious bursts of anger.

Allday. Like an oak, a rock. Over the ten years since he had been brought aboard by the press gang in Cornwall their relationship had strengthened. Allday's deep understanding of the sea, his impudence when need be, had been like an anchor for Bolitho. A friend? That was too frail a description.

He could hear him now, talking with Old Matthew Corker the coachman, while Young Matthew occasionally joined in with his piping tones from the rear box. The boy was only fourteen, and the old coachman's grandson. He was the apple of his eye, and he had brought him up from a baby after his father had been lost at sea in one of the famous Falmouth packet-ships. Old Matthew had always hoped that the boy would eventually follow in his footsteps. He was getting on in years, and Bolitho knew he had missed the right road on several occasions on the long haul from Falmouth, where weeks ago this journey had had its beginning. The old man was more used to the local harbours and villages around Falmouth, and as he had followed the road to London, pausing at inn after inn to change horses and pick up fresh post-boys to ride them, he must have wondered when he would eventually step down from his box.

The coach had been Bolitho's idea. The thought of being taken ill on some part of the journey, perhaps on a crowded mail coach, had haunted him. This carriage was old, and had been built for his father. Well sprung, with the motion more like a boat on these roads than a vehicle, it was painted dark green, with the Bolitho crest on either door. The motto too,

For My Country's Freedom, picked out in gold scroll-work beneath.

He thought of that motion now as the carriage rolled past the endless bank of shining trees and fields. In his pocket were his written orders, the wording so familiar to him, and yet, in these circumstances, so barren.

To proceed to the Nore. The great River Medway, the towns which marked the miles to the Royal Dockyard at Chatham, and then on to the open sea.

To command what? As far as he could discover he was under the local control of a Commodore Ralph Hoblyn. His name at least was familiar, and he had served with distinction in the Americas before being badly wounded at the decisive battle of the Chesapeake in '81. Another misfit perhaps?

Ferguson yawned and then collected his wits.

"Must be close to Rochester, sir?"

Bolitho pulled his watch from his breeches and felt his jaw stiffen as he flicked open the guard. She had given him the watch to replace one lost in battle. Viola Raymond. He had tried to recapture her in his thoughts a million times. To hear her laugh, see the light dance in her eyes because of something he had said. Dear, lovely Viola. Sometimes in the night he would awake, sweating, calling her name, feeling her slip from his arms as she had on that terrible day in the open boat. She above all, who had shared the misery of what had appeared a hopeless passage under relentless sunlight, deprived of food and water with some of the men half-mad in their suffering. She had somehow sustained all of them, wearing his coat, bringing grins to their scorched faces and cracked lips. The Captain's Lady, they called her.

11

Then, on that final day, when Bolitho knew they had found *Tempest* again, she died without even a murmur. In the nightmares which had followed, one scene always stood out stark and terrible above all else. Allday, holding her slim body, and with a boat's anchor tied about her waist, lowering her into the sea. Her figure, white in the dark water, fading and fading, then nothing. But for Allday, he would have gone mad. He was still unable to think of her without pain.

He stared at the watch in his palm, the engraved inscription which he knew by heart.

> "Conquered, on a couch alone I lie
> Once in dream's conceit you came to me
> All dreams outstripped, if only thou wert
>   nigh—"

Bolitho said, "We shall see the Medway directly."

Something in the dullness of his voice made Ferguson watch him uneasily. The same dark, intelligent features, the eyes which could laugh or show compassion; and yet something was lost. Perhaps forever.

Old Matthew called out to the leading post-boy and the carriage came slowly to a halt where the road met with the gradient of a shallow hill.

Old Matthew disliked using post-boys when he had handled four horses, even six at a time, from the age of eighteen in the Bolitho service. But it was a long journey back to Falmouth, to the last inn where he would recover his own two pairs of chestnut horses, which he was said to love more than his wife.

Bolitho heard Allday mutter, "Not here, matey. I can manage without *his* blessing!"

The carriage moved forward again, the horses scraping their shoes on the damp ground and shaking their harness like sleigh bells.

Bolitho lowered a window and saw the reason for his coxswain's agitation.

They were at a dreary crossroads; a stone which read, *To London, thirty miles* shared the deserted place with a gibbet which swung slightly in the wet breeze.

A tattered, eyeless thing hung in irons. It was hard to believe it might have once lived and loved like other men. A felon, a common thief, now denied even the dignity of burial.

Bolitho climbed down from the carriage and stamped his feet to restore the circulation. He could smell salt from here, and beyond a ragged procession of trees he saw the great curving outline of the river. It looked flat and unmoving, more like pewter than water hurrying to join the sea.

Through the haze of distant rain he saw the old town of Rochester, the ruins of some ancient fortification near the water's edge. A town which, like many others around this part of Kent, lived off the navy and its great dockyard and victualling jetties. In times of war the townspeople listened at their locked doors when darkness fell, for fear of the hated press gangs which roamed the streets in search of men for the fleet. To begin with they combed the inns and lodging houses for prime seamen, but as the toll of war mounted, and every King's ship cried out for still more hands, the press gangs had to be content with anyone they could find. Ploughmen and boys, tailors and saddle-makers, none was spared.

Many a ship would be forced to put to sea with only a third of her company trained seamen. The remainder, punched, threatened, and chased by boatswain's mates with their "starters", learned the hard way. Many were killed or injured in the process long before their captain had to face an enemy. Falls from aloft in a screaming gale, bones broken by waves surging inboard to sweep a man against a tethered cannon, and those who merely vanished, lost overboard with nobody able to help, or even to hear them go.

And now, with the clouds of war rising above the Channel, the press gangs were out again. This time they were seeking deserters and unemployed seamen. The press would never be popular, but as yet there was no other way. England needed ships; the ships needed men. The equation had not altered in a hundred years.

Bolitho looked up and felt a shaft of watery sunlight touch his cheek. *A captain of his own ship.* Once an impossible dream, the greatest step anyone could make from wardroom to the privacy of the great cabin. But to gain it and then have it taken away was even harder to accept.

His new command consisted of three topsail cutters, fast, highly manoeuvrable craft similar to those used by the Revenue Service. One was completing a refit in the dockyard, and the others doubtless awaited his arrival with curiosity or displeasure, and probably wondered why their world was to be invaded by a post-captain.

Bolitho had studied all the available reports with

care, hoping to discover some glimmer of purpose which might make this appointment bearable. But it seemed as if in south-east England, and the Isle of Thanet in particular, the cat and the dog lived side by side. The revenue cutters hunted for smugglers, and the press gangs searched for unwilling recruits and deserters. The law-breakers, the smugglers who in many cases seemed better equipped and armed than their opposite numbers, seemed to do much as they pleased.

Bolitho remounted the coach and saw Allday watching him, his pigtail poking over the collar of his coxswain's blue jacket.

Their eyes met. "Back again, Cap'n. Frigate or no, 'tis still the sea. Where we belong."

Bolitho smiled up at him. "I shall hold to that, old friend."

Allday settled down again and watched the horses lean forward to take the strain.

He had seen the tightening of Bolitho's jaw. Like those other times when the deck had been raked with the enemy's iron, and men had fallen on every side. And when he had forced himself to accept that his lady had gone, fathoms deep, to a peace he had been too late to offer her. And like the times when they had ventured from the old grey house, for those first pitiful walks together after the fever had released its grip. A few yards at first, and the next day, then the next, until Bolitho had thrust him away, pleading with him to let him go the rest of the way unaided. Once he had fallen in sight of the headland where the sea surged endlessly amongst the rocks. He had cried out brokenly, "She would have liked it here, old friend!"

15

And together they had won the battle. The hardest one Allday had ever shared.

Now he was back, and God help anyone who tried to stand against him. Allday touched the heavy cutlass beneath his seat. *They'll have to take me first, and that's no error.*

But they had not even driven into the outskirts of Rochester before trouble showed itself.

Bolitho had his orders spread on his knees as the carriage gathered speed down another hill when he heard Allday exclaim, "On the road, by God—looks like a riot! Better turn back, Old Matthew!"

The coachman was yelling at the post-boys, and Bolitho thought he heard Allday groping for a loaded piece from the weapons box.

"Stay!" Bolitho swung out of the door and held on to the handrail. The carriage was almost broadside across the road, the horses steaming and agitated by the baying sound of voices.

Bolitho drew a small telescope from his coat and levelled it on the road. There was a surging crowd of people, some waving their arms and sticks, others laughing and drinking from flasks. Two of them were mounted. They were all men.

Allday laid a short, heavy-muzzled blunderbuss on the carriage roof and covered it with a piece of canvas from his seat.

He said harshly, "I don't like it, Cap'n. Looks like a hanging mob."

Ferguson was examining his small pistol and said, "I agree, sir. We should pull back. There must be a hundred of them heading this way." He did not sound

16

frightened. The Saintes had taught him to overcome fear. It was more like concern.

Bolitho held the small telescope steady. It was much easier with the carriage halted.

In the centre of the yelling crowd two figures, each with a halter tied around his neck, were being dragged along, their hands pinioned, their feet bare and bloodied on the rough road. One was naked to the waist, the other had had his shirt almost ripped from his back.

Ferguson said, "One of the mounted men, sir. He looks well dressed."

Bolitho had already noted that. A heavy, bearded man with a fine hat and a cloak lined with scarlet. If anything he was inciting the mob, his words lost in distance.

Allday said, "Maybe they've caught a pair of thieves, Cap'n." He glanced back up the hill as if still expecting to see the gibbet with its ragged skeleton.

Bolitho snapped, "Drive on!" He looked at Allday and saw his anxiety. "Those two *thieves* are wearing sea-officers' breeches."

Ferguson protested, "But, sir! That may be nothing to do with it!"

Bolitho looked steadily at Old Matthew. "When you are ready."

The carriage rolled on to the road again. Even above the rattle of wheels and hooves Bolitho could hear the rising din of angry voices as they bore down on the procession.

"Whoa, there!" Old Matthew's voice was harsh with anger. "Yew stand away from those horses, yew buggers!" Then the carriage halted.

Bolitho stepped down on to the road, aware of the

sudden silence, the staring faces, many flushed with drink, others gaping as if he had just appeared from hell.

He could feel Ferguson watching from the carriage window, his pistol just out of sight. Allday too, measuring the distance to jump to the ground. By then it might be too late.

It was Young Matthew who unknowingly broke the spell. He ran from behind the carriage to help quieten the lead horses. It was as if the mob did not exist.

The mounted man with the beard spurred his horse through the watching figures.

"What have we here, sir? A King's officer, no less." He made a mock bow in the saddle. "On his way to take charge of a fine ship at Chatham, no doubt! To protect us all from the Frenchies, eh, lads!"

There was some derisive laughter, but many of them were studying Bolitho more closely, as if they expected a trap of some kind.

Bolitho said shortly, "And what are *you* about, sir?" His hand dropped to his sword. "I'll not be asking twice!"

The bearded man stared past him. Looking for an escort? It was hard to tell.

But he grinned confidently as he replied, "I am the deputy sheriff of Rochester, *Captain*."

"That is something. Now we know each other's rank."

At that moment one of the captives threw himself to his knees and almost choked as someone dragged hard on the halter.

Bolitho recognised just one word. *Lieutenant*. It was enough.

18

"I would suggest you release these men at once. They are both sea-officers in the King's service."

He saw the significance of his words sink in, the way that some of the mob were attempting to drift away and dissociate themselves from the incident.

But the bearded man yelled, "And be damned to them *and* their bloody press gang, I say!" He stared around and showed his teeth as a few men shouted in support.

Like baying hounds at the kill, Bolitho thought.

He repeated, "Remove their ropes." He nodded to Young Matthew. "Do it, boy." He turned towards the deputy sheriff. "And you, sir, will dismount. *Now.*"

The half-naked lieutenant, his face and body cut and bruised from several blows, staggered to his feet.

"They *attacked* us, sir." He was almost incoherent. His companion was much younger, a midshipman probably. One sign of panic now, and the rioters might rush them. They would be swamped.

Bolitho watched the bearded man dismount. "Where are their uniforms?"

He stared at Bolitho, then burst out laughing. "You are a cool one, Captain—I'll give you that, for what it's worth!" His mood changed. "They came without asking consent from the mayor. We taught them a lesson." He tried to meet Bolitho's gaze and added thickly, "They'll not forget it!"

Bolitho waited. "Their uniforms?"

The man looked up at his mounted companion. "Tell him, Jack."

The other man shifted uneasily in his saddle. "We threw 'em into a pigpen." Nobody was laughing or jeering now.

19

Bolitho removed his hat and tossed it into the carriage.

"They are King's officers, sir."

"I know that, damn it. We were just doing it—"

"Then I suggest you insulted the King."

"What?" The deputy sheriff's eyes were bulging beneath his hat.

"You may take your choice. Draw that fine sword you wear so bravely." He touched the old hilt at his side. "I think this may be a good place for it." His voice hardened. "Nothing to say? No words for your courageous mob?"

A mist seemed to swirl across his eyes and for a moment he thought the fever had returned. Then he realised what it was. The same madness he had felt in the past when a battle had seemed hopeless and all but lost.

He had wanted to bluff this arrogant bully. Now he actually wanted him to take up the challenge, merely for the satisfaction of killing him. All the weeks of frustration, the anger and bitterness which had tested him throughout the months of despair, the waiting and pleading at the Admiralty, seemed to be joining in one terrible, vindictive force.

"I—I ask your pardon, Captain." It was almost a whisper.

Bolitho eyed him with contempt. "I do not pardon cowards." He glanced at the two shivering victims who had probably believed they were about to be hanged. "Get into the coach, gentlemen."

He turned once more to the deputy sheriff. "Your sword." He took it from him. The man seemed twice his size and yet his hand was shaking as if with a palsy.

Even now the crowd might regain its temper. But something had cooled them—the sight of his uniform, or the knowledge of their own guilt? He would never know. He drove the splendid blade beneath the rear box of the carriage, then leaned on it until it snapped like a carrot. Then he tossed it at the man's feet.

"Cowards have no use for fine steel, sir. Now be off with you."

The crowd parted and seemed to fade into the fields on either side of the road.

Bolitho climbed on to the step and looked up at his coachman. "A brave lad you have there, Matthew!"

Corker wiped his brow with a red handkerchief.

"By God, Cap'n, yew 'ad me fair scared just then!"

Allday gently eased the hammer of his blunderbuss. "You've made a bad enemy, Cap'n, an' that's no error."

Bolitho closed the door and said, "And so, by God, has he!"

Then, as the carriage gathered speed, he folded his arms and asked the rescued men gently, "Now tell me in your own time what happened."

As they spoke he had to clutch his arms tightly to his body to prevent them from shaking. It had been a near thing, although right from the beginning he had known instinctively that on such a deserted road the incident had been carefully planned for his benefit.

He smiled at his reflection in the rain-streaked glass. They had not been prepared for his reaction. *And neither was I.*

Ferguson saw the brief smile. For a few moments he had imagined everything was about to end. Now he saw that it was, for Bolitho, a beginning.

21

2

Trust

CAPTAIN RICHARD BOLITHO stood with his shoes sinking into the wet sand of a sloping foreshore and stared across the widening stretch of the River Medway. The sun was hard and bright, so that the trees on the opposite bank were almost lost in steaming haze. But it was without warmth, although to look at it was like being reminded of a tropical shore elsewhere. He moved his shoulders inside his coat and wondered if he would ever feel warm again. Even the breeze from the river was cool and damp.

He tried to push the thought aside. It was a typical spring day; he had to keep remembering that. *He* was the one at fault with his memory forever rooted in another place, another time.

Allday, standing a little apart and a few paces behind him on the slope, remarked casually, "Well, Cap'n, there's one of your brood right enough." He waited, gauging the mood as he had since their arrival here.

Bolitho nodded and shaded his eyes to study the little ship which lay above her own reflection beyond an islet and two shining sandbars. A topsail cutter, *Telemachus*, the one which had been undergoing a refit in the dockyard upriver from here.

Bolitho looked at her spartan outline, a vessel so different when under full sail. It was hard to realise

22

that these cutters, so small after a frigate, had for their size a bigger sail area than any other craft afloat. They might not be able to outrun all the rest, but in any sort of wind they could outmanoeuvre anything.

One of his brood. Allday, in spite of his forced casualness, must know what he was thinking. Comparing her with *Tempest*, the Great South Sea, everything. Without effort he could picture the three tall pyramids of pale, fair-weather canvas, reaching up to the cloudless blue sky. The deck seams sticking to your shoes as you moved about in search of a shadow while the horizon lay sharp and empty in all directions. A *real ship*. A thoroughbred. Yes, Allday would know and feel it too.

Bolitho had reported his arrival to the admiral in command at the Royal Dockyard, a distant but affable man, who had seemed to regard the affair on the road with the two bound and humiliated officers as little more than an irritation.

He had said, "The midshipman—well, he knew less than nothing, but the lieutenant in charge should have known better than to search premises and arrest suspected deserters without first informing the local authorities. I shall make my displeasure felt, of course, and I dare say that someone might be made to pay a fine, but—" He did not need to continue.

Bolitho had persisted, "I am told that the same thing happened at Rochester last year, sir. Then it was no less than the mayor who led a mob to attack the guardhouse where some pressed men were awaiting an escort."

The admiral had frowned. "That's true. The devil even fined our officers heavily before he would release them." He had become angry. "But they'll sing a different tune when the Frogs are on the rampage again. It will be *good old Jack Tar* then, sure enough, when these self-righteous hypocrites think that their rotten skins are in danger once more and they whimper for sailors to defend them!"

Bolitho had not yet met Commodore Hoblyn. The admiral had explained that he was visiting some local shipyards with a view to the Admiralty's purchasing small, handy craft, in the event of war. The admiral had commented wryly, "With letters of marque no doubt, to enlist a few more cutthroats for the King!"

Bolitho had left the admiral's house, his final words still in his ears. *"Don't take it so to heart, Bolitho. You have three fine cutters at your command. Use them as you will, within the scope of your orders."*

It was strange, Bolitho thought, that in the two days since his arrival here he had sensed more than once that every move he made was being watched. More so perhaps because of the efforts some had made to look away when he had passed. Which was why he had sent his carriage with a protesting Ferguson back to Falmouth. He had even arranged for the local dragoons to provide a small escort until they were out of Kent and on the road to London and beyond.

Bolitho looked down the slope again and saw the boy, Young Matthew, peering at the anchored cutter, barely able to stand still with his excitement.

That had been almost the hardest part, he thought. The boy had pleaded with his grandfather to be allowed to go with Bolitho as a servant, a groom, anything.

The old coachman had blown his nose and had said eventually, "Well, sir, 'e's more trouble underfoot than 'e knows. Mebbee a bit o' time with some discipline will tame the little puppy!" But his eyes had told another story, and his voice had been as heavy as his heart.

Allday murmured, "I'll go an' hail the vessel, Cap'n."

"Aye, do that." He watched Allday stride down the slope to join the boy at the water's edge. *Probably thinks I'm imagining all of it.* It was why Bolitho had asked for a carriage to bring him here, instead of joining the *Telemachus* in the dockyard. They knew too much already. He needed a few surprises of his own.

The other two cutters, named *Wakeful* and *Snapdragon*, were already lying downriver towards Sheerness, where the Medway surged out into the great estuary with the Thames.

Small ships perhaps, but each one a private world like every vessel in the fleet.

He shaded his eyes again. *Telemachus* was just a few inches short of seventy feet but had the surprisingly ample beam of twenty-four feet. Sturdily built with a rounded bow, the after part narrowed down to a typical mackerel-tail shape. How she shone above her own image, the cat's-paws rippling down her side, more like a toy than a ship-of-war. The sunlight played on her buff hull with its single, broad black wale below the gunports. But it was always the rig which took a sailor's attention, he decided. A single, large mainmast mounted forward of midships, made even taller by a tapering fidded topmast. She had a long, horizontal bowsprit and a boom to carry the huge loosefooted mainsail which protruded well beyond her low counter. With all her canvas furled

25

or brailed up to the topsail yard she looked unfinished. But once at sea . . .

Bolitho sighed. Enthusiasm, like warmth to his body, defied him.

Allday's powerful voice echoed across the water, and after a few seconds some faces appeared at the *Telemachus*'s bulwark. Bolitho wondered what the cutter's commander must think of this unorthodox arrival.

He saw a jolly-boat appear around the stern, the oars taking charge as a deceptively slow current carried them clear of the hull. There were already many more people on deck now. *A visitor, a break in the monotony.*

A fraction under seventy feet and yet she carried a complement of sixty souls. It was hard to accept that they could cram themselves into that hull and share it with guns, powder, shot and stores enough to sustain them, and still find room to breathe.

He saw Allday watching the jolly-boat with a critical eye.

"Well?"

Allday shrugged one massive shoulder. "*Looks* smart enough. Still—"

Then he glanced at the boy beside him and grinned. "Like a dog with two tails, he is."

"Can't think why. A safe bed, with nothing fiercer than horses to meet each day. In exchange for this—" He gestured towards the river and the other anchored men-of-war. "It might help him to make up his mind, I suppose." He sounded bitter.

Allday looked away. What was the point of piping up and offering an argument? Young Matthew worshipped Bolitho, just as his father had done after he had obtained a berth for him in the packet company. He shook his head. Later on perhaps. But right now the captain was all aback. Maybe they had only half-won the battle after all.

The boat lurched alongside a waterlogged piece of slipway and a young lieutenant splashed up towards Bolitho, his face astonished and full of apology.

He doffed his hat and stammered, "Lieutenant Triscott, sir. I am the senior in *Telemachus*." He stared round in disbelief. "I—I had no idea that you were expected, sir, otherwise—"

Bolitho touched his arm. "*Otherwise*, Mr. Triscott, you would have borrowed the admiral's barge and been planning a guard-of-honour for the occasion, am I right?" He looked again at the river. "This way is better." He gestured to the road. "There is a chest yonder. Be so good as to have it brought over."

The lieutenant stared at him blankly. "You are staying aboard, sir?"

"It was my intention." Bolitho's grey eyes settled on him and he added gently, "If you have no objection, that is?"

Allday hid a grin. Mr. Triscott was the senior. He had refrained from mentioning that apart from the commander he was the *only* commissioned lieutenant in the ship.

Bolitho watched the oars rising and falling, the way some of the seamen glanced quickly at him, then looked away when he saw them. Experienced, strong hands, every one.

He asked quietly, "You have a good company, Mr. Triscott?"

"Aye, sir. Most were volunteers. Fishermen and the like—" His voice trailed away.

Bolitho rested his chin on his sword hilt. Triscott was about nineteen at a guess. Another young hopeful, glad to serve in a lowly cutter rather than spend his most precious years on the beach.

He watched the tall, solitary mast rising to meet them. Well built, with her name in scrollwork across her counter. He noticed that a carved dolphin appeared to be supporting the name; a fine piece of craftsmanship, he thought.

Then he remembered. Telemachus, in legend, the son of Ulysses and Penelope, had been rescued from drowning by a dolphin.

The cutter might not be grand enough to warrant a proud figurehead in her bows, but the unknown carver had made certain she would be honoured all the same.

As they made for the chains Bolitho glanced at the closed ports. The sides were pierced for fourteen guns, originally only six-pounders, with a pair of swivels mounted aft by the tiller. But there were now two powerful carronades up forward, "smashers" as the Jacks called them, a match for any vessel which drifted under their lee in a fight.

There was a bark of commands as the boat hooked on to the chains and Bolitho stood up to seize a small ladder. At any other time he would have smiled. Standing in the boat he was almost level with the entry port itself, where a tall lieutenant with a press of figures behind him waited to receive the post-captain.

Small fragments stood out like pieces of a partly cleaned painting. The lieutenant's grim expression, Allday rising from a thwart in case Bolitho should slip or feel suddenly faint. And the boy, Young Matthew Corker, with his round, open face shining with sheer pleasure at this moment when his fourteen years had suddenly changed.

Calls shrilled and then Bolitho found himself on deck. As he raised his hat towards the narrow poop where the White Ensign streamed out to a lively breeze, he said shortly, "I am sorry for this lack of warning."

Lieutenant Jonas Paice bit back a retort and said gruffly, "I thought, sir, that is—"

He was a powerful man in every way. Bolitho knew the essentials about him. Paice was old for his rank, perhaps two years younger than himself, but had once commanded a collier-brig out of Sunderland before entering the King's service as a master's mate. It would be sufficient to begin with. Later, Bolitho intended to know the man behind every face in his small flotilla of three cutters.

"You imagined I might be spying on you."

Paice stared at him as if he could scarcely believe it. "I did think that you intended to take us unawares, sir."

"I am glad to hear it." Bolitho glanced over and beyond the silent figures. "The flag stands out well from Beacon Hill, Captain. May I suggest you up-anchor and get under way without fuss." He gave a slight smile. "I can assure you I will attempt not to get under your feet."

Paice tried again. "You'll find this somewhat different from a fifth-rate, sir. A wild animal if she's not handled to her liking."

Bolitho eyed him calmly. "I served in a cutter years ago. The *Avenger*. She was commanded by my brother."

A few seconds and he saw it all. The sudden prick

of memory, the mention of his brother. Something like relief too. As if Paice was glad to know, or think he knew, why Bolitho had been given this humble appointment. Perhaps it was even true. Dead or not, Hugh had made too many enemies to be forgotten, or his family forgiven.

He looked forward along the deck again. It was full of people. They probably resented his arrival. He said, "We will join *Wakeful* and *Snapdragon* without delay."

Paice stared at Allday and then at the boy as if he could still not accept what was happening.

"But, sir, don't you need any others to assist you?"

Bolitho watched some gulls rising to circle lazily around the mainmast truck, their wings straight and motionless.

"I have all I need, thank you." He grimaced at Allday. "I fear the first lesson has begun."

They all stared at Young Matthew. In those few minutes his face had changed to a startling green.

Paice cupped his hands. "Man the capstan! Prepare to break out the anchor! Mr. Hawkins, hands aloft, loose tops'l!"

Bolitho walked aft as the crowded figures surged into a new and ordered pattern. He half-listened to the squeal of blocks as men hauled on halliards and braces, while from the capstan the stamp of bare feet, accompanied by the groan of incoming cable, seemed to rouse him from a deep sleep.

Like hearing the sea calling to him without pain or mockery. He removed his hat and felt his hair ruffle in the damp air.

He recalled Rear-Admiral Drew's dry comment: "*Were* a frigate captain."

A last show of pride would have cost him even this. He would still be haunting the corridors of the Admiralty, or returning beaten and sick to the grey house at Falmouth.

Allday said, "I'll show you to the cabin, Cap'n." He chuckled. "Falmouth rabbits have more room!"

He watched as Bolitho groped his way to the small companion ladder near the tiller, beside which a master's mate and two helmsmen were already pointedly at their stations.

Once at sea things might seem better, he thought.

Allday heard the boy's desperate retching and hurried to find him. Once he paused, his chin just level with the deck coaming, and watched the land sway over as the anchor tore free from the ground.

Sails banged and thundered in confusion and he saw the great shadow of the boomed mainsail slice overhead like a banner.

They had done with the land. This was their place. It was enough.

Allday tapped on the cabin door and had to bend almost double to peer inside. He saw Bolitho with his back to the bulkhead, the three commanding officers of the anchored cutters packed in around the table as best they could.

"All secure, Cap'n." Just a brief exchange of glances, but Bolitho understood that he would be outside the door and make sure that nobody should hear what he was not intended to. Allday knew from experience. Little ships had the biggest ears, and Bolitho needed his first meeting to be undisturbed.

Before he withdrew, Allday also noticed that Bolitho was wearing his old seagoing coat, with its tarnished buttons, displaying no epaulettes on the shoulders. A coat stitched and repaired so many times that, when his sister Nancy had held it up with dismay and tried to persuade him to get rid of it, Allday had realised just how close he had become to the family.

Nancy had been helping to pack two chests for Bolitho's journey to London to plead for an appointment. During the long illness which they had shared in their various ways Allday had stood firm, knowing it was his strength which Bolitho depended on. But the mention of the coat, such a simple thing, had broken his defences, taken him by surprise like boarders in the night.

"No, Miss Nancy! Leave it be!" Then in a defeated voice, his eyes downcast, he had explained, "It was what the Captain's Lady wore in the boat, afore she—" He had been unable to go on.

Get rid of that coat? It would have to fall apart first.

The door closed and Bolitho glanced around at their various expressions.

On the short passage to this anchorage he had spoken to Paice as much as he could without interfering with his duties of ship-handling. A tall, powerful figure, but one who rarely raised his voice when passing commands. He did not seem to need it. The combined wardroom and cabin had no headroom at all, and only directly beneath the skylight was it possible to stand upright. But Paice had to stoop even there.

He was an excellent seaman, with a master's eye for wind and current. He seemed to *feel* the moods of his sturdy command even before the helmsmen

32

who stood on either side of the long tiller bar. But he was slow to answer questions; not resentful, more defensive. As if he searched for any possible criticism, not of himself but of his *Telemachus*.

It was a perfect evening after all. Pink clouds as dusk moved across the headland which sheltered the anchorage, with the first lamps already glittering like fireflies from the homes of Queenborough.

The three cutters might look as alike as peas in a pod to any watching landsmen, but Bolitho had already marked their small differences, no more apparent than right here with their commanders. Lieutenant Charles Queely of the *Wakeful* was in his mid-twenties, a dark-haired man with a hooked nose and deepset eyes, ever-alert like a falcon. The face of a scholar, a clergyman perhaps; only his speech and dress marked him as a sea-officer. He hailed from the Isle of Man, and came of generations of deepwater sailormen. Lieutenant Hector Vatass of the *Snapdragon* was a direct contrast. Fair-haired, with a homely face and blue eyes which would deceive no one. An English sailor from almost any century. He was twenty-five, and had served originally in a frigate until she was paid off.

Bolitho said, "Please light up your pipes if you wish; I am sure that *Telemachus* has a good store of tobacco!" They smiled politely but nobody moved. It was too soon for confidences.

Bolitho said, "*Snapdragon* will be entering the dockyard in a few days."

He saw Vatass start with surprise. "Er—yes, sir."

"Make the most of it. It seems likely that overhauls will soon be a thing of the past, and I need—no, I *want* this flotilla to be ready for anything."

33

Vatass prompted carefully, "Will it be war, sir?"

Before Bolitho could answer, Queely snapped disdainfully, "Never! The Frogs have their King and Queen in jail, but they'll let them out soon enough when their bloody-minded National Convention realise they need them!"

Bolitho said, "I disagree. I believe there *will* be war, and very soon. Ready or not, it is not unknown for a country to provoke a conflict if only to cover its own failings." His tone hardened. "And England is even less prepared!"

Paice folded his arms. "But where do we come into this, sir? We carry out patrols, stop and search some homebound vessels, and occasionally find deserters amongst their people. We also offer support to the revenue vessels when asked—"

Queely showed his teeth in a grin. "Which ain't too often!"

Paice glanced at the sealed skylight. "It's a mite hot, sir. Could I—"

Bolitho smiled. "I think not. I need to speak without others lending their attention."

He saw Paice's immediate, defensive frown and added bluntly, "We can trust nobody. Even the most loyal seaman would be hard put to resist a few pieces of gold for what he might see as harmless information."

Vatass said vaguely, "But what *do* we know, sir?"

Bolitho looked at each face in turn. "Smuggling is rife here, and on the Isle of Thanet in particular. From the Nore to the Downs the trade is barely checked, and there are insufficient revenue vessels to hunt them down." He placed his hand flat on the table and added, "From what I have seen and heard already, I am certain that smuggling is condoned, even aided, by some in authority. The lieutenant who was stripped and beaten when I found him on the London Road did not obey the letter of his orders. He *should* have applied for permission from the town before he raided houses and recaptured deserters, men who bad or not are desperately needed in the fleet." He saw his words sinking in. "Why did he not ask? Why instead did the young lieutenant choose to ignore his orders?" His hand rose and fell with a slap. "He knew that the very authority he looked to would probably warn or offer refuge to the deserters. I have no doubt that there are many such prime seamen earning their keep in the Trade as we sit right here."

Queely cleared his throat. "With respect, sir, we have tried in the past to seek out smugglers. Perhaps, and I mean no offence for I know you to be a gallant officer, being away for so long in the Indies and the Great South Sea, you have—" He hesitated as Bolitho's eyes settled on his.

Bolitho smiled grimly. "Lost touch? Is that what you meant?"

Paice said in his gruff voice, "I hate the scum too, sir. But we are so few against so many, and now that you have spoken out, I'll say my piece if I may."

Bolitho nodded. Their guard was down. He had spoken to them like companions, not as a senior officer to his subordinates. Low in rank maybe, but they were all captains, and had the right to be heard.

Paice said bluntly, "It's as Charles Queely says." He gave what might have been a cautious smile. "You being a Cornishman, sir, will know a lot about the Trade and those who live by it. But with respect, it's nothing compared to this coast. And as you said, sir,

35

it seems that there are more who commit these crimes outside the jails than in them!" The others nodded in agreement.

Vatass said, "The revenue officers are often outnumbered, and outgunned by the smugglers. Many of their captains are loath to work close inshore for fear of being wrecked and overrun, and ashore their riding-officers risk their lives when there is a big haul being unloaded. They strike terror into anyone who raises a hand against them. Informers are butchered like pigs. Even revenue men are not safe any more."

Bolitho asked, "What information do we receive?"

Paice said, "The coastguard help, so too the revenue officers *if* they get enough time."

Bolitho stood up and banged his head sharply on a beam. He looked at Paice and gave a rueful smile. "You are right. Quite different from a fifth-rate!" This time they all laughed.

It was a small beginning. He said, "It takes too long. They hold all the advantages. Send for dragoons, and the beach will have been emptied by the time a courier is able to raise the alarm."

Queely murmured angrily, "*If* the poor devil gets through without having his throat slit!"

Paice said, "And the buggers watch us at anchor, sir. Out there at this moment there'll be one of them, a fast horse nearby. We'd need fifty cutters and even then—"

Bolitho stood up again to lift one panel of the skylight and felt the salt air on his lips.

"Then we will mark them down at sea, gentlemen. It may stir up a hornet's nest, but we shall have results. The more trouble we can make for them, the

36

less interference we shall get with our work. We are ordered to obtain men for the fleet. That we shall do." His eyes flashed in the reflected sunset. "The navy has never taken second place to pirates. I see these smugglers as no different. We will press or prosecute, but first we will try a little action of our own."

He rapped on the door and eventually Young Matthew bowed into the cabin with a tray of goblets and wine.

Bolitho looked at Paice. "Some wine from my home in Falmouth, *not* smuggled, I trust!" *Telemachus* was after all Paice's command; it would be seen as highhanded to offer drinks when he was only a guest here. He glanced at the boy and saw that his face was almost back to normal, his cheeks like Devon apples again. But his gaze was glassy, and he had not been seen at all on the passage downriver. One of Allday's sworn-by remedies no doubt. A ship's biscuit ground up to a powder and soaked under a powerful measure of rum. Kill or cure, Allday claimed. Young Matthew was learning more every hour of the day.

Bolitho said, "I can rely on all of you to share this discussion with no one. When the time is ripe, we will hit them."

He lifted his goblet and thought he heard Allday leaning against the door.

"I give you a sentiment, gentlemen. To those across the Channel who are suffering terror which is not of their making, and to our three ships!" He saw Queely's surprised glance.

But they drank deeply, the air touched with rum as the boy refilled the goblets.

The wine was hock, chilled like a Cornish stream in the bilges. Young Matthew had often helped at table under Mrs. Ferguson's watchful eye; he was proving that he had forgotten nothing.

Bolitho raised his goblet again and said simply, "To His Majesty. Damnation to all his enemies!"

That night, while *Telemachus* swung easily to her anchor cable, Bolitho, cramped though he was in a small cot like any junior lieutenant, slept for the first time without the dream's torment. Near the cot, lying on a chest, was his old coat, the watch she had given him tucked carefully into a pocket.

A reminder, that with her memory he could never be alone.

3

Decoy

LIEUTENANT JONAS PAICE stood with his legs spread while he watched *Telemachus*'s long running bowsprit as it lifted, then lunged forward again like a lance. It was as if the cutter was taking on the endless ranks of short, steep waves in personal combat.

The sky overhead was streaked with tattered clouds, all hurrying before a strong north-easterly breeze which felt more like autumn than spring.

It would soon be dusk. Paice shifted his position but barely staggered as his command heeled even further over, her huge mainsail, like the jib and foresail, set tightly almost fore-and-aft as she butted up to windward. How she could sail, he thought, and to confirm his appreciation the helmsman yelled, "Full an' bye, sir! Nor' by West!" But for once the pleasure of sailing so close to the wind failed to sustain him. This was the third day of it, beating back and forth in a great triangle above the approaches to the northeast foreland of Kent.

Perhaps he should have held his tongue and waited for Captain Bolitho to grow tired of hunting smugglers and turn to an easier life in some shore-based headquarters like the commodore. Paice had received news from an old and trusted informant that there was to be a "run", somewhere along the shores of Deal, either last night or tonight. He had been surprised at Bolitho's interest and immediate reaction. He had sent *Telemachus* to sea, while he himself had sailed in Queely's *Wakeful*. Then at a pre-arranged rendezvous Bolitho had changed back to Paice's own command.

Bolitho was down below now studying the chart, comparing his notes with the ship's log. Like a man being driven to the limit, Paice thought. He heard the acting-master, Erasmus Chesshyre, giving some instructions to the two helmsmen, then his slithering footsteps as he joined him at the bulwark.

Together they watched the grey-green sea lifting almost to the rail, spurts of spray coming through the sealed gunports as she heeled right over to the wind.

Chesshyre was a master's mate, with one other to assist him. But his skill had distinguished him long ago, and with luck he would soon be promoted to sailing-master. And if there was to be war, he would be snatched away from *Telemachus* to watch over the sailing and pilotage of some lively frigate.

Paice frowned. If Bolitho failed to recover more deserters or find more men for the fleet, the cutters would be the first to lose their people. It was unfair, just as it was unavoidable. The cutters were like a navy within a navy. Their companies were mostly volunteers from inlets and villages where the fishing had died out, and skilled seamen had turned to the navy for work. Many of the men had known each other before signing on, so that discipline rarely needed harshness, and the qualities of leadership were respected far more than gold lace.

Chesshyre gauged his moment. "After tonight, sir—"

Paice turned towards him. "We shall continue until ordered otherwise."

Chesshyre nodded glumly. "Aye, aye, sir."

The deck fell beneath them and a deluge of spray from high over the side swamped the waterlogged jolly-boat which had been double-lashed at the beginning of the watch. Astern, far across the taffrail, was the Kentish coast, but it was completely shrouded in mist and spindrift and when night came it would be as black as a boot.

Paice urged, "Look at the weather, man. Do you not see it?"

Chesshyre shrugged, unconvinced. "I know, sir. A perfect night for a run. But out here we could ride past the buggers."

"Aye." Paice thought of Bolitho's elaborate care to disguise their movements, even changing ships so that any observer on the shore might pass the word that *Wakeful* was the cutter to be watched. He thought of young Vatass in *Snapdragon*, snug in the dockyard by now. He was well out of it.

Paice glanced around at the stooping figures of his men. Every one a seasoned sailor who did not have to be told when to splice a piece of frayed cordage, or take another turn on a halliard. They were even trusted to go ashore on the rare occasions when *Telemachus* was resting in harbour. That was more than could be said for most of their grander consorts in peace *or* war.

He squinted up at the topsail yard where two lookouts clung like bedraggled monkeys, the spray running from their bodies like rain. With her topsail tightly furled while she surged and lifted into the

41

teeth of the wind, *Telemachus* stood a fair chance of seeing another vessel before she was sighted herself.

They had barely sighted anything since putting to sea. It was as if local traders and the merchantmen from the Channel were unwilling to move any distance without the visible presence of a man-of-war. Across the water France lay like a mad beast, resting one moment, spitting blood the next. There were few honest seafarers prepared to run afoul of that.

Chesshyre persisted, "Everybody knows about the Trade in Kent, sir." He faltered as Paice's eyes fastened on him and he could have bitten out his tongue for speaking.

When he had first joined *Telemachus* he had wondered why the master of a collier-brig, to all intents a free agent, would choose to enlist in the navy as a lowly master's mate. When Chesshyre had been accepted by *Telemachus*'s tight little company he had slowly learned the truth about this tall, powerful lieutenant.

Paice had been married a short time to a girl he had known for several years. On her way home from visiting her father and mother she had been horrified to see a dozen or more known smugglers attacking a solitary revenue officer. A crowd of people, too afraid or too indifferent to interfere, had watched them beating the man to death. Paice's wife had called the onlookers to assist, and when they had hung back she had tried to drag one of the smugglers off the revenue officer who was by then dead.

One smuggler had raised his pistol and shot her down. A savage warning to all those who watched, far more chilling than the death of a revenue man.

"I—I'm fair sorry, sir." Chesshyre looked away. "I was forgetting—"

"Well, *don't!* Not now—not ever, while you serve in my ship!"

There was a step on the companion ladder and Bolitho climbed up beside them. He was hatless, and his black hair rippled in the wind as he studied the hard press of canvas, the sea boiling along the leeside. Like his brother's cutter *Avenger*, so long, long ago.

The acting-master touched his forehead. "I'll attend the helm, sir."

He made to move aft but Bolitho asked, "You are from Kent?"

"Aye, sir." Chesshyre watched him warily, Paice's heated outburst momentarily forgotten. "Maidstone, sir."

Bolitho nodded. His voice, the easy Kentish accent, had so reminded him of Thomas Herrick, who had been his first lieutenant; his firm friend. Even Chesshyre's eyes, clear blue, were much the same. So many times he had watched Herrick's eyes change. Stubbornness, concern, hurt; and Bolitho had been the cause of most of it. They had parted when *Tempest* had set sail for England after that last savage battle with Tuke's ships. Bolitho, half-dead from fever, had followed at a more leisurely pace in a big Indiaman. Where was Herrick now, he wondered? At sea somewhere. Remembering what they had done and suffered together.

He realised that he was staring at the acting-master. "You reminded me of a friend. Did you ever meet a Lieutenant Herrick?"

For a brief moment Bolitho saw the man's caution

change to warmth. Then he shook his head. "No, sir." The contact was broken.

Paice said, "We can come about in two hours, sir." He glanced at the sky. "After that, it will be too dark to see anything."

Bolitho glanced at his strong profile. "You think me mistaken?" He did not wait for a reply; it was wrong to make Paice commit himself. He smiled tightly. "Mad too, probably."

Paice watched him although his mind was still grappling with his inner pain. Would he ever forget how she had died?

He said, "There are some who may ask why you care so much, sir."

Bolitho wiped his face with the sleeve of his old coat. "I realise that smuggling is a great temptation and will remain so. You can hang for it, but in some parishes you can dangle from the gibbet for stealing a chicken, so where's the comparison?" He shivered as spray pattered against his shoulders. "The navy must have men. Smugglers or not, a firm hand will soon break them to our ways!"

During his brief passage in *Wakeful* her commander with the falcon's features had told him about Paice's wife. Bolitho had heard Paice's voice as he had left the cabin, but had only guessed the content.

He said, "Like me, you grieve. Some think it leaves you vulnerable." He gripped a swivel gun on the bulwark as the deck slanted down again and added sharply, "But I believe it makes you—care, as you put it."

Paice swallowed hard. It was like being stripped

and made defenceless. How did he know? What memory did *he* carry to distress him?

He said gruffly, "Never fear, sir, I'm with you—"

Bolitho touched his arm and turned away. He seemed to hear the admiral's words in his brain. *Use them as you will within the scope of your orders.* Spoken words, not written ones. Valueless if things went wrong.

He said, "You may live to regret that, Mr. Paice, but I thank you."

Allday appeared from the companionway, a tankard held carefully in one fist while he waited for the deck to rear upright again.

He held it out to Bolitho, his eyes swiftly examining the men nearby, Chesshyre the master, with his mate Dench who was shortly taking over the watch. Luke Hawkins the boatswain, a great cask of a man. It was hard to see him at the tender age of seven when he had been packed off to sea as a ship's boy. *Telemachus* carried no purser as she did not rate one. The clerk, Percivale Godsalve, a reedy little man whose pale features had defied all the months at sea, did duty as purser too. Evans, a tough gunner's mate, had said to Allday, "No passengers in this ship, matey! We all does a bit of everythin'!"

Allday knew most of what was said about Bolitho being aboard. They saw him as a threat, something from the *other navy* that only a few of the petty officers knew anything about.

Deep in his heart Allday thought Bolitho, a man he had nearly died for and would do so again without a second's thought, was wrong to press on with this task. He should take things quietly—hell's teeth, he had earned it ten times over. Let others take the risks

45

and the blame, which, unlike prize money, were equally shared out.

Allday would never have returned to the sea but for Bolitho. But Bolitho loved the navy; it was his whole life. Only once had Allday seen that love waver, but now the Captain's lady was gone. Only the sea was left.

He watched Bolitho swallow the steaming coffee gratefully. They had seen so much. Allday stared out at the frothing yellow wave crests. They'd get another ship together. If only . . .

"Deck there! *Sail ho!*"

Paice stared up at the two waving lookouts, his face creased with disbelief.

The voice pealed down again. "Fine on the lee quarter, sir!"

Bolitho saw the instant change in the tall lieutenant as he snatched a telescope from its rack and swung himself on to the weather ratlines with the agility of a cat.

Bolitho tried to contain the shiver of excitement as it coursed through him like icy water.

It was probably nothing, or a ship, alone and running for shelter before darkness closed in. The Channel was a treacherous place on any night, but in these times it was a blessing to hear the anchor safely down.

Bolitho recalled his own desperate efforts to go aloft without the awful fear of it. Many were the times he had had to force himself up the madly shaking ratlines, clinging to a stay and trying not to peer down at the deck and the creaming water far below.

Paice had no such qualms. But he was soon clambering on to the deck again, and his face, masklike in the dying sunlight, was composed by the time he had strode aft.

He said, "She's the *Loyal Chieftain*, sir. A Deal vessel. Know her well." He spat out the words. "*Loyal*— the last word I'd use for that pig!"

There was no time for further discussion. At any moment the other vessel would see *Telemachus*'s sails.

Bolitho said, "Bring her about, Mr. Paice. As fast as you will."

"Hands aloft and loose tops'l!"

"Stand by to come about!"

Feet padded over the streaming planks, and more figures crowded up from between decks as the calls shrilled through the hull.

"Let go an' haul!" Hawkins's thick voice made the men lie back on the braces and halliards to bring the boom over.

"Helm a-lee!"

Bolitho gripped a stanchion and watched the sails flapping like insane banners as the rudder was heaved over, the helmsmen backed up by two more hands as the ship fought against sea and wind. Then all at once they were round, and running with the breakers, the spray bursting beneath the stem so that they seemed to be flying.

Paice mopped his face and shouted above the thunder of more canvas as the topsail filled and hardened from its yard like a breastplate. "'Nother minute and the bugger would have slipped across our stern!" He saw Bolitho's expression and said, "Her master is Henry Delaval, a known smuggler, but he's never been taken with any evidence, God rot him! His vessel's a brig, well found and armed." Here was

47

the bitterness again. "That's no crime either, *they* say!"

"There she is, sir, larboard bow!" It was Lieutenant Triscott, who had been preparing to take over the watch, and had run on deck with some butter and crumbs sticking to his lapel.

Paice thrust his big hands behind him. His eyes spoke volumes, but all he said was, *"Got you!"*

Bolitho wedged his hip against the companion hatch in an attempt to keep steady enough to train a telescope on the other vessel.

Above the leaping wave crests, broken here and there into ragged spectres by stronger gusts of wind, he saw the brig's topsails, now copper-coloured against the evening sky. Her hull was still hidden and he guessed that Paice had recognised her only after climbing aloft. Never before had he seen Paice show so much emotion, hatred even, and he guessed that the memory of his young wife was linked in some way with the man Delaval.

Hawkins bellowed, "She's settin' 'er forecourse, sir!"

Bolitho nodded, oblivious to the spray which was soaking him from head to toe. The brig was using the wind to full advantage and was already standing away, her two masts seeming to draw closer together above the tumbling water.

Paice glanced at him, his eyes in shadow. "Sir?" He could barely conceal his eagerness.

Bolitho lowered the glass. "Aye, give chase." He was about to add that the brig's master might have taken *Telemachus* for a French privateer, and was heading away to safety. But seeing Paice's intent expression killed the thought instantly. Paice knew

48

this man, so Delaval would know him and his cutter equally well.

"Alter course, Mr. Chesshyre! Let her bear up two points and steer South-West by West!"

As the men ran to braces to haul the long boom further out above the water, Dench the master's mate was already crouching by the compass box, his hair plastered to his forehead while the rudder went over.

One helmsman lost his footing on the tilting deck, but another took his place at the long tiller bar, his bare toes digging for a grip.

"Steady she goes, sir! Sou'-West by West!"

"Damn his eyes, he's making a run for it, Cap'n." Allday seemed the calmest one on the deck as he watched the other vessel's blurred topsails with apparently little more than professional interest.

Bolitho knew him too well to be deceived. *Like me, perhaps?* Holding it all inside, showing just a mask to others who looked to you for hope or fear.

Paice heard Allday's comment and snapped, "God, I'll not lose the bastard now!"

Bolitho said, "Put a ball across her, Mr. Paice."

Paice looked at him, unused to anyone's methods but his own.

"We're supposed to fire well clear, sir, as a signal."

Bolitho smiled briefly. "As close as your gunner can arrange it. In a long chase we might lose her when the night finds us, eh?" From the corner of his eye he saw one of the seamen grinning and nudging his companion. Was it because they thought him mad, or because they were beginning to discover their true role as a man-of-war, albeit a small one?

George Davy the gunner supervised the foremost six-pounder personally, one horny hand on the gun-captain's shoulder while the crew worked with their handspikes and tackles until he seemed satisfied.

Paice cupped his hands. "Load the larboard smasher as well, Mr. Davy."

Bolitho balled his hands into fists to discipline his shivering limbs. Paice was thinking for himself. If the brig was prepared to fight, even if she tried merely to cripple *Telemachus*'s rigging and sails, it was sensible to have the deadly carronade loaded and ready to rake her poop.

"Fire!"

Bolitho had been too long away from the sea, longer still from the harsh roar of a frigate's broadside; the crack of a six-pounder was sharp enough to bring pain to his ears.

Allday muttered, "Bloody little popgun!"

Bolitho saw the boy Matthew Corker kneeling near the aftermost gun, his hands gripping a bucket of sand as he stared at the scene on deck where the six-pounder's crew were already tamping home another ball, each man very aware of the post-captain beside Paice.

Bolitho snapped, "Keep down, boy!"

The youth peered up at him. No trace of fear. But it was because he knew nothing. Nor would he, Bolitho decided grimly.

There was far too much spray to see the fall of shot, but the angle of the *Loyal Chieftain*'s masts and topsails was unchanged, and she was moving fast with the soldier's wind right under her coat-tails.

Paice looked at Bolitho. "Into her this time, if you please."

The six-pounder hurled itself inboard on its tackles and as Bolitho lifted his glass he was in time to see

50

the brig's main topsail jerk, then split from head to foot. The wind greedily explored the ball's puncture and reduced the whole sail to wildly flapping ribbons.

Someone gave a derisive cheer then Hawkins shouted, "She's puttin' about, sir!"

Paice retorted, "Even if she is heaving-to, Mr. Triscott, I want her under our lee, do you understand?" Urgency had set an edge to his voice.

Bolitho stood aside as Paice strode this way and that, his tall frame moving with remarkable ease amongst his men and the litter of cordage and tackles.

"Load the larboard battery, Mr. Triscott, but do not run out!" He pivoted round. "Shorten sail, Mr. Hawkins! Take in the fores'l!" His eyes moved across Bolitho and he exclaimed, "If that suits, sir?"

The brig had taken in her forecourse, and under topsail and jib only was floundering round into the wind. She was much closer now, less than a cable away, her masts and rigging glowing warmly in the copper light.

There were not many hands on her yards, or indeed working about the deck. But she was under control, and as *Telemachus*'s gun-captains faced aft and held up their fists, Bolitho knew that the brig could be swept with grape and canister before she could hit back.

Paice loosened the hanger at his side and said, "Lower the jolly-boat. Your best oarsmen, Mr. Hawkins. It'll be a hard pull in this sea!"

Bolitho said, "I would like to come with you." Their eyes met and held. "You *are* going yourself, I take it?"

Paice nodded. "The first lieutenant can manage, sir."

51

"It is not what I asked."

Paice shrugged. "It is my right, sir."

"Very well." He could feel the lieutenant's strength like something physical, barely controlled. He added, "It were better I am present. For both our sakes, eh?"

The calmness of his tone seemed to stay Paice's emotion, although Bolitho felt anything but calm. He knew that if this man Delaval was caught on board the brig with contraband Paice would likely kill him. Equally, as senior officer, he would be seen as having condoned a murder by a subordinate.

Bolitho watched the boat being swayed up and over the side. The brig's people might attack the boarders as soon as they climbed aboard and still make off in escape.

Bolitho said, "Mr. Triscott, if they attempt to make sail, fire into them." His voice hardened. "No matter what you may see."

Triscott stared from him to his commander. He looked suddenly very young and vulnerable.

He stammered, "Aye, aye, sir, if you so order."

Paice said sharply, "He does, and I am in agreement!"

The jolly-boat was manhandled alongside and once again Bolitho was impressed by the quality of the seamanship, the scarcity of spoken orders, let alone the use of a rope's end. He found himself wondering if all cutters were like this one. He glanced quickly at Paice as he scrambled down beside him in the sternsheets. Or was it just because of this impassive, haunted lieutenant?

"Out oars! Give way all!"

The sound of Allday's resonant voice brought a few

stares from the boat's crew. But Allday had no intention of being left behind as a helpless onlooker. He was doing what he knew best. Nor would Bolitho deny him after all he had gone through.

The boat lifted and plunged wildly until Allday had steered her clear of the choppy water around the cutter's quarter. Bolitho saw the White Ensign streaming out from the gaff above his head and thought suddenly of Hugh, his dead brother. What a waste, and for no purpose. He turned to watch the brig's tapering topgallant masts spiralling against the sky and found that he was gripping the old sword closely against his thigh. Hugh had lost his chance to wear it, and now, perhaps within minutes, there would be no one left to carry it with pride. There were faces along the bulwark now, strangely silent, with no sign of defiance or fear.

Paice lifted a speaking trumpet. "We are boarding! Do not resist!"

Allday said beneath his breath, "It'll be now or never. They could make a bloody gruel of us with one whiff of canister, an' that's no error!" He pushed it from his thoughts and shouted, "Bowman! Lively there! Stand by!" He eased the tiller bar and saw the bowman's grapnel soar into the brig's main chains, clatter down and hook on.

"Boat your oars!" Allday supported Bolitho's arm as he crouched ready to leave the pitching boat. He hissed, "Right with you, Cap'n!" He gave a throaty chuckle. "Old times!"

Then they were taking their turn to leap from the boat and scramble their way through the small entry port.

Bolitho glanced quickly around. He saw the vessel's

53

master, a short, neat figure in a fine blue coat standing almost indifferently by the wheel. He knew it was Delaval even before Paice opened his mouth.

Paice had his hanger drawn and strode aft, his voice carrying easily above the slap of canvas and the sea's protests beyond the bulwarks. "Stand where you are!"

Delaval retorted, "So it's you. By what *right*—"

Paice gestured to a seaman by the wheel and the cutlass he had seen in his belt clattered to the deck.

"In the King's name, so hold your noise." He nodded his head to the petty officer who had accompanied the boat and the man hurried away, calling names, ignoring the brig's sailors as if they were not there.

Paice said, "I intend to search this vessel. After that—"

"You are wasting your time. More important, you are wasting mine." His dark eyes moved suddenly to Bolitho, taking in the plain blue coat, the outdated sword which was still sheathed at Bolitho's side. Delaval said, "I will make the strongest protest. I was going about my lawful business."

Bolitho asked, "What cargo?"

Delaval's eyes flashed. There could have been triumph there. "None. I am in ballast, as your worthy boarding party will soon discover." He did not attempt to hide the sneer in his voice. "I intended to sail for Amsterdam. You will see from the log that I have regular transactions with agents there."

Bolitho could sense Paice's anger and impatience. He asked quietly, "And you changed your mind?"

"The weather, news of more trouble in France, several things."

The petty officer returned but stood so that Delaval could not see his face. He swallowed hard. "Nuthin', sir. In full ballast." He seemed almost afraid of his discovery.

Delaval said, "I told you." He lifted his chin and stared at Paice. "You will pay for this." His arm shot out and he pointed to an inert shape covered by a piece of canvas. He continued, his voice almost caressing, "You fired on my ship—"

Paice snapped, "You tried to run, you refused to heave-to! Don't pretend with me, damn you!"

A seaman pulled the canvas aside and Bolitho saw it was a man in sailor's clothing. Beside him lay a heavy block, its sheaves sticky with blood and hair. The man's forehead and skull had been crushed. Only the features were unmarked.

"I did not try to run away. But as you see, my vessel is short-handed, some of my men are working another. It took twice as long to bring her round and heave-to." He nodded several times. "I shall be certain to mention all this in my complaint to the proper authority!"

Bolitho gripped his sword to his leg again. It was bad luck. The ball must have severed some rigging and allowed the block to fall and kill the man. It happened often enough in any ship, but this could not have occurred at a worse time.

He said, "We shall return to *Telemachus*, Mr. Paice."

Even a bloody hand-to-hand fight would have been better than this, he thought. Lady Luck, as Thomas always called it, had been against them from the beginning. He glanced at Paice and was surprised to see his face was stiffly controlled, his anger apparently gone.

Even when they clambered down to the jolly-boat nobody aboard the brig called out or abused them in any way. Delaval was not going to spoil his victory by putting a foot out of place.

Bolitho did not wait for the boat to be hoisted inboard before going below to the cabin.

He half-listened to the usual bustle and noise of a vessel getting under way once more, the creak of the rudder below the transom, a goblet clattering from the table as the cutter heeled over to the wind. Allday was outside the door, having made certain the boat was safely secured. Poor Allday; he would hate to see him disgraced. He bit his lip. There would be others who would be less displeased when he was sent back to Falmouth.

Paice ducked through the door, his coat still black with spray. It was his command but he waited for Bolitho to ask him to be seated. He looked tired and strained, a different person.

Bolitho did not waste time. "I am sorry. You were right, I was mistaken. I shall see that no blame is attached to you. I ordered the chase—" He lifted his hand heavily as if his sleeve was filled with lead shot. "No, hear me out. I told you to fire into her. It is enough. Perhaps I still thought—"

Paice waited and then said, "No, sir, you were *not* mistaken. If anyone is to blame it's me for thinking, even for a moment, that Delaval would be stupid enough to be caught so easily."

Bolitho looked across the small cabin with its leaping shadows made by the spiralling lanterns.

"Then tell me, what has changed your mind?"

Paice said calmly, "Delaval *knew* we were out there, sir. And he needed us to know that he had outwitted us."

"You mean it was all a lie?"

"Not all of it." Paice clenched his fists several times, as if they were detached from the apparent calm he was displaying. "That dead man was never killed by a falling block, sir. That's why the bastard wanted me to see his face."

"You knew him?"

"He was my informant. The one who told me about the run."

"And there's nothing we can do about it."

Paice gave a deep sigh. "Delaval is a Channel Islander by birth. It's rumoured he had to leave Jersey because of his cruelty when he commanded a privateer there."

Bolitho tried to shut out the picture of the vicious mark Tuke had branded on Viola's naked shoulder when he had held her captive. But the picture would not fade, and he could still hear Tuke's sneers as they had circled around each other on *Narval*'s bloodied deck, their swords seeking an opening.

He heard himself say quietly, "I knew another like that."

Paice watched him for several seconds. "Probably tortured him after they had discovered he was informing on the smugglers. Then murdered him. Or maybe he was trading information to others. Either way they've done for him, and we can't prove a thing." He took a long, deep breath which seemed to come from his shoes.

"So you see, sir, you *were* right. *Loyal Chieftain* acted as a decoy for something else, but Delaval couldn't resist putting his own touch to it for my benefit. But one day—" He did not continue. He had no need.

Paice groped his way bent double to the door. "Do you wish to rendezvous with *Wakeful*, sir?"

Bolitho stared at him. "*Wakeful*? That's it, by God! Only *Wakeful* knew I was transferring back to your ship!"

Paice rubbed his chin fiercely even though he was still bent over in the doorway.

"Surely you don't think—"

Bolitho felt the shivers again up his spine.

"I don't know Delaval, but I *do* understand men like him. He showed no interest in me, not even curiosity—it was you he wanted to humiliate and impress—do you not see that?"

Paice nodded grimly. "I'm afraid I do, sir."

Bolitho said, "Let us take a glass together before you change tack." He reached over and impetuously touched the big lieutenant's arm.

"The battle's not lost after all. But I fear for the casualties when the fight is over!"

Allday heard the change in Bolitho's voice, could almost see his shoulders lifting again.

He gave a slow grin as Bolitho added, "So let's be about it, eh?"

4

Divided Loyalties

THE house which Commodore Ralph Hoblyn occupied and used as his personal headquarters was an elegant, square building of red brick with a pale, stone portico.

Bolitho reined in his horse and looked at the house for a full minute. It was not an old building, he decided, and the cobbled driveway which led between some pillared gates was well kept, with no trace of weeds to spoil it. And yet it had an air of neglect, or a place which had too many occupiers to care. Behind him he heard the other horse stamping its hooves on the roadway and could almost feel Young Matthew's excitement as he shared the pride and privilege of accompanying Bolitho on this warm, airless evening.

Bolitho recalled the angry waves and the brig's sail being ripped apart by it. It could have been another ocean entirely. There was a smell of flowers in the air, mixed as ever with that of the sea which was never far away.

The house was less than a mile from the dockyard at Sheerness where the two cutters had returned that morning.

A lieutenant had brought the invitation to Bolitho. It had been more like a royal command, he thought grimly.

He saw the glint of steel and the scarlet coats of two

marines as they stepped across the gateway, attracted possibly by the sound of horses.

He had seen several pickets on the way here. It was as if the navy and not the local felons and smugglers were under siege. His mouth tightened. He would try to change that—always provided Commodore Hoblyn did not order him to leave.

He tried to recall all he could about the man. A few years older than himself, Hoblyn had also been a frigate captain during the American Rebellion. He had fought his ship *Leonidas* at the decisive battle of the Chesapeake, where Admiral Graves had failed to bring de Grasse to a satisfactory embrace.

Hoblyn had engaged a French frigate and a privateer single-handed. He had forced the Frenchman to strike, but as he had closed with the privateer his own ship had exploded in flames. Hoblyn had continued to fight, and even boarded and seized the privateer before his ship had foundered.

It had been said that the sight of Hoblyn leading his boarders had been enough to strike terror into the enemy. His uniform had been ablaze, one arm burning like a tree in a forest fire.

Bolitho had met him only once since the war. He had been on his way to the Admiralty to seek employment. He had not even looked like the same man. His arm in a sling, his collar turned up to conceal some of the terrible burns on his neck, he had seemed a ghost from a battlefield. As far as Bolitho knew he had never obtained any employment. Until now.

Bolitho urged his mount forward. "Come, Matthew, take care of the horses. I shall have some food sent to you."

He did not see the awe on the boy's face. Bolitho

was thinking of Allday. It was so out of character not to ask, to demand to accompany him. Allday mistrusted the ways of the land, and hated being parted from Bolitho at any time. Perhaps he was still brooding over their failure to catch the smugglers. It would all come out later on. Bolitho frowned. But it would have to wait.

He had spoken with Lieutenant Queely aboard *Wakeful* before leaving Sheerness. It was like a missing part of a puzzle. *Wakeful* had seen nothing, and the revenue men had had no reports of a run. Testing him out? Like Delaval's elaborate and calculated display of the dead man, Paice's informant. Cat and mouse.

He nodded to the corporal at the gate who slapped his musket in a smart salute, the pipeclay hovering around him in the still air. Bolitho was glad he had declined a carriage. Riding alone had given him time to think if not to plan. He smiled ruefully. It had also reminded him just how long it was since he had sat a horse.

Young Matthew took the horses and waited as a groom came forward to lead him to the stables at the rear of the house. Bolitho climbed the stone steps and saw the fouled anchor above the pillars, the stamp of Admiralty.

As if by magic the double doors swung inwards noiselessly and a dark-coated servant took Bolitho's hat and boat cloak, the latter covered with dust from the steady canter along an open road.

The man said, "The commodore will receive you shortly, sir." He backed away, the cloak and hat carried with great care as if they were heated shot from a furnace.

Bolitho walked around the entrance hall. More pillars, and a curved stairway which led up to a gallery. Unlike the houses he had seen in London, it was spartan. No pictures, and few pieces of furniture. *Temporary*, that described it well, he thought, and wondered if it also indicated Hoblyn's authority here. He looked through a window and caught the glint of late sunlight on the sea. *Or mine*. He tried not to think about Queely. He could be guilty, or one of his people might have found a way to pass word to the smugglers. News did not travel by itself.

It was like being in a dark room with a blind man. Uniform, authority, all meaningless. A fight which had neither beginning nor end. Whereas at sea you held the obedience and efficiency of your ship by leadership and example. But the enemy was always visible, ready to pit his wits against yours until the final broadside brought down one flag or the other.

Here it was stealth, deceit, and murder.

As a boy Bolitho had often listened to the old tales of the Cornish smugglers. Unlike the notorious wreckers along that cruel coastline, they were regarded as something vaguely heroic and daring. The rogues who robbed the rich to pay the poor. The navy had soon taught Bolitho a different story. Smugglers were not so different from those who lured ships on to the rocks where they robbed the cargoes and slit the throats of helpless survivors. He found that he was gripping his sword so tightly that the pain steadied his sudden anger.

He felt rather than heard a door opening and turned to see a slim figure framed against a window on the opposite side of the room.

At first he imagined it was a girl with a figure so

slight. Even when he spoke his voice was soft and respectful, but with no trace of servility.

The youth was dressed in a very pale brown livery with darker frogging at the sleeves and down the front. White stockings and buckled shoes, a gentle miniature of most servants Bolitho had met.

"If you will follow me, Captain Bolitho."

He wore a white, curled wig which accentuated his face and his eyes, which were probably hazel, but which, in the filtered sunlight, seemed green, and gave him the quiet watchfulness of a cat.

Across the other room and then into a smaller one. It was lined from floor to ceiling with books, and despite the warmth of the evening a cheerful fire was burning beneath a huge painting of a sea-fight. There were chairs and tables and a great desk strategically placed across one corner of the room.

Bolitho had the feeling that all the worthwhile contents of the house had been gathered in this one place.

He heard the young footman, if that was his station here, moving to the fire to rearrange a smouldering log into a better position. There was no sign of the commodore.

The youth turned and looked at him. "He will not be long, sir." Then he stood motionless beside the flickering fire, his hands behind his back.

Another, smaller door opened and the commodore walked quickly to the desk and slid behind it with barely a glance.

He seemed to arrange himself, and Bolitho guessed it came of long practice.

Just a few years older than himself, but they had been cruel ones. His square face was deeply lined, and he held his head slightly to one side as if he was still in pain. His left arm lay on the desk and Bolitho saw that he wore a white fingerless glove like a false hand, to disguise the terrible injuries he had endured for so long.

"I am pleased to see you, Bolitho." He had a curt, clipped manner of speech. "Be seated *there* if you will, I can see you the better."

Bolitho sat down and noticed that Hoblyn's hair was completely grey, and worn unfashionably long, doubtless to hide the only burns which probed above his gold-laced collar.

The youth moved softly around the desk and produced a finely cut wine jug and two goblets.

"Claret." Hoblyn's eyes were brown, but without warmth. "Thought you'd like it." He waved his right arm vaguely. "We shall sup later." It was an order.

They drank in silence and Bolitho saw the windows changing to dusky pink as the evening closed in.

Hoblyn watched the youth refilling the goblets.

"You've been luckier than most, Bolitho. Two ships since that bloody war, whereas—" He did not finish it but stared instead at the large painting.

Bolitho knew then it was his last battle. When he had lost his *Leonidas* and had been so cruelly disfigured.

Hoblyn added, "I heard about your, er—misfortunes in the Great South Sea." His eyes did not even blink. "I'm told she was an admirable woman. I am sorry."

Bolitho tried to remain calm. "About this appointment—"

Hoblyn's disfigured hand rose and fell very lightly. *"In good time."*

He said abruptly, "So this is how they use us, eh? Are we relics now, the pair of us?" He did not expect or wait for an answer. "I am bitter sometimes, and then I think of those who have *nothing* after giving their all."

Bolitho waited. Hoblyn needed to talk.

"It's a hopeless task if you let it be so, Bolitho. Our betters bleat and protest about the Trade, while they filch all they can get from it. Their lordships demand more men for a fleet they themselves allowed to rot while they flung those same sailors on the beach to starve! *Damn them*, I say! And you can be sure than when war comes, as come it must, I shall be cast aside to provide a nice posting for some admiral's cousin!" He waited until his goblet was refilled. "But I love this country which treats her sons so badly. You know the French as well as I—do you see them stopping now?" He gave a harsh laugh. "And when they come we shall have to pray that those murderous scum have lopped off the heads of all their best sea-officers. I see no chance for us otherwise."

Bolitho tried to remember how many times the youth had refilled his goblet. The claret and the heat from the fire were making his mind blur.

He said, "I have to speak about the *Loyal Chieftain*, sir."

Hoblyn held his head to a painful angle. "Delaval? I know what happened, and about the man who was killed too." He leaned forward so that his fine shirt frothed around the lapels of his coat. A far cry from the tattered veteran Bolitho had seen years ago on his way to the Admiralty.

Hoblyn dropped his voice to a husky growl. "Someone burned down the man's cottage while you

65

were at sea—I'll lay odds you didn't know *that!* And his wife and children have vanished into thin air!" He slumped back again, and Bolitho saw sweat on his face.

"Murdered?" One word, and it seemed to bring a chill to the overheated room.

"We shall probably never know." He reached out to grasp his goblet but accidentally knocked it over so that the claret ran across the desk like blood.

Hoblyn sighed. "Damn them all." He watched his footman as he deftly mopped up the wine and replaced the goblet with a clean one.

"But life can have its compensations—"

Just for a brief instant it was there. The merest flicker of an exchange between them. The youth did not smile and yet there was an understanding strong enough to feel.

Hoblyn said offhandedly, "You have *Snapdragon* in Chatham dockyard?"

Bolitho shook himself. Maybe he was mistaken. He glanced quickly at the footman's pale eyes. They were quite empty.

"Yes, sir. I thought it best—"

"Good thinking. There'll not be much time later on. Our lords and masters want results. We shall give them a few." He smiled for the first time. "Thought I was going to bite your head off, did ye? God damn it, Bolitho, you're what I need, not some knothead who's never heard a shot fired in bloody earnest!"

Bolitho pressed his shoulders against the chairback. There was something unnerving about Hoblyn. But under the bluster and the bitterness his mind was as sharp and as shrewd as it had ever been. If he was

66

like this with everyone the slender footman must have heard every secret possible. Was he to be trusted?

Hoblyn added, "The big East Indiamen are among the worst culprits, y'know. They come up-Channel after months at sea and they meet with smugglers while they're under way, did you know that?"

Bolitho shook his head. "What is the purpose, sir?"

"John Company's captains like to make a little extra profit of their own, as if they don't get enough. They sell tea and silks directly to the Trade and so avoid paying duty themselves. The Customs Board don't like it, but with so few cutters to patrol the whole Channel and beyond, what can they expect?" He watched Bolitho calmly. "Wine and brandy is different. Smaller runs, less chance of the buggers getting caught. But tea, for instance, is light but very bulky." He tapped the side of his nose with the little white bag. "Not so easy, eh?"

Bolitho waited, not knowing quite what he had expected.

"I have received information." He must have seen doubt in Bolitho's grey eyes. "From a better mouth than some wretched turncoat's." Hoblyn calmed himself with an effort. "There's a cargo being landed at Whitstable ten days from now." He sat back to watch Bolitho's expression. "It will involve a lot of men." His dark eyes seemed to dance in the candlelight as the youth placed a silver candelabrum on the desk. "Men for the fleet, *or* the gallows, we'll strike no bargains, and a cargo to make these bloody smugglers realise we're on the attack!"

Bolitho's mind was in a whirl. If it was true, Hoblyn was right. It would make all the difference to their presence here. He pictured Whitstable on the

chart, a small fishing port which lay near the mouth
of the Swale River. More proof if any were needed of
the smugglers' audacity and arrogance. At a guess,
Whitstable was no more than ten miles from this very
room.

"I'll be ready, sir."

"Thought so. Nothing like a bit of humiliation to
put fire in your belly, eh?"

A clock chimed somewhere and Hoblyn said,
"Time to sup. The rest can keep. I know you're not
one to loosen your tongue. Something else we have in
common, I suspect." He chuckled and then struggled
around the desk while the youth waited to lead the
way to another room.

As he bent over Bolitho saw the livid scars lift
above his collar. He must be like that over most of
his body. Like a soul banished from hell. They moved
out into the same hallway where a servant waited at
another pair of doors. There was a rich smell of food,
and Bolitho noticed the cut and material of Hoblyn's
clothes. His fortunes had changed if nothing else.

He was about to ask that a meal be sent for Young
Matthew when he saw Hoblyn's hand brush against
that of the footman.

Bolitho did not know if he felt disgust or pity.

As Hoblyn had said, *the rest can keep.*

Bolitho awoke shocked and dazed and for a few agonising seconds imagined that he was emerging from the
fever again. His skull throbbed like hammers on an
anvil, and when he tried to speak his tongue felt as if
it was glued to the roof of his mouth. He saw Young
Matthew's round face watching him in the gloom,

only his eyes showing colour in a feeble glow from the cabin skylight.

"What is it?" Bolitho barely recognised his voice. "Time?" His senses were returning reluctantly and he realised with sudden self-abhorrence that he was still fully clothed in his best uniform, his hat and sword on the table where he had dropped them.

Matthew said in a hoarse whisper, "You bin sleeping, sir."

Bolitho propped himself on his elbows. The hull was moving very sluggishly on the current, but there were only occasionally some footfalls on the deck above. *Telemachus* still slept although it must soon be dawn, he thought vaguely.

"Coffee, Matthew." He lowered his feet to the deck and suppressed a groan. Blurred pictures formed in his mind and faded almost as quickly. The laden table, Hoblyn's face shining in the candlelight, the comings and goings of servants, one plate following the next, each seemingly richer than that which had preceded it. And the wine. This time a groan did escape from his lips. It had been a never-ending stream.

The boy crouched down beside him. "Mr. Paice is on deck, sir."

He remembered what Hoblyn had revealed, the information he had gained on a Whitstable landing. The need for secrecy. How had he got back to *Telemachus*? He could remember none of it.

His mind steadied and he looked at the boy. "You brought me here?"

"It were nothing, sir." For once he showed no excitement or shy pride.

69

Bolitho seized his arm. "What is it? Tell me, Matthew."

The boy looked down at the deck. "It's Allday, sir."

Bolitho's brain was suddenly like clear ice. "What has happened?"

Pictures flashed through his thoughts. Allday standing over him, his bloodied cutlass cleaving aside all who tried to pass. Allday, cheerful, tolerant, always there when he was needed.

The boy whispered, "He's gone, sir."

"Gone?"

The door opened a few inches and Paice lowered his shoulders to enter the cabin.

"Thought you should know, sir." He added with something like the defiance he had shown at their first meeting, "He's not borne on the ship's books, sir. If he was . . ."

"He's my responsibility, is that what you mean?"

Paice must have seen the pain in his face even in the poor light.

"I did hear that your cox'n was once a pressed man, sir?"

Bolitho ran his fingers through his hair as he tried to assemble his wits. "True. That was a long while ago. He has served me, and served me faithfully, for ten years since. He'd not desert." He shook his head, the realisation of what he had said thrusting through him like a hot blade. "Allday would not leave me."

Paice watched, unable to help, to find the right words. "I could pass word to the shore, sir. He may meet with the press gangs. If I can rouse the senior lieutenant I might be able to stop anything going badly for him." He hesitated, unused to speaking so openly. "And for you, if I may say so, sir."

Bolitho touched the boy's shoulder and felt him shiver.

"Fetch me some water and fresh coffee, Matthew." His voice was heavy, his mind still groping.

Suppose Allday *had* decided to leave? Bolitho recalled his own surprise when Allday had not insisted on accompanying him to the commodore's house. It was all coming back. Bolitho felt his inner pocket and touched the written orders which the commodore had given him. It was a wonder he had not lost them on the way back to the cutter, he thought wretchedly.

Allday might have felt the affair of the *Loyal Chieftain* badly. God knew he had put up with enough over the past months—and with what reward for his faith and his unshakeable loyalty?

Now he was gone. Back to the land from which Bolitho's own press gang had snatched him all those years back. Years of danger and pride, loss and sadness. Always there. The oak, the rock which Bolitho had all too often taken for granted.

Paice said, "He left no message, sir."

Bolitho looked up at him. "He cannot write." He remembered what he had thought when he had first met Allday in *Phalarope*. If only he had had some education Allday might have been anything. Now that same thought seemed to mock him.

Somewhere a boatswain's call twittered like a rudely awakened blackbird.

Paice said heavily, "Orders, sir?"

Bolitho nodded and winced as the hammers began again. Eating and drinking to excess, something he rarely did, and all the while Allday had been here, planning what he would do, awaiting the right moment.

"We shall weigh at noon. See that word is passed to *Wakeful*." He tried to keep his tone level. "Do it yourself, if you please. I want nothing in writing." Their eyes met. *"Not yet."*

"All hands! All hands! Lash up an' stow!" The hull seemed to shake as feet thudded to the deck, and another day was begun.

"May I ask, sir?"

Bolitho heard the boy returning and realised that he would have to shave himself.

"There is to be a run." He did not know if Paice believed him, nor did he care now. "The commodore has a plan. I shall explain when we are at sea and in company. There will be no revenue cutters involved. They are to be elsewhere." How simple it must have sounded across that overloaded table. And all the while the handsome youth in the white wig had watched and listened.

Paice said haltingly, "I sent the first lieutenant ashore to collect two of the hands, sir. They were found drunk at a local inn." He forced a grin. "Thought it best if he was out of the way 'til I'd spoken with you."

The boy put down a pot of coffee and groped about for a mug.

Bolitho replied, "That was thoughtful of you, Mr. Paice."

Paice shrugged. "I believe we may be of one mind, sir."

Bolitho stood up carefully and thrust open the skylight. The air was still cool and sweet from the land. Maybe he no longer belonged at sea. Was that what Allday had been feeling too?

He glanced down and saw Matthew moving a small roll of canvas away from the cot.

Paice backed from the cabin. "I shall muster the hands, sir. No matter what men may believe, a ship has no patience and must be served fairly at all times."

Bolitho did not hear the door close. "What is that parcel, Matthew?"

The boy picked it up and shrugged unhappily. "I think it belonged to Allday, sir." He sounded afraid, as if he in some way shared the guilt.

Bolitho took it from him and opened it carefully on the cot where he had lain like some drunken oaf.

The small knives, tools which Allday had mostly made with his own hands. Carefully collected oddments of brass and copper, sailmaker's twine, some newly fashioned spars and booms.

Bolitho was crouching now, his hands almost shaking as he untied the innermost packet and put it on the cot with great care.

Allday never carried much with him as he went from ship to ship. He had placed little importance on possessions. Only in his models, his ships which he had fashioned with all the skill and love he had gained over the years at sea.

He heard the boy's sharp intake of breath. "It's lovely, sir!"

Bolitho touched the little model and felt his eyes prick with sudden emotion. Unpainted still, but there was no mistaking the shape and grace of a frigate, the gunports as yet unfilled with tiny cannon still to be made, the masts and rigging still carried only in

Allday's mind. His fingers paused at the small, delicately carved figurehead, one which Bolitho remembered so clearly, as if it were life-sized instead of a tiny copy. The wild-eyed girl with streaming hair, and a horn fashioned like a great shell.

Young Matthew said questioningly, "A frigate, sir?"

Bolitho stared at it until he could barely see. It was not just any ship. With Allday it rarely was.

He heard himself murmur, "She is my last command, Matthew. My *Tempest*."

The boy responded in a whisper, "I wonder why he left it behind, sir?"

Bolitho turned him by the shoulder and gripped it until he winced. "Don't you see, Matthew? He could tell no one what he was about, nor could he write a few words to rest my fears for him." He looked again at the unfinished model. "This was the best way he knew of telling me. That ship meant so much to both of us for a hundred different reasons. He'd never abandon it."

The boy watched as Bolitho stood up to the skylight again, barely able to grasp it, and yet knowing he was the only one who was sharing the secret.

Bolitho said slowly, "*God damn him* for his stubbornness!" He bunched his hand against the open skylight. "And God protect you, old friend, until your return!"

Marching in pairs the press gang advanced along yet another narrow street, their shoes ringing on the cobbles, their eyes everywhere as they probed the shadows.

At the head a tight-lipped lieutenant strode with his hanger already drawn, a midshipman following a few paces behind him.

Here and there the ancient houses seemed to bow across the lanes until they appeared to touch one another. The lieutenant glanced at each dark or shuttered window, especially at those which hung directly above their wary progress. It was all too common for someone to hurl down a bucket of filth on to the hated press gangs as they carried out their thankless patrols.

The lieutenant, like most of them in the local impressment service, had heard all about the two officers being stripped, beaten and publicly humiliated on the open road, with no one raising a hand to aid them. Only the timely appearance of the post-captain and his apparent total disregard for his own safety had saved the officers from far worse.

The lieutenant had been careful to announce his intentions of seeking prime seamen for the fleet, as so ordered. He slashed out angrily at a shadow with his hanger and swore under his breath. You might just as well ring the church bells to reveal what you were about, he thought. The result was usually the same. Just a few luckless ones, and some of those had been lured into the hands of the press gangs, usually by their own employers who wanted to be rid of them. A groom who had perhaps become too free with a landowner's daughter, a footman who had served a mistress better than the man who paid for her luxuries. But trained hands? It would be a joke, if it were not so serious.

The lieutenant snapped, "Close up in the rear!" It was unnecessary; they always kept together, their heavy cudgels and cutlasses ready for immediate use if attacked, and he knew they resented his words. But he hated the work, just as he longed for the chance of a ship. Some people foolishly wrung their hands, and clergymen prayed that war would never come.

The fools. What did they know? War was as necessary as it was rewarding.

There was a sudden crash, like a bottle being smashed on the cobbles.

The lieutenant held up his hanger, and behind him he heard his men rouse themselves, like vixens on the scent of prey.

The midshipman faltered, "In that alley, sir!"

"I know that!" He waited until his senior hand, a hard-bitten gunner's mate, had joined him. "Did you hear that, Benzie?"

The gunner's mate grunted. "There be a tavern through there, sir. Should be closed now, o'course. This be th'only way out."

The lieutenant scowled. The idiot had left the most important fact to the end. He swallowed his revulsion and said softly, "Fetch two men and—"

The gunner's mate thrust his face even closer and whispered thickly, "No need, sir, someone be comin'!"

The lieutenant thankfully withdrew his face. The gunner's mate's breath was as foul as any bilge. Chewing tobacco, rum and bad teeth made a vile mixture.

"Stand to!" The lieutenant faced the narrow alley and cursed their lordships for the absurdity of it. The hidden figure with the slow, shambling gait was probably a cripple or as old as Neptune. What use was one man anyway?

The shadow loomed from the shadows and the lieutenant called sharply, "In the King's name, I order you to stand and be examined!"

The gunner's mate sighed and tightened his hold on the heavy cudgel. How the navy had changed. In his day they had clubbed them senseless and asked questions later, usually when the poor wretch awoke with a split head to find himself in a man-of-war already standing out to sea. It might be months, years, and in many cases never, that the pressed man returned to England. Who would care anyway? There had even been a case of a bridegroom being snatched from the steps of a church on his wedding day.

But now, with regulations, and not enough ships ready for sea, it was unsafe to flout the Admiralty's rules.

He said, "*Easy*, matey!" His experienced eye had taken in the man's build and obvious strength. Even in this dawn light he could see the broad shoulders and, when he turned to stare at the press gang, the pigtail down his back.

The lieutenant snapped, "What ship?" His nervousness put an edge to his voice. "Answer, or you'll be the worse for it, man!"

The gunner's mate urged, "There be too many o' us, matey." He half-raised his cudgel. "Tell the lieutenant, like wot 'e says!"

Allday looked at him grimly. He had been about to give up his hazy plan, when he had heard the press gang's cautious approach. Were it not so dangerous it might have made him smile, albeit secretly. Like all those other times when he had dodged the dreaded press in Cornwall, until the day when His Britannic Majesty's frigate *Phalarope* had hove into sight. Her captain had been a Cornishman, one who knew where landsmen ran to ground whenever a King's ship topped the horizon. It was strange when you thought of it. If a Frenchie ever drew close inshore every fit man would stand to arms to protect his home and country from an enemy. But they would run from one of their own.

Allday said huskily, "I don't have a ship, sir." He had spilled rum over his clothing and hoped it was convincing. He had hated the waste of it.

The lieutenant said coldly, "Don't lie. I told you what would happen if—"

The gunner's mate gestured at him again. "Don't be a fool!"

Allday hung his head. "The *London*, sir."

The lieutenant exclaimed. "A second-rate, so you are a prime seaman! *Yes?*" The last word was like a whip-crack.

"If you say so, sir."

"Don't be bloody insolent. What's your name, damn you?"

Allday regarded him impassively. It might be worth it just to smash in the lieutenant's teeth. Bolitho would have a useless pipsqueak like him for breakfast.

"Spencer, sir." He had neglected to invent a name, and the slight hesitation seemed to satisfy the officer that it was because of guilt.

"Then you are taken. Come with my men, or be dragged in irons—the choice is yours."

The press gang parted as Allday moved amongst them. Their eagerness to be gone from this deserted street was almost matched by their relief.

One of the seamen muttered, "Never mind, mate, could be worse."

Somewhere, far away, a trumpet echoed on the morning air. Allday hesitated and did not even notice the sudden alarm in their eyes. He had done it. At this moment Bolitho might be looking at the little *Tempest*. But would he see a message there? Allday felt something like despair; he might see only desertion and treachery.

Then he squared his shoulders. "I'm ready."

The lieutenant quickened his pace as he heard someone drumming on a bucket with a piece of metal. The signal for a mob to come running to free their capture.

But this patrol at least had not been entirely wasted. Only one man, but obviously an experienced sailor. No excuses either, nor the last-moment, infuriating production of a Protection like those issued to apprentices, watermen, and the likes of the HEIC.

The gunner's mate called, "Wot's yer trade, Spencer?"

Allday was ready this time. "Sailmaker." Chosen carefully, not too lowly, so that they might have disbelieved him, nor too senior, so that they might have sent him back to the *London*, a ship he had never laid eyes on.

The man nodded, well satisfied. A sailmaker was a rare and valuable catch.

They topped a rise and Allday saw the masts and crossed yards of several men-of-war, their identities still hidden in deep shadow. Bolitho was there. Would they ever meet again?

If not it will be because I am no longer alive.

Strangely enough the realisation brought him immediate comfort.

5

Out Of The Mouths Of Babes . . .

BOLITHO gripped the swivel-gun mounting on
the weather bulwark, and used it to steady
himself as *Telemachus* dipped and lifted to a
steady north-easterly, her forward rigging running
with spray. Eight bells had just chimed out from the
forecastle and as in any man-of-war, large or small,
the watches changed to a routine as old as the navy
itself.

Lieutenant Triscott touched his hat to Paice. "The
watch is aft, sir."

Bolitho sensed the stiffness in his manner, something unusual for one so young and usually so
buoyant.

"Relieve the wheel, if you please."

The helmsman chanted, "West Nor'-West, sir! Full
an' bye!"

The members of the last dogwatch hurried to the
hatchway while the relief took over and began to
check running rigging, and the lashings of countless
pieces of equipment and the guns which lined either
side.

It was not just the first lieutenant who was showing
strain, Bolitho thought. It was never easy in a small
overcrowded hull at the best of times, and he was
well aware of their resentment as day followed day,
beating up and down, holding on to visual contact
with *Wakeful* running far down to leeward, and

80

preparing for what most of them thought was another empty rumour.

Bolitho blamed himself for much of it. It was Paice's command, but he watched everything himself, and tried to plan for whatever lay ahead.

Paice had had little to do with Commodore Hoblyn and was unwilling to voice an opinion as to the value of his information. Perhaps he was still brooding over the murder of his own informant and the calculated arrogance with which Delaval had displayed the man's corpse. Or he might place Hoblyn in the category of senior officers who had been too long ashore to understand the stealth and cunning of this kind of work.

Whenever he was alone in his cot Bolitho was unable to lose himself in his plans. Allday would return to his thoughts again and again, so that he lay tossing and turning until he fell into an exhausted sleep, his anxieties still unresolved.

He noticed that neither Paice nor Triscott ever mentioned Allday in his presence. Either they were afraid to arouse his displeasure, or, in the way of sailors, they were convinced that Allday was already dead.

Paice crossed the narrow poop and touched his hat, while his eyes watched the clear sky of evening.

"Might get some mist later, sir." His gaze moved to Bolitho's profile, assessing the mood. "But we can hold contact with *Wakeful* for a few more hours before we tell her to close with us for the night."

Bolitho glanced up at the quivering mast where the lookouts squatted on the topsail yard. They had the other cutter in sight, but down here on deck the sea might have been empty.

They had twice met with a revenue lugger. Once she had carried a curt despatch from the commodore, a confirmation that his information was still valid.

The second time the lugger had carried news of a more disturbing nature. It seemed that there had been several daring runs made along the south coast, from as far afield as Penzance in Cornwall and Lyme Bay in Dorset. A revenue cutter had chased one schooner as far as the Isle of Wight before the smuggler had give her the slip in a sudden rain squall.

Paice had commented, "Seems that all the excitement is elsewhere, sir."

A criticism of Bolitho's strategy, perhaps, and the fact that their two cutters were placed as far as possible from any of the landings. The Customs Board had taken them very seriously, and had diverted every available vessel to seize or destroy any boats suspected of dropping smuggled cargoes. The navy had even loaned a thirty-two-gun frigate from Plymouth to offer support if the revenue vessels were outgunned or fought on to a lee shore.

Paice remarked, "First of May tomorrow, sir."

Bolitho turned and said shortly, "I am aware of it. You may assure your people it is also the last day they will be required on this patrol."

Paice held his gaze and replied stubbornly, "I implied no lack of faith, sir. But it could mean that the commodore's intelligence, with all respect to him for I believe him to be a brave officer, was falsely offered. Any failure might be seen as something personal."

Bolitho watched some fish leaping across the crisp wave which surged back from *Telemachus*'s plunging stem.

"You think the commodore would be ordered to withdraw our cutters?"

"It crossed my mind, sir. Otherwise why are we out here, and not even in the Strait of Dover? If it was a ruse, we are too far away to be of any use."

"Is that the opinion of your whole command?" There was steel in his voice.

Paice shrugged heavily. "It is *my* opinion, sir. I do not ask others while I command here."

"I am glad to know it, Mr. Paice."

It was reaching him now, like the rest of the vessel. No room to escape, no place to hide from others at any time of the day or night. Only the masthead lookouts had any sort of privacy.

After this Bolitho knew he would have to go ashore and set up his own headquarters like Hoblyn. And without even Allday to make the sea's rejection bearable. He pounded his hand against the swivel gun's wet muzzle. Where was he now? How was he faring? Perhaps some press gang had already taken him to a ship at Chatham where his explanation had fallen on deaf ears. What could he have hoped to achieve anyway? The endless, unanswered questions seemed to roar through his head like surf in a cave.

He turned his thoughts to Hoblyn, and Paice moved away to consult with Scrope, the master-at-arms, who had been hovering near the tiller for some time, trying to catch his commander's eye. Paice had probably taken Bolitho's silence as another rebuff, the slamming of a door which both had imagined was open between them.

What then of Hoblyn? He did not come from a successful family or even from a long line of sea-officers. He was, as far as Bolitho knew, the first to

83

enter the navy which he had served without sparing himself until the terrible day he had been changed into a broken and disfigured *relic*, as he had described himself. Officially he was under the orders of the flag officer in command at the Nore, but like Bolitho was expected to act almost independently. Part of his work was making a list of vessels which in time of war could be purchased from their merchant service and used for the navy. Vessels under construction in the many yards around Suffolk and Kent would also have to be listed.

There were certainly openings for bribery. Money could soon change hands if a shipowner or builder could persuade a senior officer to pay a high price which could then be shared to mutual profit. Some vessels had changed hands several times in peace and war, and like the ill-fated *Bounty* had made good profits with each transaction.

If Hoblyn depended solely on a commodore's pay, he was certainly living far above it. The house was spartan Admiralty property, but the food and wine Bolitho had seen would have found favour on the table of the Lord High Admiral himself.

The yards Hoblyn visited would also be well known to the smuggling fraternity. Bolitho turned, and allowed the cold spray to dash across his face to clear his mind, like that first morning after Allday disappeared. His imagination was running wild, with a suspected felon in every shadow.

Hoblyn had tried to tell him in his own way; so had the admiral at Chatham. Let others fret over it, and content yourself with your daily lot until something better offers itself.

He was trying too hard. At the Admiralty he had

been told in a roundabout way that he had been chosen because of his gallant record, something which might inspire young men to sign on, to wear the King's coat because of his own service. It was a bitter reward.

The Nore and Medway towns were known for their distrust in the stirring words of a recruiting poster. In other wars the harbours and villages had been stripped of their young men, some who had gone proudly to volunteer, others who had been dragged away from their families by the desperate press gangs. The aftermath had seen too many cripples and too few young men to encourage others to follow their example.

Relic. The word seemed to haunt him.

He watched some seamen clambering up the weather ratlines to whip some loose cordage which had been spotted by the boatswain's eagle eye.

This was their ship, their home. They wanted to be rid of the officer who had once been a frigate captain.

There was a slithering footfall on deck and Matthew Corker moved carefully towards him, his young face screwed up with concentration. He held out a steaming mug. "Coffee, Cap'n." He smiled nervously. "'Tis half-empty, I'm afraid, sir."

Bolitho tried to return the smile. He was doing everything he could to please him, do the things which he had seen Allday do. He had even called him Cap'n, as Allday did and would allow no other. He had overcome his seasickness for most of the time.

"D'you still want to go to sea, Matthew?" The coffee was good, and seemed to give him strength.

"Aye, sir. More'n ever."

What would his grandfather, Old Matthew, think of that?

A shaft of red sunlight ran down the mainmast, and Bolitho stared at it as the great mainsail rattled and boomed in the wind. A few more hours and all pretence would be over.

He would not be remembered as the frigate captain, but as the man who tried to use a cutter like one. *Relic*.

"I forgot to tell you something, sir." The boy watched him anxiously. "Us being so busy an' worried like."

Bolitho smiled down at him. *Us*, he had said. It had not been easy for him either. The crowded hull, and doubtless some language and tales which he would barely understand after his sheltered existence at Falmouth.

"What is that?"

"When I took the horses to the stables at the commodore's house, sir, I had a walk round, looked at the other horses an' that." Bolitho saw him screwing up his face again, trying to picture it, to forget nothing.

"There was a fine carriage there. My grandfather showed me one once, when I was very young, sir."

Bolitho warmed to him. "That must have been a *long* time ago."

It was lost on him. "It's got a special kind of springing, y'see, sir—I've never seen another, until that night."

Bolitho waited. "What about it?"

"It's French, sir. A berlin, just like the one which came to Falmouth that time with some nobleman an' his lady."

Bolitho took his arm and guided him to the bulwark so that their backs were turned to the helmsmen and other watchkeepers.

"Are you quite sure?"

"Oh yes, sir." He nodded emphatically. "Somebody had been varnishing the doors like, but I could still see it when I held up the lantern."

Bolitho tried to remain patient. "See what?"

"I forget what they calls them, sir." He pouted. "A sort of flower with a crest."

Bolitho stared at the tilting horizon for several seconds.

Then he said quietly, "Fleur-de-lys?"

The boy's apple cheeks split into a grin. "Aye, that's what my grandad called it!"

Bolitho looked at him steadily. *Out of the mouths of babes* . . .

"Have you told anyone else?" He smiled gently. "Or is it just between *us?*"

"I said nuthin', sir. Just thought it a bit strange."

The moment, the boy's expression, the description of the fine carriage seemed to become fixed and motionless as the lookout's voice pealed down to the deck.

"Sail on th' weather quarter, sir!"

Paice stared across at him questioningly.

Bolitho called, "Well, we know she's not the *Loyal Chieftain* this time, Mr. Paice."

Paice nodded very slowly. "And we *know* there's naught 'twixt her and the land but—"

Bolitho looked at the boy. "*Us*, Mr. Paice?"

"Aye, sir." Then he raised his speaking trumpet. "Masthead! Can you make out her rig?"

"Schooner, sir! A big 'un she is, too!"

Paice moved nearer and rubbed his chin with agitation.

"She'll take the wind-gage off us. It would be two hours or more before we could beat up to wind'rd, even in *Telemachus*." He glanced meaningly at the sky. "Time's against that."

Bolitho saw some of the idlers on deck pausing to try and catch their words.

He said, "I agree. Besides, when she sights *Telemachus* she might turn and run if she thinks we are about to offer a chase."

"Shall I signal *Wakeful*, sir?" Once again that same hesitation.

"I think not. *Wakeful* will stand a better chance downwind if this stranger decides to make a run for the Dover Strait."

Paice gave a tight grin. "I'll say this, sir, you never let up."

Bolitho glanced away. "After this, I hope others may remember it."

Paice beckoned to his first lieutenant. "Call all hands, Andrew—" He glanced anxiously at Bolitho. "That is, *Mr* Triscott. Clear for action, but do not load or run out."

Bolitho watched them both and said, "This is where *Telemachus*'s ability to sail close to the wind will tell. It will also offer our small broadside a better chance should we have to match the enemy's iron!"

He crossed to the lee side and looked down at the creaming wake. There was only this moment. He must think of nothing further. Not of Allday, nor that this newcomer might well be an honest trader. If that were true, his name would carry no weight at all.

He heard the boy ask, "What'll *I* do, sir?"

Bolitho looked at him and saw him falter under his gaze. Then he said, "Fetch my sword." He nearly added *and pray*. Instead he said, "Then stand by me."

Calls trilled although they were hardly needed in *Telemachus*'s sixty-nine-foot hull.

"All hands! Clear for action!"

Tomorrow would bring the first day in May. What might it take away?

Bolitho lowered the telescope and spoke over his shoulder. "What do you estimate our position, Mr. Chesshyre?"

There was no hesitation. "'Bout ten miles north of Foreness Point, sir."

Bolitho wiped the telescope with his sleeve to give himself time to digest the master's words.

Foreness Point lay on the north-eastern corner of the Isle of Thanet, and the mainland of Kent. It reminded him briefly of Herrick, as had Chesshyre's voice.

Paice said hoarsely, "If he *is* a smuggler he'll be hard put to go about now, sir."

Bolitho levelled the glass again and saw the big schooner's dark sails standing above the sea like bat's wings. Paice was right. The north-easterly would make it difficult, even hazardous to try and claw round to weather the headland. The lookouts would be able to see it from their perch, but from the deck it looked as if the two vessels had the sea to themselves.

Bolitho glanced at the sky, which was still cloudless and clear. Only the sea seemed darker, and he knew that sooner or later one of them would have to show his hand.

He pictured the coast in his mind. They were steering towards the old anchorage at Sheerness, but before that lay Whitstable, and as the two vessels maintained their same tack and speed they were slowly converging, drawing together like lines on the chart.

Paice said, "He'll have to stand away soon, sir, or he'll end up with Sheppey across his bows."

Bolitho glanced along the deck, at the gun crews crouching or lounging by the sealed ports, each captain having already selected the best shot from the garlands for the first loading.

Bolitho had been in so many actions that he could recognise the casual attitudes of the seamen, the way they watched the schooner's steady approach with little more than professional interest. With Allday it was different; but these men were not accustomed to real action. A few might have fought in other ships, but most of them, as Paice had explained, were fishermen and workers driven from the land because of falling trade.

Bolitho said, "You may load now, Mr. Paice." He waited for the lieutenant to face him. "He is not going to run, you know that, don't you?"

Paice swallowed. "But I don't see that—"

"*Do it*, Mr. Paice. Tell the gunner's mates to supervise each piece personally. I want them double-shotted but with no risk of injury from an exploding cannon!"

Paice yelled, "All guns load! Double-shotted!"

Bolitho ignored the curious and doubtful stares as several of the seamen peered aft to where he stood by

90

the taffrail. He raised the glass again and watched the big sails leap into view. People too, at the bulwarks, and moving around the tapering masts. How would *Telemachus* look to them, he wondered? Small and lively, her guns still behind their port lids. Just one little cutter which stood between them and the land.

"D'you know her?" Bolitho lowered the glass and saw young Matthew staring at him unblinkingly, as if fearful of missing something.

Paice shook his head. "Stranger, sir." To the master he added, "What about you?"

Chesshyre shrugged. "Never laid eyes on her."

Bolitho clenched his fists. It had to be the right one. A quick glance abeam; the light was slowly going, the sun suddenly misty above the hidden land.

He said, "Bring her up two points, Mr. Paice."

Men scampered to their stations, and soon the blocks squealed, and the great mainsail thundered from its long boom.

"Steady she goes, sir! Nor'-West!"

"Run up the Colours!"

Bolitho dragged his eyes from the schooner and watched the gun crews. Some of them were still standing upright, gaping at the other ship.

Bolitho snapped, "Tell those bumpkins to stand to, damn them!"

He heard the big ensign cracking in the wind above the deck, then shouted, "Fire one of the larboard guns, Mr. Paice!"

Paice opened his mouth to dispute the order, then he nodded. By firing a gun from the opposite side they would keep the whole starboard broadside intact.

Moments later the foremost six-pounder banged

out, the smoke dispersing downwind before the crew had begun to sponge its barrel.

Bolitho folded his arms and watched the schooner, like the boy at his side, not daring to blink.

Paice said, "He's ignored the signal, sir." He sounded dazed, as if he scarcely believed it was happening. "Maybe he's—"

Bolitho did not know what Paice intended to say for at that second there was a great flash from the schooner's forecastle, and as smoke belched over the wave crests a ball smashed through *Telemachus*'s bulwark and burst apart on a six-pounder. Splinters of wood and iron shrieked away in all directions, and as the gun's echo faded the sound continued, but this time it was human.

One of the seamen was on his knees, his bloodied fingers clawing at his face and then his chest, his scream rising until it sounded like a woman in terrible agony. Then he pitched on his side, his life-blood pumping across the sloping deck and into the lee scuppers. Several of the other sailors stared at the corpse with utter horror; and there were more yells and screams as another ball crashed into the bulwark and hurled a fan of splinters across the deck.

"Open the ports! *Run out!*" Paice was standing silhouetted against the surging water alongside, his face like a mask as men whimpered and crawled across the shattered planking, marking the pain and progress with their blood.

Bolitho called, "On the uproll, Mr. Paice! It's our only hope at this distance!" So it had happened just as Hoblyn had predicted. His mind cringed as Triscott's hanger sliced down and the six guns on the starboard side crashed out in unison. The carronade was useless at anything more than point-blank range, and undoubtedly the schooner's master knew it.

He saw the sails dancing above the schooner's deck and watched as some blocks and cordage plummeted over the side to trail like creeper in the water.

"Reload! Run out!" Triscott's voice was shrill. "As you bear, lads!" He dropped his hanger again. *"Fire!"*

Bolitho saw several of the men peering round at their fallen comrades—how many had died or been cruelly wounded it was impossible to tell. At the same time Bolitho thought he saw their anxiety and sudden terror changing its face to anger, fury at what had been done to them.

Chesshyre yelled, "Down here—take over from Quin!" The helmsman in question had been hit in the head and had slumped unnoticed and unheard across the tiller bar, his eyes fixed and staring as they lowered him to the deck.

Chesshyre caught Bolitho's glance and said, "They've a bit to learn, sir, but they'll not let you down." He spoke so calmly he could have been describing a contest between boats' crews.

Bolitho nodded. "We must hit her masts and rigging." He shouted in the sudden lull. "Gun-captains! Aim high! A guinea for the first sail!" *"Fire!"*

Paice said harshly, "That bastard's using nine-pounders if I'm any judge!" He gasped as a ball smashed hard down alongside and flung spray high over the bulwark.

Bolitho saw his expression as men ran to the pumps. Like pain. As if he and not the cutter had been hit.

93

There was a wild cheer and Bolitho swung round to see the schooner's foresail tearing itself apart, the wind bringing her down as she fought against the confusion of sea and helm.

Bolitho bit his lip as another ball screamed overhead and a length of halliard whirled across the deck like a wounded snake. It could not last. One ball into *Telemachus*'s only mast would finish it.

Paice said wildly, "He can't depress his nine-pounders, sir!"

Bolitho stared. Paice was more used to this kind of vessel and would know the difficulty of mounting a long nine-pounder on the deck of a merchantman.

"He's trying to put about!" Triscott waved at his gun crews. "Into him, lads!" He watched as their grimy hands shot up. *"Fire!"*

Paice whispered, *"Holy Jesus!"*

Luck, the skill of an older gun captain, who could say? Bolitho saw the schooner's bowsprit shiver to fragments, the forecastle suddenly enveloped in torn shrouds and writhing canvas.

Paice searched through the drifting smoke for his boatswain.

"Mr. Hawkins! Stand by the arms chest!" He tugged out his own hanger, his eyes back on the schooner. "By God, they'll pay for this!"

Bolitho saw the distance dropping away as the crippled schooner continued to pay off downwind. His eyes narrowed and he heard the vague bang of muskets, the balls slamming against the cutter's hull. How long? He gestured urgently. "Can you manhandle the other carronade to the starboard side?"

Paice nodded, his eyes blazing. "Clear the larboard

94

battery, Mr. Triscott! Lay the smasher to starboard and prepare to fire!" He glanced at Bolitho and added, "They may outnumber us, but not for long!"

Bolitho watched the punctured sails rising above the cutter as if to swoop down and enfold her, smother her into the sea. Fifty yards. Twenty yards. Here a man fell coughing blood, there another clapped one hand to his chest and dropped to his knees as if in prayer.

Bolitho pushed the boy down beside the companionway.

"Stay there!" He drew the old sword and pictured Allday right here beside him, his cutlass always ready.

"Stand by to board!" He saw their faces, some eager, others fearful now that the enemy was alongside. They could hear them yelling and firing, cursing while they waited for the impact.

Bolitho walked behind the crouching seamen, his sword hanging loosely from his hand.

Some glanced at him as his shadow fell over them, stunned, wild, filled with disbelief as he showed himself to the schooner's marksmen.

"Ready!" Bolitho winced as a ball cut through the tail of his coat. Like a gentle hand plucking at it. *"Now!"*

The two carronades exploded in adjoining ports with a combined roar which shook the cutter from truck to keel. As the smoke fanned inboard and men fell about coughing and retching in the stench, Bolitho saw that most of the schooner's forecastle had been ripped aside, and the mass of men who had been waiting to attack or repel boarders were entwined in a bloody tangle, which turned and moved as if one hideous giant had been cut down. The weight of grape with canister from the poop swivel had turned the deck into a slaughterhouse.

Bolitho gripped the shrouds and shouted, "To me, lads! Grapnels there!" He heard them thudding on the schooner's bulwark, saw a crouching figure beside an upended gun, as if watching the attack. But it was headless.

The two hulls ground into each other, lurched apart, and then responding to the hands at the grapnels came together in a deadly embrace. *"Boarders away!"* Bolitho found himself carried across to the other vessel's deck, men thrusting past and around him in their need to get at their adversary.

Figures fell screaming and dying, and Bolitho saw *Telemachus*'s anger and jubilation change yet again to an insane sickness. With cutlass and pike, bayonets, even their bare hands, they fell on the schooner's crew with a ferocity which none of them would have believed just an hour earlier.

Bolitho shouted, *"That's enough!"* He struck down a man's cutlass with his own blade as he was about to impale a wounded youth on the reddened planks.

Paice too was yelling at his men to desist, while Hawkins the boatswain and a picked party of seamen were already taking charge of halliards and braces, to prevent the two hulls from destroying each other in the swell.

Cutlasses were being collected by the victors, and the schooner's company herded together, their wounded left to fend for themselves.

Bolitho said breathlessly, "Send men below, Mr. Paice—some brave fool might try to fire the magazine." More orders and some cracked cheers rose around him, and he saw Triscott waving his hat from

Telemachus's poop. The boy was standing near him, trying to cheer but almost choked by tears as he saw the devastation and the hideous remains left by the carronades.

Hawkins squeaked through blood and pieces of flesh, his boots like a butcher's as he reported to his commander.

"All secured, sir." He turned to Bolitho and added awkwardly, "Some of us was no 'elp to you, sir." He gestured with a tarred thumb. "But you was right. The 'olds is full to the deck-beams with contraband. Tea, spices, silk, Dutch by the looks o' it." He lowered his voice and watched without curiosity as a badly wounded smuggler crawled past his boots. "I've set some armed hands on the after 'old, sir. Spirits by the cask, Hollands Geneva I'll wager, and there may be more."

Paice wiped his face with his sleeve. "Then she *is* a Dutchie."

Hawkins shook his head. "Only the cargo, sir. The master is, or *was*, from Norfolk. Most of the others is English." His lip curled. "I'd swing the lot of 'em!"

Bolitho sheathed his old sword. Hoblyn had been right about that too. The cargo intended for Whitstable had probably begun its journey in the holds of some Dutch East Indiaman. A quick profit.

He looked at the dead and dying, then across at *Telemachus*, her own pain marked in blood. There had been little profit this time.

Paice asked anxiously, "Are you well, sir?" He was peering at him. "You're not hurt?"

Bolitho shook his head. He had been thinking of Allday, always close at times like these, and they had seen more than enough between them.

"I feel as if I have lost my right arm." He shook himself. "Have the vessel searched before nightfall. Then we shall anchor until we can attend to our repairs." He watched as one of the smugglers, obviously someone of authority, was marched past by two seamen. "That is good. Hold them apart. There is much we don't yet know."

Paice said simply, "My bosun spoke for us all, sir. We fought badly because we had no heart for it. But you are a man of war. We shall know better in future."

Bolitho walked to the side, his whole being revolted against the sights and stench of death.

Hoblyn should be pleased; their lordships of Admiralty also. A fine schooner which after repair could either go to the prize court or more likely be taken into the navy. An illegal cargo, and desperate men who would soon hang in chains as a warning to others.

His glance moved over some of the huddled prisoners. A few of them might be pressed into service like their ship, provided they were found guiltless of murder.

It should have been enough. He felt a seaman offer his hard hand to assist him over the bulwark to *Telemachus*'s deck.

But if victory there was, it seemed an empty one.

6

The Brotherhood

JOHN ALLDAY sat on a stone bench with his back resting against the wall. There was only one window, small, and too high to see out of this damp, cell-like room, but he had kept his eyes open since he had surrendered to the press gang and knew that the lockup house was somewhere on the road to Sheerness. They had passed a small cavalry barracks, no more than an outpost for a handful of dragoons, but enough, it seemed, to allow the press gangs to come and go without fear of being attacked by those who might try to release their captives.

Allday guessed it was about noon and tried to disperse his own sense of uneasiness, the conviction that he had acted rashly and might find himself in worse trouble.

His companions, just five of them, were a poor collection, he thought. Deserters probably, but no loss to any ship of war.

Feet clattered on cobbles and somewhere a man laughed. There was an inn just a few yards from the lockup house, and he had seen two fine-looking girls watching from its porch as they had hurried past. He had thought of the inn he visited in Falmouth. He felt suddenly alone, and lonely.

He recalled too the time he had been taken by Bolitho's press gang in Cornwall. He had tried to lie his way out of it, but a gunner had seen the tattoo on his arm, the crossed cannon and flags which he had gathered along the way when he had served in the old seventy-four, *Resolution*. If what he had suspected was a fact, this same tattoo would help rather than hinder his hazy plan. If not, he might find himself aboard a seagoing ship, outward bound to some hell on the other side of the world before he could make himself believed. Even then, a captain short of trained men would scarcely be willing to listen.

What would Bolitho do without him? He screwed up his brows in a deep frown. He had watched Bolitho's despair as he had met one barrier after another, and then the affair with the *Loyal Chieftain* had been more than enough.

He glanced at the door as a key grated in it and the same gunner's mate with the foul breath peered in at them.

He gestured with his key. "Outside and get cleaned up. Then there's some bread and cheese, ale too if you behaves yerselves!" He looked directly at Allday. "You stay 'ere. We need some more words about you."

Allday said nothing as the others hurried away, already lost. Was the gunner's mate merely dragging it out for no purpose, or was there something behind his remarks?

But it was another who finally entered the dank room. Allday recognised him as a member of the press gang, the one who had spoken to him on the way here.

"Well, Spencer?" The man leaned against the wall

and regarded him bleakly. "Got yerself in a right pot o' stew, eh?"

Allday shrugged. "I ran once. I'll do it again."

"Mebbe, mebbe." He cocked his head to listen to some horses cantering along the roadway.

"With them bloody dragoons on yer tail you'd not get far, matey!"

"Then there's no way." Allday lowered his head, to think, to hide his eyes. It was something like a wild animal's sixth sense, an instinct which he had always possessed, and which had saved his skin too many times to remember. Something Bolitho admired and respected, and had told him as much.

The man said, "Sailmaker, y'say?"

Allday nodded. He had no fears there. He had learned to stitch and use a sailmaker's palm before he was eighteen. There were not many tasks aboard ship he could not manage.

"Does it matter now?"

"Look, matey, don't take that tone with me—"

Allday sighed. "You know how it is."

The other hid his relief. For a moment he had felt something akin to fear when the big man had stirred from smouldering anger.

"Right then. There are ways. An' there's those who needs the likes o' you." He gestured contemptuously at the closed door. "Not like them bilge rats. They'd rob an' cheat anyone, gallows meat th' lot of 'em!"

He moved closer to Allday and added quietly, "We're movin' tonight. So wot's it to be? Another poxy ship-o'-th'-line, or a berth in somethin' a bit more—" he rubbed a finger and thumb together "—*rewardin'*, like?"

101

Allday felt cold sweat on his chest. "Can it be done?"

"No questions. But yes, it can, an' it is!" He grinned. "You be ready, see?"

Allday leaned over to pick up his old jacket and was careful that the other man saw his tattoo. "I can't stomach being locked up."

"Right you are. But make no mistake. If you betray those who might be willin' to 'elp you, you'll pray for death on a halter. I've seen things—" He straightened up. "Just *believe* me, see?"

Allday thought of the corpse on the *Loyal Chieftain*'s deck, the rumours he had heard from some of the *Telemachus*'s hands that the murdered man's family had vanished too. It did not need a magician to discover why.

The door opened and the gunner's mate came in. "You can get yer grub now, er—Spencer."

Allday watched for a hint of understanding between them, but there was none. In this game nobody trusted anyone. Perhaps the gunner's mate was controlling this strange business?

Any deserter would probably take an offer of help, even if it landed him in the midst of a gang of smugglers. Being retaken by a press gang at best meant the same life from which he had tried to escape. At worst it could mean real hardship, plus a savage flogging as a warning to others.

The gunner's mate walked beside him to a long, scrubbed table where the others were already eating bread and cheese as if it was their last meal on earth.

He said, "Stick to the sea, Spencer. Don't get like them scum."

Allday asked casually, "What did you want to talk about?"

The gunner's mate picked up a tankard and waited for a seaman to fill it with ale for him.

"Don't matter now. Your ship, the *London*, 'as sailed for the Caribbean. You'll just 'ave to take what you're given."

When Allday had been pressed and taken to Bolitho's frigate *Phalarope* he had seen nothing like this. From a quiet Cornish road to the messdeck of a man-of-war. He smiled grimly. Him and Ferguson who had later lost an arm at the Saintes. Now they would serve no other. It was more like love than duty.

He glanced around the yard. Small groups of men were being mustered and checked by the lieutenant and some other members of a press gang.

His heart sank. Not a good seaman amongst them . . . he almost laughed. How could he care about the needs of the fleet when at any moment his own life might be in danger?

But there *had* to be a way of doing it. If not the gunner's mate, then who? No ordinary seaman, press gang or not, could manage it alone. It would be more than his life was worth. A brief court martial, a few prayers, and then run aloft to some big ship's mainyard to kick your breath to the wind. No, there had to be more involved than that.

He watched the lieutenant, the same one who had called on him to stand and be examined. Allday knew ships, and he knew officers. This lieutenant would not have the brains even to be dishonest.

The lieutenant shouted, "Pay attention. I'll not say it twice!"

Silence settled over the uneasy gathering.

He continued, "In view of the situation here you must move at dusk to Sheerness. You will go in separate parties, and obey all orders without hesitation. I shall personally see that any disorder is treated as mutiny." He glared around. "I need not say more, I think?"

Allday heard someone whisper, "Sheerness, up the road! Christ, Tom, we'll be signed into some ship afore the week's out!"

A tall figure with white patches on his collar moved from one of the outhouses.

Allday watched, his heart suddenly beating hard. The midshipman looked old for his lowly rank, about the same age as *Telemachus*'s Lieutenant Triscott. A pale, embittered face, the mouth turned down like someone permanently out of humour. Passed-over for lieutenant, or held back because of a senior officer's disfavour? There could be a dozen reasons.

Allday reached out to pick up some cheese and saw the midshipman give him a quick glance, then another at the seaman who had made him the offer.

So this was it. Allday tried to think clearly and calmly so that the chunk of dry cheese almost choked him.

There had to be an officer mixed up in it, even if it was an unimportant, passed-over midshipman.

The gunner's mate said, "That's Mr. Midshipman Fenwick. 'E'll be with your lot." He glanced at him curiously. "Between us, 'e's a pig, so watch yer step!"

Allday faced him. "I'll remember."

He returned to the cell-like room, his mind already busy on the next tack. If Bolitho discovered what was happening, it would be Mr. bloody Fenwick who would need to watch his step.

Allday grinned. *And that's no error*.

Commodore Ralph Hoblyn climbed up from the schooner's cabin and leaned heavily on an ebony stick while he looked along the upper deck.

Bolitho watched him and tried to read his thoughts. The schooner, originally Dutch, had been renamed the *Four Brothers*, and, according to her papers, was used for general trading from the port of Newcastle. Her owner and master were one and the same, a man named Darley who had died in the brief but savage fight with *Telemachus*.

Now she lay at anchor off Sheerness, with the scarlet coats of a full marine guard at bow and stern in case anyone inside or outside the dockyard might be tempted to pilfer her cargo.

Hoblyn regarded the great bloodstain which had defied all attempts of the captured smugglers to remove it. The remains of those cut down by the carronades' devastating bombardment had been thrown unceremoniously overboard, but the stain, and the shattered timbers and planking were evidence enough of the battle.

Hoblyn wiped his mouth with his handkerchief. Bolitho had noticed that he seemed to tire very easily. Was it just that he had become unused to the sea, or did this schooner's deck act as a cruel reminder of his last command?

He said, "I am extremely gratified, Bolitho. A full cargo, and a well-found vessel to boot." He glanced up at the rigging, some of which had been spliced by Paice's hands for the passage to Sheerness. "She'll fetch a good bounty at the next prize court, I

105

shouldn't wonder. The dockyard can patch and paint her beforehand, of course."

Bolitho asked, "You'll not take her into the service, sir?"

Hoblyn shrugged and winced. "I should be *delighted* to act on their lordships' behalf, naturally, Bolitho, but money first—theirs or someone else's." He turned towards him. "*No favours.*"

Hoblyn walked to the vessel's wheel and touched it thoughtfully. "I shall send word immediately. To the Customs Board too."

"So there were no arrests at Whitstable, sir?"

Bolitho half-expected Hoblyn to show concern or discomfort. If he felt either he concealed it well.

Only two smugglers had been caught on the shore by a patrol of dragoons who had been forewarned by Hoblyn about the expected run. In the skirmish both had been killed.

"No, more's the pity. But you took the *Four Brothers*, and that will make these felons think before they try again." He half-smiled. "I'm afraid you'll not get many recruits from the prisoners, though."

Bolitho stared across the water at the anchored cutter. He had never seen such a change in any vessel. The whole company seemed shocked and unable to believe what had happened. The fight had left five of their people dead and three more who were unlikely to recover from their wounds. In their small, tight company the losses had left a gap which new hands would be hard put to fill. Of the dead, the helmsman named Quin had been one of the most popular aboard. Ironically he had originally come from Newcastle, the *Four Brothers'* home port.

"Had we been able to take her by boarding, sir, then . . ."

Hoblyn made as if to touch his arm but withdrew it to his side. Another constant reminder.

He replied harshly, "It was not to be. They fired on a King's ship. There's not a judge in the land who would let them escape the scaffold, and rightly so!" He seemed to overcome the passion in his tone and added, "Be patient, Bolitho, you will have your men." He waved his stick towards the shore. "They're there, *somewhere*."

Bolitho turned away as Allday returned to his thoughts. It was not the first time he had acted alone. But now it was different. This enemy flew no flag. It could be anyone.

He watched as Hoblyn limped to another hatch where some men were preparing tackles for hoisting smaller items of cargo on deck. His mind kept returning to the boy Matthew Corker's discovery. The berlin concealed in Hoblyn's stables. Where did it come from? Hoblyn had arrived at the dockyard in an expensive carriage of his own, so had proved once again, if proof was needed, that he was a rich man. There could be no connection between Hoblyn and the schooner. It was far too risky. Any one of her hands might have turned King's evidence to save his neck, and damn anyone who was left secure.

Hoblyn remarked, "I suggest you do your utmost to get *Snapdragon* out of Chatham. I think you're going to need her. After your escapade with this schooner their lordships will likely feel more inclined to off-load some of these patrols from the revenue cutters to *your* shoulders." He turned so that the sunlight glittered in his eyes. "Who knows? I may discover more intelligence for you to act upon." He shaded his eyes with his disfigured hand and watched as his carriage moved slowly along the waterfront.

Bolitho followed his gaze and saw what he imagined was the white wig of Hoblyn's servant inside the carriage.

A lieutenant of the guard called to the boat alongside as Hoblyn limped carefully to the entry port.

Then he paused and glanced once more along the scarred decks.

"Speak to Paice's people, Bolitho. It would come better from you." He gave him a searching stare. "Your man was unhurt, I trust? I know how you value his services."

So casually said. Or was it?

Bolitho replied, "He is on an errand for me, sir."

He felt something like sick relief as Hoblyn lowered himself into the boat.

I wish to God I knew where he was.

The marine lieutenant watched him impassively and said, "We shall have a guardboat pulling around us until all the cargo is unloaded, sir."

Bolitho looked at him. A young, untried face. He remembered Paice's words. A man of war. *Am I really like that?*

"Good. Keep your men away from the spirits too." He saw the sudden indignation in his expression. "Even marines have been known to *drink*, you know." He saw *Telemachus*'s boat hooking on to the chains. "I shall leave it to you, Lieutenant."

On the short pull to the anchored cutter he noticed the way that the oarsmen watched him when they thought he was not looking. What was it now, he wondered? Respect, fear, or to learn what they were expected to become?

Paice greeted him at the cutter's side and touched his hat.

"All the wounded have been removed, sir. I fear that another of them died just before they left." He shifted unhappily. "His name was Whichelo, but then you'd not know him, sir."

Bolitho looked at the tall lieutenant and said, "*Know* him? Yes, of course. The one who was standing in full view by his gun. I am sorry the lesson had to be learned in death." He walked towards the companionway. "May I have the aid of your clerk, or is he the purser today?" He stepped down and almost expected to see Allday on the deck below, watching and waiting. "I have some despatches to be copied." He turned on the companion ladder, his face warm in the sunlight. "After *that*, prepare for sea, Mr. Paice."

Paice stared after him, his mind still grappling with Bolitho's cool acceptance of what had happened. Such a short while in their midst and yet he had even recalled the man who had just died.

Paice clenched his big hands. Bolitho had somehow managed to use that information like part of a lesson as well as a warning. Perhaps what he had seen and done since he had first gone to sea as a twelve-year-old midshipman had honed all the pity and compassion from him.

Paice thrust through the throng of seamen who were working on repairs to seek out Godsalve the clerk, so he did not see the man who had just left him in turmoil.

Bolitho knelt in the small cabin, the uncompleted model ship grasped in both hands like a talisman.

A man of war?

Allday groped his way around the small timbered outhouse feeling for anything he might use as a weapon.

All afternoon the party of six prisoners with an armed escort of seamen had marched along the road towards Sheerness. When dusk came, the midshipman named Fenwick who commanded the group ordered a halt at a small inn where he was received with familiarity, although not with warmth. The other five prisoners were locked in an outbuilding with their legs in irons as an extra precaution. Allday, apparently because of his superior status as a sailmaker, was kept apart.

Allday returned to a crate where he had been sitting. The stage was set, he thought vaguely. He had heard the midshipman explaining just a bit too loudly to the seamen in the press gang why he was separating them in this fashion.

Once, the man who had first approached Allday came to the outhouse with some water and a hunk of bread.

"Is this all?" Allday had smelled the rum on the man's breath. It was what he needed more than anything.

The man had grinned at his anger. "The others ain't gettin' nuthin'!"

Allday had tried to question him about the proposed escape. How would the midshipman explain it to his superior?

The man had held up his lantern to study him more closely. "Leave it to us. Yer talks too much. Just remember wot I told yer!"

If only he could lay hands on a dirk or a cutlass. Maybe they had already seen through his feeble disguise? Someone might even have recognised him, and they were holding him apart so that he could be silenced for good when night came.

At sea Allday could tell the time almost by the pitch of a hull, and on land, when he had spent a short while guarding sheep in Cornwall, he had grown used to reading the stars and the moon's position for the same purpose.

But sealed up in this dark hut he had no way of telling and it made him more uneasy.

He wondered what Bolitho was doing. It worried him to think of him managing on his own. But something had to be done. He tensed as he thought he heard a slight sound through the door.

Now the truth. He could feel his heart pounding, and tried to control his breathing.

If it is to be murder—he would take one with him somehow.

Lanternlight made a golden slit up one side of the door, and a moment later a bolt was drawn. Then the seaman peered in at him.

Allday saw the midshipman's white collar-patches glowing beyond the lantern, and sensed the sudden tension. Even the seaman seemed ill at ease.

"Ready?"

Allday left the hut and almost fell as the lantern was shuttered into darkness.

The midshipman hissed, "Stay together!" He peered at Allday. "One foul move and by God I'll run you through!"

Allday followed the midshipman, his eyes on his white stockings. It was not the first time *he* had made

111

this trip, he thought grimly. Rough ground, with scrub and bushes, the smell of cows from a nearby field. Then over a flint wall and towards a dark copse which loomed against the early stars like something solid. Allday's ears told him that nobody else from the press gang was coming with them. He heard the seaman behind him stagger, and tensed, expecting the sudden agonising thrust of steel in his back. But the man uttered a whispered oath and they continued on through the darkness. The trees appeared to move out and surround them like silent giants, and Allday knew from the midshipman's uneven breathing that he was probably doubly afraid because of his own guilt.

"This is far enough!" Midshipman Fenwick raised an arm. "Here it is!"

Allday saw him stopping to peer at a large, half-burned tree trunk. The meeting point. How many others had come here to sell themselves, he wondered?

The seaman spat on the ground and Allday saw the glint of a pistol in his belt, a cutlass bared and held in his fist; no doubt he was ready to use both.

Allday pricked up his ears. The creak of harness, perhaps, but if so the horses must have muffled hooves. Where was it? He strained his eyes into the darkness, so that when the voice spoke out he was surprised at its nearness.

"Well, well, Mr. Fenwick, another of your adventures."

Allday listened. The speaker had a smooth, what he would call an educated voice. No accent which he could recognise, and Allday had heard most of them on all the messdecks he had known.

Fenwick stammered, "I sent a message."

"You did indeed. A sailmaker, you say?"

"That is so." Fenwick was replying like a frightened schoolboy to his tutor.

"It had better be, eh?"

"There is just one thing." Fenwick could barely form his words for trembling.

The voice snapped, "More money, is it? You are a fool to gamble. It will be your undoing!"

Fenwick said nothing, as if he was unable to find the courage.

Allday watched the shadows. So it was gambling. The midshipman was probably being threatened because of debts. Allday stiffened and felt the hair rise on his neck. He had heard a footfall somewhere to his left, a shoe kicking against loose stones. He could still see nothing, and yet he sensed that there were figures all around them, unseen among the trees.

Fenwick must have felt it too. He suddenly blurted out, "I need help! It's this man—"

Allday crouched, ready to spring, and then realised that Fenwick was pointing at his armed seaman.

"What about him?" The voice was sharper now.

"He—he's been interfering, doing things without coming to me. I remembered what you said, how it was planned—" The words were pouring out in an uncontrollable torrent.

The voice snapped, "Put down your weapons, *both of you!*" When neither of them moved, Allday heard the metallic clicks of pieces being pulled to full cock. Then two shadows emerged from the opposite side, each armed with what appeared to be a hanger or, perhaps, a cutlass.

The seaman dropped his own blade and then tossed his pistol to the ground.

He rasped, "It's a bloody lie! The *young gentleman*'s gutless! You can't take 'is word fer nuthin'!"

Allday waited. There was defiance in the man's tone, anxiety too.

The voice asked, "And Spencer, if that is your name, why are *you* here?"

"I'll repay my escape by working, sir."

"Mr. Fenwick, how have you left matters at the inn?"

Fenwick seemed completely stunned by the change of manner. The unseen questioner was smooth, even jocular again.

"I—I thought we could claim Spencer had escaped—"

The seaman sneered, "See? Wot did I tell yer?"

"I have a better idea." There was a creak, as if the man was leaning out of a window of his carriage. "To have this sailmaker make good his escape, we need a victim, eh? A poor dead sailorman murdered as he tried to prevent it!"

The two shadows bounded forward and Allday heard the seaman gasp in pain as he was beaten to his knees.

"Here!" Allday felt the cold metal of a cutlass grip pushed into his fingers.

The voice said calmly, "Prove your loyalty to the Brotherhood—Spencer. That will bind both you and our gallant midshipman closer than ever to our affairs."

Allday stared at the kneeling figure while the others

114

stood clear. The cutlass felt like lead, and his mouth was as dry as a kiln.

The voice persisted, "Kill him!"

Allday stepped forward but at that moment the seaman threw himself on one side, scrambling for the pistol which he had dropped.

The explosion and the flash which lit up the motionless figures by the burned tree was like a nightmare. It all happened in seconds and Allday gritted his teeth as he saw the pistol fall once more, still gripped by the sailor's hand, which had been severed at the wrist by one blow from a cutlass. Even as the man rolled over and gave one last shrill scream the same attacker raised his blade and drove it down with such force Allday heard the point grate into the ground through the man's body.

The sudden silence was broken only by the sudden muffled stamp of nervous horses, the far-off barking of a farm dog, then the sound of wheels on some kind of cart-track.

The figure by the corpse bent down and picked up the fallen cutlass, but left the pistol still gripped by its severed hand.

He stared at Allday, his expression invisible. "Your turn'll come." To Fenwick he added, "Here, take this purse for your gaming table." There was utter contempt in his voice. "You can raise the alarm in an hour, though, God knows, some picket might have heard the fool shoot!"

Fenwick was vomiting against a tree, and the man said softly, "I'd finish him too, but—" He did not go on. Instead he watched as Fenwick picked up his weapons and the small bag of coins before adding,

"We had best be moving." He could have been grinning.

"You can keep the cutlass. You'll need it."

Allday looked back at the untidy corpse and wondered if Fenwick would be the next victim.

He followed the other man through the trees, the shadowy figures of his companions already on the move.

Allday had had cause to kill several men in his life. In anger, and in the fury of battle, sometimes in the defence of others. So why was this any different? Would he have killed the seaman to give his story more value, if the other man had not struck first?

Allday did not know, and decided it was better to keep it that way until the danger was past.

How quickly fate could move. Soon the midshipman would raise the alarm, and later they would find the corpse. A common seaman who had been murdered by an escaping prisoner named Spencer.

Allday thought of the unseen man in the carriage. If he could only manage to learn his name—he shook himself like a dog. One thing at a time. At present he was still alive, but the knowledge he had gained so far was enough to change that just as quickly.

7

In Good Company

LIEUTENANT CHARLES QUEELY clattered down *Wakeful*'s companion ladder and after a small hesitation thrust open the cabin door. Bolitho was sitting at the table, chin in hand while he finished reading the log.

He glanced up. "Good morning, Mr. Queely."

Queely contained his surprise. He had expected to find Bolitho asleep, not still going through his records and examining the chart.

He said, "I—I beg your pardon, sir. I was about to inform you that dawn is almost upon us." He glanced quickly around the cabin as if expecting to see something different.

Bolitho stretched. "I would relish some coffee if you could provide it." He knew what Queely was thinking, and found himself wondering why he did *not* feel tired. He had allowed himself no rest, and when *Telemachus* had sighted the other cutter he had arranged to be pulled across to Queely's command without delay or explanation.

Queely was usually well able to conceal his innermost feelings, and, despite his youth, had already slipped easily into a commander's role. But Bolitho's arrival, and the sight of *Telemachus* hove-to, displaying her powderstains, and areas of pale new timber where her carpenter and his crew had begun their repairs, had taken him all aback.

117

Queely had asked, "Will they return to the yard, sir?"

"I think not. I have told Lieutenant Paice that working together at sea to complete their overhaul, even though they are short-handed because of those killed and wounded, will do far more good. It will draw them into a team again, keep them too busy to grieve or to fall into bad ways."

Queely had been shocked to see the damage and had said immediately, "I knew nothing about it, sir. I carried out my patrol as you ordered, and after losing signalling contact with you I decided to remain on station."

That had been yesterday. Now, after a full night's sailing, they had continued to the south-east in spite of tacking again and again into the wind.

It was possible that Queely had been totally ignorant of the fierce close-action with the *Four Brothers*. With his studious features, hooked nose and deepset eyes he seemed to be a man who was well able to make up his own mind and act upon it. *I decided to remain on station*. What Bolitho might have said under the same circumstances.

As Queely pushed through the door to send for some coffee Bolitho looked around the cabin once more. *Telemachus* and this vessel had been built in the same yard with just a couple of years between them. How could they be so different? Even the cabin gave an air of intentional disorder, or temporary occupancy. As if Queely used it just for the purpose *Wakeful* was designed for, not as something to be coddled. Uniforms swayed from various hooks, while sidearms and swords were all bundled together in a half-open chest. Only Queely's sextant lay in pride of place, carefully wedged in a corner of his cot where it would be safe even in the wildest weather.

He thought of Paice's unspoken protest at being ordered immediately to sea after *Telemachus*'s first battle. Was it really the true reason he had sent him, the same explanation he had made to Queely? Or was it to protect Allday from sailors' casual gossip once they were able to get ashore?

If Allday was still alive . . . He ran his fingers through his hair with quiet desperation. *He was alive.* He must believe it.

The door opened and Young Matthew entered with a pot of coffee. His round face had lost its colour again, and his skin looked damp and pallid. He had been fighting his own battle with the motion. That was another difference between the two cutters. Paice *sailed* his *Telemachus*, Queely seemed to drive his command with the same lack of patience he exhibited in his daily routine.

Bolitho thought of Queely's second-in-command, a reedy lieutenant named Kempthorne. He came of a long line of sea-officers, and his own father had been a rear-admiral. Bolitho suspected that it was tradition rather than choice which had brought Kempthorne into the King's navy. Chalk and cheese, he thought. It was hard to see him having much in common with Queely. Bolitho had never seen so many, well-used books outside of a library. From them he had gathered that Queely was interested in many subjects, as widely ranged as tropical medicine and astronomy, Eastern religions and medieval poetry. A withdrawn, self-contained man. It would be useful to know more about him.

Bolitho looked at the boy over the top of his tankard. "Feeling a mite better, Matthew?"

The boy gulped and gripped the table as the sea surged along the hull and brought an angry exchange between the watchkeepers around the tiller.

"*Easier*, sir." He watched Bolitho drinking the coffee with despair. "I—I'm trying—" He turned and fled from the cabin.

Bolitho sighed and then slipped into his old, seagoing coat. For a few moments he fingered a faded sleeve and its tarnished buttons. Remembering it around her sun-blistered shoulders, her beautiful body lolling against him in the sternsheets. *And then* . . .

He almost fell as the hull rolled again and did not even notice the pain as his head jarred against the deckhead. He stared round wildly, the anguish sweeping over and through him like a terrible wave.

Will it never leave me?

He saw Queely angled in the doorframe, his eyes watching warily.

Bolitho looked away. *"Yes?"* He may have called out aloud. But Viola would never hear him. The picture haunted him, of Allday lowering her over the boat's gunwale while the others stared, unbelieving, their burned faces stricken as if each and every man had found and then lost something in her. And now Allday was gone.

Queely said, "Land in sight, sir."

They clambered up the ladder, the steps running with the spray which cascaded through the companionway each time *Wakeful* dipped her bowsprit.

Bolitho gripped a stanchion and waited for his eyes

120

to accept the grey half-light. The sky was almost clear. It held the promise of another fine day.

The watch on deck moved about with practised familiarity, their bodies leaning over to the cutter's swooping rolls and plunges, some wearing rough tarpaulin coats, others stripped to the waist, their bare backs shining like statuary in the flying spray. The "hard men" of *Wakeful*'s company. Every ship had them.

Bolitho wondered briefly what they thought about the *Four Brothers*. They had had no contact with *Telemachus* until yesterday, but he knew from experience that the navy created its own means of transmitting information: fact and rumour alike seemed to travel faster than a hoist from any flagship.

"Do you have a good lookout aloft?"

Queely watched his back, his hooked nose jutting forward like a bird of prey.

"Aye, sir." It sounded like *of course*.

"Have a glass sent aloft, if you please." Bolitho ignored Queely's angry glance at his first lieutenant and lifted a telescope from its rack beside the compass box.

As he wiped the lens with a handkerchief already damp in the spray, he said, "I want to know if anything unusual is abroad this morning."

He did not need to explain, but it gave him time to think.

He waited for a line of broken waves to sweep past the larboard beam, then braced his legs and levelled the glass beyond the shrouds. A shadow at first, then rising with the hull, hardening into an undulating wedge of land. He wiped his mouth and handed the telescope to Kempthorne.

France.

So near. The old enemy. Unchanged in the poor light and yet being torn apart by the Terror's bloody aftermath.

He heard the master say in a loud whisper, "We'm gettin' a bit close."

Queely raised his speaking trumpet and peered up at the lookout. "D'you see anything? *Wake up*, man!"

He sounded impatient; he probably thought it a waste to send a good telescope aloft where it might be damaged.

"Nuthin', sir!"

Queely looked at Bolitho. "I'd not expect much shipping here, sir. The Frogs maintain their inshore patrols all the way from the Dutch frontier, right down to Le Havre. Most ships' masters think it prudent to avoid arousing their attention."

Bolitho walked to the bulwark and thought of Delaval, and the *Four Brothers'* dead captain. The smuggling gangs seemed to come and go no matter whose ships were on patrol.

Queely explained, "The Frenchies have a stop, search and detain policy, sir. Several ships have been reported missing, and you'll get no information from Paris." He shook his head. "I'd not live there for a King's ransom."

Bolitho eyed him calmly. "Then we must ensure it cannot happen *here*, eh, Mr. Queely?"

"With respect, sir, unless we get more ships, the smugglers will ignore us too. The fleet is cut to virtually a handful of vessels, and now that they see a richer living in the Trade, able-bodied seamen are becoming a rare commodity."

122

Bolitho walked past the vibrating tiller bar and saw there were three men clinging to it, a master's mate nearby with his eyes moving from the mainsail's quivering peak to the compass and back again.

"That is why our three cutters must work together." Bolitho saw Young Matthew run to the lee bulwark and lean over it to vomit although his stomach had been emptied long ago. A passing seaman grinned, seized his belt and said, "Watch yer step, nipper, it's a long fathom down there!"

Bolitho looked past him but was thinking of *Telemachus*. "You are all unique, and because of the trust and loyalty shared by your people you are an example to others."

Queely watched him then said, "You were examining the log, sir?"

"Is that a question?" Bolitho felt the spray soaking into his shirt, but kept his eyes on the far-off ridge of land. "Whenever I have been given the honour of command I have examined the punishment book first. It always gives me a fair idea of my predecessor's behaviour, and that of his company. You should be grateful that your command is free of unrest and its inevitable repression."

Queely nodded uncertainly. "Aye, sir, I suppose so."

Bolitho did not look at him. He knew his comment was not quite what Queely had expected.

Some of the hands working at the halliards were chattering to each other when Queely shouted, "Belay that!" He held up his hand. "*Listen*, damn you!"

Bolitho clenched his hands together behind his back. Sharp hammer-like explosions. Small artillery, but firing in earnest.

"Where away?"

The master called, "Astern, starboard quarter, sir." The others stared at him but he faced them defiantly. "No doubt in my mind, sir."

Bolitho nodded. "Nor mine."

Queely hastened to the compass. "What must I do, sir?"

Bolitho turned his head to listen as another series of shots echoed across the water.

"Bring her about." He joined Queely beside the compass. "In this wind you can run free to the south-west." It was like thinking aloud. It was also like *Telemachus* all over again. The doubt, hesitation, opposition, even though nobody had raised a single protest.

Queely glanced at him. "That will surely take us into French waters, sir."

Bolitho looked at the straining mainsail, the way the long boom seemed to tear above the water with a mind of its own.

"Maybe. We shall see." He met his eyes and added, "It would seem that *someone* is abroad this morning after all?"

Queely tightened his jaw then snapped, "All hands, Mr. Kempthorne! Stand by to come about." He glared at the master as if he had caused his displeasure. "We shall steer south-west."

The master's face was blank. "Aye, aye, sir."

Bolitho suspected he was used to Queely's moods.

"Ready ho!"

"Put the helm down!"

Bolitho gripped the companion head for support again as with her headsail sheets set free and the sails flapping in wild confusion, *Wakeful* butted around and across the wind's eye.

"Mains'l *haul!*"

Bolitho dashed the spray from his face and hair and could have sworn that the long fidded topmast was curving and bending like a coachman's whip.

Queely's impatience matched Paice's pride.

"Meet her! Steady as you go—*steady*, man!"

Heeling over on the opposite tack *Wakeful* responded again to wind and rudder, but with the lively north-easterly hardening her sails like armour plating, she held firmly to her course, the motion less violent.

"Sou'-West, sir! Steady she goes!"

Bolitho walked stiffly to the larboard side and watched the first thin sunlight touch the land. It looked much nearer, but it was a trick of light and colour which often happened in coastal waters.

Bolitho snatched up a telescope as the lookout yelled, "Deck there! Ships on th' larboard bow!" He sounded breathless, as if the violence of the manoeuvre had almost hurled him down.

It was still too far. Bolitho watched the waves looming and fading as he trained the glass carefully on the bearing.

Smaller vessels. Perhaps three of them. One of them firing, the sound reaching him now through the planks under his feet. Like driftwood striking into the hull.

"Deck there! 'Tis a chase, sir! Steering sou'-west!"

Bolitho tried to picture it. A chase, using the same wind which made *Wakeful*'s canvas boom like thunder. What ships must they be?

"Let her fall off two points, Mr. Queely. Steer south-south-west."

He forced himself to ignore Queely's stifled resentment. "Make as much sail as you can safely carry. I want to catch them!"

Queely opened and closed his mouth. Then he beckoned to Kempthorne. "Loose the tops'l!"

Bolitho found time to think of his dead brother as under extra canvas the cutter seemed to throw herself across the short crests. No wonder he had loved his *Avenger*. The picture faded. If he ever really cared for anything.

He looked up and saw the sunshine touching each sail in turn, the canvas already steaming in the first hint of warmth.

The guns were still firing, but when he raised the glass again he saw that the angle of the sails had increased, as if the furthest craft was being headed off and driven towards the land when before she had been making for open water. Like a sheep being tired and then harried by the shepherd's dog until all thought of escape was gone.

A voice said, "We're overhaulin' the buggers 'and over fist, Ted!"

Another exclaimed, "They ain't even seen us yet!"

The coastline was taking on personality, while here and there Bolitho saw sunlight reflecting from windows, changing a headland from purple to lush green.

"Deck there!" Everyone had forgotten about the masthead. "Two French luggers, sir! Not certain about t'other, but she's in bad trouble! Canvas shot through, a topmast gone!"

Bolitho walked this way and that. Two luggers,

perhaps after a smuggler. "We shall discover nothing if the French take her." He saw the others staring at him. "*More sail*, Mr. Queely. I wish to stand between them!"

Queely nodded to the master then said in a fierce whisper, "We shall be inside their waters in half-an-hour, sir! They'll not take kindly to it." He offered his last card. "Neither will the admiral, I'm thinking."

Bolitho watched more men swarming aloft, their horny feet moving like paddles on the jerking ratlines.

"The admiral, fortunately, is in Chatham, Mr. Queely." He glanced round as more shot hammered over the crests. "Whereas we are here."

"It is my right to lodge a protest, sir."

"It is also your duty to fight your ship if need be, to the best of your ability." He walked away, angry with Queely for making him use authority when he only wanted co-operation.

"One of 'em's seen us, sir!"

The other lugger had luffed and was spilling canvas as she thrust over into the wind to meet *Wakeful*'s intrusion.

Queely watched the lugger, his eyes cold. "Clear for action."

Kempthorne strode aft from the mainmast, his gaze questioning.

"Sir?"

"Then stand by to shorten sail!"

Bolitho looked across the deck, feeling his displeasure, his resistance.

"Have your gunner lay aft, Mr. Queely. I wish to speak with him."

Something touched his coat and he turned to see

127

the boy staring up at him, the old sword clutched in both hands.

Bolitho gripped his shoulder. "That was *well* done, Matthew."

The boy blinked and stared at the frantic preparations to cast off the gun's breechings without hampering the men at halliards and braces. There was no longer awe there, nor excitement. His lips quivered, and Bolitho knew that fear, and the reason for it, had replaced them. But his voice was steady enough, and only Bolitho knew what the effort was costing him. As he helped Bolitho clip the sword into place he said, "It's what *he* would have done, sir, what he would have expected of me."

Once again, Allday's shadow was nearby.

Luke Teach, *Wakeful*'s gunner, waited patiently while Bolitho described what he wanted. He was a thickset, fierce-looking man who hailed from the port of Bristol, and was said to boast that he was a true descendant of Edward Teach, or Blackbeard as he was known. He had also come from Bristol, a privateer who soon found piracy on the high seas was far more rewarding.

Bolitho could well believe it, for the gunner had a jowl so dark that had the King's Regulations allowed otherwise he might have grown a beard to rival that of his murderous ancestor.

Bolitho said, "I intend to drive between the luggers and the other vessel. The French may not contest it, but if they do—"

Teach touched his tarred hat. "Leave 'un to me, zur." He bustled away, calling names, picking men

128

from various stations because he knew their ability better than anyone.

Queely said, "That ship is in a poor way, sir." But his eyes were on the preparations around the carronades. "I fear we may be too late."

Bolitho took the telescope and examined the other vessels.

The luggers would be wary of the English cutter, for although they served their navy and were well-handled, probably by local men, like *Wakeful*'s, they would be unused to open combat.

He watched the nearest one tacking steeply under a full press of tan-coloured sails and saw the new French ensign flapping from her gaff, the little-known Tricolour set in one corner of the original white flag.

He glanced up and saw that Queely had already made his own gesture, although he doubted if the French would need to see an English flag to know her nationality and purpose.

The craft being chased had lost several spars and was barely making headway, some rigging and an upended boat trailing alongside to further pull her round. A fishing vessel of some kind, Bolitho thought, their own or English did not matter. It seemed very likely she might be employed in the Trade—few revenue officers dared to venture into the fishermen's tight community.

"God, she's taking it cruelly." Kempthorne was standing on the mainhatch to get a better look as more shots pursued the stricken vessel, some striking the hull, others tearing through rigging and puncturing her sails.

"Run out, Mr. Queely." Bolitho rested his hand on his sword hilt and watched as the *Wakeful*'s men

129

hauled and guided their guns up to their open ports.

The French lugger would know what that meant. *Baring her teeth*. Making it clear what she intended.

The lugger changed tack and began to fall down-wind to draw nearer to her consort.

Teach the gunner was creeping along the bulwark like a crab, pausing to peer through every port, to instruct each man, a handspike here, a pull on a tackle there. *Wakeful* was no fifth-rate but at least she was prepared.

Queely exclaimed, "The Frogs are hauling off!"

Bolitho thought he knew why but said nothing. The explosion when it came was violent and unexpected. A tongue of flame shot from the fishing boat's deck and in seconds her canvas was in charred flakes, the rigging and upperworks savagely ablaze.

A boat was pulling away, and must have been in the water, hidden by the shattered hull before the explosion was sparked off. One of the luggers fired, and a ball passed above the little boat to hurl a water-spout high into the air.

Queely stared at Bolitho, his eyes wild. "*Engage*, sir?"

Bolitho pointed to the fishing boat. "As close as you dare. I don't think—" The rest was lost in a second explosion as a ball crashed directly into the oared boat, and when the fragments had finally ceased splashing down—there was nothing to be seen.

Queely banged one hand into his palm. "*Bastards!*"

"Shorten sail, if you please." Bolitho trained his glass on the sinking fishing boat. By rights she should have gone by now, but some trick of buoyancy defied both the fire and the gashes in her hull.

Kempthorne whispered to his commander, "If there is another explosion we shall be in mortal danger, sir!"

Queely retorted, "I think we are aware of it." He looked hotly at Bolitho. "*I* certainly am."

There was a far-off, muffled bang, and it seemed an eternity before a great fin of spray cascaded across the sea near the capsizing hull. Fired at maximum range from some shore battery which was watching the drama through powerful telescopes. Probably a thirty-two-pounder, a "Long Nine" as the English nicknamed them, an extremely accurate gun, and the largest carried by any man-of-war. For that purpose it was also used on both sides of the Channel to determine the extents of their territorial waters.

Wakeful was out of range for any accurate shooting. But it would only need one of those massive iron balls, even with the range all but spent, to dismast her, or shatter her bilges like a battering ram.

It was why the luggers were keeping well clear, and not just because they were unwilling to match the cutter's carronades.

Bolitho said, "No time to put down the boat. I want grapnels." He looked at the men not employed at the guns. "*Volunteers* to board that wreck!"

Nobody moved, and then one of the half-naked seamen swaggered forward. "Right ye be, sir."

Another moved out. "Me too, sir."

A dozen hands shot up, some of the gun crews too.

Bolitho cleared his throat. Allday might have got volunteers; he had not expected to do it himself with total strangers.

"Take in the mains'l!" Queely had his hands on

131

his hips, pressing against his waist to control his agitation.

"Tops'l and jib, Mr. Kempthorne, they will suffice!"

Bolitho walked amongst the volunteers as they prepared their heaving lines and grapnels.

The first volunteer peered at him and asked, "Wot we lookin' fer, sir?" He had the battered face of a prize-fighter, and Bolitho's mind clung to yet another memory, that of Stockdale, his first coxswain, who had died protecting his back at the Saintes.

"I don't know, and that's the God's truth." He craned over the bulwark and watched the sinking hull moving dangerously near. The surrounding sea was covered with dead fish and shattered casks, flotsam, charred remains, but little else.

There was another distant bang and eventually the ball slammed down just a few yards from the wreck. The fishing boat was an aiming mark for the invisible shore battery, Bolitho thought. Like a lone tree in the middle of a battlefield.

The shock of the heavy ball made the wreck lurch over and Bolitho heard the sudden inrush of water as the seams opened up to speed its end.

"Grapnels!"

Four of them jagged into the wreck and within seconds the seamen were clawing their way across, urged on by their messmates, the luggers all but forgotten except by Teach and his handpicked gun crews.

The shore battery fired again, and spray fell across the sinking vessel and made the seamen there peer round with alarm.

132

Queely said hoarsely, "They'll catch us at any moment, sir!"

A grapnel line parted like a pistol shot; the wreck was starting to settle down. There was no point in any further risk.

"Cast off! Recall those men!"

Bolitho turned as the man with the battered face yelled, *"'Ere, sir!"*

He floundered through a hatchway where the trapped water already shone in the sunlight like black glass. If the hull dived nothing could prevent it, and he would certainly go with her.

"Call him back!"

Bolitho watched, holding his breath as the man reappeared. He was carrying a body over his bare shoulders as effortlessly as a sack.

Queely muttered, "God's teeth, it's a woman!"

Willing hands reached out to haul them on board, then as the wreck began to dip, and another line snapped under the strain, Bolitho said, "Carry on, Mr. Queely, you may stand your ship out of danger."

A ball smashed across the water and hit the wreck beneath the surface.

"Loose the mains'l! More hands aloft there!"

Wakeful gathered way, flotsam and dead fish parting beneath her long bowsprit.

When Bolitho looked again, the fishing boat had vanished. He walked slowly through the silent seamen then felt his head swim as he saw the woman lying on the deck. She was just a girl, wearing rough, badly made clothing, a coarse shawl tied under her long hair. One foot was bare, the other still encased in a crude wooden *sabot*.

They stood around staring until Queely pushed

between them, and, after glancing questioningly at Bolitho, knelt beside her.

The man who had carried her aboard said, "She be *dead*, sir." He sounded stricken, cheated.

Bolitho looked at her face. The eyes tightly shut, with saltwater running from them like tears, as if she was asleep, trapped in some terrible dream.

Some poor fishergirl probably, caught up in a conflict in which she had no part.

But looking at her pale features reminded Bolitho of only one thing, that moment when Viola had been given to the sea.

Queely opened the front of the girl's clothing and thrust his hand underneath and around her breast.

Apart from the wind in the sails there was no other sound.

Queely withdrew his hand and tidied her wet garments with unexpected care.

"Dead, sir." He looked up at him dully. "Shall I have her put over?"

Bolitho made himself move closer, his hands bunched so tightly that he could feel the bones cracking.

"*No*. Not yet." He looked at the watching faces. "Have her sewn up." He lowered himself to the deck and touched her hair. It was like sodden weed.

Then he looked at her bare, outthrust foot. "What are those marks?"

Queely glanced at him. He had been looking at the sails, and the men at the tiller, to make certain there was no chase, no further threat from the battery.

"Sir?"

Bolitho made himself hold her ankle. It was like

134

ice. There were scars on the skin, raw, like the marks of irons.

Queely explained. "The wooden *sabots*, sir. They did it. Look at the other one."

"Yes. I see." Bolitho wanted to cover her. To hide her pain from their eyes.

Then he stared at the lieutenant across her body. "I should have seen it." He ignored Queely's surprise and took her bare foot in his fingers. It was all he could do not to cry out as the memory probed through him.

Her foot was soft, and not from the sea. Too soft for a rough wooden shoe, and one more used to happier times, to dancing and laughter. He lowered his face until it was almost touching hers. "Come here." He felt Queely kneel beside him. "Can you smell it?"

Queely hesitated. "Aye, sir. Very faint." He pushed the wet hair from the girl's stricken face so that it still seemed it might awaken her, open her eyes to his touch. He said, "Perfume, sir."

Bolitho examined her small hands, stiffening now in spite of the warm sunlight. Dirty, but smooth and well kept.

Queely said quietly, "No fishergirl, this one, sir."

Bolitho stood up and held on to a backstay for support. He looked abeam but the luggers were partly hidden in low haze, the land already meaningless.

He knew Queely was searching her body but could not watch.

Queely stood up and held out a lace-edged handkerchief. It had the initial *H* in one corner. Soaked in seawater but quite clean. A last link perhaps with a life which had rejected her.

Queely said heavily, "That's all, sir."

Bolitho took it. "One day perhaps—" He could not go on.

Later at the lee bulwark the small, canvas-sewn body was raised on a grating.

Lieutenant Kempthorne had asked if a flag was required but Bolitho had replied, "She has been destroyed by her own, and ours cannot help her now."

With heads uncovered the seamen stood about and watched in silence.

Bolitho steeled himself, then turned as Queely, his hat crushed beneath one arm, said something aloud in French.

Then he repeated to his men around him, "We cannot kneel beside her grave, but we commend her to the sea from which she came."

There was a brief slithering sound, a splash alongside, and in twos and threes the men broke up and returned to their duties.

Queely replaced his hat and said, "Well, sir?"

"How strange it should be a young, unknown French girl who has become our first ally in this wretched business."

Watched by Queely he took out the handkerchief and shook it in the warm breeze.

"She *will* be remembered." He stared astern at *Wakeful*'s frothing progress. "She is safe now, and in good company."

8

By Sea And By Stealth

THE hoofbeats of the three horses became more muffled as they turned off the narrow road and on to rough moorland, the grass still glittering from overnight rain.

Bolitho kneed his horse forward and watched the sunlight uncovering the trees and some scattered farm buildings. Opening up the land, like the sunshine of that morning when they had sighted the pursued fishing boat.

Wakeful had anchored before dawn and within the hour Bolitho had been mounted, and with Young Matthew following close behind had set off to this place.

In the early sunlight he saw the trooper of dragoons pausing to peer back at them, his scarlet coat and white crossbelt very bright against the dripping trees.

The man had been waiting to escort him as soon as the cutter was anchored. The commodore's aide had sent the message, although he had been unable to offer any more intelligence regarding the reason. Hoblyn it appeared was away again visiting some boatyard.

He heard the boy yawning hugely behind him. Half-asleep still, dazed by the events he had shared and witnessed, and obviously grateful to feel the land under him again.

The trooper called, "Not much further, sir." He eyed Bolitho curiously. "Am I ridin' too fast for 'e, sir?"

"I'm a Cornishman." Bolitho's voice was unusually curt. "I am used to riding."

The trooper hid a grin. "Oi be from Portsmouth, sir, but Oi knows nowt about ships!" He spurred his horse into a trot.

Bolitho noticed that the trooper had a short carbine, favoured by the dragoons, already drawn and resting across his saddle. Like a skirmisher in enemy territory. In such peaceful countryside it seemed unreal.

Again and again Bolitho's mind returned to the dead girl. She was his only link, and yet he still did not know how to use it. Instead he saw her face, tight with shock when she must have realised she had only seconds to live. He imagined he could still feel the icy skin of her ankle in his grip. *Viola*.

Whom could he trust? Who would believe him, or even want to believe him?

"'Ere we be, sir."

Bolitho gave a start and realised that they were cantering into a widespread copse of tall trees. There was a clearing now, almost circular, with a burned-out tree in the centre. The perfect place for a duel, he thought grimly.

Amongst the trees he saw several scarlet-clad figures, the occasional nervous swish of a horse's tail. There was something sinister about the clearing. A place of danger.

An officer was sitting on a small stool, drinking from a silver tankard while his orderly stood attentively at his elbow. He saw Bolitho and handed his man the tankard before rising to his feet.

His uniform was beautifully cut, but could not disguise his slight belly. A man who lived well, despite his calling, Bolitho thought.

The officer raised his hat and smiled. "Major Philip Craven, 30th Regiment of Dragoons." He gave a slight bow. "Would you care for a taste?"

He had an easy, pleasant manner, and was younger than Bolitho had first imagined.

Bolitho noticed that, despite his relaxed air, his eyes were rarely still. On his men, the horses, or the track which they had just left.

Bolitho replied, "I should enjoy that." It surprised him, for he was usually ill-at-ease with the army, foot *or* cavalry.

As the orderly busied himself with a basket on the ground, Bolitho noticed a naval lieutenant and a tall, pale-faced midshipman for the first time.

The major gestured. "Two officers of the press."

Bolitho took the proffered tankard and was glad he could keep it so steady.

More trouble. Was it Allday?

He asked, "Why was I informed?"

The major shrugged. "I've heard of your—er, exploits of course. When the commodore is away, I try to keep in contact with the navy and the civil authority." He frowned suddenly. "God, you'd think we were an army of occupation!" He beckoned for the orderly to refill his tankard and added, "One of the sailors was murdered here, trying to retake a man who had escaped from their custody."

Bolitho sipped the wine. It was, he suspected, very expensive claret.

139

The major explained, "The midshipman was here too, but they were rushed by some mob or other, and his sailor was cut down." He walked slowly to a patch of trampled grass. "Found his severed hand just here, the pistol still in it. It had been fired, so he may have winged one of the scum. But luck in that direction is thin on the ground. I've had my fellows search the area." He added bitterly, "By God, they're getting used to that, I can tell you, sir! But there was nothing. I did not expect there would be." He looked around at the watching trees, the way that the sunlight seemed shut out, beyond reach.

Then he said, "I can see that you feel it too. This is a place of ill repute. Nobody comes here now." His eyes sparked in a memory. "However there was a carriage here recently. But we lost the tracks as soon as it left the copse."

"A local man of importance?"

The major observed him shrewdly. "I have my own ideas. But what can I do? To think that within a year perhaps, I shall be ordered to lead my dragoons—" he waved vaguely in the direction of the sea, "against French invaders, to protect the same people who lie, cheat, and if necessary murder anyone who stands up to them!"

"Is it really as bad as that?"

The major smiled. "My colonel will tell you, given half a chance. He was in Thanet, about eight years ago when he was a captain. He was ordered to Deal, with a troop of fifty dragoons, to put down a smugglers' gang and burn their boats." His eyes hardened as he saw it in his mind, imagining himself and not his colonel. "They were set upon by an armed mob of well over a thousand, and were cut off. But for

140

the timely arrival of the 38th Regiment of Foot, who, God bless 'em, had marched all the way from Canterbury to assist, my colonel's troop would have been massacred. I am a soldier, and I have seen some terrible sights, just as you have. But this kind of work leaves me sick with disgust."

Bolitho saw Young Matthew leading his horse towards the trees, then pausing as a dragoon held up his hand and shook his head.

"Why don't people come here?"

The major shrugged. "You see that burned-out tree? A smuggling gang caught a man from the nearby village. He had been spying on them, was well known for it apparently. Sometimes he was said to have sold information to the revenue officers, even to the army."

"So they killed him here?" Bolitho looked hard at the clearing.

"No. They set fire to that tree, then burned out his eyes. A warning to others, if one such were needed!"

Bolitho felt his shirt clinging clammily to his body. "Thank you for telling me all this." He beckoned to the two watching sea-officers. "I'll be quick."

The major smiled. "I'm willing to fight in the open. But here? I'd prefer to use infantry!"

The lieutenant touched his hat and explained that he had been in charge of a press gang, and had ordered his midshipman to march some prisoners to Sheerness.

Bolitho said sharply, "I will attend to that matter presently." The lieutenant's obvious eagerness to shift any blame to his subordinate's shoulders was sickening.

"Who are you?" Bolitho eyed the pale midshipman,

and immediately sensed his fear. "Tell me exactly what happened."

"Midshipman Fenwick, sir." He looked anywhere but at Bolitho's eyes. "I—I had halted my party at a small inn, as is customary, sir, and whilst doing rounds I discovered that one of my charges had escaped. There was no time to rouse the guard, so I decided to give chase along with—" His eyes moved nervously to the trampled grass. "We were outnumbered. They were everywhere—"

The major interrupted gently, "It was at *night*, Captain Bolitho."

"I see." Bolitho watched the midshipman's hands. Fingers opening and twitching. More like an old man than one at the start of his chosen calling. Passed over for promotion, failed his lieutenant's examination, but opportunity was still with him, something too often denied others altogether.

Bolitho asked, "Who was the man who escaped?"

"He—he was a sailmaker, sir, we'd kept him apart from the rest because—" His voice trailed away, then he exclaimed, "I did my best, sir!"

The lieutenant stared at Fenwick angrily. "He should have known better, sir. The one good man we'd been able to catch, a deserter from the *London*, and this fool let him run!"

Bolitho snapped, "Pray be silent." Then to the midshipman he said, "Can you recall the sailmaker's name?" He did not really care, but there was more to this than was out in the open. The midshipman was hiding something. Perhaps he had run away and left the seaman to die alone, a memory which would haunt him for the rest of his life.

The midshipman screwed up his eyes. "I—I—"

Then he nodded. "Yes, sir. It was Spencer. I recall it now!"

The major remarked, "Probably already at sea in some smuggling vessel."

Bolitho turned away to conceal his expression from them. He walked a few paces, feeling their eyes following him. Perhaps Allday could not read or write, but he knew and loved animals. Especially the old sheepdog at the great grey house in Falmouth, whom Bolitho had named Spencer.

He turned abruptly and said to the lieutenant, "You will place this midshipman under open arrest, and you will remain with him at the dockyard, until a proper enquiry has been carried out."

He ignored the lieutenant's dismay and Fenwick's shocked gasp. If they were involved it would be better if they were safely under supervision. Either way they would lose if implicated. A court martial, and death at a yardarm, or—he looked at the burned-out tree —much worse if others discovered they had been unmasked.

The major followed him to the horses and said admiringly, "I *liked* that."

Bolitho glanced at him and smiled briefly. He might not like it so much if he knew the real reason.

He raised his boot to the stirrup and saw Young Matthew watching him from the other horse.

Allday was alive. Was risking his life once again, for him.

It was all he could do to keep his voice normal.

"I shall go to the commodore's residence, Major. He may have returned."

"Then I shall escort you, sir." The major was pleased to leave.

As they moved out of the trees into the welcoming sunshine, and the dragoons formed into pairs behind their officer, Bolitho turned in his saddle and looked back towards the sinister copse. He saw rooks circling above the trees, their raucous voices breaking the stillness like taunting cries.

No wonder people avoided the place. He felt his jaw tighten as he saw the dead girl's face in his mind again.

She may have died alone when the fishing boat had blown up, but he doubted it. His heart rebelled against it as he recalled the small boat pulling frantically away before the explosion had blasted the fisherman apart. Whoever they had been must have locked the girl on board before lighting a fuse, something prepared long in advance should they be found by one of the French patrol vessels.

There may have been only a few terrified people; there could have been hundreds who had fled the Terror, selling all their possessions, even themselves, for the chance to escape.

Smugglers? Slavers would be a closer description, and that was too good for them.

Wakeful had been the only witness, and now, because of it, Allday's own life was doubly at risk.

He waited until the major had cantered up beside him and then asked, "That man you mentioned to me." He looked at him directly. "Is he still alive?"

The dragoon nodded, his eyes on the surrounding hedges. "In his own crazed world. People give him food, though they are careful to keep secret their Christian generosity. My own men toss him some scraps, I suspect. He were better dead. Alive he is a

144

living reminder of what will happen to those who inform on the Brotherhood."

Bolitho asked, "Could you find him for me?" He saw the disbelief in his eyes. "It is just a straw. I can ignore nothing, no matter how futile it may appear."

The major nodded. "I shall *try*." He glanced at Bolitho's profile. "I am with you in this affair, sir, for I too am heartily sick of waiting."

Bolitho reached out and impetuously took his gloved hand.

"So be it!"

He shivered despite the warm air. The time for caution was over.

Apart from the usual marine sentries, the commodore's residence appeared to be deserted, but after asking the corporal of the guard point-blank, Bolitho said, "He's back."

Major Craven's orderly stood with Young Matthew holding the horses' heads, and Bolitho noticed that the rest of the small detachment of dragoons remained mounted in the road outside the gates.

The door swung inwards noiselessly and Bolitho saw it was Hoblyn's personal footman.

"I must see the commodore."

The youth glanced beyond the two officers as if he was about to deny that Hoblyn had returned. Bolitho saw his hazel eyes widen with alarm at the sight of the mounted dragoons, then he said, "I shall take you to him." He drew back from the steps, then led the way towards that same room.

The major grimaced. "Like a tomb. Needs a woman's touch."

The commodore was sitting behind his massive

desk but made no attempt to rise as they were ushered in.

Hoblyn said in his clipped fashion, "Why the urgency? I've much to accomplish. There are not enough hours in the day."

Bolitho began, "I sent a report—"

"Did you indeed?" Hoblyn glanced coldly at the major. "Do *you* wish to see me too?"

Craven stood firm. "Captain Bolitho thinks it might be better for all of us if I did, sir."

"I see." Hoblyn waved towards two chairs and shuffled some papers on his desk. "Ah yes, the *report*. I did see it, I remember now. The fishing boat and the two French luggers." He looked up suddenly, his eyes hard. "You moved too hastily, Bolitho. The French will swear you acted unlawfully in their waters. Right or wrong, they will certainly use the incident to endanger peace, something that His Majesty is trying to preserve. He does not wish to antagonise the French, no matter what state their country is in."

Bolitho retorted, "I would have thought that His Majesty might have an even greater desire to retain his head on his shoulders!"

Hoblyn snapped, "That is *impertinent!* In any case, why should it matter about one fishing boat? Surely you can use your talents to better advantage?" He was becoming angrier by the minute, his maimed hand tapping the desk to emphasise each point.

Bolitho said, "I believe they were smuggling émigrés across the Channel, sir. Human cargo, with no thought for the consequences." Even as he told Hoblyn about the dead girl he saw the commodore's eyes give just the briefest hint of anxiety.

146

Then Hoblyn snapped, "Who will say, one way or the other? It is just your word, Bolitho, which I am afraid will carry little weight in Admiralty." He leaned forward and stared at him, the major ignored or forgotten. "They will break you if you persist with this obsession. You know from your own experience in London that there are a hundred captains who would grasp your appointment and be grateful!"

Bolitho replied stubbornly, "I cannot believe that you think that the tolerance of a crime should be in the same boat as the fear of annoying the French government. If so, then I want no part of it. I will return to London and resign." He heard the major's boots squeak as he shifted his position in the chair. It was surprising he could hear anything above the pounding of his own heart.

Hoblyn dabbed his brow with his handkerchief. "Let us not be hasty, Bolitho."

Bolitho said simply, "I am asking you, sir, *pleading* if you will, that you will forget the security of this appointment and use your influence to intervene. It seems that every man's hand is against us here, and the smugglers laugh at our attempts to run them to earth."

Hoblyn stared at his desk. "You have so much passion, Bolitho, yet so little trust in authority."

"I have no cause to be trusting, sir."

Hoblyn appeared to be wrestling with his innermost thoughts. "You are quite determined to continue in this fashion, regardless of the hornets' nest you will most surely rouse?"

"I have no choice, sir, but I must have support."

"Yes." Hoblyn moved his shoulder as if it was hurting him. "You may be correct to assume that there is a direct link between the smugglers and the oppression in France. It is certainly true that our prime minister has been urging stronger action against these gangs." He added bitterly, "I fear that William Pitt has done precious little to supply the money to enforce the necessary prevention!"

Major Craven murmured, "Everyone sends for the dragoons, sir."

Hoblyn gave a deep sigh. "I will send a despatch to the Admiralty, Bolitho. It will be up to their lordships, of course, but I shall explain that I am in favour of a more aggressive policy."

Bolitho said, "Thank you, sir." He hoped that his surprise did not show in his voice. From anger to agreement; it was too sudden, too easy. Not like the captain who had once stormed an enemy privateer with his body ablaze.

Hoblyn pressed his fingertips together and stared at him impassively.

"Draw your three cutters to Sheerness."

"They are here, sir. *Snapdragon* left Chatham dockyard in my absence."

Hoblyn gave a thin smile. "I hope you can continue to stay ahead of events, Bolitho. There are some who will wish you dead. I suggest you move ashore as soon as is prudent. I will arrange quarters inside the dockyard here at Sheerness. It will be safer for you.

The door opened silently and the slim footman stood watching from the hallway. It was as if he could read his master's thoughts.

"Jules will show you out, gentlemen."

Bolitho and the major got to their feet. Apparently there was to be no wine this time.

Hoblyn said, "Inform me of your every intention."

He eyed both of them for several seconds. "My head will not rest on any block because of your personal ambitions!"

The interview was over.

Outside on the cobbles Bolitho said grimly, "A victory or a reverse, I am uncertain which."

The soldier frowned. "Far better than sitting still. It is high time that the authorities understand what we are facing. You need men for the fleet—"

Bolitho saw Young Matthew leading the horse towards him. "If and when a fleet is refitted in time!"

"Either way, you'll not get the men until you scatter the Brotherhood and lessen their power over ordinary people."

The major climbed into his saddle and looked down at him.

"I am with you."

Bolitho smiled. "Do not forget what I asked of you."

The soldier grinned. "I said, I shall *try!*" Then he cantered from the yard, touching his hat to the sentries as he rejoined his troop on the road.

A good officer, Bolitho thought, and for some reason one he knew he could trust.

At the dockyard they left the horses with a marine, and walked to the jetty where some boats were loitering.

For a moment longer Bolitho stared at the three anchored cutters, riding above their reflections like graceful seabirds. *His little brood.* Even that reminded him of Allday.

He said to a waterman, "Take me to *Telemachus.*"

As the boat moved slowly amongst the anchored vessels Bolitho saw the glint of sunlight on a raised telescope from *Wakeful*'s taffrail. He looked away. It was most likely to be Queely, watching his progress, glad to be rid of him—or was he?

Paice greeted him at the entry port and touched his hat. Bolitho was surprised to see his apparent pleasure.

"I was not certain you would return to us, sir." He grinned. "Welcome."

He waved one big hand around the busy figures on deck. "You were right, sir. They've all worked so hard together that most of the pain is behind them."

Bolitho nodded approvingly. Apart from the strong smells of tar and paint, there was virtually nothing to show of the damage.

As he caught the glances of some of the seamen he saw them nod self-consciously, before turning back to their tasks. Like a homecoming.

Paice became serious again. "No news of your cox'n, sir."

"What do you know?" Bolitho met his gaze.

"Only that he is on a mission for you, *officially* that is." He glanced at his men. "But news has wings. The longer it takes . . ." He did not finish.

Bolitho touched his arm. "I know. Please let it lie, for his sake if not for mine."

He glanced at the waterfront, the bright sunshine, the sense of peace.

"I shall write some fresh orders for you." He turned and looked at him steadily. "You will command here if anything happens to me."

Paice's strong features were a mixture of pleasure and anxiety.

"They'd not *dare*, sir!"

Bolitho's gaze seemed to embrace all three cutters.

"I might lose this appointment at the whim of some quill-pusher in Admiralty. I might even fall in a fight. It is *our way*, Mr. Paice, so be ready for anything."

Paice walked with him to the companionway. "Hell's teeth, sir, you've changed the people here and in the other cutters. You'll not find us wanting next time."

Bolitho closed the door of the cabin behind him and stared up at the open skylight.

Was Hoblyn guilty of some conspiracy, or did he really not care for involvement of any kind? Bolitho thought of the graceful footman, and grimaced. *Jules*. It suited him well.

He did not remember falling asleep, but awoke with his forehead resting on his arm, the pen still in his fingers from the moment he had signed Paice's new orders.

Paice was sitting opposite him on a sea chest, his eyes doubtful.

"You've not slept for two days, I'll wager, sir." It sounded like an accusation. "I was most unwilling to rouse you, but—"

Bolitho saw the wax-sealed envelope in his fist and was instantly alert. Since the tender age of twelve his mind and body had been hardened to it. Years of watchkeeping in all weathers, moments of anxiety to banish any craving for sleep when the watch below was turned up to reef sails in a screaming gale, or to repel enemy boarders. It was the only life he had ever known.

"What is it?"

He slit open the envelope and first read the signature at the bottom. It was from Major Craven, the hand neat and elegant, like the man. He read it through twice very carefully. He was aware that the cutter was moving more than she had been when his head had dropped in sleep, just as he was conscious of Paice's measured breathing.

He looked up and saw the gleam in the lieutenant's eyes.

"Where is 'the old abbey'?"

Paice withdrew a chart from a locker without questioning him. He jabbed the coastline with one big finger. "Here, sir. 'Bout three miles to the east'rd. A quiet, dismal spot, if you ask me."

Bolitho peered at it and nodded. The ideal place for a meeting. To move by road, as Craven had pointed out, would soon draw somebody's notice, and the words would go out like lightning. The troublesome Cornish captain was on the move again.

By sea then, and by stealth.

He said, "We will weigh before dusk and steer for the Great Nore." He moved some brass dividers to the north-east from Sheerness. "Once in the dark we will come about and make a landfall here—" the dividers rested on the point marked as an ancient abbey. "Nobody must see us, so you will anchor off shore."

Paice's hand rasped over his chin. "Beg pardon, sir, but I *am* in the dark right now. Are you intending to send a press gang ashore? Because if so—"

Bolitho stared at the much-used chart. "No, I am meeting someone. So I shall need a good boat's crew and someone who knows these waters like his own right arm."

Paice replied without a second's hesitation, "The master, Erasmus Chesshyre, sir. Feel his way inshore like a blind man."

152

Bolitho glanced sharply at him, but Paice's remark was an innocent one.

Paice added, "I'd like to go with you, sir."

"No." It was final. "Remember what I told you. If anything should happen—"

Paice sighed. "Aye. I know, sir."

"One last thing, Mr. Paice. If the worst should happen, send Young Matthew back to Falmouth, with an escort if need be."

"Aye, sir." He stood up carefully, bowed beneath the deckhead beams. "I'll tell Mr. Triscott to prepare the hands." He hesitated in the low doorway. "An' I'm *right proud* to serve alongside you, sir."

The sentiment seemed to embarrass him and he hurried to the companion ladder, calling names as he went.

Bolitho drew a fresh sheet of paper towards him and decided he would write a letter to his sister Nancy. If he did fall, her husband the squire, known around Falmouth as the King of Cornwall, would soon get his hands on the big grey house below Pendennis Castle, the home for generations of Bolithos.

The thought disturbed him more than he thought possible. No more would the local people see a Bolitho returning from the ocean, or hear of another who had died in some far-off battle.

He glanced momentarily at Craven's instructions, then with a sad smile held the note up to a candle and watched it dissolve in flames.

He had recalled something which his father had made him and his brother Hugh learn by heart before they had left that same house for the navy.

"They have outlived this fear, and their
    brave ends
Will ever be an honour to their friends."

It could have been written for them.

"Out yer get, matey!"

Allday groaned and rolled painfully on to his side,
and felt somebody guiding his feet over the back of
a cart.

If they trusted him, it was the wary trust of one
wild animal for another. He had no idea how far he
had been carried, and as the cart had bumped and
staggered over rutted tracks, once through a field, he
had felt as if every bone was broken.

He stood upright and felt his hands being untied,
a rough bandage being removed from his eyes.

One of his escorts grinned and handed him the
cutlass. "No 'ard feelin's, matey. Under this flag you
takes no chances, see?"

Allday nodded and looked around him. It was
dawn, another day, the air busy with birdsong and
insects. His nostrils dilated. The strong smell of
saltwater and tar, oakum and freshly hewn timber. A
boatbuilder's yard.

He was pushed, rather than guided, into a long
shed where a crude slipway ran the full length and
vanished through some heavy canvas awnings at the
lower end. Newly built or repaired boats could be
launched straight into the water from here, he
supposed.

He blinked his eyes as he saw some twenty or more
men sitting at tables wolfing food and draining jugs
of ale as if they had been here all night. They all

154

looked up as the man who had accompanied Allday said harshly, "This 'ere's Spencer, sail-maker. It's all you need to know. Get 'im some grub."

Allday crossed his leg over a bench and regarded his new companions thoughtfully. A mixed bunch, he decided. Some had been honest sailormen; others would have been rogues in any marketplace.

As his eyes grew accustomed to the windowless shed he realised that the man who had been with him in the cart had been the one who had hacked off the sailor's hand. Now he was laughing and sharing a joke with one of his companions as if he hadn't a care in the world.

Allday took a jug of ale and grunted his thanks. It would be wise to say as little as possible.

The ale was tasteless but strong on an empty stomach; it made him feel slightly better.

Another step. He eyed his new companions warily. Deserters to a man. If what he had seen of his "rescuers" was anything to judge by, they had stepped from one captivity into another.

He leaned over and asked casually, "What now?"

The man at his side darted him a suspicious glance. "We waits, see? We'll be part of a crew." He nodded, reassured by Allday's massive presence. "We'll all be stinkin' rich!"

Allday took another swallow of ale. Or bloody dead, he thought darkly. Then he looked around the boatshed, probably well guarded too. It was so simple. A boatyard, the last place you would expect to find seamen on the run. But where was it? He had to discover that or all the risks were pointless. The Captain must be told where—

He stiffened as a voice rapped, "I'll let you know

when *I'm* ready. You just do as you're told, damn your eyes!"

Allday raised his head very slowly and stared between two men who were in deep conversation.

The sunlight was stronger now, and he could see a half-completed hull standing amidst a litter of planks and wood shavings, and beyond that a line of tall trees. He knew the incisive, irritable voice—but how could he?

He heard someone murmuring what sounded like an apology and then part of a canvas awning was pulled aside like a curtain.

Allday held his breath as the dark eyes moved over the listless figures around the tables.

The man said, "Well, they'd better show more steel than the last lot!"

When Allday dared to look again the awning had fallen back into place. *He didn't see me*. He almost gasped his relief out loud.

The face had been that of *Loyal Chieftain*'s master, Henry Delaval . . .

It was all that Bolitho needed to know. But the plan would not settle in his mind.

All he could hear was a scream. All he could see was the smoking pistol in a severed hand.

156

9

Enemy Territory

BOLITHO gripped the jolly-boat's gunwale and looked up at the endless canopy of small stars. Only an undulating black shadow which broke the foot of the pattern gave a true hint of land, and he could sense Chesshyre's concentration as he peered above the heads of the oarsmen, or directly abeam.

Once he said, "Tide's on the ebb, sir."

Bolitho could hear it rippling and surging around the boat's stem, the deep breathing of the oarsmen as they maintained a regular stroke without an order being passed.

The man in the bows called aft in a loud whisper, "Ready with the lead, sir!"

Chesshyre came out of his concentrated attention. "Is it armed, Gulliver?"

"Aye, sir."

"Start sounding."

Bolitho heard the splash of the boat's lead and line being dropped over the bows, then the man named Gulliver calling, "By th' mark three!"

Chesshyre ordered, "Pass it aft!" He waited for the leg-of-mutton-shaped lead to be handed from thwart to thwart, then he rubbed the tallow in its base between his fingers before holding it up to his nose. He passed the lead back again and muttered, "Shell and rough sand, sir. We're making headway. So long

157

as we stand away from the sandbars at low water we shall—"

The bowman called, "By th' mark *two!*"

Chesshyre swore silently and eased over the tiller bar. "Like *that*, sir!"

Bolitho understood. It was common enough in his own West Country for sailors to be able to feel their way by using a lead and line, know the state of the seabed by what they found on the tallow which "armed" it. In another twenty years he guessed it would be a lost craft of seamanship.

"How far?"

Chesshyre raised himself slightly as something white broke the pitch-darkness. Then he sank down again. It was not a rock or sandbar but a leaping fish.

"'Nother half-hour, sir." He kept his voice low so that the oarsmen would not know the extent of their labour. They were used to it, but the boat was crowded with extra hands and weapons, including a heavy bell-mouthed musketoon already packed with canister and metal fragments, in case they were attacked.

Bolitho listened to the creak of oars—how loud they sounded despite being muffled with greased rags. But he knew from experience that it would be swallowed completely in the other noises of sea and wind.

Suppose it was a wasted journey? Perhaps the man would take fright and hide when he heard the sailors with their weapons?

Chesshyre hissed, "There, sir! See the old abbey?"

Bolitho strained his eyes and saw a sharper shadow rising amongst the stars.

Chesshyre breathed out. "Better'n I thought."

158

Bolitho thought how like Herrick he sounded. Another memory. A different ship.

"Less than a fathom, sir!"

"Haul in the lead, Gulliver. Stand by, boys!" Chesshyre crouched half-upright, his silhouette like a dark gargoyle. "Be ready to beach!"

The bowman was busy with his boathook and called, "Comin' in now, sir!"

"*Oars!* Lively there!" After that it all happened in seconds.

The extra hands leaping outboard and splashing in the shallows to guide the hull safely on to a small, unusually steep beach. Oars lowered with great care across the thwarts while Christie, one of Paice's boatswain's mates, growled, "Drop that bloody gun an' I'll see yer backbones!"

In spite of the tension Bolitho heard somebody chuckle at the threat. Then he was out of the boat, the receding water dragging at his shoes, clawing him back as if to claim him.

Chesshyre passed his instructions and two men hurried away in either direction, while others grouped around the beached boat to make certain it could be quickly launched, but was in no danger of drifting away.

Bolitho found a moment to recall the other times when he had seen it done. *The sailor's way*. Give him a boat or even a raft and he is in good heart. But with only the sea at his back it is a different story.

Chesshyre rejoined him and said, "There's a small track to the left, sir. That'll be the one."

Shadows moved in around them and Bolitho said, "Draw your blades, but do not cock your pistols. One shot by accident, and we'll awaken the dead."

159

Somebody murmured, "An' there are plenty o' them round 'ere, sir!"

Another jester.

Chesshyre waited as Bolitho drew his old sword and balanced it in his fist.

"You must be an old hand at this, sir?"

It was strange coming from him, Bolitho thought, as they were the same age.

"I admit it's more like landing on enemy soil than I expected in England."

He tested his bearings and then walked carefully towards the track. It was little more than a fox's path, but the sandy soil made it easy to follow.

He half-listened to the sea's lazy grumbling as it laid bare rocks in the falling tide, and pictured Paice somewhere out in the darkness, unable to help, unwilling to be left out.

The sea sounds suddenly faded and Bolitho felt the warm air of the countryside fanning his face. The smells of the land. The old abbey lay to the left although he could see less of it now than from the boat.

Chesshyre touched his arm and stopped in his tracks. *"Still!"*

Bolitho froze and heard someone gasp, feet kicking in the long grass. Then two figures loomed from the darkness, one with his hands above his head, the other, a small, darting man with a drawn cutlass, pushing him none too gently ahead of him.

Bolitho said, "I have good ears, but—"

Chesshyre showed his teeth. "Inskip was a poacher afore he saw the light, sir. Got ears in his arse, beggin' your pardon."

The man with raised hands saw Bolitho, and

perhaps recognised some sort of authority when seconds earlier he had been expecting his life to be cut short.

He exclaimed, "I was sent to meet you, sir!"

Chesshyre rapped, "Keep your voice *down* for Christ's sake, man."

Bolitho gripped his arm; it was shaking so violently that he knew the man was terrified.

"Where is the blind man? Did he not come?"

"Yes, yes!" He was babbling. "He's here, right enough. I did just what the major told me—now I'm off afore someone sees me!"

A seaman strode along the path. "'Ere 'e is, sir." He directed his remarks to the master but they were intended for Bolitho.

"Don't go too close, sir. 'E stinks like a dead pig."

Bolitho walked away from the others, but heard Chesshyre following at a careful distance.

The blind man was squatting on the ground, his head thrown back, his eyes covered by a bandage.

Bolitho knelt beside him. "I am Captain Bolitho. Major Craven said you would help me."

The man moved his head from side to side, then reached out and held Bolitho's arm. Through the coat sleeve his fingers felt like steel talons.

"I need your aid." Bolitho's stomach rebelled, but he knew this contact was his only hope. The blind man stank of filth and dried sweat, and he was almost grateful for the darkness.

"Bolitho?" The man moved his head again as if trying to peer through the bandage. "Bolitho?" He had a high piping voice, and it was impossible to determine his age.

161

Chesshyre said thickly, "The poor bugger's off his head, sir."

Bolitho retorted, "Wouldn't *you* be?"

He tried again. "That night. When they did this to you." He felt the hand jerk free, as if it and not its owner was in terror. "What did you see? I wouldn't ask, but they took a friend of mine—you understand?"

"See?" The blind man felt vaguely in the grass. "They took a long while. All th' time they laughed at me." He shook his head despairingly. "When the fire was lit they branded my body, an'—an' then—"

Bolitho looked away, sickened. But he was so near to Allday now. This poor, demented creature was all he had. But he felt as if he were applying torture, as they had once done to him.

"I used to watch for 'em. Sometimes they come with pack-horses—bold as brass, they was. Other times they brought men, deserters. That night—"

Chesshyre said, "He knows nowt, sir." He peered around at the trees. "He should be put out of his misery."

The man turned as if to examine the *Telemachus*'s master, then said in a flat, empty voice, "I bin there since, y'know." He wrapped his arms around his ragged body and cackled. "I was that well acquaint with the place!"

Bolitho kept his voice level. "What place? Please help me. I shall see you are rewarded."

The man turned on him with unexpected venom. "I don't want yer stinkin' gold! I just wants revenge for what they done to me!"

Chesshyre bent over him and said, "Captain

162

Bolitho is a fine an' brave officer. Help him as you will, and I swear he'll take care of you."

The man cackled again. It was an eerie sound, and Bolitho could imagine the small party of seamen drawing together nearby.

Chesshyre added, "What's your name?"

The man cowered away. "I'm not sayin'!" He peered towards Bolitho and then seized his arm again. "I don't 'ave to, do I?" He sounded frantic.

"No." Bolitho's heart sank. The link was too fragile to last. It was another hope gone wrong.

In a surprisingly clear voice the blind man said, "Then I'll take you."

Bolitho stared at him. "When?"

"Now, o' course!" His reply was almost scornful. "Don't want the 'ole o' Sheppey to know, does we?"

Chesshyre breathed out loudly. "Well, I'll be double-damned!"

That, too, was what Herrick said when he was taken aback.

Bolitho took the man's filthy hand. "*Thank* you."

The bandaged head moved warily from side to side. "Not with nobody else though!"

Christie the boatswain's mate murmured, "Not bloody askin' for much, is 'e?"

Bolitho looked at Chesshyre. "I must do as he asks. I must trust him. He is all I have."

Chesshyre turned away from his men. "But it's *asking* for trouble, sir. He may be raving mad, or someone might have put him up to it, like the fellow who brought him here, eh, sir?"

Bolitho walked to the men who were guarding the messenger. "Did you tell anybody about this?" To

163

himself he thought, *more to the point, will he tell someone after he has left us?*

"I swear, sir, on my baby's life—I swear I've told nobody!"

Bolitho turned to Chesshyre. "All the same, take him aboard when you leave. I think he is too frightened to betray anyone at the moment, but should the worst happen and you discover it, see that he is handed to Major Craven's dragoons." His voice sharpened. "He can join the other felons at the crossroads if it comes to that."

Chesshyre asked desperately, "What shall I say to Mr. Paice, sir?"

Bolitho looked at him in the darkness. Then he raised his voice and saw the bandaged head move towards him again. "Tell him I am with a friend, and that we are both in God's hands."

Chesshyre seemed unable to grasp it. "I just don't know, sir. In all my service—"

"There is always a first time, Mr. Chesshyre. Now be off with you."

He watched as the sailors began to fade away into the shadows and noticed how they seemed to pass him as closely as they could before they groped their way to the fox's path. To see for themselves, as if for the last time.

Chesshyre held out his hand. It was hard, like leather. "May God indeed be at the helm this night, sir." Then he was gone.

Bolitho reached down and aided the man to his feet. "I am ready when you are."

He felt light-headed, even sick, and his mouth was suddenly quite dry. This man might only think he

164

knew where he was going, his mind too broken to distinguish fact from fantasy.

The blind man picked up a heavy piece of wood, a branch found somewhere in the course of his despairing ramblings.

Then he said in his strange, piping voice, "This way." He hesitated. "Watch yer step. There's a stile up yonder."

Bolitho swallowed hard. Who was the blind one now?

An hour later they were still walking, pausing only for the bandaged head to turn this way and that. To gather his bearings, to listen for some sound, Bolitho did not know. Perhaps he was already lost.

He heard dogs barking far away, and once he almost fell with alarm as some birds burst from the grass almost under his feet.

The blind man waited for him to catch up, muttering, "Over yonder! Wot d'you see?"

Bolitho stared through the darkness and discovered a deeper blackness. His heart seemed to freeze. A different bearing, but there was no doubt about it. It was the same sinister copse, which they were passing on the opposite side.

The blind man could have been studying his expression. He broke into a fit of low, wheezing laughter. "Thought I'd lost me way, did ye, Captain?"

About the same time, Chesshyre was explaining to Paice and his first lieutenant what had happened, the jolly-boat's crew lolling on the deck like dead men after the hardest pull they had ever known.

Paice exploded, "You *left* him? You bloody well left the captain unsupported!"

165

Chesshyre protested, "It was an order, sir. Surely you know me better than—"

Paice gripped his shoulder so that the master winced. "My apologies, Mr. Chesshyre. Of *course* I know you well enough for that. God damn it, he wouldn't even let me go!"

Triscott asked, "What shall we do, sir?"

"Do?" Paice gave a heavy sigh. "He told me what I must do if he sent back the boat without him." He glanced at Chesshyre sadly. "That was an *order* too." Then he gazed up at the stars. "We shall haul anchor. If we remain here, dawn will explain our reasons to anyone who cares to seek them." He looked at the messenger who was sitting wretchedly on a hatch coaming under guard. "By the living Jesus, if there is a betrayal, I'll run him up to the tops'l yard myself!"

Then in a calmer voice he said, "Hoist the boat inboard, Mr. Triscott. We will get under way."

A few moments later there was a splash, and a voice yelled with surprise, "Man overboard, sir!"

But Paice said quietly, "No. I was a fool to speak my mind. That was the lad—Matthew Corker. He must have heard me."

Triscott said, "Even the jolly-boat couldn't catch him now, sir."

Paice watched the regular splashes until they were lost in shadow.

He said, "Good swimmer."

Chesshyre asked, "What can he do, sir?"

Paice made himself turn away from the sea, and from the boy who was going to try and help the man he worshipped above all others.

He was like the son Paice had always wanted, what

they had prayed for, before she had been brutally shot down.

He said harshly, "Get the ship under way! If anything happens to that lad, I'll—" He could not go on.

Thirty minutes later as the glass was turned, *Telemachus* spread her great mainsail and slipped out into the North Sea, before changing tack and steering westward for Sheerness.

Paice handed over to his second-in-command and went aft to the cabin. He opened the shutter of a lantern and sat down to complete his log when his eye caught a reflection from the opposite cot.

He leaned over and picked it up. It was a fine gold watch with an engraved guard. He had seen Bolitho look at it several times, and not, he guessed, merely to discover the hour. The parcel containing the uncompleted ship-model was nearby.

With great care he opened the guard. Somehow he knew that Bolitho would not mind. Afterwards he replaced it beside Allday's parcel.

In the navy everyone thought a post-captain was junior only to God. A man who did as he pleased, who wanted for nothing.

Paice thought of him now, out there in the darkness with a blind man. Apart from this watch he had nothing left at all.

Bolitho lay prone beside a thick clump of gorse and levelled his small telescope on a boatyard which lay some fifty yards below him. He winced as a loose pebble ground into his elbow, and wondered if this really was the place which the blind man had described.

He laid the glass down and lowered his face on to his arm. The noon sun was high overhead, and he dared not use the glass too much for fear of a bright reflection which might betray their position.

He would have to go down as soon as it was safe. How could he lie here all day? He cursed himself for not thinking of a flask when he had left the *Telemachus*. His mind shied away from water and he placed a pebble in his mouth to ease his parched throat.

He raised himself briefly on one elbow and glanced at his companion. The blind man was a pitiful sight, his clothing stained and in rags, the bandage covering his empty sockets foul with dirt.

The man remarked, "You gets used to waitin'." He nodded firmly. "When it's dark—" He shook with silent laughter. "Dark—that's rich, ain't it?"

Bolitho sighed. How did he know night from day? But he no longer doubted him after that demonstration of his uncanny abilities.

He stiffened and raised the small telescope again, but was careful to hold it in the shade of a clump of grass.

A few figures were moving through the boatyard. Two were armed, one carried a stone jar. Probably rum, he thought. Nobody was working there, and tools lay abandoned near an uncompleted hull, an adze still standing on a length of timber.

The men walked like sailors. They showed no sign of fear or wariness. There had to be a reason for such confidence.

Bolitho closed the little telescope, recalling how he had used it on the road from London when he had confronted the mob and the two frightened press gang

officers. He watched some tiny insects busying themselves around his drawn sword. He *must* decide what
to do next. If he left this place to fetch help, he might
miss something vital. He glanced again at his ragged
companion, and was moved by what he saw. He was
rocking back and forth, his voice crooning what
sounded like a hymn. Once a gentle man, perhaps.
But when he had said he wanted his revenge for what
they had done to him, he had been like a man from
the fires of Hell.

When he looked again he realised that he was alone,
but not for long. The blind man crawled through
some bushes, a chipped mug in his clawlike hand. He
held it out in Bolitho's direction. "Wet yer whistle,
Captain?"

It must be from some stream, Bolitho thought. It
tasted rancid, and was probably used by sheep or
cows. Bolitho drank deeply. It could have been the
finest Rhenish wine at that moment.

The blind man took the empty mug and it vanished
inside one of his tattered coats.

He said, "They brings 'em 'ere sometimes,
Captain. Men for the Trade. From 'ere they goes to
smugglin' vessels, see?" He cocked his head, like a
schoolmaster with some backward pupil.

Bolitho considered it. If it was so easy, why did
the authorities not come and search the place? Major
Craven had hinted at powerful and influential people
who were more interested in profit than the enforce-
ment of a law they insisted could not be maintained.

"Whose land is this?"

The blind man lay down on his side. "I'll rest now,
Captain."

For the first time since their strange rendezvous

there was fear in his voice. The true, sick fear of one who has been on the brink of a terrible death.

He could almost envy the man's ability to sleep—perhaps he only ventured out at night. For Bolitho it was the longest day. He busied his thoughts with the commodore and the three cutters, until he felt his mind would crack.

And then, quite suddenly, or so it seemed, the light began to fade, and where there had been green trees and the glittering sea beyond, there were shadows of purple and dark pewter.

A few lights appeared in the boatyard's outbuildings, but only once or twice had he seen any movement, usually an armed man strolling down to the waterfront to relieve himself.

Bolitho examined every yard of the distance he would have to cover. He must avoid catching his foot or slipping in some cow dung. Surprise was his only protection.

He realised that the blind man was wide awake and crouching beside him. How could he live in such filth? Or perhaps he no longer noticed even that.

"What is it?"

The man pointed towards the sea. "A boat comin'."

Bolitho seized his telescope and swore under his breath. It was already too dark, as if a great curtain had been lowered.

Then he heard the creak of oars, saw a shaded lantern reflecting on the water where a man stood to guide the boat in.

The blind man added, "A *ship*, Captain."

Bolitho strained his eyes into the darkness. If ship there was, she showed no lights. Landing a cargo? He dismissed it instantly. The blind man knew better than anyone what they were doing—he had more than proved it. They were collecting sailors: men who had been marked *run* in their ships' logs; others who had managed to escape the gibbet; soldiers of fortune. All dangerous.

He heard the creak of oars again. Whatever it was, it had been quickly done, he thought.

He stood up, the cooler air off the sea making him shiver. "Wait here. Don't move until I return for you."

The blind man leaned on his crude stick. "They'll gut you, sure as Jesus, if they sees you!"

"I have to know." Bolitho thought he heard a door slam. "If I don't return, go to Major Craven."

"I ain't goin' to no bloody redcoats! Not no more!"

Bolitho could hear him muttering querulously as he took the first steps down the grassy slope towards a solitary lighted window. He heard laughter, the sound of a bottle being smashed, then more laughter. So they had not all gone. Perhaps Allday . . . He reached the wall of the building and leaned with his back against it, waiting for his breathing to steady.

Then, very slowly he peered around the edge of the window. The glass was stained and covered with cobwebs, but he saw all he needed. It was a shipwright's shed, with benches and fresh planks piled on racks. Around a table he saw about six figures. They were drinking rum, passing the jar round, while another was cutting hunks of bread from a basket. Only one man was armed and stood apart from the rest. He wore a blue coat with a red neckerchief and an old cocked hat tilted rakishly on thick, greasy hair.

Bolitho glanced behind him. There was no other

sound. So these men were also deserters, awaiting the next boat which could use them? There was an air of finality about the place, as if once they had gone, it would be abandoned, or returned to its proper use. Then there would be no evidence. *Nothing*. And Allday would be just as lost as ever.

Bolitho licked his lips. Six to one, but only the armed man, who was obviously one of the smugglers, presented real danger. He found that his heart was beating wildly, and he had to lick his lips repeatedly to stop them being glued with dryness.

They were all together, but any second one might leave the building and raise the alarm. They would soon arm themselves then.

Bolitho moved carefully along the wall until he reached the door. He could see from the lantern's flickering light that there were no bolts or chains.

It seemed to taunt him. *Have you been stripped of your courage too?* He was committed, and knew that he had had no choice from the beginning.

Bolitho eased the pistol from his belt and tried to remember if he had kept it clear of the water when he had waded ashore. He winced as he cocked it. Then he stood clear of the door, held his sword angled across his body, and kicked it with all his strength.

"In the King's name!" He was shocked at the loudness of his voice in the confined space. "You are all under arrest!"

Someone yelled, "God damn, it's the press!"

Another gasped, "They told us we was *safe!*"

The armed man dropped his hand to the hanger at his belt and rasped, "He's not the press! I knows who he is, damn his eyes!"

172

Bolitho raised his pistol. "Don't move!" The man's face was twisted with anger and hatred and seemed to swim over the end of the muzzle like a mask.

Then he seized his hanger and pulled it from its scabbard.

Bolitho squeezed the trigger and heard the impotent click of a misfire. The man crouched towards him, his hanger making small circles in the lantern-light, while the others stared in disbelief, probably too drunk to register what had happened.

The man snarled, *"Get out! Fetch weapons!* He's alone—can't you see that, you gutless swabs?"

He lunged forward but held his legs as before. Sparks spat from the two blades, and Bolitho watched the man's eyes, knowing that whatever happened now, he could not win. They would set upon him like a pack, more afraid of the gallows than of killing a King's officer.

He could hear the rest of them clambering through a window, one already running through the darkness yelling like a madman. They would soon return.

He said, "You have no chance!"

The man spat at his feet. "We'll see!" Then he laughed. "Blade to blade, Captain bloody Bolitho!"

He slashed forward, and Bolitho parried it aside, locking hilts for a second so that he could thrust the man away, and hold him silhouetted against the lantern.

The man yelled, "Kill him, you bilge-rats!" He had sensed that despite his strength he was no match for Bolitho's swordsmanship. He vaulted over a bench, then faced Bolitho across it, his hanger held out like a rapier.

Not long now. Bolitho heard running feet, a man

173

falling over some obstruction in the darkness, the rum making him laugh insanely. Then there was a single shot, and for an instant Bolitho thought one of them had fired at him through the window. He heard somebody sobbing, the sudden trampling thud of horses, and Major Craven's voice rising above all of it.

The door burst open and the place was filled suddenly with scarlet coats and gleaming sabres.

Craven turned as a sergeant shouted, "One o' the buggers 'as done for Trooper Green, sir." Craven looked at Bolitho and gave the merest nod, then faced the armed smuggler. "You heard that? My men will be happy to end your miserable life here and now, *unless*—"

The man tossed his hanger on the bench. "I know nothing."

Bolitho took Craven's arm. "How did you know?"

Craven walked to the door. "Look yonder, Captain."

A dragoon was helping a small figure to climb down from his saddle. The boy walked slowly and hesitantly into the lantern-light, his eyes running with tears. Fear, relief, it was all there.

Craven said quietly, "Lift your foot, boy."

Aided by the dragoon Young Matthew raised one bare foot. It was ripped and bloody, almost to the bone.

Craven explained, "One of my pickets found him running along the road." He looked at his men outside as they rounded up the deserters and bound their wrists behind them. One trooper lay dead on the ground.

Bolitho seized the boy and held him against his coat, trying to ease away the shock and the pain.

"There's no harm done, Matthew, thanks to you. That was a brave thing you did."

Craven nodded. "Damned dangerous, too."

Bolitho looked at the dragoon who had carried the boy from his horse. "Care for him. I have something to do." He confronted the man who minutes earlier had been urging his companions to arm themselves and cut him down, and said, "If you tell me what I want to know, I might be prepared to put in a word. I can promise nothing."

The man threw back his head and roared with laughter. "D'you think I fear the hangman?"

Craven murmured, "He is far more frightened of his masters, the Brotherhood."

He offered no resistance as the sergeant tied his hands behind him and sneered, "They'll have you yet —*Captain!*"

A dragoon shouted, "'Ere—where d'you think you're goin', mate?"

Then, like the others, he fell silent as the ragged figure with the broken branch held out before him moved slowly into the circle of light.

Bolitho sensed it immediately, like a shaft of lightning between them.

The blind man whispered, "It's 'im, Captain!" There was a sob in his voice now. "I 'ad to come, then I 'eard 'is laugh. 'E's the one wot did this to me!"

The man shouted, "You bloody liar! Who'd take the word of a blind lunatic?"

Bolitho had an overwhelming desire to strike him. To kill him, tied and helpless though he was.

"*I* would, whoever *you* are." How calm his voice sounded. It was like hearing a complete stranger.

175

"When all this was begun, *this man*—who has become my friend, let it be known—asked no reward."

There was absolute silence now and Bolitho saw the bound man staring at him uncertainly, the bluff gone out of him.

"He asked only for revenge, and I think I know what he meant." Bolitho glanced at the others. "Major Craven, if you will take your men outside?" The dragoons filed out, some shocked at what they had witnessed, others with the light of cruel revenge in their faces. They had just lost one of their own. What did outsiders understand of loyalty, and their sacrifice?

Bolitho watched as the realisation crossed the man's cruel features. Spittle ran from a corner of his mouth. *"You lie! You wouldn't dare!"* When Bolitho walked towards the door he screamed, *"Don't leave me!"*

The blind man felt his way around the seated prisoner, and then touched his eyes from behind. Very gently, as he crooned, "Like trapped butterflies."

The man screamed and struggled. *"Christ, my eyes!"*

Bolitho opened the door, his throat retching.

Then he heard the man shriek, "I'll tell you! I'll tell you! Call him off, for Christ's sake!"

Bolitho crossed the room in two strides. "I want names. I need to know things which only you will be a part of."

The man's chest was heaving as if he was drowning. "I felt his claws in my eyes!"

"I am waiting." He rested one hand on the blind man's scrawny shoulder and saw him turn his bandaged eyes towards him. In his own way he was

176

telling Bolitho he had already had his revenge. Perhaps he had found no reprieve in it.

Together they listened to the man's desperate flood of information. The hangman's halter, or death in a sea-fight were commonplace. But against the prospect of torture at the hands of someone he had blinded and broken he had had no defences.

Bolitho said, "You will be kept in the barracks, alone and under guard at all times. If one word you have told me is false, you will have this man as your sole companion."

He reached out and slammed the smuggler's head back against the chair. "*Look at me, damn you!* Do you see any bluff in *my* eyes?"

There was naked terror in the man's face now and Bolitho could smell the stench of it. Then he said quietly, "So be warned."

He walked out of the building and leaned against the wall, staring at the tiny stars.

Craven said, "Thank God I was in time."

"Aye." He watched the blind man touching the muzzle of one of the horses. "There's much we have to thank him for tonight." He knew that in a few more minutes he would have vomited. "Now where is that boy?"

But Young Matthew had fallen asleep across the dragoon's saddle.

Craven said, "Time to leave. I sent word for assistance before I came. I felt this would be the place. My men have never been allowed to come here." He glanced at the sky. "There's a troop of fifty horse or more on the road from Chatham by now, but we'll take no chances."

He watched his dead dragoon being tied across an

empty saddle. "Is it worth the cost this time?" He removed his hat as the horse was led past.

Bolitho nodded. "I believe so." He waited for the major to order a spare mount for him. "You have done so much." His tone hardened. "Now it is up to me."

The blind man waited beside the horses as Bolitho leaned down and touched his arm. "Will you come with us?"

The man shook his head. "I'll be close by if you needs me, Captain."

As the troop, with the prisoners running beside the horses moved away from the buildings, the blind man looked into his perpetual darkness and murmured, "'E called me 'is *friend*."

Then, like a ragged shadow, he too was swallowed up.

10

The Spark Of Courage

THE brig *Loyal Chieftain*, drifting and rolling under close-reefed topsails, was a death-trap for any landsman or the unwary. In pitch-darkness she lay between two sturdy luggers while men from all three crews hauled on tackles, levered, and stowed an endless collection of cargo. In the brig's forward hold, Allday marvelled at the speed of the transfer from the two luggers in spite of several stupid blunders. The brig carried twice her normal company, but most of them had never worked together before, and he had heard more kicks and obscenities than in any man-of-war.

Each time he went on deck he looked hopefully towards the land. But there was no sign of it, not even a light to reveal how near or far it lay. He knew they were lying-to off the Dutch coast, somewhere near Flushing, but it might easily have been on the other side of the world.

His prowess as a seaman had soon been noted, and Allday had found himself thanking his Maker more than once that Delaval was not aboard. The brig *Loyal Chieftain* was under the charge of his lieutenant and mate, a tight-lipped man called Isaac Newby who hailed from Dorset. He had been arrested twice for smuggling but each time he had been released for lack or loss of evidence.

He had remarked to Allday, "I've friends in high

179

places." Otherwise he had said little, and after they had made contact with the two luggers there had been no time even to eat or drink.

Men fumbled over unfamiliar tackles, or were knocked senseless by a cargo net of brandy casks. In the holds, another team was busily lashing hemp halters and floats to ranks of casks almost before they had been stowed for the passage. A man Allday had befriended, once a foretopman named Tom Lucas, had explained that once off the English coast the casks would be dropped overboard in moored trots, like lobster pots, to be collected later by some of the long, oared smuggling galleys. After that, the cargo would be distributed in caves and small inlets, to be carried to the next "drops" by packhorse or donkey.

Lucas was a tall, grave-faced sailor, very much the landsman's idea of a typical Jack Tar of Old England. Once, on passage from Kent, he had been stitching a patch on his shirt. Allday, watching, was used to the navy's ways and harsh discipline, but Lucas's bare back was scarred and mangled beyond recognition. He had been serving in a seventy-four at the Nore, a ship plagued by a bad captain, undermanning and appalling food.

He had complained on behalf of his mess to the first lieutenant who to all accounts had been a fair man. He in turn had approached the captain. The result: three dozen lashes at the gangway for mutinous behaviour. Lucas had made up his mind to desert but had been surprised by another lieutenant on the night he had chosen. He had struck the officer only with his fist, but he had fallen from the gangway to the gundeck below. Lucas did not know if the lieutenant was dead or alive, and had no intention of returning to find out.

He had stared at Allday grimly. "A flogging round th' fleet? Well, you knows what that means. I couldn't take it. An' if the lieutenant died, it'll be the yardarm dance anyway!"

But it was obvious to Allday that he had no heart for smuggling. It was an escape, without hope or future, until fate caught up with him. Allday had heard some of the others discussing it in the dogwatches. So far, there had been plenty of back-breaking work, and precious few rewards. It did not balance the scale, but it was some consolation, he thought.

Allday was with Lucas tonight, supervising the hold, and in some cases putting the right lines into unfamiliar hands while the hulls groaned and lurched together in a steep offshore swell.

Allday muttered, "Black as a boot on deck."

Lucas paused and sniffed the air, which was heavy with brandy. "I could use some o' that." He seemed to realise what Allday had said. "Yeh. Well, I've done a couple of runs in this brig. The captain always 'as a decoy. So if our—" He seemed to grin in the gloom. "I mean, if *their* patrols or revenue cutters appear, it gives 'im time to stand clean away."

Allday lowered his head to conceal his expression. So that was how it was done. Maybe the smuggling fraternity took turns to play decoy, then shared the spoils afterwards?

Isaac Newby, the mate, peered down past the shaded lanterns. "Ready below?" He sounded on edge, impatient.

Allday raised his fist. "Soon enough. One more net to be stowed."

Newby vanished, probably to examine the other hold.

Lucas said bitterly, "What next, I wonder? Gold for the captain, an' a gutful of rum for us, eh?"

Allday watched him thoughtfully. How many good seamen had gone rotten because of uncaring officers and ruthless captains? It was a pity there were not many more like Our Dick, he thought.

A voice yelled, "Stand by to cast off, starboard! Lively, you scum!"

Lucas swore. "Just like home."

First one lugger was cast off, then the other, with more curses and squealing blocks, the canvas unmanageable with the brig floundering downwind. Then just as suddenly she had set her topsails and jib and was leaning over to the larboard tack. Hatches were battened down, and the disorder removed.

Lucas stared out at the heaving, black water and gritted his teeth. "Christ, they've brought women aboard!" He seized the ratlines and hung on them despairingly. "God, *listen* to 'em. Don't the buggers know it's bad luck?"

Allday listened and heard someone cry out. It was little more than a sound, like a gull's mew, soon lost in the thunder of spray-soaked canvas.

The boatswain shouted, "You lot! Stand by to loose the forecourse! Hands aloft, and shift your bloody selves!" A rope's end found its target and a man yelped with painful resentment.

The boatswain joined Allday at the weather shrouds. "Fair wind." He squinted aloft but the men strung out on the forecourse yard were hidden in darkness. "Should be a good run this time."

Allday heard it again, and asked, "Women, eh?" For some reason it disturbed him.

The boatswain yawned. "The captain likes to have his way." He gave a hard laugh. "It's all money, I reckon, but—" He shrugged as a piercing scream broke from the after skylight.

Allday tried to moisten his lips. "Delaval, d'you mean?"

The boatswain glared impatiently as the big foresail flapped and writhed out of control. "Yeh, he came aboard from one of the Dutchie luggers." He cupped his hands. "Catch a turn there, you idle bugger! Now *belay!*"

But Allday scarcely heard him. Delaval was here. But he might not remember. He had had eyes only for Bolitho and Paice at their last meeting. Even as he grasped the hope, Allday knew it was a lie.

More bellowed orders, and one watch was dismissed below for another foully cooked meal.

Allday walked aft, his powerful frame angled to the slanting deck, his mind in great trouble. He saw the faces of the helmsmen glowing faintly in the binnacle light, but it was too weak to be seen more than yards beyond the hull.

What should he do now? If he stayed alive long enough he might—

A larger wave than the previous one swayed the deck hard over. He saw the spokes of the wheel spin, heard the two helmsmen cursing as they fought to bring the vessel back under command.

Allday gripped a rack of belaying pins, and found himself looking directly down through the cabin skylight. There was a girl there—she could not be more than sixteen. One man, Newby the mate, was pinioning her arms, another, hidden by the skylight's coaming, was tearing at her clothes, laying her breasts naked while she struggled and cried out in terror.

Too late did he feel the closeness of danger.

"So this is the sailmaker? I never forget a face, *Mister* Allday!"

The blow across the back of his head brought instant darkness. There was no time even for fear or pain. *Oblivion*.

Bolitho loosened his shirt and stared around at the intent faces. *Telemachus*'s small cabin was packed to bursting-point with not only the lieutenants from all three cutters but their sailing-masters as well.

He spread his hands on the chart and listened to the wind sighing through the rigging, the regular creak of timbers as the hull tugged at her cable.

It was evening, but the air was humid rather than warm, and the sky broken by ridges of heavy-bellied clouds.

He found time to compare it with his first meeting with the cutters' commanders. In so short a while they had all changed. Now there was no doubt, no suspicion; events had somehow welded them together in a manner Bolitho had first believed impossible.

The others had also rid themselves of their coats and Bolitho wondered how they would appear to some landsman or outsiders. More like the men they were hunting than sea-officers, he thought.

"We will weigh at dusk, and have to risk arousing interest—" His glance fell on Chesshyre. "I see that you have already noted the change?"

Chesshyre nodded, startled to be picked out before all the others. "Aye, sir, wind's backed two points or more." He shivered slightly as if to test the weather. "I'd say fog afore dawn."

They looked at each other, the suggestion of fog moving amongst them like an evil spirit.

Bolitho said, "I know. When I consulted the glass—" He glanced up at the open skylight, plucking his shirt away from his body. It felt like a wet rag, like the moment he had kicked open the door and had faced the men around the table. It seemed like an age past instead of days. He hurried on, "The information is that two vessels are heading for the Isle of Thanet from the Dutch coast. One will be deep-laden, the other a decoy." He saw them exchange glances and added, "I have no doubt that this intelligence is true." He pictured the smuggler tied to a chair, his screams of terror as the blind man's hands had touched his eyes. No, he had little doubt of this information.

Paice said, "May I speak, sir?" He looked at the other lieutenants and Queely responded with a curt nod, as if they had already been discussing it. Paice said, "If this fails, and we lose them, what will happen to *you?*"

Bolitho smiled; he had been half-expecting an objection to his plan. "I shall doubtless be ordered to a place where I can no longer disrupt matters." Even as he said it, he knew he had never uttered a truer word. Even with Midshipman Fenwick under close arrest, and the smuggler in the hands of Craven's dragoons, his evidence would leak like a sieve without Delaval and a cargo.

He pushed the thought from his mind and said

flatly, "I believe that the information which led to the capture of the *Four Brothers* was deliberately offered to us to allay suspicion. Probably a competitor anyway, a most suitable sacrifice with the stakes so high."

He held his breath and watched their expressions. If they accepted this, they were implicating themselves. Only Commodore Hoblyn had known about the *Four Brothers*. By accepting Bolitho's word they too could be charged with conspiracy.

Paice said resolutely, "I agree. We've been held away from that piece of coastline for as long as I can recall. There are several small boatyards there, most of 'em on the land which belongs to—" He looked at Bolitho and said bluntly, "Sir James Tanner, a person of great power and authority." He gave a slow grin as if to show he was aware of his own disloyalty and added, "Some of us *suspected*. Most saw only the hopelessness of any protest with us against so many." His grin widened, "Until, with respect, sir, you came amongst us like a full gale of wind!"

Lieutenant Vatass of *Snapdragon* pulled at his crumpled shirt and said, "I think that speaks for us all, sir. If we *are* to stand alone?" He gave an elegant shrug. "Then let us get on with it."

There was a muttered assent around the airless cabin.

Bolitho said, "We will leave as arranged. I have left word with Major Craven, and sent a despatch to our admiral at the Nore." He would have smiled but for Allday. Even the admiral would have to climb down from his eyrie when this news was exploded before him. If Bolitho failed he would face a court martial. That he could accept. But these men, who had accepted his arrival only under pressure, he must shield at all costs.

The three sailing-masters were comparing notes and making last adjustments to their chart. Their navigation would have to be better than ever before. There was not even room for luck this time. Just three small cutters in search of a will-o'-the-wisp. Bolitho had sent word to Chatham in the hopes of calling a frigate to intervene should Delaval slip through their tightly stretched net. Even if the admiral agreed to his wishes, it was quite likely that no frigate was available.

Bolitho recalled his meeting with Sir Marcus Drew at the Admiralty. He had left him in no doubt where responsibility would lie if Bolitho misused his commission.

If Hoblyn was guilty of conspiracy with the smugglers, no matter for what reason, he could expect no mercy either from the navy or from the men he had served for his own profit.

Bolitho's mouth hardened. Allday's life was at stake because of all this. If anything happened to him he would deal with Hoblyn and the unknown Sir James Tanner in his own fashion.

As evening closed in across the anchorage Bolitho went on deck and watched the unhurried preparations to get under way.

He could sense the difference here too. The unspoken acceptance by men he had come to know in so brief a time. George Davy the gunner, even now crouching and ducking around his small artillery. Scrope, master-at-arms, with Christie the boatswain's mate, checking the heavy chest of axes and cutlasses below the tapering mast. Big Luke Hawkins, the boatswain, was hanging over the bulwark gesturing to some men in the jolly-boat to warp it closer to the tackles for hoisting inboard.

Slow, careful preparations—for what? To risk death at the hands of smugglers whom most people condoned, if not admired? Or was it out of *loyalty?* To Bolitho, or to one another, as was the navy's way with pressed man and volunteer alike.

Bolitho glanced at the waterfront and wondered if there was already a fine mist spreading towards the many anchored vessels. And although the wind still buffeted the furled sails, the sea seemed flatter, milkier out towards the Isle of Grain and Garrison Point. He shivered and wished he had brought his coat on deck.

He heard dragging footsteps and saw Young Matthew Corker resting by a six-pounder, his eyes on the land.

Bolitho said quietly, "We owe you a great deal, Matthew. One day you will realise it. What do you wish for yourself after this?"

The boy turned and faced him, his expression unusually sad and grave. "Please, Captain, I'd like to go *home.*" He was near to tears but added with sudden determination, "But only when Mr. Allday is back."

Bolitho watched him walk forward, soon hidden by the busy seamen. It was the right decision, he thought. One he had to make for himself.

Paice joined him by the bulwark and said, "Good lad, that one, sir."

Bolitho watched him, and guessed the reason for Paice's hurt.

"Aye, Mr. Paice. But for him—" He did not need to continue.

With the wind filling and puffing at the great mainsails the three cutters weighed and headed out to open water. Many eyes watched them leave, but with the mist moving slowly out to embrace the three hulls, there was little to reveal their intentions.

Major Philip Craven of the 30th Dragoons was enjoying a glass of claret when the news of their departure was brought by a hard-riding trooper.

Craven folded the message and finished the claret before calling his orderly to fetch his horse.

Commodore Ralph Hoblyn paced his great bedroom alone, his eyes everywhere whenever he reached a window. And as darkness fell, he was still striding back and forth, his stooped shoulder even more pronounced in shadows against the walls.

A messenger brought word to the gates about the cutters' leaving without fresh orders, but the corporal of the guard retorted sharply, "The commodore's made it plain in the past! 'E's not to be disturbed, *no matter wot!*"

And away in Chatham itself, the one person who had been the hinge of all these events, Midshipman Fenwick of the local impressment service, made the only firm decision of his miserable nineteen years. While the guards were changing their duties, he took his belt and hanged himself in his cell.

Down in *Telemachus*'s cabin once more, Bolitho changed into a fresh shirt and placed his watch carefully in his pocket. Around and above him the hull muttered and groaned, and he felt the wash alongside losing its power with each dragging minute.

He stared at the chart until his head throbbed.

189

It was now or never. He glanced at the parcel with the ship model inside. For both of them.

It seemed like an eternity before understanding returned. Even then it was a battle, against pain, and a sick unwillingness to believe what had happened.

Allday tried to open his eyes but with shocked horror realised that only the right one would obey. His whole body ached from bruises, and when he tried again to use his other eye he thought for an instant it had been put out.

He stared at the hazy picture which reached only to the perimeter of light cast by a gently spiralling lantern. It was barely a few feet away, and he thought he was going mad because of the confined space. He emitted a groan of agony as he tried to move. For the first time he realised that his legs were braced apart by irons bolted to the deck, his wrists dragged above his head by manacles so tight that he could no longer feel them.

He made himself wait, counting the seconds, while he attempted to muster his thoughts. He could remember nothing. But when he moved his head again he felt the force of the blow and guessed how he had come here. They must have beaten him almost to a point of death after that, although he had felt nothing. Not then.

He eased his legs and felt the irons dragging at them. He was naked to the waist, and when he peered down he saw blood, dried and stark on his body, like black tar in the lantern light.

A tiny pinprick flickered in his damaged eye and he felt more pain when he tried to open it. It must be clotted with his own blood, he thought despairingly, but what was the difference now? They would kill him. He tensed his legs in the irons. But not before they had made him suffer more.

Voices came faintly through the hull and he realised suddenly that the motion had eased; for another few dazed seconds he believed the brig was in harbour.

But as his mind tried to grasp what was happening he heard the irregular groan of the tiller, the clatter of tackle on deck. He peered round the tiny space again, each movement bringing a fresh stab of pain. No wonder it was small and low. It must be the lazaret, somewhere below the after cabin where the master's stores were usually held. Here there was nothing but a few dusty crates. Delaval—Allday sobbed at the sudden discovery of his name. It was surging back in broken pieces. The girl, half-naked in the cabin, screaming and pleading, and then . . .

That was why the tiller movements were so loud and near. His sailor's instinct forced through the despair and the pain. The brig was barely making headway. Not becalmed, so that—it came to him then. It must be a fog. God, it was common enough in these waters, especially after wind across a warm sea.

He craned his neck again. There was a small hatch from the cabin above, and another even smaller door in the bulkhead. Probably for a carpenter to inspect the lower hull if the vessel was damaged.

Allday sat bolt upright. She was the *Loyal Chieftain*, and was loaded with contraband to the deck beams. He felt close to shouting out aloud, all his distress and anguish pinned into this one small prison. It was for nothing. *Nothing*.

He dragged himself out of the sudden self-pity and

191

resignation, and listened to a new movement on deck. A brief rumbling that he had heard a thousand times, in a thousand places—the sound of gun trucks as a carriage was manhandled across deck planking. It was the long nine-pounder he had seen when he had helped to load the ship.

Suppose Bolitho was nearby? He fought against the sudden hope, because there was none. He tried to think only of dying without pleading, of escaping it all like the Captain's lady had done in the Great South Sea.

But the thought persisted, shining through the mists of pain like St. Anthony's Light at Falmouth.

Just suppose Bolitho was searching this area . . .

More thuds echoed through the decks as if to prod his thoughts into order.

Allday had never trusted a topsail cutter, or any other vessel which relied on a single mast, no matter how much sail she carried. He peered with his sound eye at the deckhead as if to see the gun-crew who were manoeuvring the nine-pounder, probably towards the quarter in readiness for a stern-chase. One good shot, and a cutter would be rendered useless. She would be left to fend for herself. Allday gritted his teeth. Or more likely, Delaval would round-up on her and loose every gun he had into the wreckage until not a soul was left alive.

He moved his arms and legs but was helpless. He must be content, accept that death was close by.

To fall in battle as old Stockdale had done was one thing—to die screaming under torture was another. Allday did not know if he could face it.

He closed his eyes tightly as the hatch in the deck-head was flung open. He heard angry voices, and then a coarse laugh as someone was pushed down into the lazaret. The hatch banged shut and Allday opened his eye once again.

The girl was crouching on her knees, whimpering and gasping like a savaged animal. There was blood on her face, and even in the poor light Allday saw the scratches on her bare shoulders as if talons had torn at her body. It was the same girl he had seen in the cabin. Close to, she was even younger than he had first thought. Fifteen or less. He watched despairingly as her hands fluttered about her torn clothing as she tried to cover her breasts.

As the lantern swung suddenly she stared up and saw him for the first time. It was all there in her face. Revulsion, terror, disgust at what had been done to her.

Allday swallowed hard and tried to think of words to calm her. God alone knew what they had done. From all the blood he guessed she had been raped several times. And now, like him, she was waiting to be disposed of.

He began carefully, "'Ere, Miss, be brave now, eh?" His voice was little more than a croak. He added, "I *know* what you've been through—" He groaned and felt the manacles tearing at his wrists. What was the use? She didn't understand what he was saying, not a bloody word; and what if she did?

The girl crouched in the same position, her eyes still and unblinking.

Allday murmured, "I hope it's quick for you." He groaned again. "If I could only *move!*" His words seemed to bounce from the curved sides to mock him.

More voices echoed through the decks, and feet

padded overhead as men ran to trim the sails yet again.

Allday's head drooped. Fog, that was it. Must be.

He glanced at the girl. She sat quite still, one breast bared. As if hope and life had already left her.

Footsteps thudded above, suddenly close, and Allday gasped hoarsely, "Come here to me, Miss! *Please!*"

He saw her eyes widen as she stared up at the small hatch, then at him with the brightness of terror. Something in his tone, perhaps, made her crawl over the filthy deck and huddle against his body, her eyes tightly closed.

Legs appeared through the hatch, then Isaac Newby the mate dropped into full view. He drew a cutlass from his belt and stabbed it into the deck out of reach where it swayed from side to side like a gleaming snake.

He looked at the girl and said, "Soon be time to drop you outboard, *Mister* Allday. But the cap'n 'as 'is own ideas, y'see—" He was grinning, enjoying it. "We shall 'ave to leave a souvenir for your gallant captain to remember you by, to remind 'im of the time he tried to outrun the Brotherhood, *right*?" He tapped the knife at his belt. "Delaval thinks your fine tattoo would make the proper sort of gift!" He threw back his head and laughed. "So the arm will have to come off, like."

Allday tasted bile in his throat. "Let *her* go. What can she do?"

Newby rubbed his chin as if in thought. "Well, seein' as you're not long for this world—" His arm shot out and he dragged the girl from the side, one hand tearing off the last covering from her shoulders.

194

"Feast yer eyes on *this*!" He gripped the girl's hair and pulled her face roughly to his own, his free hand ripping away the remainder of her clothing like some savage beast.

Allday had no way of knowing what happened next. He saw the girl slump back beside him, her breasts rising and falling in fear, while Newby propped himself on his hands and stared straight ahead. Allday watched as Newby's utter disbelief changed to sudden emptiness while he pitched forward and lay still. Only then did he see the knife protruding from his side. She must have seen it before he had tried to rape her again, had dragged it from its sheath, and then . . .

Allday bobbed his head towards the dead man's belt. He had seen the screw there beside the empty sheath.

"Get it for me!" He struggled to make himself understood by dragging at his leg irons. "Help me, *for God's sake!"*

She reached out and touched his bruised face, as if they were a million miles from this terrible place. Then she bowed over the man's body and unhooked the screw from his belt.

Allday watched with sick fascination as she unfastened first the leg irons then reached up to release the manacles, oblivious to her breasts brushing against him, to everything but the moment, the spark of courage which when offered she had used without hesitation.

Allday rolled over and gasped aloud in agony as the blood forced through his veins again. He felt light-headed, and knew that if he did not keep moving he might lose his wits completely.

He jerked the cutlass from the deck and gasped,

"That feels better!" Then he hobbled over to the corpse and plucked the knife from it. It did not come out easily, and he muttered, "You did for that pig well enough!"

He stared up as shouts filtered down to them from that other world of sea and canvas. He heard the clatter of handspikes and tackles. They were moving the nine-pounder again. There could only be one reason. He gripped the girl's shoulder and wondered why she did not pull away. Maybe she was beyond that, beyond everything real and decent.

Allday gestured towards the little door in the bulkhead and made a sawing motion with the knife. He noticed there was still blood on it, but she watched his gestures without fear or revulsion.

He explained carefully, "You get through there an' cut the lines to the rudder, see?" He groaned as her eyes remained empty and without understanding. They would soon come looking for Newby, especially if they intended to close with another vessel. Allday levered open the little door with his cutlass and held the lantern closer so that she could see into the darkness of the afterpart. Controlled by unseen hands, the rudder's yoke lines squeaked and rubbed through their blocks, the sea beyond the transom gurgling so loudly it seemed just feet away. Allday started as he felt her fingers on his wrist. She looked at him just once, her glance searching as if to share their resources, then she took the proffered knife and slithered through the small doorway. Once inside that confined space Allday saw her body suddenly pale in the darkness, and knew that she had tossed aside the last of her covering, as if that too was part of a nightmare.

196

He loosened his arms and winced as the pain probed through them. Then he peered up at the hatchway. It was the only way anyone could approach. He listened to the girl's sharp breathing as she sawed up and down on one of the stout hemp lines. It might take her a long while, a strand at a time. He spat on his palm and gripped the cutlass all the tighter. Now she had the strength of hatred and fear to help her. A few moments ago he had been expecting death, but only after the brutal severing of his arm.

Now, if only for a short while, they were both free, and even if he had to kill her himself, she would suffer that and nothing more.

A voice bellowed, "Where the *hell* is he?"

Allday bared his teeth. "Here we go then!" A shaft of light came down from the cabin and a voice called angrily, "Come on deck, you mad bugger! The cap'n's waitin'!"

A seabooted leg appeared over the coaming and Allday could feel the wildness surging through his mind and body like a raging fire.

He snarled, "Won't I do, matey?" The cutlass blade took the man's leg just above the knee with all his power behind it, so that Allday had to lurch away to avoid the blood and the terrible scream before the hatch was dropped into place.

As his breathing steadied he heard the regular scrape of the knife and murmured, "You keep at it, my lass. We'll show these bastards a thing or two!" He licked his dried lips. After that . . . But afterwards no longer mattered.

Bolitho walked aft to the compass box, aware of the

197

loudness of his shoes on the damp planking. The *Telemachus*'s deck was filled with silent figures, but in the drifting mist he could have been with a mere handful of companions.

Chesshyre straightened up as he recognised him and said, "Barely holding steerage way, sir." Even he spoke in a hushed whisper. Like all sailors he hated sea-mist and fog. Bolitho watched the tilting compass card. North-North-East. He watched it move again very slightly under the tiny lamp-glow. Chesshyre was right. They were holding on course, but making barely two knots, if that. It couldn't have been at a worse time.

Someone up forward began to cough, and Hawkins the boatswain rasped, "Stick a wad down yer gullet, Fisher! Not a squeak out of you, my son!"

Paice's tall shadow moved through the mist. Perhaps more than any other he understood Bolitho's predicament, the agony of seeing his one remaining chance slip away. To the smugglers it meant very little. Any landfall would do. They could rid themselves of their cargoes with ease once they were within sight of home waters.

Bolitho watched the winding tendrils of mist creeping through rigging and shrouds, while even in the darkness the big mainsail seemed to shine like metal from the moisture. It appeared as if the cutter was stationary, and only the mist was moving ahead.

It would be first light soon. Bolitho clamped his jaws together to contain his despair. It might just as well be midnight.

It was impossible to guess where the other two cutters lay. They would be lucky to regain contact when the mist cleared, let alone run down the decoy or Delaval.

Allday was out there somewhere. Unless he already lay fathoms deep, betrayed by his own loyalty and courage.

Paice remarked, "We *could* change tack again, sir."

Bolitho could not see his face but could feel his compassion. He had wanted Delaval more than anyone. Was there nothing they could do?

He replied, "I think not. Attend the chart yourself and try to estimate our position and drift." He spoke his anxiety aloud. "I know it's unlikely but there may be a ship just out there. Otherwise I would suggest more soundings. Anything is better than not knowing."

Paice thrust his big hands into his pockets. "I shall put a good man aloft as soon as there is some daylight, sir." He turned away, the mist swirling between them, the compass light vanishing. "I will check the chart."

Lieutenant Triscott shifted uneasily, unwilling to break into Bolitho's thoughts.

Bolitho said, "What is it, Mr. Triscott?" He had not meant to sound so sharp. "You are all on edge today!"

Triscott said lamely, "I was wondering, sir. Should we meet with the smuggler, I—I mean—"

"You are asking if we can overpower him without the other cutters?"

The youthful lieutenant hung his head. "Well, yes, sir."

Bolitho leaned on the bulwark, the woodwork like ice under his fingers even though his body felt hot and feverish.

"Let us *find* him, Mr. Triscott. Then you may ask me again."

Chesshyre cupped his hands behind his ears. "What was that?"

Bolitho stared aloft but soon lost the shrouds and running-rigging in the mist, as if they led up to nowhere.

The boatswain called hoarsely, "Not *riggin'*, sir!"

Bolitho held up his hand. "Quiet!" Like Chesshyre he had thought for just a few seconds that the sound had come from above, like a line parting under stress, or being too swollen with damp and carrying away inside a block. But it was not. It had come from outside the hull.

Men stood and swayed between the six-pounders; others clambered into the shrouds as if to listen more easily, all weariness and disappointment forgotten. At least for the while.

Paice appeared on deck, hatless, his thick hair moving in the wet breeze like a hassock of grass.

He said thickly, "I know *Telemachus* better'n I know myself, sir. Every sound carries down there to the cabin." He peered angrily into the darkness. "That was a musket shot, or I'm a bloody nigger!" He glanced awkwardly at Bolitho. "Begging your pardon, sir!"

This time they all heard it. Muffled, the sound barely carrying above the shipboard noises within the confines of the deck.

Chesshyre nodded, satisfied. "Close, sir. Down-wind of us. No doubt about it. The wind's poor enough, but it'll deaden the sound."

Bolitho frowned with concentration. Chesshyre's

observations were good ones. Who would be firing into mist without some kind of retaliation?

"Let her fall off a point." He gripped Paice's sleeve as he made to move aft. "Pass the word to load both batteries. Gun by gun." He let each word hang in the air. "I don't want anyone making a noise. We've not much time, but we've time enough for caution."

Triscott and the gunner moved up either side, whispering instructions, gritting their teeth at the slightest creak or thud.

Bolitho walked forward between the busy, groping figures and stood in the eyes of the vessel, his fingers gripped around a stay with the tiny gurgling bow-wave directly beneath him. Once when he looked aft he thought the mist was thicker, for he could barely see the mast. It was like standing on a pinnacle, moving ahead, seeing nothing. One slip, and they would never find him.

There was another muffled shot and he felt a new disappointment. It seemed further away, on a different bearing. Mist distorted most things at sea, even a trained seaman's judgement. Suppose—he thrust it from his mind. *There was a ship there.* He could sense it. And if that someone kept firing, the sound would lead them to it. He tried to control his sudden anger. If only the mist would depart. He stared up at the sky. It was surely brighter now? It had to be.

Triscott called softly, "All loaded, sir."

Bolitho climbed down from the stemhead and used the lieutenant's shoulder to support himself as he groped his way over the inboard end of the bowsprit.

As they walked aft between the guns a voice whispered, "We gonna fight, Cap'n?"

Another said, "There'll be prize money if we takes this 'un, eh, Cap'n?"

Someone even reached out to touch his arm as he passed, as if to regain a lost courage, to find comfort there.

Not for the first time was Bolitho grateful they could not see his face. He reached the compass-box and saw one of the helmsmen leaning backwards, his whole weight on the tiller bar, his red-rimmed eyes watching steadily for the tell-tale peak of the mainsail.

Bolitho stared at him, realising that he could see the man's stubbled face when moments earlier he had been hidden completely.

Paice exclaimed, "I'll go myself, sir!" Then he was away, swarming up the lee ratlines with the ease of a young topman.

Bolitho watched him until his outline merged into the remaining mist. His wife must have been proud of him, just as she had been ashamed of the people who had stood by and allowed a man to be murdered. She had probably been thinking of the tall lieutenant even as the pistol had cut short her life.

Paice slithered down a stay. "She's a brig, sir!" He did not seem to feel the cuts on his hands from the hasty drop. "I can just make out her tops'l yards." He stared at Bolitho without seeing him. "Must be her! That bastard Delaval!"

Bolitho could feel the power of the man, the reborn force of his hatred.

"Two good hands aloft!"

Then Paice said in a more controlled voice, "No sign of any other sail, sir." He clenched his hands and stared with disbelief at the blood on his wrists. "But by God, I'd walk on water to take that swine!"

There were more shots now and Bolitho offered silent thanks. If *Telemachus* could close the range and use her smashers it might compensate for the smuggler's heavier armament. The musket fire must be keeping them busy. Too busy even to put a lookout at the masthead.

A mutiny? He saw Delaval's cruel features in his mind. It was unlikely. A cold hand seemed to close around his heart and squeeze the life out of it.

It was Allday.

He was stunned by the flat calmness in his voice. "Alter course to engage, Mr. Chesshyre. Pass out the weapons."

He looked up at a small handkerchief of pale sky, and thought of the dead girl on *Wakeful*'s deck.

A long, painful journey. When the mist eventually cleared, it would be settled. He loosened the old sword at his hip.

For some it would be over.

Allday flung himself against the curving side and ducked yet again as a musket ball slammed through the partly open hatch.

He heard them calling to one another, the scrape of ramrods as they reloaded. He was sweating despite the chill air of the lazaret, and his whole body was streaming as if he had just dragged himself from the sea.

He gripped the cutlass and squinted up through the trapped powder smoke. It was just a matter of time. He shouted over his shoulder towards the small door, "Keep sawing, my lass! You'll get through!" Only once had he been able to watch the girl's progress. Even with a sharp blade it was hard work to cut through the stout rudder-lines. He had seen her pale outline rising and falling above the creaking lines, everything else forgotten, unimportant. She probably didn't even know why she was doing it, Allday thought despairingly, just as she understood not a word he said to her.

The hatch moved an inch, and the muzzle of a musket pointed blindly through the opening. Allday reached up and seized it, winced as he felt the heated metal, then tugged it hard, catching the man off balance so that he fell across the hatch, the musket exploding within a foot of Allday's head. Before the smuggler could release his grip Allday thrust upwards with his cutlass and yelled, "One for the pot, you bastards!"

He fell exhausted against the side, his eyes too raw from smoke to care about the blood which poured through the hatch like paint.

The people in the cabin suddenly froze into silence, and above the creak of rudder lines Allday heard a voice yell, "Stand to! Man the braces there! A King's ship, by Jesus!" And then another, calmer, more controlled; Delaval's. "It's Paice's *Telemachus*, I'll swear. This time we'll do for him and his bloody crew, eh, lads?"

Allday did not know or care about any response. The words stood out before all else. Paice's *Telemachus*. Bolitho was here.

The deck was slanting down so that the corpse of Newby rolled on one side as if awakening to the din.

Allday heard the shouted orders, the slap of canvas, and then the too-familiar sound of the nine-pounder being hauled into position.

He peered through the little door and pleaded, "Keep at it, lass. I can hold 'em off until—"

He stared blindly at the pale figure sprawled across one of the timbers. Either the last shot had caught her, or someone had fired down through the slits which held the sheaves of the rudder lines.

He reached over the sill and dragged her up and through, held her naked body against his own, turning her face with sudden tenderness until the swaying lantern reflected from her eyes.

Brokenly he whispered, "Never mind, young missy, you bloody well tried!"

The deck bounded to a sudden recoil and he heard somebody yelling directions even as the discharged gun ran inboard on its tackles.

Allday crawled over the deck and dragged the coat from Newby's back. Then he covered her with it and with a last glance at her face lifted her to the open hatch and pushed her into the abandoned cabin.

Another minute or so and she might have cut the rudder lines, then Paice's cutter would have stood a good chance of outsailing her, crossing her stern and raking her with those deadly carronades.

The deck heaved again and dust filtered down from the poop as the gun fired across the quarter.

Allday wrapped the girl's body in the coat and put her across his shoulder. For just those seconds he had seen her face in the pale light. No fear, all anguish gone. Probably the first peace she had known since the Terror had swept through her country.

Allday glanced round the cabin until his eyes fell on a bottle of rum which was about to slide from the table. With the girl's body carried easily over his shoulder he drank heavily from the bottle before picking up the reddened cutlass again and making for the companion ladder.

They could not hurt her or him any more. Out in the open he would die fighting. He shuddered as the gun crashed inboard again and the deck shook to the concussion.

There was a ragged cheer. "There goes 'er topmast, by God!"

Allday blinked the sweat from his eyes and left the cabin. At the foot of the ladder he saw the man whose leg he had nearly severed when he had climbed through the hatch. His bandage was sodden with blood, and he stank of vomit and rum. Despite his pain he managed to open his eyes, his mouth ready to scream as he saw Allday rising over him.

Allday said, "Not any more, matey!" He jammed the point of his cutlass between the man's teeth and drove it hard against the ladder. To the dead girl he muttered, "Keep with me, lass!"

As his eyes rose above the coaming he saw the backs of several men who were standing at the bulwarks to point at the other vessel. Between them Allday saw *Telemachus*, his heart sinking as he saw her despoiled outline, the topmast gone, like a great crippled seabird. The gun's crew were already ramming home another charge, and past them Allday saw Delaval watching his adversary through a brass telescope. All the fury and hatred seemed to erupt at once and Allday yelled,

"I'm here, you bloody bastard!"

For those few moments every face was turned towards him, the approaching cutter forgotten.

"Who's going to be brave enough, eh, you scum?"

Delaval shouted, "Cut him down! Bosun, take that man!"

But nobody moved as Allday bent down and laid the dead girl on the deck in the dawn's first sunlight.

"Is *this* what you want? All you have guts for?" He saw the seaman Tom Lucas staring at the girl before he shouted, "We didn't bargain for this!"

They were his last words on earth. Delaval lowered his smoking pistol and drew another.

He snapped, "Put up the helm! We'll finish this now!"

Allday stood alone, his chest heaving, barely able to see out of his uninjured eye, or keep his grasp on the cutlass.

As if through a haze he watched the helm going over, saw sudden confusion as the spokes spun uselessly and a voice cried, *"Steerin's gone!"*

Allday dropped beside the girl on the deck and grasped her hand, the cutlass held ready across her body.

"You done it, girl!" His eyes smarted. "By Christ, we're in irons!"

The brig was already losing steerage way and heeling unsteadily downwind. Allday looked at the gun's crew, their expression dazed as the distant cutter seemed to slide away from their next fall of shot.

"Well, lads!" Allday waited for the sudden, agonising impact. He knew Delaval was aiming his other pistol, just as he knew that men were moving away from the sides to stand between them.

He repeated, "Is *this* what you want?"

Delaval screamed, "Cut him down! I order it!"

Still no one moved, then some of the seamen Allday

207

had seen at the boatyard tossed down their weapons, while others defiantly faced aft towards Delaval.

Allday watched *Telemachus*'s splintered topmast rise above the *Loyal Chieftain*'s weather bulwark, knew he would have seen Bolitho were his eyes not so blind.

It seemed like a year before a grapnel lodged in the bulwark and the deck was taken over by some of Paice's armed seamen.

There was no resistance, and Paice himself walked aft until he confronted Delaval by the abandoned wheel.

Delaval faced him coldly, but his features were like chalk.

"Well, Lieutenant, your greatest triumph, I dare say. Will you murder me now, unarmed as I am, in front of witnesses?"

Paice glanced across to Allday and gave a brief nod before removing the unfired pistol from the other's hand.

"The noose is for scum like you." He turned aside as a voice yelled, "*Wakeful* in sight, sir!" Someone gave a cheer but fell silent as Bolitho climbed over the bulwark past the levelled muskets and swivels on *Telemachus*'s side.

He looked around at their tense faces. He had seen Paice's expression, his features torn with emotion when seconds earlier he might have hacked Delaval to the deck. Perhaps, like the blind man, he had discovered that revenge would solve nothing.

Then he walked to Allday, who was kneeling again beside the dead girl. Two unknown young women. A twist of fate.

He saw the cuts and cruel bruises on Allday's body

208

and wanted to say so much. Maybe the right words would come later.

Instead he said quietly, "So you're safe, John?"

Allday peered up at him with his sound eye and felt his face trying to respond with a grin, but without success.

One truth stood out. Bolitho had called him by his first name. Something which had never happened before.

11

Faces In The Crowd

THE Golden Fleece Inn which stood on the outskirts of Dover was an imposing, weather-beaten building, a place to change post horses, to rest a while after the rough roads around and out of the port.

Rear-Admiral Sir Marcus Drew waited for the inn servants to place his travelling chests in the adjoining room and walked to the thick leaded windows overlooking a cobbled square. He stared with distaste at groups of townsfolk who were chattering in the hot sunshine, some buying fruit or Geneva from women with trays around their necks.

It was just possible to see the harbour, or part of it, reassuring to know, as Drew did, that there were several small men-of-war at anchor there. On the way to the inn he had also found some comfort in the presence of scarlet-coated marines, or an occasional troop of stern-faced dragoons.

Nevertheless he felt uneasy here. But for a direct order he would still be in London, perhaps even with his young mistress. He turned away from the window as his secretary entered and paused to stare at him, wiping his small gold-rimmed spectacles with a handkerchief at the same time.

"Is it satisfactory, Sir Marcus?" He peered around the spacious room, and considered it a palace.

Drew snorted, "I dislike this place—the whole situation in fact." Coming here had stripped him of confidence, his accustomed sense of being in control. Usually he spent his days choosing officers for certain appointments; at other times he bowed to their lordships' whims and fancies by providing favours for others he might inwardly have regarded as useless.

Now here, to Dover. He scowled. Not even Canterbury where there was at least some social life, or so he had heard. Dover seen from within and not through the eyes of some homeward-bound sailor was too rough and ready, with an air of instability to match it. But for the great castle which cast its timeless gaze across the harbour and the approaches, he would have felt even more uncertain.

The secretary offered, "Captain Richard Bolitho has arrived, Sir Marcus." He laid his head on one side. "Shall I—"

"*No!* Have him wait, dammit! Fetch me a glass of something."

"Brandy, Sir Marcus?"

The rear-admiral glared at him. "Don't make mock of me, sir! The brandy is quite likely contraband—I want no part of it!"

He controlled his temper. It was not his secretary's fault. Another thought pressed through his mind. Besides, the man knew about his little affair. He said in a more reasonable tone, "Fetch me what you will. This place . . . it downs my heart."

The elderly secretary moved to the windows and stared at the crowd, which within half-an-hour had doubled. There was music down there, some masked dancers bobbing through the crowd, probably picking pockets as they went, he thought.

At the far side of the square was a great cluster of

211

horses, each held by a red-coated soldier. They looked wary, while their two officers paced back and forth in deep conversation.

He shifted his gaze to the crude scaffold, a man who was obviously a carpenter putting finishing touches to it. The secretary noticed that, as he worked, his foot was tapping in time to the cheerful music. No wonder the rear-admiral was uneasy. In London you were spared this sort of thing unless you counted the ragged scarecrows which dangled in chains on the outskirts, along the King's highway.

Sir Marcus joined him and muttered, "By God, you'd think they'd have heard enough about France to—" He said no more. He was always a careful man.

Two floors below, Bolitho walked into a small parlour and rested his back in a cool corner.

The inn seemed to be full of naval people, none of whom he knew. But he had been away from England a long while. A young lieutenant had jumped to his feet and had stammered, "I beg your attention, Captain Bolitho! Should you require a junior lieutenant—"

Bolitho had shaken his head. "I cannot say. But do not lose heart." How many times had he himself been made to beg for an appointment?

The landlord served him personally, carrying a tall tankard of local ale to his table.

"We're not used to so many senior persons, sir, and that's no mistake! War must be comin' soon, it's a sure sign!" He went off chuckling to himself.

Bolitho stared at the blue sky through one of the tiny windows. It kept coming back. Memory upon memory, and most of all, Allday kneeling on deck, his poor bruised face turned to greet him. There had been no sort of disbelief or surprise. As if they had both known in their hearts they would be reunited.

That had been weeks ago. Now he was here, summoned to Dover by the same flag officer who had offered him this appointment.

He heard shouts of laughter from the square outside and considered his feelings. Was it coincidence or purpose which had brought them here today?

At least the rear-admiral had come to him. Had it been the other way round Bolitho would have known his attachment was over.

A servant hovered by the door. "Sir Marcus will see you now, sir." He gestured towards the stairway which wound upwards past some old and stained paintings of battles, ship disasters, and local scenes. A sailors' haunt—smugglers too, he thought grimly.

He was breathing hard by the time he had reached the top floor. A shortage of breath or patience? Perhaps both.

An elderly man in a bottle-green coat ushered him into the first room, and he saw Drew sitting listlessly by one of the open windows. He did not rise, but waved for Bolitho to take a chair.

Bolitho began, "I was called here, Sir Marcus, because—"

The admiral retorted wearily, "We were *both* called here, man. Have some claret, though after the journey it may taste like bilge!" He watched Bolitho as he poured a glass for himself. The same grave features, level eyes which looked like the North Sea in the reflected sunlight. Cold, and yet . . . Drew said, "It was a lengthy report which you sent their lordships, Bolitho. You spared nothing, added no decoration."

213

He nodded slowly. "Like your Cornish houses and their slate roofs—hard and functional."

"It was all the truth, sir."

"I have no doubt of it. In some ways I would have wished otherwise." He dragged the report across his table and ruffled through it, words or sentences sparking off pictures and events, as if he had been listening to Bolitho's voice while he had read it.

Drew said, "You had a free hand and you used it, as many knew you would. The result? Most of those deserters, and many others who were in hiding, *volunteered* to return to the navy." He glanced at him severely. "I am not so certain that I would have permitted them to return to different vessels from which they had originally run, or accepted them without an example of punishment to deter others." He sighed and continued, "But you gave them your word. That had to be sufficient. All told we gained two hundred men; perhaps others will take your word as a bond. It will encourage wider areas, I hope."

He cleared his throat. "I would like you to tell me about Commodore Hoblyn."

Bolitho got to his feet and walked to a side window overlooking a narrow street, like the one which Allday had described, where he had been taken by the press gang.

He said bitterly, "That too is in my report, Sir Marcus."

He expected a rebuke but Drew said quietly, "I know. I would like you to tell me, as man to man. You see, I served with Hoblyn in that other war. He was a different being then."

Bolitho stared at the empty street and tried to shut out the mounting buzz of voices from the crowd which waited to observe the spectacle of a man being hanged.

"I did not know, Sir Marcus." He knew the admiral was watching his back but did not turn. "It was too much for him in the end." How could he sound so calm and casual? Like all the events which had led up to taking the *Loyal Chieftain*, and which now lay safe in memory. Like being in a calm in the eye of a typhoon where everything was sharp and clear, desperately so, perhaps, while you waited to enter the second path of the storm. "I suspected Hoblyn was involved with the smuggling gangs, although I wanted to disbelieve it. He was a poor man, rejected by the one life for which he cared, and then all at once he was rich. Gifts which he treasured as acts of friendship—perhaps he too refused to see them as bribes. A carriage from a French nobleman, a world in which he thought he held control. They needed him, and when they thought he had betrayed them they took their revenge."

Bolitho rested his hand on the sill, praying that the admiral had had enough, that he could let the pieces fall into distance like the moment you lower a telescope from another craft.

But the room was still, and even the distant voices in the square seemed afraid to intrude.

"I had told Major Craven what I intended before we weighed anchor." He stared into the little street, his grey eyes very still. "When he saw us return with our prizes—" That too had been like a dream, *Snapdragon* following them to the anchorage, her jubilant prize-crew aboard the smuggling schooner intended as a decoy. That unknown seaman aboard *Telemachus* who had called to him through the fog would get his prize money after all. Bolitho continued, "Craven had two troops of his men and a magistrate to read the warrant." He barely listened to his own voice as he relived that night, when he had reached Hoblyn's house to join Craven's dragoons and a magistrate who had been almost too terrified to speak.

The marine picket was outside the gates, and most of Hoblyn's servants had been clustered in the gardens in their night attire. They had described how Hoblyn had ordered them from the house, and when one had requested a few moments to return to his room he had fired a pistol point-blank into a chandelier.

Craven had said, "The doors are locked and bolted. Can't understand it, Bolitho. He must know why we're here." He added with sudden anger, "By God, some of my own men have died because of his treachery!"

Bolitho had been about to ring the bell himself when he had seen Allday walking carefully between the dragoons.

Bolitho had said, "You should be resting, old friend. After this—"

But Allday had replied stubbornly, "I'm not leaving you again, Cap'n."

Craven had settled it by calling for his farrier sergeant. A tall, bearded dragoon who had marched up to the doors with his huge axe, the one he sometimes used for slaughtering animals to feed the soldiers, and in just two minutes he had laid both doors on the ground.

It had been a macabre scene which had greeted their eyes. In the light of guttering candles Bolitho

216

had seen the shattered fragments of a chandelier, and then when he had approached the great staircase he had seen the blood, on the carpets, against the wall, even on a banister rail. They had halted halfway up the staircase, and Major Craven's drawn sabre had glinted in the flickering candles as he had gripped Bolitho's arm. "In God's name what was that fearful sound?"

No wonder the servants had been terrified out of their wits, and the picket had stayed by the gates until Craven's men had arrived in force. It was a terrible, inhuman cry, rising and falling like a wounded wolf. Even some of the older dragoons had glanced at one another and had clutched their weapons all the tighter.

Bolitho had hurried to the big door at the top of the stairs, Allday limping behind him, that same cutlass still in his hand.

Craven had shouted, "In the King's name!" Then he had kicked the door inwards with his boot.

Bolitho knew he would never forget the sight which had waited in that room. Hoblyn crouching beside the huge bed, rocking from side to side, his hands and arms thick with dried blood. For a moment longer they had imagined that he was injured, or had attempted to kill himself without success. Until a sergeant had brought more candles, and together they had stared at the bed, at what was left of the naked body of Jules, the youthful footman and companion.

There was not a part of his body which had not been savagely mutilated or hacked away. Only the face was left unmarked, like the murdered informer aboard the *Loyal Chieftain* when Bolitho had first confronted Delaval. From the youth's contorted

217

features it was obvious that the horrific torture had been exercised while he had been alive. The bed, the floor, everything was soaked in blood, and Bolitho had realised that Hoblyn must have carried the corpse in his arms round and round the room until he had collapsed, broken and exhausted.

The Brotherhood had thought that he had betrayed them, not realising that Bolitho's search for Allday had provoked the attack on the boatyard.

From all the rewards Hoblyn had gained from them by his help and information, they had selected the possession he had prized the most, and had butchered the youth, then left him like a carcass at the gates.

Craven had said huskily, "In the King's name you are charged this day—" He had broken off and had choked, "Take him. I can stand no more of this charnel house!"

It had been then that Hoblyn had come out of his trance and stared at them without recognition. With a great effort he had got to his feet, and almost tenderly covered the mutilated corpse with a blanket.

In a steady voice he had said, "I am ready, gentlemen." He had turned only briefly to Bolitho. "You *would not heed* me." Then he had tried to shrug his shoulders, but even that had failed him.

At the door he had said, "My sword. I am entitled."

Bolitho and Craven had looked at one another. Maybe each had known in his own way.

They had waited outside the door, while the dragoons lined the hallway below, where some dazed servants were peering in at the bloodstains and the plaster which had fallen to Hoblyn's pistol.

The bang of the shot brought more cries and shouts

from the waiting servants. They had found Hoblyn lying on the bed, one arm over the blanketed shape, the other crooking the pistol which had blown away the back of his skull.

Bolitho realised he had stopped speaking, that the din outside the inn was louder now.

Sir Marcus Drew said quietly, "I am distressed to learn it, Bolitho, and I grieve that you should have been forced to witness it. In the long run, it will have been the best way out. Perhaps the only way for him."

Bolitho moved to the large window and watched the scene below. The pattern had changed, and the dragoons were mounted now, lined, saddle to saddle, across the square, each sabre drawn and shouldered, the horses restless, uneasy in the presence of death. A mounted major was patting his own horse's neck, but his eyes were on the swaying crowd. It could have been Craven, but it was not.

Drew stood beside him and sipped at his claret, his mind still with the image of Hoblyn's death.

"He was a fool, not the man I once admired. How did he come to—" He could not continue.

Bolitho eyed him coldly. "Come to *love* that youth? It was all he had. The woman who had waited for him during the war would not even look at him when she was told of his terrible scars. So he searched elsewhere, and found that boy." Bolitho was again surprised at the emptiness of his voice. "He learned too late that there are no pockets in a shroud, no money box in a coffin."

Drew licked his lips. "You are a strange fellow, Bolitho."

"Strange, sir? Because the truly guilty go free, or

hide in safety behind rank or privilege?" His eyes flashed. "One day—"

He stiffened as he saw Delaval's slight figure mounting the scaffold, a trooper on either side. Dressed in a fine velvet coat, his dark hair uncovered, his appearance brought a chorus of cheers and jeers from the expectant crowd.

Bolitho looked down and saw Allday directly below him, leaning against one of the inn's pillars, a long clay pipe held unlit to his mouth. In the ensuing weeks he had lost the scars and his eye was as clear as before. But he had changed nonetheless; he seemed quieter, less ready to make a joke of everything. In one way he had not changed. Like dog and master, Bolitho had often thought, each fearful that the other might die first. Loyalty? That was no description of it. Probably Paice was there too, watching, remembering.

The horses were more restless, and the major raised his arm to steady the line.

Drew said softly, "A rogue, but you can pity him this moment."

Bolitho retorted equally quietly, "I pray he rots in hell."

It was nearly done. An official from the sheriff's office, a quavering clergyman whose words, if there were any, were quite lost in the hubbub of shouts and jeers.

Bolitho had seen hangings before—too many, and mostly those of sailors, men found guilty of mutiny or worse, run up to the mainyard by their own messmates.

But this display was little better than Madame Guillotine across the Channel, he thought.

The noose was placed around Delaval's neck but he shook his head when one of the executioners made to blindfold him.

He looked composed, even indifferent as he called something to those nearest the scaffold.

At that last moment an elegant, dark red phaeton with a fragile gold crest painted on the door, cantered around the fringe of the crowd until the coachman reined it to a halt.

Delaval must have seen it too, for he stared until his eyes almost bulged from his head. He tried to scream something, but at that instant the trap was sprung and his legs thrashed wildly in space, the air choked from his lungs while excreta ran down his fine nankeen breeches.

Bolitho saw the phaeton move away, but noticed a man's face watching from the open window. The face was smiling until it withdrew out of sight, and the fine carriage gathered speed away from the square.

The crowd was silent now in a mixture of disgust and disappointment that the spectacle was almost over. The puppetlike figure still twisted and flinched on the rope, and it would take another few minutes for the man who had been murderer, rapist, and smuggler to snuff out his life completely.

Delaval's last bravado might have carried him across the threshold of darkness but for that face in the carriage window.

Bolitho turned away from the window, his limbs shaking uncontrollably. He had seen it before, on the road to Rochester when it had been in company with the deputy sheriff and his mob. The missing piece of the pattern.

He faced the rear-admiral and asked calmly, "So, may I ask why I am here, Sir Marcus?"

Bolitho watched the purple shadows standing out across the square and felt the cooler air of evening against his face. It had been a long day spent with Rear-Admiral Drew, a man so obviously worried by the prospect of implicating himself in anything which might damage his secure position in Admiralty that conversation had been stilted and fruitless.

All he had discovered of any value was that they were here to meet a man of great importance. His name was Lord Marcuard.

Bolitho had heard Marcuard discussed in the past, and seen brief mentions of him in the Gazette. Someone of supreme influence, above the rules of Parliament, who was called frequently to offer his advice on matters of policy to no less than the King himself.

Drew had said at one point, "Do not provoke or irritate His Lordship, Bolitho. It can do nothing but harm and you will be the poorer."

Bolitho saw some men working on the empty scaffold. Two highwaymen who had prowled together on the Dover Road would share Delaval's fate tomorrow. They might attract an even larger crowd. Yet another myth, that highwaymen were somehow different from murderers and thieves.

Drew was so typical, he thought bitterly. When war came, young captains would be expected to obey the commands and instructions of men like him. Admirals who had gained their advancement in times of peace, who had become soft in the search for their own advantages.

222

The old secretary opened the door and darted a quick glance between them.

"Lord Marcuard's carriage approaches, Sir Marcus."

Drew twitched his neckcloth and glanced at himself in a mirror.

"We are to wait here, Bolitho." He sounded incredibly nervous.

Bolitho turned away from the window. The carriage had not arrived by the square. The meeting was to be a secret affair. He felt his heart beat faster. He had imagined it might be one of routine, a few words of encouragement perhaps for future aggressive tactics against the smugglers. Lord Marcuard was rarely known to leave his grand house in Whitehall. Even when he did he usually remained secure in his great estate in Gloucestershire.

He heard boots on the stairs and saw two grooms, each armed with a pistol and sidearm, take up a position on the landing beyond the open door. Despite their livery they looked more like seasoned soldiers than servants.

He murmured, "It seems we are to be *protected*, Sir Marcus."

The admiral turned on him. "Don't be so damned flippant!"

A shadow crossed the doorway and Bolitho bowed his head. Marcuard was not what he had expected. He was tall and slender, of middle age, with a finely chiselled nose and chin, and eyes which turned down in a fixed expression of melancholy disdain. He was dressed in a finely cut coat and breeches of pale green which Bolitho guessed to be pure silk, and carried an ebony stick. His hair, which was gathered to the back

223

of his collar in an un-English fashion was, Bolitho noticed, heavily powdered. It was a small enough vanity, but Bolitho had always disdained men with powdered hair. This was most certainly a man of the Court, and not of any field of battle.

Drew stammered, "I am *honoured*, m'lord."

Lord Marcuard seated himself carefully on a chair and arranged the tails of his elegant coat.

"I would take some chocolate. The journey—most tiresome. And now this place." His eyes turned to Bolitho for the first time. He sounded bored, but his glance was as sharp as any rapier.

"So you are the man of whom I have heard so much. Splendid exploit. Tuke was a dangerous threat to trade."

Bolitho tried not to show his surprise. He had imagined that Marcuard was referring to the seizure of the *Loyal Chieftain*. At the same time he guessed that he had been intended so to think. Like being tested.

Drew was flushing badly, taken aback by the switch from hot chocolate to Bolitho's last command in the Great South Sea.

Bolitho was glad that unlike the rear-admiral he had taken hardly any wine during the day. Marcuard might dress and act like a fop, but he was nobody's fool.

He said, "I had a good company, m'lord."

Marcuard gave a cool smile. "Perhaps in their turn they were fortunate in having an excellent captain?" He touched his chin with the knob of his stick. "But I doubt that would occur to you." He did not wait for a reply.

"His Majesty is concerned about France. William

224

Pitt is attempting to take precautionary steps, of course, but—"

Bolitho watched the stick's silver knob. Fashioned like an eagle, its claws around a globe—the world perhaps? Marcuard had not said so, but Bolitho felt he did not like Pitt very much.

Marcuard added in the same bored tones, "His Majesty's perspective does tend to alter from day to day." Again the faint smile. "Like the winds to France." He gave a small frown. "Do see if you can distract someone long enough to procure the chocolate."

Bolitho made to move for the door but he snapped, "*No*. I must hear your voice in this."

Bolitho felt almost sorry for Drew. Was the snub real, or only another demonstration of this man's immense authority?

As Drew hurried away Marcuard said, "I was too late to see Delaval swing. The roads. I'd have laid a wager otherwise." Then he said sharply, "Your taking of the brig and the decoy schooner was brilliant. A frigate captain you once were, and no matter what fate awaits you, I suggest that in your soul you will remain one until you are in your grave!"

Bolitho knew his remarks were not casual. He had not come to Dover for idle conversation.

He replied, "I was determined, m'lord. Much was at stake."

"Yes." The eyes passed over him again without curiosity. "So I have heard. The matter of Commodore Hoblyn, well—" He gave a slight grimace. "Once a brave man. A knave nonetheless. You are still troubled, Bolitho, that I can see without difficulty. Speak out, man."

Bolitho glanced at the door. Drew would have a seizure if he knew he was being asked to reveal his thoughts like this.

He said, "I was convinced that Delaval expected to be saved from the gallows, m'lord. Despite all the evidence and the discovery of his foul murders of young Frenchwomen, he was confident to the end." He paused, expecting Marcuard to silence him, pour scorn on his ideas as Drew had tried to do. But Marcuard said nothing.

Bolitho continued, "Sir James Tanner owns much of the land where deserters and smugglers were given shelter between their runs across the Channel. I obtained evidence that he, and only he could have controlled the organisation which such movements required. He *bought* people, anyone who could offer duplicity, from that wretched midshipman to the commodore, and many others respected in high places."

"I can see why you are oft unwelcome here, Bolitho. What are you telling me now?"

"This man Tanner has been able to ignore every suggestion of involvement. There is not a judge or magistrate who will listen to any criticism. How can the government expect, no, *demand* common seamen to risk their lives, when they see the guilty flouting the same laws which have impressed them?"

Marcuard nodded, apparently satisfied. "I was influenced by your last action. In a fog too. Your three cutters must think most highly of you now."

Bolitho stared at him as if he had misheard. Had all the rest fallen on deaf ears?

Marcuard said, "If, nay, *when* war comes, we cannot depend upon the French remaining a leaderless rabble. Many of their best officers have been beheaded because of the lust and madness of this present revolution. But there will always be other leaders, as there were in England when Charles lost his head on the block." He reached out with the long ebony stick and tapped the floor to emphasise every word. "Perhaps there will be a counter-revolution; only time will allow this. But France must have her King on his rightful throne." He saw Bolitho's astonishment and smiled openly for the first time. "I see I have confused you, my gallant captain! That is good, for if others penetrate my mind, our hopes will be dashed before we are begun!"

Marcuard stood up lightly and crossed to a window. "We need an officer we can trust. No civilian will do, especially a man of Parliament who sees only his own advancement no matter what his tongue might proclaim!" He turned on his toes, like a dancer, Bolitho thought dazedly. "I have chosen you."

"To go where, m'lord? To do what?"

Marcuard ignored it. "Tell me this, Bolitho. Do you love your King and country above all else?"

"I love England, m'lord."

Marcuard nodded slowly. "That at least is honest. There are people in France who are working to release their monarch. They need to be assured they are not alone. They will trust no spy or informer. The slightest flaw, and their lives end under the blade. I have seen it. I *know*." He eyed him steadily. "I am partly French, and your report of the two girls who died at sea interested me very much. My own niece was guillotined in the first month of the Terror. She was just nineteen. So you see—" He turned irritably

227

as voices came from the landing. "Damn their eyes, they make chocolate too fast in Kent!"

Then he said evenly, "You will be advised, but will tell nobody until a plan is made. I am sending you to Holland." He let his words sink in. "When war comes, Holland will fall to the French. There is no doubt of that, so you must be doubly careful. Spain will throw in her lot with France for her own good."

Bolitho stared at him. "But I thought that the King of Spain—"

"Was against the Revolution?" He smiled faintly. "The Dons never change, and I thank God for it. They value their Church and gold above all else. His most Catholic Majesty will soon convince himself where his loyalty lies."

The door opened and Drew followed by two inn servants bowed his way forward.

"I regret the delay, m'lord!" Drew's eyes moved like darts between them.

"It will be worth it, Sir Marcus."

As Lord Marcuard leaned forward to examine the tray his eyes met Bolitho's and he added softly, "It *has* to be worth it."

Then he looked away as if it was a dismissal.

"You may leave us, Bolitho. Your admiral and I have weighty matters to discuss."

Bolitho walked to the door and turned to give a brief bow. In those seconds he saw Drew's relief, shining from his face like a beam of light, in the knowledge that Marcuard, the King's man, was not displeased, that life might continue as before.

He also saw Marcuard's final gaze. It was that of a conspirator.

228

12

The Power And The Glory

FOR Bolitho, the weeks which followed the capture of the *Loyal Chieftain* and the decoy schooner were uneventful and frustrating. Commodore Hoblyn was not replaced by a senior officer; instead, a studious official came from the admiralty to supervise the purchase of suitable vessels, and to list possible applicants for letters of marque should war be declared in the near future.

The house where Hoblyn had killed himself remained empty and shuttered, a landmark of his disgrace and final grief.

Bolitho found himself with less and less to do, and had to be content with his three cutters acting without his personal supervision, while they carried out their patrols or assisted the revenue vessels in the continuing fight against smugglers.

He found little comfort in the varying successes of his recruiting parties and the press gangs although there had been a surprising increase in volunteers for the fleet, especially from the more inland villages where news of Bolitho's victory over Delaval's ships and gangs had preceded his visits.

The news of the murdered girls had spread like wildfire, and fresh information had come from many different sources to prove that their wretched deaths had not been isolated incidents.

After the first bloodbath in the streets of Paris the

229

mobs had turned their hatred towards the professional classes, then lower still to mere shopkeepers and artisans. Anyone who was branded as a traitor to the revolution, a lackey to the feared and loathed *aristos*, was dragged to prison for harsh interrogation and the inevitable journey through the streets to the waiting guillotine. Some parents had tried to assist their children to escape by selling all they owned; others had attempted to bribe their way into small vessels in the hope of reaching safety in England. Some smugglers like Delaval had found the latter the most profitable of all. They would take everything from these poor, terrified refugees, then murder them in mid-Channel or in the North Sea. Dead men told no tales. If young girls were amongst their human cargo they could expect no mercy at all.

Once, when supping with Major Craven at his small barracks, Bolitho had said angrily, "We are dealing with the scum of the earth. Any enemy who sails under a known flag, no matter what cause he represents, has more respect and honour."

And now there was not even the major to pass the time with. He and most of his regiment had been ordered to Ireland, in readiness for disturbances there after an overall famine had failed to produce food and warmth for the approaching winter.

And winter was coming early, Bolitho thought. You could see it in the tide-race, and in the tossing white horses of the Channel.

The new detachment of soldiers was composed mainly of recruits and some of the freshly-formed militia, more concerned with their drills and exercises than they were with Bolitho's warnings about smugglers. But the Trade had slackened, if not died, since the *Loyal Chieftain* incident. It should have given him satisfaction, but when he walked the shoreline with Allday a constant companion, he found little consolation.

From the urbane Lord Marcuard he had heard nothing. That had been the biggest disappointment of all. Perhaps it had been another ruse to keep him quiet. Even Craven's removal might be connected in some way, although it was impossible to prove it. Officers and officials whom he was forced to meet if only to maintain the co-operation he had painstakingly built up, treated him with a certain wariness—respect or awe, he did not know.

To some he seemed to represent the man of war, to others an interference with a life they knew would soon change but still refused to abandon.

Rear-Admiral Drew's departure had been swift after the meeting at Dover. He had left with an air of profound relief and perhaps a new determination to remain uninvolved in anything beyond the walls of Admiralty.

There had been one hope when Drew had left written orders that he should not invade the property or privacy of Sir James Tanner without express instruction from higher authority. There was little point anyway, for it was said that Tanner was elsewhere, maybe out of the country altogether. But Bolitho had nursed the idea that the orders had come through Drew from Lord Marcuard. Even that was difficult to believe now.

Late one afternoon Bolitho stood on a bluff watching a frigate working her way downstream towards Sheerness. Her paintwork shone in the grey light; the gilt gingerbread around her stern windows and counter was proof that the lucky man who commanded her had money to spare to present such a fine display. Like Bolitho's *Undine* and *Tempest* had been when he had assumed command first of one, then the other, after the American Revolution.

He watched her resetting her topsails, the men strung out like black dots on her braced yards. A ship to be proud of. The greatest honour of all. He thought of Viola's animation and interest when she had made him speak freely of his ship, as he had done to no one before, or since.

He heard Allday murmur. "A good 'un, Cap'n."

Bolitho smiled, moved by the supply of ruses which Allday used to prevent him brooding, or remembering too much.

Suppose Allday had been killed? He felt a pain in his chest like a stab. Now he would have been quite alone.

Bolitho turned and looked at him, his hat tugged down to cover his scar. She had touched and kissed that scar and had told him more than once that it was a mark of pride and honour, not something to shame him.

"I wonder if she carries any of the people we gained as volunteers after we had offered them a choice?"

Allday gave a lazy grin. "Just so long as their cap'n knows how to treat 'em!"

Bolitho turned up the collar of his boat-cloak and watched the frigate again as she changed tack towards more open water. It was tearing him apart. Where bound? Gibraltar and the Mediterranean? The West Indies and the dark green fronds which lined each perfect beach?

He sighed. Like the young lieutenant who had

232

offered himself for a ship, any ship, he felt cut off. Discarded, as Hoblyn had been. He ground his heel on the loose sand. *No. Not like Hoblyn*.

He asked, "And you never saw the man in the carriage that night, the one who ordered you to kill the sailor from the press?"

Allday watched the rebirth of something in those searching, grey eyes.

"Not a peep, Cap'n. But his voice? I'd recognise that even in hell's gateway, so to speak. Like silk it was, the hiss of a serpent." He nodded fervently. "If I hears it again I'll strike first, ask the wherefores afterwards—an' that's no error!"

Bolitho stared towards the frigate but her lee side was already clothed in deepening shadows. By tomorrow, with favouring winds, she would be abreast of Falmouth. He thought of the great house. Waiting. Waiting. How small the family had become. His sister Nancy, married to the "King of Cornwall", lived nearby, but his other sister Felicity was still in India with her husband's regiment of foot. What might become of her, he wondered?

There were too many little plaques and tablets on the walls of Falmouth Church which recorded the women and children who had died of fever and native uprisings, in places few had even heard of. Like the Bolitho tablets which filled one alcove in the fine old church, each one reading like part of the navy's own history. From his great-great-great-grandfather, Captain Julius, who had died in 1646 during the Civil War which Lord Marcuard had touched upon, when he had been attempting to lift the Roundhead blockade on Pendennis Castle itself. And his great-grandfather, Captain David, who had fallen to pirates off the shores of Africa in 1724. Bolitho's fingers reached under his cloak and touched the old hilt at his side. Captain David had had the sword made to his own specifications. Tarnished it might be, but it was still lighter and better-balanced than anything which today's cutlers could forge.

Bolitho walked towards the sunset, his mind suddenly heavy. After his own name was added to the list, there would be no more Bolithos to return to the old house below the headland and its castle.

Allday's eyes narrowed. "Rider in a hurry, Cap'n." His fist dropped to the cutlass in his belt. The land had made him wary and suspicious. In a ship you knew who your friends were, whereas—he exclaimed, "By God, it's Young Matthew!"

The boy reined his horse to a halt and dropped lightly to the ground.

Bolitho asked, "What is it, lad?"

Young Matthew fumbled inside his jerkin. "Letter, sir. Came by courier." He was obviously impressed. "Said it must be handed to you, an' you only, sir."

Bolitho opened and tried to read it but the dusk had made it impossible. But he picked out the gold crest at the top, the scrawled signature, *Marcuard*, at the foot of the page and knew it had not all been a figment of imagination, or some plan to keep him in the background until he could be discreetly disposed of.

The others were staring at him, the horse looming over the boy's shoulder as if it too wanted to be a part of it.

Bolitho had managed to read just three words. *With all despatch*.

Afterwards he remembered that he had felt neither

anxiety nor surprise. Just a great sense of relief. He was needed again.

Wakeful's gangling first lieutenant groped through the waiting figures and eventually found Queely standing beside the compass.

He said quietly, "I have been right through the ship, sir, as ordered. All lights doused." He peered blindly across the bulwark at the occasional fin of white spray and added, "I'll not argue when we come about for open water!"

Queely ignored him and stared first at the reefed mainsail, then the tiny flickering glow of the compass light.

The air was cold like steel, and when spray and spindrift pattered over the deck he could feel winter in it.

He said, "My respects to Captain Bolitho. Please tell him we are in position."

"No need. I am here." Bolitho's shadow detached itself from the nearest group and moved closer. He wore his boat cloak, and Queely saw that he was hatless, only his eyes visible in the gloom.

It was halfway through the middle watch, as near to two o'clock as their cautious approach to the Dutch coastline could make possible.

Queely turned away from the others and said abruptly, "I am not content with these arrangements, sir."

Bolitho looked at him. From the moment he had stepped aboard Queely's command and had ordered him to the secret rendezvous, this scholarly lieutenant had not once questioned his instructions. All the way across the bleak North Sea to a mark on the chart,

235

and he had held his doubts and apprehensions to himself. For that Bolitho was grateful. He could only guess at the danger he was walking into, and was glad that whatever confidence he retained was not being honed away. Paice might have tried to dissuade him, but *Telemachus* was still in the dockyard completing the refitting of her rigging, and the replacement of her lost topmast. He saw Paice's strong features in his thoughts in the moments which had followed *Loyal Chieftain*'s capture.

Paice had exclaimed, "We didn't lose a man, sir! Neither did *Wakeful!*"

It was strange, but nobody else had even asked him about that, not even Drew. He smiled grimly as he recalled the rear-admiral's agitation; *especially* him, might be more apt.

It was like the reports in the newsheets after a great battle or a storm's tragedy at sea. A flag officer or individual captains might be mentioned. The people and their cost in the ocean's hazards were rarely considered.

He replied, "It is all we have, Mr. Queely." He guessed what he was thinking. Lord Marcuard's information had taken weeks to reach him, longer again to be studied and tested. In the meantime anything might have happened. Holland was still standing alone, but it would not be difficult for French spies to infiltrate even the most dedicated circle of conspirators. "I shall remain ashore for four days. You will stand away from the land until the exact moment as we planned. That will prevent any vessel becoming suspicious of your presence and intentions." He did not add that it would also stop anyone aboard *Wakeful* from spreading gossip, willingly or otherwise. Queely was a quick-witted officer. He would recognise the unspoken reason.

He persisted, "I think you should be accompanied to the shore at least, sir."

"Impossible. It would double your time here. You must be well clear before dawn. If the wind should back or drop—" There was no point in further explanations.

Queely held his watch close to the feeble compass glow.

"We will soon know." He peered around for his lieutenant. "Mr. Kempthorne! Silence on deck." He raised a speaking trumpet and held it to his ear to try to shut out the restless sea.

Bolitho felt Allday beside him and was glad of his company, moved that he should be prepared to risk his life yet again.

Allday grunted. "Mebbe they've changed their minds, Cap'n."

Bolitho nodded and tried to remember each detail of the chart and the notes he had studied on the passage from Kent.

A small country, and not many lonely places suitable enough for a secret landing. Here it was supposed to be a waterlogged stretch of low land, not unlike the marshes and fens of south-east England. Eventually the hard-working Dutch would reclaim the land from the sea and perhaps farm it. They rarely wasted any of their overcrowded resources. But if the French came—

Bolitho tensed as a light shuttered across the heaving water. In the blackness of night it seemed like a beacon.

237

Queely muttered, "Hell's teeth! Why not just fire a welcome salute!"

It was the first hint that he was more anxious than his manner had revealed.

"Bear up a point! Stand by, forrard! We don't want to run them down!" In a whisper he added, "Depress that swivel, Robbins! If it's a trick we'll leave a card to be remembered by!"

The other boat seemed to rise from the seabed itself, and several attempts to take heaving lines and stave off a collision made even more noise, although Bolitho doubted if it would carry more than a few yards.

He noticed muffled figures rising and falling in the swell, a stumpy mast with a loosely brailed-up sail. Above all, the stench of fish. Something was handed to one of the seamen and passed swiftly aft to Bolitho. It was part of an old bone coat-button. Bolitho withdrew his piece from his pocket and held them both together. They were parts of the same button. He wondered what might have happened if one of the sailors had dropped it in the darkness. Would trust have overcome suspicion? It was a crude but tested form of recognition, far less complicated or dangerous than a written message.

Bolitho said, "I am leaving now, Mr. Queely." He gripped his arm tightly. "You know what to do if—"

Queely stepped aside. "Aye, sir. *If*."

Then they were scrambling down the cutter's side and into the small fishing boat. Rough hands reached out to guide them through the dangerous traps of nets and pots, stacked oars, and what felt like the entrails of gutted fish.

238

The sail banged out from its boom and the boat swayed steeply in a welter of fine spray.

When Bolitho looked again, *Wakeful* had disappeared, without even the disturbed white horses to betray her position.

Allday settled down on a thwart and muttered, "I'll never grumble at a King's ship again!"

Bolitho glanced at the purposeful figures around them. Nobody had said a word, or offered any sort of greeting.

Marcuard's words seemed to ring out in his ears. *Be doubly careful.*

As he strained his eyes for a first glimpse of land Bolitho knew he would not need reminding again.

The journey to the rendezvous took longer than Bolitho had expected. He and Allday were transferred to a different craft, the final one being so cramped that it was necessary to remain almost bent double in the forepeak.

From the chart and what he had gathered from his sparse orders Bolitho knew they had passed Walcheren Island before the transfer, then after they had entered the Ooster Scheldt River they had touched sides with the second boat, barely pausing even to exchange a grunted greeting. The place seemed to be a mass of waterways and inlets although the crew were careful not to encourage Bolitho to look closely at their route.

A desolate, flat landscape, Bolitho thought, marked here and there by tall windmills, like giants against the sky. There were plenty of small craft on the move, but he had seen nothing of any uniforms which might indicate a naval or military presence.

When night closed in for the second time, the boat was pulled and manhandled into some long reeds, so that but for the gentle motion they could have been on a patch of dry land. It was too dark to see anything, with just a few tiny stars showing occasionally between the clouds. The wind had changed slightly, but not too much to concern *Wakeful*, he thought.

Allday craned his head over the side and listened to the regular creak of another great windmill. There was a strong smell too. "Pigs," he said without enthusiasm. "Are we here, Cap'n?"

Bolitho heard voices, then two figures approached the boat—so there must be a spit of land hereabouts, he thought.

One figure was the boat's skipper, a round-faced Dutchman with an eye-patch. The other was stepping delicately over the wet reeds, a handkerchief clasped to his nose.

He stared down at them and then said, "Er, Captain Bolitho? You are most prompt!" His English was almost flawless but Bolitho knew he was French.

Bolitho climbed from the boat and almost slipped into deeper water. As he eased his cramped muscles he asked, "And whom do I have the honour—"

The man shook his head. "We have no names, Captain. It is safer that way." He gave an apologetic shrug. "And now I am afraid I must blindfold you and your—" he glanced warily at Allday's powerful figure, "—companion." He sensed their instant caution. "You might see something, no matter how unimportant it may be in your eyes, which could be dangerous for us all, yes?"

Bolitho said, "Very well." The man was nervous.

240

One of gentle breeding. Certainly no soldier. An experienced campaigner would have blindfolded them hours ago. He shivered. If he had to, he knew he could find his way back here without difficulty. Boyhood in the county of Cornwall, and years of service in small vessels had left him its own heritage.

They sloshed through the reeds and then on to rough ground, the windmill's regular groans then being joined by another. Bolitho knew that someone from the boat was walking in the rear. Apart from the wind it was very still, the air as keen as sleet.

The man held Bolitho's elbow, murmuring occasional warnings about their progress. Bolitho sensed they were close to a large building, but not one of the windmills.

His guide whispered, "You are meeting Vice-Amiral Louis Brennier." He seemed to feel Bolitho's sudden attention. "You know him?"

He did not reply directly. "I thought there were to be no names, m'sieu?"

The man hesitated, then said, "It is what he wishes. His life has no value but to this great cause."

He sounded as if he was repeating a lesson.

Bolitho fell in step again. Vice-Amiral Louis Brennier, an officer of distinction during the American Revolution when he had directed the operations of French privateers and, later, men-of-war who were working alongside the rebels. He had been taking passage for Jamaica in de Grasse's flagship *Ville de Paris* when he had met up with Admiral Rodney's fleet off the little islands called the Saintes. The battle had been devastating and complete, with the French ships either destroyed or taken. It had seemed only right that the mighty *Ville de Paris* should have struck to the *Formidable*, Rodney's own flagship.

Brennier had been a mere passenger at the time, a hard role for a man of action like him, Bolitho had -thought. It had been the French intention to attack and seize Jamaica and for Brennier, a very senior officer, to be installed as governor. The Saintes had changed all that, as it had for so many on such a fine April day. Ordinary, decent men. Like Stockdale who had fallen without a word, Ferguson who had lost an arm; the list was endless. His own ship, *Phalarope*, had only stayed afloat by working the pumps all the way to the dockyard at Antigua.

He heard a door being unbolted, felt sudden warmth in his face. The blindfold was removed and he found that he was in a broad stone-built room. It was a farm, although the true owners were nowhere to be seen.

He faced the old man who sat across the scrubbed table from him and bowed his head.

"Vice-Amiral Brennier?" He knew he must be old now, but it was still a shock. The admiral's hair was white, his skin wrinkled, his eyes half-hidden by heavy lids.

He nodded slowly, his eyes never leaving Bolitho's.

"And you are Capitaine Bolitho." His English was not so good as his aide's. "I knew your father." His face crinkled into a tired smile. "That is, I knew *of* him. It was in India."

Bolitho was taken off balance. "I did not know, m'sieu."

"Age has its compensations, Capitaine, or so they tell me."

He raised his thin hands towards a roaring fire and

242

said, "Our King lives, but matters worsen in our beloved Paris."

Bolitho waited. Surely the hope of the King's reclaiming the French throne was not being entrusted to Brennier? He had been a gallant officer, and an honourable opponent, trusted by the King and all who had served him. But Brennier was an old man, his mind wandering now over the disaster which had overtaken his country.

Bolitho asked, "What will you have me do, m'sieu?"

"Do?" Brennier seemed reluctant to rejoin him in the present. "It is our intention and sworn duty to obtain the King's release, by any means, no matter the cost!" His voice grew stronger, and despite his doubts Bolitho could see the younger man emerging. "Here in the Low Countries we have amassed a fortune. Precious jewels, gold—" He lowered his forehead on to one hand. "A King's ransom, the English might call it." But there was no mirth in his tone. "It is close by. Soon it must be moved and put to work."

Bolitho asked gently, "Where did it come from, m'sieu?"

"From the many whose families have suffered and died under the guillotine. From others who seek only a return to a cultured, inventive life." He looked up, his eyes flashing. "It will be used to free the King, by bribery, by force if it must be so, and some to mount a counter-revolution. There are many loyal officers in the South of France, m'sieu, and the world shall witness such a reckoning! We will do to these vermin what they have done to us!" His outburst seemed to weaken him. "We shall speak further when some of my friends arrive." He gestured towards another door. "Go there, Capitaine, and meet your fellow *agent-provocateur*."

His aide entered again and waited to assist him to some stairs. At their foot he turned and said firmly, "France lives! Long live the King!"

The aide gave what might have been a small shrug. To Allday he said curtly, "Wait here. I will send for some food and wine."

Allday muttered, "Little puppy! It's them like him who lost France, if you ask me, Cap'n!"

Bolitho touched his arm. "Be easy, old friend. There is much we have yet to understand. But do as he says, and keep your eyes open." He did not have to say any more.

Then he pressed on the other door and walked into a more comfortable room.

As the door closed behind him, a figure who had been sitting in a high-backed chair facing another lively fire, rose and confronted him.

"Bolitho? I trust the journey was none too arduous?"

Bolitho had only seen the man twice before and each time at a distance. But there was no mistaking him. About his own age, with the arrogant good looks and cruel mouth he remembered from the Rochester Road, and that brief moment in the coach window at Dover.

He felt his hand fall to his sword. "Sir James Tanner." He was calmed by the flatness in his voice. "I never thought I'd meet a cur like you here!"

Tanner's face tightened but he seemed to control his immediate reaction with a practised effort.

244

"I have no choice. It is Lord Marcuard's wish. Otherwise—"

Bolitho said, "When this is over I intend to see you brought to justice."

Tanner turned his back. "Let me tell you things, Bolitho, before your damned impertinence puts us both in jeopardy. Be assured, I would like nothing better than to call you out *here and now*."

Bolitho watched his squared shoulders. "You will find me ready enough, *sir!*"

Tanner turned and faced him again. "Your life is so clean and well charted, Bolitho. It lies 'twixt forecastle and poop with no bridge in between, where a captain's word is law, when no one shall defy it!" He was speaking faster now. "Why not try stepping outside and into the real world, eh? You will soon discover that the politics of survival tend to create strange bedfellows!" He seemed to relax slightly as he gestured casually between them. "Like us, for instance."

"It sickens me even to share the same room."

Tanner eyed him thoughtfully. "You would never prove it, you know. Never in ten thousand years. Others have tried before you." He became suddenly reasonable. "Take yourself, Bolitho. When you returned from the American War you discovered your family estate pared away, sold to pay for your brother's debts, is that not correct?" His voice was smooth and insistent. "You fought bravely, and that was your reward."

Bolitho held his expression as before but only with difficulty. At every corner, in every turn, there was always Hugh's disgrace, the memory used to shame or belittle the family as it had killed their father.

Tanner was saying, "*My* father lost nearly everything. His debtors were measured in leagues, believe me. But I got all of it back on my own."

"By organising a smuggling trade that was unrivalled anywhere."

"*Hearsay*, Bolitho. And even if it were so, nobody will stand up and swear it." He leaned over the chair and tapped the leather with his hand. "D'you imagine I want to be here, involved in a wild scheme which has about as much chance of succeeding as a snowman in a furnace!"

"Then why are you?"

"Because I am the only one Lord Marcuard trusts to execute the plan. How do you imagine you reached here unscathed? You do not know the country or its language, and yet here you are. The fishermen are in my employ. Oh yes, they may be smugglers, who can say? But you came here in safety because *I* arranged it, even to suggesting the exact point at which to bring you ashore."

"And what of Delaval?"

Tanner became thoughtful. "He worked for me, too. But he had grand ideas, became less and less prepared to take orders. So you see—"

"He thought you were going to gain his discharge."

"Yes, he did. He was a boaster and a liar, a dangerous combination."

Bolitho said, "Is that all there is to it?"

"Not completely. Lord Marcuard will have his way. You still do not understand this real world, do you? If he chose, Marcuard could use his power against me, and all my land and property would be forfeit. And if you are thinking I could still live at ease elsewhere, then I beg you to dismiss the idea.

From Marcuard there is no hiding place. Not on this earth anyway."

They faced each other, Tanner breathing hard, his eyes watchful, a man too clever to reveal the triumph he now felt.

Bolitho was still numbed by the fact that he was here. Had even planned his arrival.

Tanner said easily, "We have to work together. There was never any choice for either of us. I wanted to meet you before that old man did, but he suggested it might be *difficult*."

Bolitho nodded, in agreement for the first time. "I'd have killed you."

"You would have tried to do so, I dare say. It seems to run in your family." He spread his arms. "What can you hope for? If you go to the Dutch Customs House they will laugh at you. If French spies discover what you are about here, many will die, and the treasure will go to the revolutionary government." He tapped the chair with his hand again. "To use for supplying ships and weapons which *your* sailors will have to face before much longer!"

He seemed to tire of it. "Now I shall take my leave. M'sieu will wish to speak at length about this matter, and of course on the *glory which was France*." His voice was still smooth as he added, "Do not delay too long. *My* men will not wait forever."

He used a small side-door, and Bolitho heard horses stamping on some sort of track.

Bolitho left the room and saw Allday staring at him. Despite his bronzed features his face looked ashen.

"What is it? Speak, man!"

Allday watched the closed door.

"That man you just met. *His voice*. It was him. I'd not forget that one in a lifetime!"

Bolitho saw his eyes spark with memory. It was as he had suspected. The man in the carriage who had ordered Allday to kill the sailor from the press gang, and Sir James Tanner, were one and the same.

Bolitho touched his arm and said, "It is well he did not know it. At least we are forewarned." He stared into the shadows. "Otherwise he would see us both dead before this is over and done with."

"But what happened, Cap'n?"

Bolitho looked up as voices floated from the stairway. *The glory which was France.*

He said quietly, "I was outmanoeuvred." He clapped him on the arm. Allday needed *him* now. "This time."

13

Last Chance

THE footman took Bolitho's dripping cloak and hat and regarded them disdainfully.

"Lord Marcuard will receive you now, sir."

Bolitho stamped his shoes on the floor to restore the circulation, then followed the servant, a heavy-footed man with stooped shoulders, along an elegant corridor. He was a far cry from the wretched Jules, Bolitho thought.

It had been a long and uncomfortable journey from Sheerness to London. The roads were getting worse, deeply rutted from heavy rain, and now there was intermittent snow, touching the grand buildings of Whitehall like powder. He hated the thought of winter and what it might do to his health. If the fever returned—he closed his mind to the thought. There were too many important matters on his mind.

When *Wakeful* had moored at the dockyard, Bolitho had left immediately for London. There had been a brief message awaiting his return from Marcuard. He would meet him on his own ground this time.

He heard sounds from the hallway and said, "That will be my coxswain. Take good care of him." He spoke abruptly. Bolitho felt past even common courtesy. He was heartily sick of the pretence and false pride these people seemed to admire so much.

He thought of the old admiral in Holland, of the

great fortune amassed and ready to be used for a counter-revolution. It had seemed like a dream when he had outlined it; back in England the plan seemed utterly hopeless.

Bolitho's silent guides had conveyed him to the rendezvous on time but only with minutes to spare. Even in the darkness there had been shipping on the move, and the fishermen had almost given up hope when *Wakeful*'s wet canvas had loomed over them.

Lieutenant Queely's relief had been matched only by his eagerness to get under way and head for open waters. He had confirmed Bolitho's suspicions; there were men-of-war in the vicinity, Dutch or French he had not waited to discover.

Some of Bolitho's anger at Tanner's involvement had eased on the journey to London. Noisy inns, with more talk of Christmas than what might be happening across the Channel. As the coach had rolled through towns and villages, Bolitho had seen the local volunteers drilling under the instruction of regular soldiers. Pikes and pitchforks because nobody in authority thought it was yet necessary to train them to handle muskets. What was the matter with people, he wondered? When he had commanded *Phalarope* the navy's strength had stood at over one hundred thousand men. Now it was reduced to less than a fifth of that number, and even for them there were barely enough ships in commission and ready for sea.

He realised that the footman was holding open a tall door, Bolitho's cloak held carefully at arm's length.

Marcuard was standing with his back to a cheerful fire, his coat-tails lifted to give him all the benefit of the heat. He was dressed this time in sombre grey, and without his ebony silver-topped stick looked somehow incomplete.

Bolitho examined the room. It was huge, and yet lined on three walls with books. From floor to ceiling, with ladders here and there for convenience, like the library of a rich scholar. Queely would think himself in heaven here.

Marcuard held out his hand. "You wasted no time." He observed him calmly. "I am needed here in London. Otherwise—" He did not explain. He waved Bolitho to a chair. "I will send for some coffee presently. I see from your face that you came ready for an argument. I was prepared for that."

Bolitho said, "With respect, m'lord, I think I should have been told that Sir James Tanner was involved. The man, as I have stated plainly, is a thief, a cheat and a liar. I have proof that he was engaged in smuggling on a grand scale, and conspired with others to commit murder, to encourage desertion from the fleet for his own ends."

Marcuard's eyebrows rose slightly. "Do you feel better for that?" He leaned back and pressed his fingertips together. "Had I told you beforehand you would have refused to participate. Not because of the danger, and I better than you know there is danger aplenty on either side of that unhappy border. No, it was because of your honour that you would have refused me, just as it was because of it that I chose you for the mission."

Bolitho persisted, "How can we trust that man?"

Marcuard did not seem to hear. "There is an hypocrisy in us all, Bolitho. You offered your trust to Vice-Amiral Brennier, because he too is a man of honour. But a few years ago, or perhaps even next

251

week, you would kill him if the need arose because war has dictated how you shall think, and what you must do. In affairs like this I trust only those whom I need. Tanner's skills may not appeal to either of us but, believe me, he is the best man, if not the only man, who can do it. I sent you because Brennier would recognise you as a King's officer, someone who has already proved his courage and loyalty beyond question. But what do you imagine would occur if I had directed others to Holland? I can assure you that the Admiralty of Amsterdam would have been displeased, and would have closed every port against us. They have cause to fear the French and would likely confiscate the Royalist treasure to bargain with them."

Despite his hatred of the man, Bolitho thought of Tanner's words about the possibility of the vast hoard of jewels and gold being used to strengthen French power to be thrown eventually against England.

Marcuard said, "You look troubled, Bolitho. What do you feel about this affair, and of Brennier's part in it?" He nodded very slowly. "Another reason why I selected you. I wanted a thinking officer, not merely a courageous one."

Bolitho stared through one of the tall windows. The sky was growing darker, but he could see the roof of the Admiralty building where all this, and so many other ventures in his life, had begun. Full circle. The roof was already dusted with snow. He gripped his hands together to try and stop himself from shivering.

"I believe that the prospect of an uprising is hopeless, m'lord." Just saying it aloud made him feel as if he had broken a trust, that he was being disloyal to that old man in Holland who had been captured

252

by Rodney at the Saintes. He continued, "He showed me one of the chests. I have never seen the like. So much wealth, when the people of France had so little." He glanced around at the fine room. An equation which should be learned here, he thought bitterly.

"Are you not well, Bolitho?"

"Tired, m'lord. My cox'n is with me. He is finding quarters for us."

It was to sidestep Marcuard's question.

Marcuard shook his head. "I will not hear of it. You shall visit here, while you are in London. There are some who might wish to know your movements. And besides, I doubt that there are many—*quarters* —as you quaintly describe them, freely available this near to Christmas."

He regarded Bolitho thoughtfully. "While you were in Holland, I too was forming opinions."

Bolitho felt his limbs relaxing again. Perhaps it was the fire.

"About the treasure, m'lord?"

"Concerning it." Marcuard stood up and tugged gently at a silk bell rope. There was no sound but Bolitho guessed it would reach one of the many servants who were needed for such an extensive residence.

Bolitho did not trust the so-called "real world" as described by Sir James Tanner, but he had learned a lot about people, no matter what their rank or station might be. From a tough foretopman to a pink-faced midshipman, and Bolitho knew that the bell rope was to give him time, to test his own judgement before he shared any more secrets.

Marcuard said bluntly, "There is no hope for the King of France."

Bolitho stared at him, and was struck by the solemnity of his voice. While the King was alive there had always been hope that somehow things might return, halfway at least, to normal. In time, the murder of aristocrats and innocent citizens in the name of the Revolution might fade into history. The death of a King would have the brutal finality of the guillotine itself.

Marcuard watched him, his eyes smoky in the reflected flames. "We cannot rely on Brennier and his associates. That vast fortune belongs here in London, where it will be safe until a counter-revolution can be launched. I could tell you of lasting loyalties which would rise up against the National Convention once a properly managed invasion was mounted."

"That would cause a war, m'lord."

Marcuard nodded. "The war is almost upon us, I fear."

"I believe that Admiral Brennier understands the danger he is in." Bolitho pictured him, a frail old man by the fire, still dreaming and hoping when there was no room left for either.

The door opened and another footman entered with a tray and some fresh coffee.

"I know you have a great liking for coffee, Captain Bolitho."

"My cox'n—"

Marcuard watched the servant preparing to pour.

"Your Mr. Allday is being well taken care of. He seems a most adaptable fellow, to all accounts. Your right arm, wouldn't you say?"

Bolitho shrugged. Was there nothing Marcuard did

254

not know or discover from others? *No hiding place*, Tanner had said. That he could believe now.

He said, "He means all that and more to me."

"And the young lad, Corker, wasn't it? You packed him off to Falmouth, I believe."

Bolitho smiled sadly. It had been a difficult moment for all of them. Young Matthew had been in tears when they had put him on the coach for the first leg of the long haul to Cornwall, the breadth of England away.

He said, "It seemed right, m'lord. To be home with his people in time for Christmas."

"Quite so, although I doubt that was your prime concern."

Bolitho recalled Allday at that moment, his face still cut and bruised from his beating aboard the *Loyal Chieftain*. He had said, "Your place is on the estate, my lad. With your horses, like Old Matthew. It's not on the bloody deck of some man-o'-war. Anyway, I'm back now. You said you'd wait 'til then, didn't you?"

They had watched the coach until it had vanished into heavy rain.

Bolitho said suddenly, "I fear he would have been killed if I had allowed him to stay."

Marcuard did not ask or even hint at how the boy's death might have come about. He probably knew that too.

Marcuard put down his cup and consulted his watch. "I have to go out. My valet will attend to your needs." He was obviously deep in thought. "If I am not back before you retire do not concern yourself. It is the way of things here." He crossed to a window and said, "The weather. It is a bad sign."

Bolitho looked at him. He had not said as much,

but somehow he knew Marcuard was going to have a late audience with the King.

Bolitho wondered what the prime minister and his advisers thought about it. It was rumoured more openly nowadays that His Majesty was prone to change his mind like the wind, and that on bad days he was totally incapable of making a decision about anything. He might easily be prepared to discuss his anxieties with Marcuard rather than Parliament. It would make Marcuard's authority all the greater.

He was standing by the window now, looking down at the road, his eyes deep in thought.

"In Paris it will be a bad winter. They were near to starvation last year; this time it will be worse. Cold and hunger can fire men to savage deeds, if only to cover their own failings."

He looked deliberately at Bolitho, like that time at The Golden Fleece in Dover.

"I must make arrangements for the treasure to be brought to England. I feel that the sand is running low." The door opened silently and Marcuard said, "Have the unmarked phaeton brought round at once." Then to Bolitho he said softly, "Leave Brennier to me."

"What of me, m'lord?" Bolitho was also on his feet, as if he shared this new sense of urgency.

"As far as I am concerned, you are still my man in this." He gave a bleak smile. "You will return to Holland only when I give the word." He seemed to relax himself and prepare for his meeting. "Anyone who opposes you will have me to reckon with." He let his gaze linger for a few more seconds. "But do not harm Tanner." Again the bleak smile. "Not yet, in any case." Then he was gone.

Bolitho sat down and stared at the wall of books, an army of knowledge. How did men like Marcuard see a war, he wondered? Flags on a map, land gained or lost, investment or waste? It was doubtful if they ever considered it as cannon fire and broken bodies.

Below his feet, in the long kitchen Allday sat contentedly, sipping a tankard of ale while he enjoyed the pipe of fresh tobacco one of the footmen had offered him.

In any strange house the kitchen was usually Allday's first port of call. To investigate food, and also the possibilities of female companionship which most kitchens had to offer.

He watched the cook's assistant, a girl of ample bosom and laughing eyes, her arms covered in flour to her elbows. Allday had gathered that her name was Maggie.

He took another swallow of ale. A proper sailor's lass she would make. He thought of Bolitho somewhere overhead, alone with his thoughts. He had heard his lordship leave in a carriage only moments ago, and wondered if he should go up and disturb him.

He thought of the dead girl in his arms, the touch of her body against his. Poor Tom Lucas had sworn it would bring bad luck to take a woman aboard against her will. That had been true enough for both of them. Allday tried to see into the future. Better back in Falmouth than this shifty game, he thought. You never knew friend from foe. Just so long as they didn't go back to Holland. Allday usually clung to his same old rule. *Never go back*. The odds always got worse.

The cook was saying,"'Course, our *Lady*

Marcuard's down at the estate. 'Is lordship'll not be 'ome for Christmas this year, *I* reckon!" She looked meaningly at Allday and added, "Young Maggie's 'usband is there too, as second coachman, see?"

Allday glanced at the girl and saw her blush faintly before she returned her attention to her work.

The cook watched them both and added encouragingly, "Pity to waste it, *I* always says!"

His Britannic Majesty's Ship *Ithuriel*, a seventy-four-gun two-decker, made a handsome picture above her reflection on the flat water of the Royal Dockyard. Her black and buff hull and checkered gunports, her neatly furled sails and crossed yards shone with newness, as did the uniforms of her lieutenant and midshipman, facing inboard from their divisions of silent seamen. Across her poop the marines stood in scarlet lines, and above their heads a matching ensign curled listlessly against a washed-out sky in the hard sunlight.

There was pride and sadness here in Chatham today. *Ithuriel* was the first new man-of-war of any size to be commissioned since the American Revolution, and now, stored and fully manned, she was ready to take her place with the Channel Fleet.

Below her poop Bolitho watched the official handing-over of the new ship, her captain reading himself in to the assembled officers and men he would lead and inspire for as long as their lordships dictated, or as long as he remained in command.

Nearby, the officers' ladies stood close together, sharing this alien world of which they could never truly become a part. Some would be grateful that their husbands had been given appointments after all the waiting and disappointment. Others would be cherishing each passing minute, not knowing when, or if, they would see their loved ones again.

Bolitho looked at the sky, his heart suddenly heavy. He was only an onlooker. All the excitement and demands of a newly commissioned ship were cradled here, and would soon show their true value and flaws once the ship began to move under canvas for the first time.

He saw the admiral with his flag lieutenant standing a little apart from the rest, dockyard officials watching their efforts become reality as the company was urged to cry their *Huzzas* and wave their hats to honour the moment.

If only the command were his. Not a frigate, but a newly born ship nonetheless. The most beautiful creation of man yet devised; hard and demanding by any standards. He dropped his eyes as the captain finished speaking, his voice carrying easily in the still January air.

That too was hard to accept, Bolitho thought. Danger there had certainly been, but the promise of action had sustained him. Until now. In his heart he believed he had ruined his chances by his dogged and stubborn attack on Sir James Tanner. Marcuard must have found him wanting.

He looked up as he heard the new captain speak his name.

He was saying, "A fine ship which I am proud to command. But for the inspiration and leadership given by Captain Richard Bolitho over the past months I doubt if we would have enough hands to work downstream, let alone put to sea and face whatever duty demands of us!" He gave a slight bow in

259

Bolitho's direction. "*Ithuriel* shall be worthy of your trust, sir."

Bolitho flinched as all the faces turned towards him. Pressed and volunteers, men who had accepted his offer to quit the smuggling gangs and return to their calling, but now they were of one company. It was only their captain's qualities which could carry them further. And Bolitho would be left far behind and soon forgotten.

Perhaps there would be no war after all? He should have felt relief, but instead was ashamed to discover he had only a sense of loss and rejection.

The ship's company was dismissed and the boatswain's mates refrained from their usual coarse language with so many ladies gathered on the quarter-deck and poop. Extra rum for all hands, and then, when the honoured guests had departed, the hovering bumboats and watermen would come alongside and unload their passengers under the watchful eyes of the first lieutenant and afterguard. Trollops and doxies from the town, the sailor's last freedom for a long while. For some, it would be forever.

The admiral was making a great fuss over the captain, which was not surprising as he was his favourite nephew. The groups were breaking up and making for the entry port below which the many boats thronged like water beetles. There were desperate embraces and tears, brave laughter, and, from the older ones, resignation, a lesson learned from many repetitions.

Allday emerged from the shadows beneath the poop and said, "I've signalled for the boat, Cap'n." He studied him with concern, recognising all the signs. "It'll *come*, Cap'n, just you see—"

Bolitho turned on him, and relented immediately. "It was only that I had hoped—"

The senior officers had gone now; calls trilled and barges glided away to other ships and to the dockyard stairs.

Bolitho said wearily, "I would that they were my men and our ship—eh, old friend?"

Allday made a passage to the entry port. In many ways he felt vaguely guilty. He should have done more. But in London while they had been staying in that great house, he had soon found his time fully occupied with the amorous Maggie. It was just as well Bolitho had been ordered back to Kent, he thought. It had been a close-run thing.

"Captain Bolitho?" It was the flag lieutenant, poised and eager, like a ferret. "If you would come aft for a moment, sir?"

Bolitho followed him and saw the curious stares, heads drawn together in quick speculation. Rumour was firmer than fact. They would be speaking of Hoblyn and Delaval, even Hugh, and the strange fact that men who had managed to evade the dreaded press gangs had openly volunteered for service whenever Bolitho had been seen in their locality. Myth and mystery. It never failed.

In the great cabin, still smelling of paint and tar, new timber and cordage, Bolitho found another unknown captain waiting for him. He introduced himself as Captain Wordley; the papers he produced proved that he had been sent by Lord Marcuard.

Wordley watched him impassively as he examined his bulky envelope and said, "You may read them at leisure, Bolitho. I am required to return to London forthwith." He gave a wry smile. "You will know his lordship's insistence on haste."

Bolitho asked, "Can you tell me?" He could still scarcely believe it.

"You are to return to Holland. All details are listed in your orders. There is some *urgency* in this matter. Information is hard to come by, but Lord Marcuard is convinced that time is short. Very short. You are to supervise the removal of the . . . stores . . . from Holland, and see them safely to these shores." He spread his hands unhappily. "It is all I can tell you, Bolitho. In God's name it is all I know!"

Bolitho left the cabin and made his way to the entry port where Allday was waiting by the side-party and marine guard.

Like walking in the dark. A messenger-boy who was told only the briefest facts. But excitement replaced the bitterness almost immediately. He said, "We are returning to Holland, Allday." He eyed him keenly. "If you wish to stand fast I shall fully understand, especially so because of your—recent attachment."

Allday stared at him, then gave a self-conscious grin. "Was it that plain, Cap'n? An' I thought I was keeping hull-down, so to speak!" His grin vanished. "Like I said afore. We stay together this time." His eyes were almost desperate. *"Right?"*

Bolitho gripped his thick forearm, watched with astonishment by the marine officer of the guard.

"So be it."

He doffed his hat to the quarterdeck and lowered himself to the waiting boat.

Only once did Bolitho glance astern at the shining

new seventy-four, but already she seemed like a diversion, part of that other dream.

Now only Holland lay ahead. And reality.

Lieutenant Jonas Paice placed his hands firmly on his hips and stared resentfully at the anchored *Wakeful*. In the harsh January sunlight she was a hive of activity, her sails already loosened, the forecastle party working the long bars of the windlass, their bodies moving in unison as if performing some strange rite.

"I'll not be in agreement, sir. Not now, not ever."

Bolitho glanced at his grimly determined features. Time was all-important, but it was just as vital he should make Paice understand.

"I explained why I had to go before. It was a secret then. I could not share it at the time, you must realise that."

"This is different, sir." Paice turned and stared at him, using his superior height to impress each word. "Half the fleet will know what you're about." He waved his hand towards *Wakeful*. "You should let me take you if go you must."

Bolitho smiled. *So that was it*. He said, "Lieutenant Queely knows that coast well. Otherwise—" He saw *Wakeful*'s jolly-boat cast off and pull towards *Telemachus*. He said, "Try to pass word to *Snapdragon*. She is working her station off the North Foreland. Either the revenue people or the coastguard might be able to signal her. I want her back here." He studied his stubborn features. It was Herrick all over again. "We are in this together."

Paice replied heavily. "I know, sir. I have read your instructions."

He tried again. "In any case, apart from the risks, there is the weather. Last time you had mist and fog. A hazard maybe, but also a protection." He added scornfully, "Look at this! As bright and clear as the Arctic! Even a blind man could see you coming!"

Bolitho looked away. He had been thinking as much himself. *Bright and clear*, the waves outside the anchorage pockmarked with choppy white horses from the cold south-westerly. "I must go now." He held out his hand. "We shall meet again soon." Then he was climbing down to the boat where Lieutenant Kempthorne removed his hat as a mark of respect.

"Cast off! Give way all!" Allday sat by the tiller, his hat pulled down to shade his eyes from the reflected glare. He had seen the light in Bolitho's eyes, the way that the call to action had somehow strengthened him. Allday had watched him aboard the new two-decker. The longing and the loss, side by side.

He gave a long sigh. Allday had no liking for what they were doing and it had cost him dearly not to speak his mind, that privilege he valued above all else. Bolitho could strike back with equal conviction and his anger had been known to hurt as well as sting. But he had never once used his rank and authority when others would have thought of nothing else. Now, as he watched the set of Bolitho's shoulders, the black hair gathered above the fall-down collar of that old, faded coat, he was glad he had kept his peace, no matter what.

They climbed aboard the cutter, and the boat was hoisted up and inboard almost before Bolitho had reached the narrow poop where Queely was in deep conversation with his sailing-master.

Queely touched his hat and nodded. "Ready when you are, sir." He looked at the green elbow of land, the rime of frost or recent snow dusting some of the port buildings. The air was like a honed knife, but it roused a man from the boredom of routine, put an edge on his reactions. Queely said, "Doesn't much matter who sees us leave this time, eh?"

Bolitho ignored it. Like Paice, he was trying to dissuade him. It moved him to realise it was not for their own sakes, but for his.

Allday strode aft, then drew his cutlass and aimed its blade at the sun. "I'll give this a sharpen, Cap'n." He held out his hand. "I'll take the sword, if I may?"

Bolitho handed it to him. Others might see and think they understood. But how could they? This was a ritual shared with nobody else, as much a part of each man as the moment before a battle when the ship was cleared for action, screens down, the people standing to their guns. Allday would be there. *Always.* After clipping the old sword to his belt. As his father's coxswain must have done for him and those who had gone before.

"Anchor's hove short, sir!"

"Loose mains'l! Stand by heads'l sheets!" Feet padded on the damp planking, bare despite the bitter air.

Bolitho saw it all. If only more of the people at home could have seen them, he thought. Men who had so little, but gave their all when it was demanded of them. He thought of the faces he had seen aboard the new *Ithuriel*. It might be months before her company worked even half as well as the men of his three cutters.

"Anchor's aweigh, sir!"

265

Wakeful came round into the breeze, her huge mainsail scooping all of it without effort and filling out with a crack of taut canvas.

"Hold her steady!" Queely was everywhere. "Let go and haul. Mr. Kempthorne, they are like *old women* today!"

Bolitho heard one of the helmsmen chuckle. "Wish they was, matey!"

He turned and looked for *Telemachus*. How tiny she looked when set against the tall buff-and-black hull of the new two-decker.

Allday saw the look and gave a rueful grin.

There would be no stopping him now.

By evening the wind still held steady enough from the southwest, and the sea showed no sign of lessening. Spray swept regularly over the duty watch, reaching for the hands working aloft on the yards. When it caught you unawares it was cold enough to punch the breath out of your body.

Bolitho was in the cabin, going over Queely's calculations, the notes which he had made from their last rendezvous. Nothing must go wrong. He thought of Tanner and tried not to let his anger break out again. Tanner was under Lord Marcuard's orders, and on the face of it had far more to lose than Bolitho if things went badly wrong. Unless you counted life itself, Bolitho thought. He was surprised he could face it with neither qualms nor surprise. It might mean that he was truly restored, that the fever which had all but killed him had finally released him, as a receding wave will toss a drowning sailor to safety, as if for a last chance.

He heard shouts on deck and Queely clattered

down the companionway, his body shining in a long tarpaulin coat.

"Sail to the nor'-east, sir."

More yells came from above. Queely remarked, "I'm changing tack. No sense in displaying our intentions." He smiled faintly. "Yet, anyway."

The hull staggered and then reared upright again, and Bolitho heard the sea rushing along the lee scuppers like a bursting stream.

"What is she?"

"I've got Nielsen aloft, a good lookout." Again the ghostly smile. "For a Swede, that is. He reckons she's a brig. Square-rigged in any case."

They looked at each other. Bolitho did not have to consult the chart to know that this stranger stood directly between them and the land.

"Man-of-war?" It seemed unlikely to be anything else out here and at this time of the year.

Queely shrugged. "Could be."

They heard the helmsman yell, "Steady she goes, sir! Nor' by East!"

Queely frowned, seeing the complications in his thoughts. "Don't want to bring her up too much, sir. I know the nights are long, but we've precious little room for mistakes."

Bolitho followed him on deck. The sea was covered with leaping white clusters of spray, but beneath them the water looked black, a vivid contrast to the sky which despite some early stars was still clear and pale.

The hull plunged her long bowsprit down like a hunting marlin and the water surged over the forecastle and hissed aft between the gleaming guns.

Queely cupped his reddened hands. "Where away, Nielsen?"

267

"Same bearing, sir! She changed tack when we did!"

Even from the deck amidst the din of spray and wind Bolitho could hear the man's Swedish accent. What was *his* story, he wondered?

Queely swore. "In God's name, sir! That bugger is on to us!"

Bolitho gripped a stay and felt it quivering in his hand as if it were part of an instrument.

"I suggest you steer more to the east'rd as soon as it's dark. We should cross his stern and lose him."

Queely eyed him doubtfully. "So long as we can beat clear if the wind gets up, sir."

Bolitho gave a dry smile. "There is always *that* provision, of course."

Queely beckoned to his first lieutenant. "We shall hold this tack until—" The rest was lost in the boom of canvas and the creak of steering tackles as the helmsmen forced over the tiller bar.

Allday stood by the companionway and listened to the rudder. It was all too easy to picture the girl's pale shape as she had sawed frantically at the lines. *If only she had been spared.*

He tossed the stupid thought from his mind and groped his way to the ladder. There was always tomorrow. But now a good "wet" of rum was all he needed.

When darkness closed in, and their world had shrunk to the leaping crests on either beam, *Wakeful* came about and under reefed topsail thrust her bowsprit towards the east. Immediately before that Queely joined Bolitho in the cabin and shook his hat on the littered deck.

"That bugger's still there, sir." He stared at his cot

but shut the picture of sleep from his thoughts. "I shall call you when it's time." Then he was gone, his boots scraping up the ladder and on to the streaming deck above.

Bolitho lay down and faced the curved side. Just once he spoke her name aloud. "*Viola.*" And then, with his eyes tightly shut as if in pain, he fell asleep.

14

Fair Wind . . . For France

HM CUTTER *WAKEFUL* rolled heavily in the offshore swell, the motion made worse by a swift current at odds with a falling tide. Hove-to and with her flapping canvas in wild disorder, it felt as if she might easily dismast herself.

Queely had to shout above the din of rigging and wind. Caution was pointless; the clatter of loose gear and the sluice of water alongside seemed loud enough to wake the dead.

He exclaimed, "It's no use, sir! They're not coming! I have to suggest that we turn back!"

Bolitho held on to the shrouds and strained his eyes through the wind-blown spray. Queely was in command; he had plenty of reasons to be alarmed, and had been right to speak his mind.

Bolitho cursed the unknown vessel which had made them take a more roundabout course towards the Dutch coast. But for that they would have reached the rendezvous in good time. He felt Queely peering at the sky, imagining it was already getting lighter.

Bolitho said tersely, "They have orders to return on the hour."

But they were fishermen, smugglers too, not disciplined sailors like those who stood or crouched around him.

Queely said nothing in reply. He was probably thinking much the same.

The wind had veered overnight, which made it even harder for Queely to maintain his position without the risk of being driven onto a lee-shore.

Bolitho tried to think what he must do. *What is the point? There is no other way.*

Allday stood close by, his arms folded as if to show his contempt for the sea's efforts to pitch him to the deck. Occasionally he glanced up at the furled mainsail, the huge mast which leaned right over him, then staggered away to the opposite beam as the cutter rolled her gunports under.

He could tell from Bolitho's stance, the way he barely spoke, that he was tackling each of his problems in turn. Earlier Allday might have been satisfied to know this might happen. But now, having come this far, he wanted to go ahead, get it over with, like Bolitho.

Men scampered down the larboard side as a line parted and the boatswain called for them to make it fast.

Bolitho wondered what Tanner was doing, how he would react when he discovered he had been delayed.

"Boat, sir! *Lee bow!*"

Bolitho tried to moisten his lips but they felt like leather. A few more minutes, and then—

Queely rasped, "The same one as before! By God I thought they'd cut and run!"

Bolitho wrapped his boat-cloak around him, able to ignore the busy seamen with their ropes and fenders, pointing arms and angry voices as the two hulls swayed together for the first impact.

He said, "You know what to do. I'd not ask you to risk your command, but—"

They clung together as the two hulls lifted and

271

groaned in a trough, men falling, others heaving on ropes, their bare feet skidding on the wet deck.

Queely nodded. "I'll be here, sir. If the Devil himself should stand between us."

Then Bolitho followed Allday into the fishing boat. This time, her skipper gave him what might have been a grin. With the sea surging over the two vessels it could have been a grimace.

Bolitho sat inside a tiny hutchlike cabin and was thankful that the hold was empty of fish. Experienced though he was in the sea's moods, after the buffeting out there any stench might have made him vomit. Like when he had first gone to sea at the age of twelve.

The arrangements were exactly as before, although he sensed the Dutch crew's haste and nervous anxiety whenever they passed an anchored vessel, or riding lights betrayed the nearness of other craft. Merchantmen sheltering for the night, waiting for a favourable wind, men-of-war—they might have been anything. The final part of the journey was quieter, the sounds of sea and wind suddenly banished, lost beyond the endless barrier of waving rushes.

It was so quiet that Bolitho held his breath. Nobody bothered to conceal their approach and Allday whispered, "Even the mills are still, Cap'n."

Bolitho watched a tall windmill glide above the rushes, stiff and unmoving. It was eerie, as if nothing lived here.

The crew exchanged comments and then one clambered over the gunwale, his sea-boots splashing through shallows before finding the spur of land. One man ran on ahead, but the skipper stayed with Bolitho and waited for Allday to join them.

Bolitho felt a chill run up his back. The skipper had drawn a pistol from his coat and was wiping it with his sleeve. Without looking he knew that Allday had seen it too and was ready to cut the man down if need be. Was the Dutchman frightened—did he sense danger? Or was he waiting for the chance to betray them, as Delaval had done to so many others?

Allday said, "Someone's coming, Cap'n." How calm he sounded. As if he was describing a farm cart in a Cornish lane. Bolitho knew that he was at his most dangerous.

He heard feet slipping on the track and saw the shadowy figure of Brennier's aide stumble, gasp aloud as the other Dutchman pulled him to his feet again.

He stopped when he saw Bolitho and turned back towards the house. *No blindfold*. He seemed close to panic.

Bolitho and the Dutch skipper pushed open the door, and Bolitho stared at the disorder around him. Cupboards ransacked, contents spilled on the floor, even some of the charred logs raked from the fire. The search had been as thorough as it had been quick.

Bolitho looked at the Dutch skipper. They were totally separated by language.

Then he turned towards the aide and was shocked at his appearance as he revealed himself beside a lantern.

His clothes were filthy, and there were pale streaks down the grime on his cheeks, as if he had been weeping.

"What is it, man?" Bolitho unbuttoned his old coat to free the butt of his pistol. "*Speak out!*"

The man stared at him with disbelief. Then he said in a broken whisper, *"Il est mort! Il est mort!"*

Bolitho seized his arm; it felt lifeless in his grip. "The admiral?"

The aide gaped at him as if only now did he realise where he was, that Bolitho was the same man.

He shook his head and blurted out, *"Non! It is the King!"*

Allday rubbed his jaw with his fist. "God, they've done for him after all!"

The Dutchman thrust his pistol into his belt and spread his hands. It needed no language. The blade had fallen in Paris. The King of France was dead.

Bolitho wanted to find time to think. But there was none. He shook the man's arm and asked harshly, "Where is Vice-Amiral Brennier? What has become of him?" He hated to see the fear in the man's eyes. All hope gone. And now apparently left to fend for himself in a country which might be unwilling to offer him shelter.

He stammered, "To Flushing. We could wait no longer." He stared at the disordered room. "You were late, Capitaine!"

Bolitho released his hold and the aide almost collapsed on to a bench. He was wringing his hands, stunned by what had happened.

Allday asked, "What do we do, Cap'n?"

Bolitho looked at the broken man on the bench. Somehow he knew there was more. He asked quietly, "And the treasure, m'sieu, what of that?"

The aide stared up at him, surprised by the change in Bolitho's tone.

"It is in safe hands, Capitaine, but it was *too late!*"

Safe hands. There was only one other who knew about it. Now he was gone, taking the old admiral Brennier and the treasure with him. To Flushing. The name stood out in his mind like letters of fire. About twenty miles from here at a guess. It might as well have been a thousand.

He recalled Marcuard's remarks about the weather. News would travel slowly with the roads bogged-down or hidden in snow. Nobody here would know for certain when the King had been executed. He felt the sense of urgency running through him, chilling his body from head to toe. Anything might be happening. There was nobody here to ask. Even the farmer who owned this place had vanished—perhaps murdered.

The Dutch skipper said something to his companion, who was guarding the door, and Bolitho snapped, "Tell that man to remain with us!"

The aide murmured a few halting words in Dutch then added, "He wants paying, Capitaine."

Allday muttered harshly, "Don't we all, matey!"

"If you help me, m'sieu, I will take you to England. Maybe you will discover friends there—"

He looked at Allday's grim features as the man threw himself on his knees and seized his hand, kissing it fervently.

When he looked up, his eyes were streaming, but there was steel in his voice now as he exclaimed, "I know the ship, Capitaine! It is called *La Revanche*, but flies the English flag!" He cowered under Bolitho's cold gaze. "I heard him talk of it."

Bolitho allowed himself to speak his name aloud. "Sir James Tanner." The aide's fear told him every-thing he had not already guessed.

275

How apt a name. *The Revenge*. Tanner had outwitted them all.

Allday asked, "What can *we* do, Cap'n? Without a ship of our own—" He sounded lost and bewildered.

Bolitho said, "We had better be gone from here." He strode to a window and threw back the shutter. The sky seemed paler. He must think of the present, not anguish over what had happened. *Wakeful*'s near encounter with the stranger had been deliberate, a delay engineered by Tanner. It had given him time to execute the rest of his plan. "We must try to explain to the Dutchman that we need to be taken downriver to his fishermen friends." He stared at the aide again. "Tell him he will be well paid." He jingled some coins in his pocket to give the words emphasis. "I'll brook no argument!"

Allday tapped the floor with the point of his cutlass. "I reckon he understands, Cap'n." Again he sounded very calm, almost casual. "Don't you, matey?"

It would be a full day before *Wakeful* would dare to approach the rendezvous. Even then it might be too dangerous for Queely to draw near enough. Bolitho felt sick, and rubbed his eyes to rouse himself from despair.

Why should Tanner take the admiral, if his main intention concerned the treasure?

He walked out into the stinging air and looked up at some fast-moving cloud. It hit him like a clenched fist, as if the answer had been written in those same stars.

He heard himself say tightly, "The wind has veered yet again, Allday." He glanced at the familiar, bulky shadow framed against the fading stars.

"It blows fair, old friend." He added bitterly, "For France!"

Snapdragon's jolly-boat snugged alongside her anchored consort, and with the briefest of ceremony her commander, Lieutenant Hector Vatass, climbed aboard.

For an instant he paused and peered towards the shore. The wind was fresh to strong, but here in the Sheerness anchorage its force was lessened by the land, so that the snow flurries swirled around in an aimless dance. For a moment Vatass could see the headland beyond the dockyard; in the next it was all blotted out, with only his own vessel still visible.

Telemachus's first lieutenant guided him to the companionway and said, "Good to see you, sir."

His formality was unexpected and unusual. But Vatass's mind and body were too strained from the rigours of his entrance to the anchorage in the early morning to make much of it. He had received a message from the coastguard that he was required back at Sheerness. The order had come from Captain Bolitho. It was not one to question, even though Vatass had been fretting already over losing a speedy schooner which had evaded him in a heavier snows-quall off the Foreland.

He found Paice sitting in the cabin, his features grave as he finished writing laboriously in his log.

Vatass lowered himself on to a bench seat and said, "I wish the damned weather would make up its mind, Jonas. I am heartily sick of it." He realised that Paice was still silent and asked, "What is wrong?"

Paice did not reply directly. "Did you not meet

277

with the courier-brig?" He saw Vatass shake his head. "I thought as much."

Paice reached down and produced a bottle of brandy, half-filling two glasses. He had been preparing for this moment as soon as *Snapdragon* had been reported tacking around the headland.

He held up his glass and regarded the other man thoughtfully. "It's war, Hector."

Vatass swallowed the brandy and almost choked. "Jesus! Contraband, I'll wager!"

Paice gave a wintry smile. Vatass was very young, lucky to command a topsail cutter, to command anything at all. That would soon change now. Commands would go to officers who were barely used to their present junior ranks. *Good old Jack again*. He knew that the enormity of his announcement had taken Vatass completely aback. The weak joke was all he had to give himself time to accept it.

Paice said, "I don't care if it's stolen from Westminster Abbey." He clinked glasses solemnly. "War. I received a signal late last night." He waved his large hand across a pile of loose papers on the table. "These are from the admiral at Chatham. It has them all jumping. They should have been damned well expecting it!" He stared around the cabin. "They'll be asking us for men soon, you know that? *We* shall be using green replacements while our seasoned people are scattered through the fleet!"

Vatass was only half-listening. He did not share Paice's anxiety over the prospect of his *Telemachus* being pared away by the needs of war. All he could think was that he was young and once again full of hope. A new command—a brig perhaps, or even a rakish sloop-of-war. That would surely mean promotion.

Paice watched his emotions. Vatass had still not learned how to conceal them.

He said, "Captain Bolitho is across the water in Holland, or he could be anywhere by now." He looked at his log, and the chart which was beneath it. "*Wakeful* is with him." He downed the brandy in one swallow and refilled his glass immediately. "At least I trust to God she is."

Vatass allowed his mind to settle. Which had touched him more? Paice's news of Bolitho, or the fact he had never seen the tall lieutenant drink in this fashion before. He had heard that, after his wife had been killed, Paice had rarely been without the bottle. But that was past. Another memory.

Vatass began, "I do not understand, Jonas. What can we hope to do?"

Paice glared at him, his eyes red with anxiety and anger. "Don't you see it yet, man? What the *hell* have you been doing?"

Vatass replied stiffly, "Chasing a suspected smuggler."

Paice said in a more level voice, "The King of France has been executed. Yesterday we were told that their National Convention has declared war on England and Holland." He nodded very slowly. "Captain Bolitho is in the midst of it. And I doubt if he knows a whisper of what has happened!"

Vatass said unhelpfully, "He left you in command of the flotilla, Jonas."

Paice gave what could have been a bleak smile. "I intend to use it." He stood upright with his head inside the skylight and unclipped one of the covers.

Vatass saw tiny flakes of snow settle on his face and hair before he lowered the cover and sat down again.

"We're putting to sea as soon as makes no difference." He held up one hand. "Save the protests. I know you've only just come to rest. But at any moment I may receive a direct order from the admiral, one I cannot ignore, which will prevent our going." He lowered his voice as if to conceal an inner anguish. "I'll not leave him unsupported and without help." He kept his eyes on the young lieutenant's face as he poured him another glass, some of the brandy slopping unheeded across the neatly written orders. "Well, Hector, are you with me?"

"Suppose we cannot find *Wakeful?*"

"Damn me, we'll have tried! And I shall be able to hear that man's name without the shame of knowing I failed him, after the pride he returned to me by his own example." He waved vaguely over the chart. "The frontiers will be closed, and any alien ship will be treated as hostile. *Wakeful* is a sound vessel, and her commander a match for anything. But she's no fifth-rate." He glanced around the cabin. His command and his home; as if he could already see *Telemachus* facing up to a full broadside, with only her carronades and six-pounders to protect herself.

Vatass knew all this, and guessed that, whatever happened, his chances of an immediate promotion were in serious jeopardy. But he had always looked up to Paice's old style of leadership, even more, his qualities as a true sailor. Rough and outspoken, it was easy to picture him in his original role as master of a collier-brig.

"I'm with you." He considered his words, his

young face suddenly serious. "What about the admiral?"

Paice swept the papers from his chart and picked up some dividers.

"I have the feeling that there is someone more powerful than that fine gentleman behind our captain!" He looked across at Vatass and studied him for several seconds.

Vatass tried to laugh it off. It was war anyway. Nothing else would count now. But Paice's stare made him feel uneasy. As if he did not expect they would ever meet again.

"More vessels lying ahead, Cap'n!" Allday ducked beneath the boat's taut canvas and peered aft through the snow. It was more like sleet now, wet and clinging, so that the interior of the small boat was slippery and treacherous.

Bolitho crouched beside the Dutch skipper at the tiller and narrowed his eyes to judge the boat's progress under her two lugsails. One side of the river was lost in sleet and mist, but here and there he could see the lower portions of hulls and taut cables, probably the same ships he had passed in the night after leaving *Wakeful*. Even in the poor light the small fishing boat was a pitiful sight. Scarred and patched, with unmatched equipment which had been salvaged or stolen from other boats. He guessed that it had been used more as a link between the larger vessels for carrying contraband than for genuine fishing. The four Dutchmen who made up the crew seemed anxious to please him despite the stilted translations which passed through Brennier's aide. Perhaps they imagined that, with Tanner gone, their chance of any

281

reward was remote, and Bolitho's promise of payment was better than nothing at all.

Bolitho glanced at the aide. He had still not revealed his name. In the gloom he looked pinched up with cold and fear, his sodden clothes clinging to his body like rags. He was gripping a sword between his grimy fingers, the contrast as stark as the man's own circumstances, Bolitho thought. It was a beautiful, rapier-style weapon, the scabbard mounted in silver with a matching hilt and knuckle-bow. Like the dead French girl's handkerchief, was it his last connection with the life he had once known?

He ducked beneath the sails and saw the anchored ships up ahead. Three or four, coastal traders at a guess, their red, white and blue flags making the only stabs of colour against the drifting sleet and mist: Dutchmen waiting for the weather to clear before they worked out of their anchorage. No wonder they called Holland the port of the world. Who held the Low Countries enjoyed the rich routes to the East Indies and beyond, to the Caribbean and the Americas. Like the English, they had always been ambitious seafarers, and greatly admired, even as enemies when they had sailed up the Medway, attacking Chatham and firing the dockyards there.

He saw the Dutch skipper murmur to one of his crew, then pull out a watch from his tarpaulin coat. It was the size of an apple.

Bolitho said, "Find out what they are saying."

Brennier's aide seemed to drag himself from his despair, and after a slight hesitation said, "Very soon now, Capitaine. The other vessel is around the next . . . how you say . . . *bend?*"

Bolitho nodded. It had been quicker downstream,

and using the sails, small though they were, to full effect. Once aboard the other boat they would rest, perhaps find something hot to eat and drink before putting to sea when darkness fell. They might be unable to make contact with *Wakeful*. But they would have tried. To wait and think over what had happened would have been unbearable. Anyway, where would they have gone when the waiting was over and still nothing had been solved?

He thought of Hoblyn, the terrified midshipman, the bearded braggart on the Rochester Road, and of Delaval's anguish when he had seen Tanner even as the trap had fallen beneath his frantic legs.

Through and above it, Tanner had manipulated them all. Bolitho bit his lip until it hurt. *Even me.*

Allday said, "Over to larboard, matey!" The words meant nothing to the man at the tiller but Allday's gesture was familiar to sailors the world over.

"What is it?" Bolitho wiped his face and eyes with an old piece of bunting for the hundredth time to clear his vision.

"Bit o' bother, starboard bow, Cap'n."

Bolitho wished he had brought his small telescope, and strained his eyes as he stood upright in the boat to follow Allday's bearing.

There was a smart-looking brig anchored in the deepwater channel, and her lack of heavy tackles or lighters alongside meant she was most likely a small man-of-war, or perhaps a Dutch customs vessel.

He saw the skipper staring at her too, his face creased with sudden anxiety.

Bolitho kept his own counsel. There were no boats on the brig's deck, and none in the water unless they were tied on the opposite side. So where were they?

He called quietly, "Any movement?"

"No, Cap'n." Allday sounded on edge. "We only need half a mile and then—"

Bolitho watched as the weather decided to play a small part. A tiny shaft of watery sunlight came from somewhere to give even the drenching sleet a sort of beauty, and lay bare a part of the nearest land.

The Dutch skipper gave a sigh and raised his arm. Bolitho saw the fishing boat anchored a little apart from the others, and, even though he had not seen her before in daylight, he knew it was the one. He touched the Dutchman's arm and said, "That was well done!"

The man showed his teeth in a smile. From Bolitho's tone he had guessed that it was some kind of compliment.

"Prepare to shorten sail." He reached out with one foot and tapped the aide's leg. "You can give the word." The man jumped as if he had been stabbed.

Bolitho rubbed his hands together. They were raw with cold. Then he glanced at the dirty, patched sails and tried to gauge the final approach in this unfamiliar craft.

The sunlight was already fading, smothered by the approach of more sleet. But not before he had seen a sudden glint of metal from the fishing boat's deck, and even as he watched a figure in uniform with a white cross-belt rose into view, staring upstream for a few seconds before vanishing again below the bulwark.

"Belay that!" Bolitho seized the Dutchman's shoulder and gestured towards midstream. "Tell him the boat has been boarded—*taken*, you understand?"

The tiller was already going over, the skipper

crouching down, his eyes fixed unblinkingly on the open channel beyond.

Allday exclaimed, "God Almighty, that was close!"

Bolitho kept his eyes level with the bulwark and watched for another sign from the anchored fisherman. Boarded, it did not really matter by whom. The Dutch navy, customs men searching for contraband; or perhaps it was merely an unhappy coincidence, a routine search.

Unhappy was hardly the right description, Bolitho thought. It had seemed almost hopeless before. Without some kind of vessel, it was impossible. He glanced along the boat, shielding his face with one arm as the sleet hissed and slapped across the sails and rigging. In open water it would be more lively, even rough, if the angle of the sleet was any measure of it. He thought of *Wakeful*, plunging and rolling in the offshore swell while she waited to make the rendezvous.

This boat had nothing. Just a compass and a few pieces of old equipment. He could not even see a pump.

He looked hard at Allday's crouching shoulders in the bows. Another risk. Was it still worth that?

Bolitho said suddenly, "A good day for a shoot, Allday." He spoke quickly as if his common sense might change his mind for him.

Allday turned as if he had misheard. "*Shoot*, Cap'n?" Their gaze met and Allday nodded casually. "Oh, yes, I s'pose it is Cap'n."

When he had turned away he unbuttoned his coat and loosened the pistol in his belt where he had wedged it to keep it dry.

Bolitho glanced at his companions. The aide was

staring emptily into nothing, and all the Dutchmen were watching the fishing boat which by now had drawn almost abeam.

Bolitho felt for his own pistol, then freed his sword. Two of the Dutchmen were visibly armed, the others might be too.

He waited for the aide to look up at him then said, "In a moment I am going to take this boat away from here, m'sieu. Do you understand me?" The man nodded dully.

Bolitho continued carefully, "If they refuse to obey, we must disarm them." His voice hardened. "Or kill them." He waited, trying to guess what the man's broken mind was thinking. "It is your last chance as well as ours, m'sieu!"

"I understand, Capitaine." He crawled aft towards the tiller, his beautiful sword held clear of the filth and swilling water below the bottom boards.

Bolitho watched the oncoming curtain of sleet. It had blotted out some anchored vessels which moments earlier had been close enough to see in every detail. Once past the last few craft there would be nothing between them and the open sea.

"Be prepared, m'sieu!" Bolitho's fingers closed around the pistol. Against his chilled body it felt strangely warm, as if it had recently been fired.

Allday shouted, "Larboard bow, Cap'n! A bloody boatload!"

Bolitho saw a long, double-banked cutter pulling out from behind some moored barges, the scarlet-painted oars rising and falling like powerful wings as it swept towards them.

There were uniforms aft in the sternsheets, naval, as well as the green coats of the Dutch customs. A voice boomed over the choppy wavelets, magnified by a speaking trumpet.

The aide whispered, "They call us to stop!" He sounded completely terrified.

Bolitho prodded the Dutch skipper and shouted, "That way! *Quickly!*"

There was no need to show their weapons. The Dutchmen were, if anything, more eager to escape authority than Bolitho.

They threw themselves to work on the two flapping sails, and Bolitho felt the hull tilt to the wind's wet thrust and saw sheets of spray burst over the pursuing cutter's stem, drenching the crew and throwing the scarlet oars into momentary confusion.

Allday yelled, "They've got a gun up forrard, Cap'n!"

Bolitho tried to swallow. He had already seen the bow-gun in the eyes of the cutter. Probably a swivel or a long musketoon. One blast from either could kill or wound every man in this boat.

But the range was holding; the small fishing boat was better handled and rigged for this kind of work, and the wilder the sea the harder it would be for the cutter's coxswain to maintain his speed through the water.

Allday clung to the gunwale and choked as water reared over the bows and soaked him from head to foot.

The voice pursued them, crackling and distorted through the speaking trumpet.

Allday shouted, "They're taking aim!"

"Down!" Bolitho pulled the nearest crew member to the deck and saw Allday peering along the boat towards him, his body half-hidden by floats and nets.

The bang of the gun was muffled by the wind and sleet, so that the charge of canister hit the afterpart of the hull with unexpected violence. Bolitho heard metal fragments and splinters shriek overhead and saw several holes punched through the nearest sail. He held his breath, waiting for something to carry away, a spar to break in half, even for a sudden inrush of water.

The Dutch skipper clambered to his knees and nodded. There was something like pride in his face. Even in this sad old boat.

Allday gasped, "We've lost 'em, Cap'n!"

Bolitho peered astern. The sleet was so thick that even the mouth of the river had vanished. They had the water to themselves.

He was about to rise to his feet when he saw Brennier's aide staring at him, his eyes bulging with pain and fear.

Bolitho knelt beside him, then prized the man's hands away from his body. Allday joined him and gripped his wrists while Bolitho tore open his waistcoat and then his finely laced shirt, which was bright with blood. There were just two wounds. One below the right breast, the other in the stomach. Bolitho heard the Dutch skipper tearing up some rags which he handed over his shoulder. Their eyes met only briefly. Again, language was no barrier. For a fisherman as well as a sea-officer, death was commonplace.

Allday murmured, "Hold hard, matey." He looked at Bolitho. "Shall I lay him down?"

Bolitho covered the dying man with some canvas, held a hat over his face to protect him from the sleet. "No." He dropped his voice. "He's drowning in his own blood." He looked at the bottom boards where the trapped sleet and seawater glittered red now. Another victim.

He could not wait here. But when he got to his feet he saw the man's eyes follow him, terrified and pleading.

Bolitho said quietly, "Never fear, m'sieu. You will be safe. We will not leave you."

He turned away and stared down at the swaying compass card without seeing it. Stupid, empty words! What did they mean to a dying man? What had they ever done to help anyone?

Bolitho swallowed again, feeling the rawness of salt in his throat like bile.

"Nor' West!" He pointed at the sails. "Yes?"

The man nodded. Events had moved too swiftly for him. But he stood firmly at his tiller, his eyes reddened by sea and wind; it must have felt like sailing his boat into nowhere.

Each dragging minute Bolitho expected to see another vessel loom out of the sleet, no challenge this time, just a merciless hail of grape or canister. Tanner repeatedly came to his mind and he found himself cursing his name aloud until Allday said, "I think he's going, Cap'n."

Bolitho got down on his knees again and held the man's groping fingers. So cold. As if they had already died.

"I am here, m'sieu. I shall tell your admiral of your courage." Then he wiped the man's mouth as a tell-tale thread of blood ran unheeded down his chin.

Allday watched, his eyes heavy. He had seen it too often before. He saw Bolitho's hand moving to make the man comfortable. How did he do it? He had known him at the height of battle, and flung to the depths of despair. Few but himself had seen this Bolitho, and even now Allday felt guilty about it. Like stumbling on a special secret.

The man was trying to speak, each word bringing more agony. It was just a matter of minutes.

Allday stared across Bolitho's bowed head. *Why doesn't the poor bastard die?*

Bolitho held the man's wrist but it moved with sudden strength and determination. The fingers reached down and unclipped the beautiful sword from his belt.

In a mere whisper he said, "Give—give . . ."

The effort was too much for him. Bolitho stood up, the rapier in one hand. He thought of the sword which hung by his side, so familiar that it was a part of him.

He looked at Allday's stony features and said quietly, "Is this all that is left of a man? Nothing more?"

As the minutes passed into an hour, and then another, they all worked without respite to hold the boat on course, to bale out the steady intake of water and constantly retrim the two patched sails. In a way it saved them. They had neither food nor water, and each man ached with cold and backbreaking labour; but there was no time to despair or to give in.

In darkness, with the boat pitching about on a deep procession of rollers, they buried the unknown Frenchman, a rusting length of chain tied about his legs to take him down to the seabed. After that, they lost track of the hours and their direction, and despite the risk of discovery Bolitho ordered that the lantern should be lit and unshuttered, as arranged, into the sleet which was once again turning to snow.

If no one found them they could not survive. It was winter, and the sea too big for their small vessel. Only Allday knew that there was barely enough oil left in the lantern anyway. He sighed and moved closer to Bolitho's familiar outline in the stern. It was not much of a way to end after what they had done together, he thought. But death could have come in a worse guise, and very nearly had on board Delaval's *Loyal Chieftain*.

Bolitho moistened his lips. "One more signal, old friend."

The lantern's beam lit up the snow so that the boat appeared to be hemmed in and unmoving.

Allday muttered hoarsely, "That's the last of it, Cap'n."

It was then that *Wakeful* found them.

15

No Hiding Place

QUEELY and his first lieutenant watched Bolitho with silent fascination as he swallowed his fourth mug of scalding coffee. He could feel it warming him like an inner fire and knew someone, probably Allday, had laced it heavily with rum.

They had been unable to do anything for the small fishing boat which had given them the chance to escape, and despite protests from the Dutch skipper it had been cast adrift; it seemed unlikely it would remain afloat for much longer.

Queely waited, choosing the moment. "What now, sir?" He watched Bolitho's eyes regaining their brightness. It was like seeing someone come alive again. When *Wakeful*'s seamen had hauled them aboard they had been too numbed by cold and exhaustion even to speak.

As he had drunk his coffee, Bolitho had tried to outline all that had happened. He had ended by saying, "But for you and your *Wakeful*, we would all be dead." He had placed the silver-mounted sword on the cabin table. "I suspect this poor man had already died when he heard that his King had been executed."

Queely had shaken his head. "We knew nothing of that, sir." His jaw had lifted and he had regarded Bolitho with his dark, hawklike face. "I would still

292

have come looking for you no matter what the risk, even if I had."

Bolitho leaned back against the side and felt the cutter rolling steeply in a cross-swell as she prepared to change tack. The motion seemed easier, but the wind sounded just as strong. Perhaps his mind was still too exhausted to notice the true difference.

He replied, "Now? We shall lay a course for Flushing. It is our only chance to catch Tanner with the treasure."

Lieutenant Kempthorne made his excuses and went on deck to take charge of the hands. Bolitho and Queely leaned on the table, the chart spread between them beneath the madly swinging lanterns. Bolitho glanced at the serious-faced lieutenant. Even in his seagoing uniform he managed to make Bolitho feel like a vagrant. His clothing stank of fish and bilge, and his hands were cut and bleeding from handling the icy sheets in the boat which they had abandoned astern.

Queely said, "If, as you say, Tanner has loaded the treasure into this vessel, La Revanche, would he not make haste to get under way immediately? If so, we can never catch him, despite this soldier's wind."

Bolitho peered at the chart, his grey eyes thoughtful. "I doubt that. It would all take time, which is why I believe he was the one to cause our delay at the rendezvous. Any suspicious act might arouse the Dutch authorities, and that is the last thing he would want."

A voice seemed to cry out in his mind. Suppose Brennier's aide had been mistaken? Or that he had heard them speaking of another vessel altogether?

Queely took his silence for doubt. "She'll likely be armed, sir. If we had some support—"

Bolitho glanced at him and smiled sadly. "But we do not have any. Armed? I think that unlikely, except for a minimum protection. Which was why Delaval and his *Loyal Chieftain* laid offshore whenever he was making a run. The Dutch were searching vessels in the river. Any heavily armed ship would draw them like bees to honey."

"Very well, sir." He gave a rueful grin. "It is little enough, but I too am anxious to see what so much treasure looks like!" He pulled on his heavy coat and turned in the doorway to the companion ladder. "I thank God we found you, sir. I had all but given up hope."

Bolitho sat down wearily and massaged his eyes. The cabin was tiny and, as usual, littered with the officers' effects. But after the fishing boat's squalor it seemed like a ship-of-the-line.

Just hours later, Bolitho was roused from his sleep. Allday found him sprawled across the chart, his head resting on one arm.

"What is it?"

Allday stood balancing a steaming basin. "The cook managed to boil some water." He gave a broad grin. "I thought to meself a good shave an' a rub-down'll make the Cap'n feel his old self again."

Bolitho slipped out of his coat and peeled off his shirt. As Allday shaved him with practised ease, legs braced, one ear attuned to every sound as the cutter rolled and plunged about them, he marvelled that the big man could always adjust, no matter what ship he was in.

Allday was saying, "Y'see, Cap'n, 'tis always the

same with you at times like this. *You* feel better—that makes it better for the rest of us."

Bolitho stared up at him, the realisation of Allday's simple philosophy driving away the last cobwebs of sleep.

He said quietly, "Today, you mean?" He saw him nod: the old instinct he had always trusted. Why had he not known it himself? "We'll fight?"

"Aye, Cap'n." He sounded almost buoyant. "Had to come, as I sees it."

Bolitho dried his face and was amazed that Allday could shave him so closely with the deck all alive beneath him. He had rarely even nicked him with his formidable razor.

Allday wiped down his shoulders and back with a hot cloth and then handed him a comb. "*That's* more like it, Cap'n."

Bolitho saw the freshly laundered shirt on the bunk. "How did you—"

"Compliments of Mr. Kempthorne, Cap'n. I—mentioned it, like."

Bolitho dressed unhurriedly. A glance at his watch told him all he had to know for the present. Queely and his company were doing what they could and needed no encouragement or criticism. He wondered what had become of the four Dutchmen, and where they would end up. Probably on the next ship bound for Holland, even at the risk of being greeted by the Customs.

The shirt made him feel clean and refreshed, just as Allday had promised. He thought of all those other times, under the blazing sun, the decks strewn with dead and dying, the brain cringing to the crash and recoil of cannon fire. Like Stockdale before him,

Allday had always been there. But with that something extra. He always seemed to understand, to know when the waiting was over, and smooth words were not enough.

Queely came down from the deck and peered in at him.

"Dawn coming up, sir. Wind's holding steady, and the snow's eased to almost nothing." He noticed the clean shirt and smiled. "Oh, you honour us, sir!"

As his feet clattered up the ladder again Bolitho said, "There is still something *missing*, Allday. Fight we may, but—" He shrugged. "He might have outfoxed us again."

Allday stared into the distance. "When I heard that silky voice of his—" He grinned, but no humour touched his eyes. "I wanted to cut him down there and then."

Bolitho half-drew his sword then let it fall smoothly into its scabbard again. "We make a fine pair. I wanted that too."

He picked up his boat-cloak. It was filthy also. But it would be like ice on deck. He must not fail, would not let the fever burst in and consume him like the last time.

Some of his old despair lingered on. He said, "Hear me, old friend. If I should fall today—"

Allday regarded him impassively. "I'll not see it, Cap'n, 'cause I shall already have dropped!"

The understanding was there. As strong as ever.

Bolitho touched his arm. "So let's be about it, eh?"

Bolitho felt his body angle to the tilting deck as the wind forced *Wakeful* on to her lee bulwark. It was colder than he had expected, and he regretted taking shelter in the cabin's comparative warmth.

Queely touched his hat and shouted above the noise, "Wind's veered still further, sir! Nor'-West by North or the like, by my reckoning!"

Bolitho stared up at the masthead and thought he could see the long pendant streaming towards the larboard bow, curling, then cracking like a huge whip. He even imagined he could hear it above the wild chorus of creaking rigging, the slap and boom of canvas.

Wakeful was steering south-south-west, close-hauled on the starboard tack, her sails very pale against the dull sky. Dawn was here and yet reluctant to show itself.

Bolitho felt his eyes growing accustomed to the poor light and recognised several of the figures who were working close at hand. Even the "hard men" of Queely's command looked chilled and pinched, but for the most part their feet were bare, although Bolitho could feel the bitter cold through his shoes. Like most sailors, they thought shoes too expensive to waste merely for their own comfort.

Queely said, "According to the master, we should be well past Walcheren Island and Flushing by now. If the weather clears we will soon sight the coast of France."

Bolitho nodded but said nothing. *France*. Once there, Tanner would make his trade. A share of the treasure and probably a sure protection from the French Convention to enable him to continue his smuggling on a grand scale. He tried not to think of the old admiral, Brennier. Tanner's mark of trust, then humiliation before the mob, and the last steps up to the guillotine. Any other leading patriot would think again before he considered lending support to a counter-revolution with Brennier dead.

Bolitho watched the sky giving itself colour. The driving wind had swept the snow away; he could see no clouds, just a hostile grey emptiness, with the faintest hint of misty blue towards the horizon.

Queely was speaking to his first lieutenant. Bolitho saw Kempthorne bobbing his head to his commander's instructions. Despite his uniform and his surroundings he still managed to look out of place.

Queely walked up the slanting deck and said, "He's going aloft with the big signals glass in a moment, sir." He saw Bolitho's expression and gave a quick smile. "I know, sir. He'd be happier as a horse-coper than a sea-officer, but he tries!"

He forgot Kempthorne and added, "We shall draw near to the French coast again, sir. If Tanner intends to change allegiance and steal the King's ransom, he may stand inshore as soon as it's light enough." He was thinking about that last time, the French luggers, the boat blowing up, and the dead girl they had returned to the sea.

Bolitho said, "We shall take him anyway. I'll brook no interference from French patrol vessels!"

Queely studied him curiously. "Strange how a man of influence like Tanner could change loyalties."

"I have always seen him as an enemy." Bolitho glanced away. "This time he'll have no hope of escaping justice because of his damned toadies in high places!"

Kempthorne was hauling his lanky frame up the weather shrouds, his coat flapping in the wind as it pressed his body against the ratlines. Bolitho watched, conscious that he could now see the masthead sharply etched against the sky, the vibrating shrouds, even a solitary lookout who was shifting his perch as the lieutenant clawed his way up beside him.

Queely remarked unfeelingly, "Just the thing to clear your head on a day like this!"

He looked at Bolitho's profile and asked abruptly, "Do you regard this as a day of reckoning, sir?" He sounded surprised, but without the doubt he had once shown.

Bolitho replied, "I believe so." He shivered and pulled his boat-cloak more tightly about his body. Suppose he was mistaken, and Tanner's ship still lay at Flushing, or had never been there at all?

He added in a hard tone, "It is a premonition one has from time to time." He saw Allday lounging beside the companionway, his arms folded. There was nothing careless or disinterested in his eyes, Bolitho thought.

"As I see it, Tanner has nowhere else to run. Greed and deceit have made escape impossible."

He thought again of Tanner's own words. *No hiding place.* Even then he had lied, must have laughed as Brennier and his companions played directly into his hands.

"Deck there!"

Queely peered up. "Where away?"

Kempthorne called lamely, "Nothing yet, sir!"

Several of the seamen nearby nudged one another as Queely snorted, "Damned nincompoop!"

Bolitho took a telescope from the rack and wiped the lens carefully with his handkerchief. As he lifted it and waited for the deck to rear upright again, he saw the sea tumbling away across the larboard bow, reaching further and still further, individual banks of crested rollers and darker troughs forming into patterns in the growing daylight. A grey, blustery morning. He thought of Falmouth and wondered how young Matthew had enjoyed his Christmas. Probably had had the household enthralled with his tales of smuggling and sudden death. Bolitho was glad he was back where he belonged. The land needed boys who would grow into men like his father had been. He glanced at Allday. Let others do the fighting so that they could build, raise animals, and make England safe again.

"Deck there!"

Queely scowled.

Kempthorne's voice cracked with excitement. "Sail on the lee bow, sir!"

Queely's dark eyes flashed in the poor light. "By God, I'd never have believed it!"

"Easy now. Let us hold on to caution, eh?" But his face made a lie of his words. It was the ship. *It must be.* No other would risk running so close to the French coast.

Queely yelled impatiently, "What is she?" His foot tapped on the wet planking. "I'm waiting, man!"

Kempthorne called hoarsely, "A—a brigantine, I think, sir!"

Bolitho said, "It must be difficult to see, even from that height."

Queely turned. "You think I'm too hard on him, sir?" He shrugged. "It may save his life and a few others before long!"

Bolitho moved to the narrow poop and clung to a dripping swivel gun. A brigantine. It seemed likely. They and schooners were most favoured in the Trade,

300

and Tanner had probably selected this one as soon as Marcuard had taken him into his confidence. He thought of the grand house in Whitehall, the servants, the quiet luxury of day-to-day life in the capital. This was a far cry from Marcuard's careful planning, but Bolitho had no doubts as to where the blame would be laid if Tanner and the treasure disappeared.

The master said to nobody in particular, "A spot o' sunshine afore the glass is turned."

Queely glared at him, but knew him well enough to say nothing.

Kempthorne, his voice almost gone from shouting above the wind and sea, called, "Brigantine she is, sir! Holding same tack!"

Bolitho grasped his sword beneath his cloak. It felt like a piece of ice.

"I suggest you prepare, Mr. Queely."

Queely watched him, his features more hawklike than ever. "The people know what to do, sir. If we are wrong, they might lose confidence."

"Not in you. You can blame it all on the mad captain from Falmouth!"

Surprisingly they were both able to laugh.

Then Queely shouted, "Pipe all hands! Clear for action!"

It was still strange for Bolitho to see the preparations for battle completed without drums, the rising urgency of a ship beating to quarters. Here, it was almost by word of mouth, with only the watch below summoned by the squeal of calls.

"Cast off the breechings!"

The master let out a sigh. *"Told you."*

A shaft of watery sunlight plunged down through the spray and sea-mist, giving the water depth and

301

colour, personality to the faces and figures working around the guns.

From his dizzy perch Lieutenant Francis Kempthorne wrapped one arm around a stay until he felt it was being torn from his body. As the sturdy hull lifted and dipped beneath him, the mast itself reached out and across the surging crests far below, and he saw the mainsail's shadow on the water, as if it were rising to snatch him down. The motion was sickening although the lookout at his side seemed indifferent to it.

He gulped and tried again, counting the seconds while he levelled the heavy telescope, not even daring to think what Queely would say if he dropped it. The bows lifted streaming from a jagged breaker and Kempthorne held his breath. The brigantine must have risen at exactly the same moment. He saw her forecourse and topsail, the big driver braced hard round as she steered on the same tack as her pursuer.

Just for those few seconds he saw her name across the counter, the gilt paint suddenly sharp and bright in the feeble glare.

He shouted, "*La Revanche*, sir!" He was almost sobbing with relief, as if it would have been his fault had she been another vessel entirely.

The lookout watched him and shook his head. Kempthorne was popular with most of the hands, and never took it out of offenders like some. The seaman had been in the navy for twelve years but could still not fathom the minds of officers.

Kempthorne was glad, pleased that he had sighted the other vessel. Yet within hours he might be dead.

Of course there might easily be prize money if things went well . . .

Down on the streaming deck Queely stared at Bolitho and exclaimed, "We've found her, sir!" His eyes flashed with excitement, Kempthorne's part in it already forgotten.

Bolitho levelled his glass, but from the deck the sea still appeared empty.

"And now, we'll *take* him!"

Kempthorne shouted, "She's shaken out another reef, sir! Making more sail!"

Queely strode to the compass box and back to Bolitho's side. "They're wasting their time," he said confidently. "We've got the bugger by the heels." He cupped his hands. "Be ready to run out the stuns'ls if she opens the range!"

Bolitho trained his glass again. Now in the growing light he could see the brigantine's forecourse and topsail, her driver filled to full capacity and making the vessel's two masts lean over towards the cruising white horses.

Even in this short interval, since Kempthorne had read her name, the distance between them had fallen away considerably. It was true what they said about topsail cutters. They could outrun almost anything.

"Run up the Colours, if you please." Queely looked at Bolitho. "He may not have recognised us, sir."

Bolitho nodded. "I agree. Let's see what he does next. Have the four Dutchmen brought on deck."

The Dutchmen stood swaying below the mast, staring from Bolitho to the brigantine, wondering what was about to happen to them.

Bolitho lowered the glass. If he could see the other vessel's poop, then they, and most likely Tanner himself, would be able to recognise his erstwhile partners. He would know then that this was not some casual encounter, a time when he might risk turning towards the French coast to avoid capture. He would know it was Bolitho. It was personal. It was now.

"Fire a gun, Mr. Queely!"

The six-pounder recoiled on its tackles, the thin whiff of smoke gone before the crew had time to check the motion with handspikes.

Queely watched the ball splash into the broken crests some half-a-cable from the brigantine's quarter.

He said, "She does not seem to be pierced for any large artillery." He glanced admiringly at Bolitho. "You reasoned to perfection, sir."

A man yelled, "Somethin's 'appenin' on 'er deck, sir!"

Bolitho raised his glass in unison with Queely, and tensed as he saw the little scene right aft by her taffrail. He did not recognise the others, but in the centre of the small group he saw Brennier's white hair blowing in the wind, his arms pinioned so that he was forced to face the cutter as she continued to overhaul *La Revanche*.

Queely said savagely, "What is his game? Why does he play for time? We'll be up to him in a moment—if he kills that old man it will be the worse for him!"

Bolitho said, "Rig four halters to the mainyard." He saw Queely look at him with surprise. "Tanner will understand. A life for a life. So too will his men."

Queely yelled, "Come down, Mr. Kempthorne! You are needed *here*!" He beckoned to his boatswain and passed Bolitho's instructions. Within minutes, or so it seemed, four ropes, each with a noose at one end, flew out from the mainyard like creeper, as if they were enjoying a macabre dance.

304

Bolitho said, "Keep him to lee'rd of you. Run down on his quarter." He was thinking aloud. But all the time, Queely's question intruded. *Why does he play for time?* The game must surely be played out.

The truth touched his heart like steel. *He wants me dead. Even in the face of defeat he sees only that.*

He raised the glass again. Brennier's face loomed into the small silent picture, his eyes wide as if he was choking.

Bolitho said, "I intend to board. Prepare the jolly-boat." He silenced Queely's protest by adding, "If you try to drive alongside in this wind, you'll likely dismast *Wakeful*. We'd lose Tanner, the treasure, everything."

Queely shouted to the boat-handling party, then said stubbornly, "If they fire on you before you board, what then? We have no other boat. Why not risk the damage, I say, and damn the consequences!" He shrugged; he had seen the fight lost before it had begun. "Mr. Kempthorne! Full boarding party!" He turned his back on the men by the tiller. "And if—"

Bolitho touched his elbow. "*If?* Then you may act as you please. Disable her, but make certain they understand they will go down with the ship if they resist further!"

He watched the jolly-boat rising and dipping like a snared shark as the seamen warped it slowly aft to the quarter.

He took a last glance at the brigantine's poop as *Wakeful* bore down on her. The figures had gone. The threat of instant retribution which they had seen in the four halters run up to the yard might have carried the moment. The sight of *Wakeful*'s carronades and run-out six-pounders would demonstrate

305

that there was no quarter this time, no room to bargain.

Allday dropped into the boat and watched the oarsmen as they fended off the cutter's hull, and prepared to fight their way over the water which surged between the two vessels.

Bolitho clambered down with Kempthorne and as the bowman shoved off, and the oars fell noisily into their rowlock, Allday shouted, "Give way all!"

Kempthorne stared at *La Revanche*, his eyes filled with wonder. "They're shortening sail, sir!"

Bolitho replied grimly, "Don't drop your guard, my lad, not for a second."

Faces appeared along the brigantine's bulwark, and Bolitho raised his borrowed speaking trumpet and shouted, "Do not resist! In the King's name, I order you to surrender!"

He could ignore the sweating oarsmen, Allday crouching over his tiller bar, Kempthorne and the other boarders jammed like herrings into the stern-sheets and amongst the boat's crew.

At any second they might open fire. It only needed one. Bolitho wanted to look round for *Wakeful* and gauge her position, how long it might take Queely to attack if the worst happened.

Allday said between his teeth, "One of 'em's got a musket, Cap'n."

Bolitho shouted again, his heart pumping against his ribs as his whole body tensed for a shot.

"Stand by to receive boarders!"

Allday breathed out slowly as the raised musket disappeared. "Bowman! *Grapnel!*"

They smashed hard into the brigantine's side, lifted

over her wale and almost capsized as another trough yawned beneath the keel.

Bolitho seized a handrope and hauled himself up to the entry port, with Kempthorne and some of the seamen scrabbling up beside him. Allday stared helplessly while the boat plunged down into another trough, leaving him and the rest of the crew momentarily cut off from the boarding party. Bolitho flung himself over the bulwark and in the next few seconds saw the scene like a badly executed painting. Men gaping at him when they should have been attacking or yelling defiance; Brennier beside the wheel, his hands apparently tied behind him, a sailor with a cutlass held close to his throat.

And in the centre stood Tanner, his handsome features very calm as he faced Bolitho across the open deck.

The jolly-boat ground alongside again and broken oars spilled out into the sea. But Allday was here, with three more armed men, their eyes wild, ready to fight—no, wanting to kill now that the moment had arrived.

Tanner said, "You are making another mistake, Bolitho!"

Bolitho glanced at Brennier and nodded. He was safe now. The man who was guarding him jammed his cutlass into the deck and stood away.

Bolitho said, "Well, Sir James, you once invited me to enter your world." He gestured toward the horizon. "This is mine. On the high seas you will find no bribed judges or lying witnesses to save your skin. If you or one of your men raises his hand against us, I will see him dead—here, today—be certain of that."

307

He was astonished that he could speak so calmly. "Mr. Kempthorne, attend the admiral."

As the lieutenant made to cross the deck, Tanner moved. "I shall see you in *hell*, Bolitho!"

He must have had a pistol, a long-barrelled, duellist's weapon, concealed beneath his coat. Too late Bolitho saw his arm swing up and take aim. He heard shouts, a grunt of fury from Allday, then even as a shadow passed across his vision came the sharp crack of the shot. Lieutenant Kempthorne swung round and stared at Bolitho, his eyes wide with disbelief. The ball had penetrated his throat directly below his chin, and as he fell forwards the blood welled from his mouth and he was dead.

In the immediate silence the sea's sounds intruded like an audience, and only the man at the wheel seemed able to move, his eyes on the compass and the straining driver. What he was trained to do, no matter what.

He wants me dead.

There was a faint splash as Tanner flung the pistol over the side. He watched Bolitho's expression and said softly, *"Next time."*

Bolitho walked towards him, men falling back to let him through. It was then that he saw *Wakeful*, creeping along the side, near enough to fire directly at individual targets, but still keeping her distance to avoid collision.

Somebody shouted, "Th' chests is in the 'old, sir!"

But the others ignored him. It no longer seemed to matter.

Allday tightened his grip on the cutlass. Remembering the silky voice from the hidden carriage, when Tanner had ordered him to kill the sailor from the press gang. He could feel the flood in his veins like thunder, and knew that if any one so much as moved towards Bolitho he would hack him down.

Bolitho faced Tanner and said, "The next time is now, *Jack*—isn't that what they call you?"

"You'd kill an unarmed man, Captain? I think not. Your sense of honour—"

"Has just died with young Kempthorne." He had his sword in his hand faster than he had ever known before. He saw Tanner gasp as if he expected the point to tear into him instantly; when Bolitho hesitated, he recovered himself and jeered, "Like your brother after all!"

Bolitho stood back slightly, the point of his sword just inches above the deck.

"You did not disappoint me, Sir James." He watched the arrogance give way to something else. "You insulted my family. Perhaps on land, in 'your world', you might still go free despite your obscene crimes!"

He was suddenly sick of it. The sword moved like lightning, and when it returned to the deck there was blood running from Tanner's cheek. The blade had cut it almost to the bone.

Quietly Bolitho said, "Defend yourself, man. Or *die*."

Gasping with pain Tanner dragged out his sword, his face screwed up with shock and fear.

They circled one another, figures hurrying away, *Wakeful*'s men standing to their weapons, one near the wheel with a swivel gun trained on the brigantine's crew.

Allday watched, shocked by Bolitho's consuming

anger, the glint in his eyes which even he had never seen before.

Clash-clash-clash. The blades touched and feinted apart, then Bolitho's cut across Tanner's shirt, so that he screamed as blood ran down his breeches.

"For pity's sake!" Tanner was peering at him like a wounded beast. "I surrender! I'll tell everything!"

"You lie, damn you!" The blade hissed out once more, and a cut opened on Tanner's neck like something alive.

Vaguely Bolitho heard Queely's voice, echoing across the water through his trumpet.

"Sail to the Nor'-West, sir!"

Bolitho lowered his sword. "At last."

Allday said, "They might be Frogs!" Bolitho wiped his forehead with his arm. It was like the blind man. Exactly the same. He had wanted to kill Tanner. But now he was nothing. Whatever happened he could not survive.

He said wearily, "They'll not interfere with two English ships."

Again, it was like a stark picture. Brennier's faded eyes, his hoarse voice as he called with astonishment, "But, Capitaine, our countries are at war!"

It was the missing part of the pattern which fate, or his own instinct, had tried to warn him about. At war, and they had not known. No wonder Tanner had been prepared to wait, to play for time. He had known the French ship was on her way. She was probably the same vessel which had stood between *Wakeful* and Holland such a short while ago.

But he did not see the sudden triumph and hatred in Tanner's eyes as he came out of his trance of fear and lunged forward with his sword. Bolitho ducked

310

and made to parry it aside, but his foot went from under him and he knew he had slipped in poor Kempthorne's blood.

He heard Tanner scream, *"Die then!"* He sounded crazed with pain and the lust to kill.

Bolitho rolled over, and kicked out at Tanner's leg, taking him off balance so that he reeled back against the bulwark.

Bolitho was on his feet again, and heard Allday roar, "Let me, Cap'n."

The blades parried almost gently, and then Tanner lunged forward once again. Bolitho took the weight on his hilt, swung Tanner round, using the force of his attack to propel him towards the side, just as his father had taught him and his brother so long ago in Falmouth.

Bolitho flicked the guard aside and thrust. When he withdrew the blade, Tanner was still on his feet, shaking his head dazedly from side to side as if he could not understand how it could happen.

His knees hit the deck, and he slumped and lay staring blindly at the sails.

Allday gathered him up and rolled him over the bulwark.

Bolitho joined him at the side and watched the body drifting slowly towards the bows. He leaned against Allday's massive shoulder and gasped. "So it's not over."

Then he looked up, his eyes clearing like clouds from the sea. "Was he dead?"

Allday shrugged and gave a slow grin of relief and pride. For both of them.

"Didn't ask, Cap'n."

Bolitho turned towards the white-haired admiral.

"I must leave you, m'sieu. My prize crew will take care of you." He looked away towards Kempthorne's sprawled body. He had intended to make him prize master of *La Revanche*, give him a small authority which might drive away all his uncertainties. He almost smiled. Prize master, as he had once been. The first step to command.

Brennier was unable to grasp it. "But how will you fight?" He peered at *Wakeful*'s tall mainsail. "Tanner was expecting something bigger to come after us!"

Bolitho walked to the entry port and looked down at the pitching jolly-boat. To the master's mate who had accompanied the boarding party he said, "Put the men you can trust to work and make sail at once. Those you can't put in irons."

The master's mate watched him curiously. "Beg pardon, sir, but after wot you just done I don't reckon we'll get much bother." Then he stared across at his own ship. He knew he would probably not see her again. "I'll bury Mr. Kempthorne proper, sir. Never you fear."

Allday called, "Boat's ready, Cap'n!"

Bolitho turned and looked at their watching faces. Would he have killed Tanner but for that last attack? Now he would never know.

To the admiral he said, "Our countries are at war, m'sieu, but I hope we shall always be friends."

The old man who had tried to save his King bowed his head. He had lost everything but the ransom in the hold, his King and now his country. And yet Bolitho thought afterwards that he had never seen such dignity and pride in any man.

"Give way all!"

Allday swung the tiller bar and peered at the men along *Wakeful*'s side ready to take the bowline.

Then he looked at the set of Bolitho's shoulders. So it's not over, he had said back there. He sighed. Nor would it be, until—

Allday saw the stroke oarsman watching him anxiously and shook himself from his black mood. Poor bugger'd never been in a sea-fight before. Was likely wondering if he would ever see home again.

He glanced at Bolitho and grinned despite his apprehensions.

Our Dick. Hatless, bloody, the old coat looking as if he had borrowed it from a beggar.

His grin broadened, so that the stroke oarsman felt the touch of confidence again.

But you'd know Bolitho was a captain anywhere. And that was all that counted now.

16

A Sailor's Lot

LUKE HAWKINS, *Telemachus*'s boatswain, shook himself like a dog and waited for Paice to loom out of the wet darkness.

"I've sent four 'ands aloft, sir!" They both squinted towards the masthead but the upper yards were hidden by swirling snow. "Some o' that cordage 'as carried away!"

Paice swore. "God damn all dockyards! For what they care we could lose the bloody topmast!" It was pointless to worry about the half-frozen men working up there, their fingers like claws, their eyes blinded by snow.

Hawkins suggested, "We could reef, sir."

Paice exclaimed, "*Shorten sail?* Damn it to hell, man! We've lost enough knots already!" He swung away. "Do what you must. I shall let her fall off a point—it might help to ease the strain."

Paice found Triscott peering at the compass, his hat and shoulders starkly white in the shadows.

The first lieutenant knew it was pointless to argue with Paice about the way he was driving his command. It was so unlike him, as if the flames of hell were at his heels.

Paice took a deep breath as water lifted over the bulwark and sluiced away into the scuppers.

When daylight came there would probably be no sign of *Snapdragon*. In these conditions station-keeping was almost a joke. Perhaps Vatass would use the situation to go about and beat back to harbour. Paice toyed with the thought, which he knew was unfair and uncharitable.

The helmsman yelled, "Steady as she goes, sir! Sou' by East!"

Chesshyre said, "We'll be a right laughing stock if we have the sticks torn out of us." He had not realised that Paice was still in the huddled group around the compass.

He winced as Paice's great hand fell on his arm like a grapnel.

"You are the acting-master, Mr. Chesshyre! If you can't think of anything more useful to offer, then *acting* you will remain!"

Triscott interrupted, "We shall sight land when the snow clears. Mr. Chesshyre assured me that it will by dawn."

Paice said hotly, "In which case it will probably turn into a bloody typhoon!"

Triscott hid a smile. He had always liked Paice and had learned all he knew from him. Nevertheless he could be quite frightening sometimes. Like now.

Paice strode to the side and stared at the surging wake as it lifted and curled over the lee bulwark.

Was he any better than Vatass, and was this only a gesture? He raised his face into the swirling flakes and stinging wind. He knew that was not so. Without Bolitho the ship even felt different. Just months ago Paice would never have believed that he would have stood his ship into jeopardy in this fashion. And all because of a man. An ordinary man.

He heard muffled cries from above the deck, and guessed that some new cordage and whipping were

315

being run up to the masthead for their numbed hands to work on.

He shook his head as if he was in pain. No, he was never an ordinary man.

Paice's wife had been a schoolmaster's daughter and had taught her bluff sea-officer a great deal. She had introduced him to words he had never known. His life until she entered it had been rough, tough ships and men to match them. He smiled sadly, reminiscently, into the snow. No wonder her family had raised their hands in horror when she had told them of her intention to marry him.

He tried again. What was the word she had used? He nodded, satisfied at last. *Charisma*. Bolitho had it, and probably did not even guess.

He thought of Bolitho's mission and wondered why nobody had listened to him when he had spoken his mind on Sir James Tanner. Like a hopeless crusade. It had been the same between Delaval and Paice himself: not just a fight between the forces of law and corruption, but something personal. Nobody had listened to him, either. They had been *sorry*, of course—he felt the old flame of anger returning. How would they have felt if their wives had been murdered like . . . He stopped himself. He could not bear even to use her name in the same company.

Now Delaval was dead. Paice had watched him on that clear day, every foot of the way to the scaffold. He had heard no voices, no abuse or ironic cheering from the crowd who had come to be entertained. God, he thought, if they held a mass torture session on the village green there would not be room to sit down.

He had spoken to Delaval silently on that day. Had cursed his name, damned him in an afterlife where he hoped he would suffer, as he had forced so many others to do.

Paice was not a cruel man, but he had felt cheated by the brevity of the execution. Long after the crowd had broken up he had stood in a doorway and watched Delaval's corpse swinging in the breeze. If he had known where it was to be hung in chains as a gruesome warning to other felons, he knew he would have gone there too.

He looked up, caught off balance as a dark shape fell past the mainsail, hit the bulwark and vanished over the side. Just those few seconds, but he had heard the awful scream, the crack as the living body had broken on the impact before disappearing outboard.

Scrope the master-at-arms came running aft. "It was Morrison, sir!"

The thing changed to a real person. A bright-eyed seaman from Gillingham, who had quit fishing and signed on with a recruiting party after his parents had died of fever.

Nobody spoke, not even the youthful Triscott. Even he knew that it was impossible to turn the cutter or lie-to in this sea. Even if they succeeded they would never find the man named Morrison. It was a sailor's lot. They sang of it in the dogwatches below, in the ale shops and the dockside whorehouses. Rough and crude they might be, but to Paice they were the only real people.

He said harshly, "Send another man aloft. I want that work finished, and lively with it!"

Some would curse his name for his methods, but most of them would understand. *A sailor's lot.*

Paice stamped his feet on the deck to bring back

some warmth and feeling. He wanted to think about Bolitho, what steps he should take next if they failed to find him when daylight came. But all he could think of was the man who had just been chosen to die. For that was what he and most sailors thought. *When your name is called.* He gripped a backstay and felt it jerking and shivering in his fingers. All he had to do was lose his handhold. How would he feel then, as his ship vanished into the night, and he was left to choke and drown?

He came out of his brooding and snapped, "I'm going below. Call me if—"

Triscott stared at his leaning shadow. "Aye, aye, sir."

Paice stumbled into the cabin and slammed the door shut behind him. He stared at the other bunk and remembered Allday's model ship, the bond which seemed to shine between those two men.

He spoke to the cabin at large. "I must find him!" He glanced at the battered Bible in its rack but dismissed the idea immediately. That could wait. Charisma was enough for one watch.

On the deck above, Triscott watched the comings and goings of men up and down the treacherous ratlines. In a few weeks' time he would be twenty years old. And now it was war. Only after he had seen and spoken with Bolitho had he grasped some inkling of what war, especially at sea, might mean. Paice had hinted that their lordships at the far-off Admiralty would be pruning out trained officers and men from every ship which had been fully employed. Why, he wondered, had they not kept a powerful fleet in commission if they knew war was coming?

Hawkins strode aft and said gruffly, "All done, sir.

The blacking-down will have to wait till this lot's over."

Triscott had to shout over the hiss and patter of water. "Morrison never stood a chance, Mr. Hawkins!"

The boatswain wiped his thick fingers on some rags and eyed him grimly. "I 'ope that made 'im feel better, sir."

Triscott watched his burly shape melt into the gloom and sighed.

Another Paice.

Figures groped through the forward hatch and others slithered thankfully into the damp darkness of the messdeck as the watches changed. Dench, the master's mate, was taking over the morning watch and was muttering to Chesshyre, probably discussing the failings of their lieutenants.

Triscott went below and lay fully clothed on the bunk, the one which Bolitho had used.

From the darkness Paice asked, "All right up top?"

Triscott smiled to himself. Worrying about his *Telemachus.* He never stopped.

"Dench is doing well with the watch, sir."

Paice said fiercely, "If I could just make one sighting at first light." But he heard a gentle snore from the opposite side.

Paice closed his eyes and thought about his wife. He had the word *charisma* on his lips when he, too, fell into an uneasy sleep.

The morning, when it came, was brighter than even Chesshyre had prophesied. A bitter wind which made the sails glisten with ice-rime, and goaded every man's resistance to the limit.

Paice came on deck and consulted the chart and

319

Chesshyre's slate beside the compass box. They did not always agree, but Paice knew Chesshyre was good at his work. It was enough.

He looked up at the curving topmast, the streaming white spear of the long masthead pendant. Wind on the quarter. So they had to be doubly careful. If they covered too many miles they would be hard-put to beat back again for another attempt to seek out the missing cutter.

Paice thought about Queely and wondered if in fact he had found Bolitho for the second part of their hazy plan. *Wakeful* might be in enemy hands. His mind hung on the word. *Enemy*. It somehow changed everything. Perhaps Bolitho was taken too, or worse.

He pounded his hands together. Bolitho should never have been sent to Kent, for recruiting, if that was truly the reason, and certainly not for a wild scheme like this one.

He should be in command of a real man-of-war. A captain others would follow; whose subordinates would learn more than the rudiments of battle but also the need for humility.

Triscott came aft from inspecting the overnight repairs and splicing, a boatswain's mate close at his heels. He looked even younger in this grey light, Paice thought. His face all fresh and burned with cold.

Triscott touched his hat, testing his commander's mood. "All secure, sir." He waited, noting the strain and deep lines on Paice's features. "I've had the gunner put men to work on the six-pounder tackles. The ice and snow have jammed every block."

Paice nodded absently. "As well you noticed." The usual hesitation. Then, "Good."

Paice turned to the master's muffled figure beside the tiller. "What do you make of the weather, Mr. Chesshyre?"

Triscott saw them face one another, more like adversaries than men who served together in this tiny, cramped community.

Chesshyre accepted the flag of truce.

"It should be clear and fine, sir." He pointed across the bulwark, below which some men were man-handling one of the stocky six-pounders behind its sealed port.

"See yonder, sir? Patch o' blue!"

Paice sighed. Nobody had mentioned it, but there was no sign of *Snapdragon*.

Triscott saw him glance at the masthead and said, "I've put a good man up there, sir."

Paice exclaimed, "Did I ask you?" He shrugged heavily. "Forgive me. It is wrong to use authority on those who cannot strike back."

Triscott kept his face immobile. *Bolitho's words.* He was still fretting about it. He offered, "There is a lot of mist, sir. In this wind—"

Paice stared at him. "Did you hear?"

Chesshyre dragged the hood from over his salt-matted hair.

"I did!"

Men stood motionless at their many and varied tasks, as if frozen so. The cook halfway through the hatch on his way to prepare something hot, or at least warm, for the watchkeepers. Big Luke Hawkins, a marlinspike gripped in one iron-hard hand, his eyes alert, remembering perhaps. Maddock the carpenter, clutching his old hat to his wispy hair as he paused in measuring some timber he had brought from the

321

hold for some particular task. Chesshyre and Triscott, even Godsalve the clerk, acting purser and, when required, a fair hand as a tailor, all waited and listened in the chilling air.

Paice said abruptly, "Six-pounders, eh, Mr. Hawkins?"

His voice seemed to break the spell, so that men began to move again, staring about them as if they could not recall what they had been doing.

Triscott suggested, "Maybe it's *Wakeful*, sir."

Chesshyre rubbed his unshaven chin. "Or *Snapdragon*?"

The air seemed to quiver, so that some of the men working below deck felt the distant explosion beat into the lower hull as if *Telemachus* had been fired on.

Paice wanted to lick his lips but knew some of the seamen were watching him. Gun by gun, booming across the water.

He clenched his fingers into fists. He wanted to yell up to the masthead lookout, but knew the man needed no persuading. Triscott had chosen him specially. He would be the first to hail the deck when he could see something.

Paice heard the boatswain's mate murmur, "Could be either, I suppose."

He thrust his hands beneath his coat-tails to hide them from view.

The regular explosions boomed across the sea's face once again, and he said, "Whoever it is, they're facing the enemy's iron *this* day!"

Spray burst over *Wakeful*'s weather side and flooded down the steeply sloping deck. Even the most experienced hands aboard had to cling to something as the hull laid hard over until to any novice it would seem she must turn turtle.

Queely yelled, "She's close as she'll answer, sir!" His salt-reddened eyes peered at the huge mainsail, then at the foresail and jib. Each one was sheeted hard-in until they were laid almost fore-and-aft down the cutter's centre line, forcing her into the wind, every other piece of canvas lashed into submission.

Bolitho did not have time to consult the compass but guessed that Queely had swung *Wakeful* some five points into the wind; the lee gunports were awash, and the water seemed to boil as she plunged across the lively crests. When he looked for the brigantine she already seemed a long way astern, her sails retrimmed while she bore away on the opposite tack.

As he had been hauled aboard Bolitho had said, "We must stand between *La Revanche* and the Frenchman. The brigantine is fast enough, and given time she might reach safety, or at least lie beneath a coastal battery until help can be sent."

He had seen Queely's quick understanding. No talk of victory, no empty promise of survival. They were to save the brigantine, and they would pay the price.

Bolitho stared up at the masthead as the lookout yelled, "Corvette, sir!"

Queely grimaced. "Twenty guns at least." He looked away. "I keep seeing Kempthorne. I used him badly. That is hard to forgive."

Bolitho saw Allday moving carefully aft from the forehatch, his cutlass thrust through his belt. The words seemed to repeat themselves. *Of one company.*

Queely watched the sails shaking and banging, taking the full thrust of the wind.

He said, "Must have veered some more. From the north, I'd say." He puffed out his cheeks. "It feels like it too!"

They all heard the sudden crack of cannon fire, and then the lookout shouted, "Sail closin' the corvette, sir!"

There were more shots, the sounds spiteful over the lively wave crests.

Queely said guardedly, "Small guns, sir." He glanced at his men along either side, drenched with spray and flying spindrift, trying to protect their powder and flintlocks. "Like ours."

Bolitho frowned. It would be just like Paice. Coming to look for them. He tensed as a measured broadside thundered across the water. He saw the sea-mist waver and twist high above the surface, and for those few moments the other vessel was laid bare. Even without a telescope he saw the lithe silhouette of a square-rigged man-of-war, gunsmoke fanning downwind from her larboard battery. The other vessel was beyond her, but there was no mistaking the great mainsail, its boom sweeping across the waves as she bore down on the French corvette.

Bolitho gritted his teeth. The corvette was like a small frigate, and probably mounted only nine-pounders. But against a cutter she was a leviathan.

Queely yelled, "Another point!"

The helmsman shouted, "West-Nor'-West, sir!" He did not have to add that she was as close to the wind as she had ever sailed; there was hardly a man who could stand upright.

Bolitho said, "Bring her about." He saw Queely's indecision. "If we turn back, we may stand across his course, and still have time to turn again."

Bangs echoed against the hull as Queely yelled, "Stand by to come about! *Let go and haul!*"

As the helm went over, the cutter seemed to rise towards the sky, her bowsprit and flapping jib lifting and lifting until the sea boiled over the side and swept aft like breakers. Men fell cursing and gasping, others seized their friends and dragged them to their feet as the receding water tried to sweep them over the bulwarks.

But she was answering, and as she swayed over on the opposite tack Bolitho felt like cheering, even though each minute was one gone from his life.

Queely shouted, "Hold her! Steady as you go!" He beckoned frantically—"Two more hands on the tiller!"

The master glared at him, then called, "Steady she is, sir! East by North!"

Bolitho snatched up a glass and sought out the corvette.

There she was, now on the larboard quarter, as if their whole world had pivoted round. *La Revanche* was almost lost in mist and spray, standing away as fast as she could. Queely's master's mate had even managed to set her topsail and royal.

He waited for the deck to steady again and tried to ignore the bustle of figures around and past him as the mainsail was sheeted home on the opposite tack.

He trained the glass with care and saw the corvette fire again, the smoke momentarily blotting her out but not before he had found the other cutter, and had seen the sea around her bursting with waterspouts and falling spray. The cutter was still pressing closer, and he saw her side flash with bright orange tongues as she fired her small broadside.

Queely said savagely, "Vatass has no chance at that range, damn it!" He saw the question in Bolitho's eyes and explained, "It's him. *Snapdragon* has a darker jib than the rest of us." He winced as another fall of shot appeared to bracket the cutter. But *Snapdragon* pushed through the falling curtain of spray, her guns still firing, although, as Queely suspected, it was doubtful if a single ball would reach the French corvette.

Bolitho tried to ignore the twisting shape of the cutter and concentrated on the enemy. She was maintaining the same tack as before and steering almost south-east. Her captain had seen *La Revanche* and would let nothing stand in his way.

Queely exclaimed, "*Snapdragon* must have sighted us, sir!" He sounded incredulous as he raised his glass again, his lips moving as he identified the pinpricks of colour which had broken from *Snapdragon*'s topsail yard.

He said hoarsely, "Signal reads, *Enemy in sight*, sir!"

Bolitho looked at him, sharing his sudden emotion. It was Vatass's way of telling them that they were at war. Trying to warn him before it was too late.

Bolitho said, "Run up another flag." He looked along the crowded deck, at the men who waited for the inevitable. "It will give him heart!"

With two White Ensigns streaming from gaff and masthead, *Wakeful* prepared to come about yet again. The manoeuvre would stand her across the enemy's path and make it impossible for the corvette to avoid an embrace. Once in close action, *Snapdragon* might be able to attack her stern, with luck even rake her with a carronade as she crossed her wake. He held his breath as a hole punched through *Snapdragon*'s topsail and the wind tore it to ribbons before it could be reefed.

The corvette fired again, each broadside perfectly timed. No wonder this captain had been selected for the task, Bolitho thought. He raised the glass, but mist and gunsmoke made it impossible to see the horizon.

He looked at Allday by the compass box. *Where is Paice?*

Allday saw his expression and tried to smile. But all he could think of was the man-of-war which was closing on them with every sail set and filled to the wind. He looked at the men on *Wakeful*'s deck. Popguns against nine-pounders, an open deck with no gangways or packed hammock nettings to protect them from the splinters. How would they face up to it? Would they see there was nothing but death at the end of it?

He thought of Lieutenant Kempthorne and all the others he had seen drop in a sea-fight. Proud, brave men for the most part, who had whimpered and screamed when they were cut down. The lucky ones died then and there, and were spared the agony of a surgeon's knife.

Here there was not even a sawbones. Maybe that was all to the good. Allday watched Bolitho's fingers close around the sword at his side. It had to end somewhere, so why not here?

He winced as the guns thundered yet again, closer still, the shots churning the sea into jagged crests, or whipping off the white horses like invisible dolphins at play.

He tried to think of his time in London, the nights

in Maggie's tiny room, with her buxom body pressed against his in the darkness. Perhaps one day—the guns roared out across the shortening range and he heard several of the watching seamen give groans of dismay.

Queely shouted harshly, "Stand to, damn you! Prepare to come about! Topmen aloft, lively now!"

Bolitho heard the edge in his voice. Its finality. It was not even going to be a battle this time.

Lieutenant Paice yelled at the masthead, *"Repeat that!"* The last roll of cannon fire had drowned the man's voice.

The lookout shouted, *"Snapdragon's* signallin', sir! *Enemy in sight!"*

Paice released his breath very slowly. Thank God for a good lookout. It was what they had planned should they find *Wakeful*. Where she was, so would be Bolitho.

Paice lifted his glass and saw the mist moving aside, even the smoke thinning to its persistent thrust. He saw the French vessel some two miles directly ahead, framed in *Telemachus's* shrouds as if in a net. She was running with the wind directly under her coat-tails, her sails iron-hard. Paice saw *Snapdragon* for the first time, her frail outline just overlapping the enemy's quarter and surrounded by bursting spray from that last fall of shot. Her topsail had been shredded, and there were several holes in her main-sail; otherwise she appeared to be untouched, and as he peered through the glass until his eyes watered he saw Vatass's guns returning fire, their progress marked by thin tendrils of foam, well short of a target.

There was another vessel moving away from the embattled ships. Paice guessed it was either an unwilling spectator, or the one Bolitho was expected to escort back to England. Then he saw *Wakeful*, sweeping out of the mist, her sails flapping then filling as she completed her tack and swung once more towards the enemy.

Triscott broke into his thoughts. "Why does the Frog stay on that tack, sir? I'd go for *Snapdragon*, if I were her commander, and lessen the odds. He must surely see us by now?"

Somebody dropped a handspike and Paice was about to shout a reprimand when he remembered what Triscott had told him about the six-pounders.

"The Frenchman has been under way all night, up and down, searching for Captain Bolitho, I suspect. My guess is that her running rigging is so swollen she can barely change tack—her blocks are probably frozen solid!" He gestured towards *Telemachus*'s spread of canvas. "Here the wind does the work for us." There was contempt in his tone. "Over yonder even musclepower won't shift those yards until the day warms up!" He sounded excited. "So they'll have to reef, or stand and fight!"

There was a great sigh from some of the hands and Paice saw *Snapdragon* stagger as some of the enemy's balls slammed home. But she came upright again and pressed on with her attack.

Paice swore angrily. "Fall back, you young fool!" He swung on Triscott. "Set the stuns'ls and shake out every reef! I want this cutter to *fly!*"

As the studding-sail booms were run out from the yard, the mast bent forward under the additional strain. The sea seemed to rush down either beam, so

329

that some of the gun crews stood up and cheered without knowing why.

Paice folded his arms and studied the other vessels. *Hounds around a stag.* He swallowed hard as the tall waterspouts shot skyward along *Snapdragon*'s engaged side. The damage was hidden from view, but Paice saw rigging curling and parting, then, slowly at first, the tall mainmast began to reel down into the smoke. In the sudden lull of firing he heard the thundering crash of the mast and spars sweeping over the forecastle, tearing men and guns in its wake of trailing shrouds and rigging until with a great splash it swayed over the bows like a fallen tree. Tiny figures appeared through the wreckage where nobody should have been left alive, and in the weak sunlight Paice saw the gleam of axes as Vatass's men hacked at the broken rigging, or fought their way to messmates trapped underneath.

Some of the corvette's larboard battery must have been trained as far round in their ports as they could bear. Paice watched through his glass and saw the shadows of the enemy's guns lengthen against the hull as they were levered towards the quarter. He shifted his horrified stare to *Snapdragon*. It was impossible to see her as another graceful cutter. She was a listing, mastless wreck already down by the bows, her shattered jolly-boat drifting away from the side amidst the flotsam of planking and torn canvas.

Triscott exclaimed in a strangled voice, "They'd not fire on her now!"

The after divisions of guns belched out flame and smoke together. It was like a single, heart-stopping explosion. Paice could even feel the weight of the iron's strength as *Snapdragon* was swept from bow to

330

stern, timber, decking, men and pieces of men flung into the air like grisly rubbish. When it finally fell it pockmarked the sea with white feathers, strangely gentle in the pale sunlight.

Snapdragon began to capsize, her broken hull surrounded by huge, obscene bubbles.

Paice watched with his glass. He did not want to forget it, and knew he never would.

He saw the deck tilting towards him, a corpse in a lieutenant's coat sliding through blood and splinters, then rising up against the bulwark as if to offer a last command. Then *Snapdragon* gave a groan, as if she was the one who was dying, and disappeared beneath the whirlpool of pathetic fragments.

Paice found that he was sucking in the bitter air as if he had just been running. His head swam, and he wanted to roar and bellow like a bull. But nothing came. It was too terrible even for that.

When he spoke again his voice was almost calm.

He said, "All guns load, double-shotted!" He sought out Triscott by the mast; his face was as white as a sheet. "Did you see that? The Frenchie made no attempt to bear up on—" he hesitated, unable to say the name of the ship he had just seen destroyed. Vatass, so keen and unworldly, hoping for promotion, wiped away like the master's calculations on his slate. *Because of me. I forced him to put to sea.* He faced Triscott again. "She'd have been in irons if she had. I reckon her running rigging is frozen as solid as a rock!"

Triscott wiped his lips with the back of his hand. "But how long—"

He was close to vomiting.

"It don't matter, and it don't signify, Mr. Triscott!

331

We'll rake that bugger an' maybe Captain Bolitho can put a ball or two through *him!*"

Triscott nodded. "Prepare to shorten sail!" He was glad of something to do. Anything which might hold back the picture of *Snapdragon*'s terrible death. It was like watching his own fate in a nightmare.

Paice moved aft and joined Chesshyre beside the helmsmen. From here he could see the full length and breadth of his small command. Within the hour she might share *Snapdragon*'s grave. He was surprised that he could face the prospect without pain. His fate, his *lot* would be decided for him. There was no choice open to any one of them.

He saw the master-at-arms and Glynn, a boatswain's mate, passing out cutlasses and axes from the chest, and below the raked mast another handful of men were loading muskets under the watchful eye of a gunner's mate. It kept them busy as the enemy vessel grew in size, lying in their path like a glistening barricade. He saw the gunner's mate gesturing towards the mast, doubtless explaining that a good marksman could play havoc with men crowded together on a ship's deck. He had picked the men himself, each one an excellent shot.

Paice nodded as if in agreement; a seaman called Inskip had held up his fist and then hurried to the weather shrouds. A good choice. Inskip had been a poacher in Norfolk before he had found his way into the navy by way of the local assizes.

Chesshyre said dryly, "Better him than me, sir."

Paice knew that Inskip would be more than mindful of *Snapdragon*'s mast plunging down into the sea. Nobody working aloft or around it would have survived. The corvette's captain had made certain of those who had.

Chesshyre muttered, *"My God!"*

Paice walked to the side as *Telemachus*'s stem smashed through some drifting wreckage. A torn jacket, what looked like a chart, splinters as thick as fingers, and the inevitable corpses, bobbing and reeling aside as *Telemachus* surged through them.

He said roughly, "I'll lay odds you wish you was in the East India Company!"

A puff of smoke drifted from the corvette's side, and seconds later a ball sliced across the sea before hurling up a waterspout half-a-cable beyond the bows.

Paice growled, "Close enough, Mr. Chesshyre." He crossed to the compass box and peered at the card. "Bring her up two points." He eyed him impassively. "We'll go for his flanks, eh?"

Chesshyre nodded, angry with himself because his teeth were chattering uncontrollably.

He said, "Ready aft! Put the helm down! Steer South by West!" Then he watched as the corvette showed herself beyond the shrouds as if she had only now begun to move.

Paice watched the enemy loose off another shot, but it was well clear.

Shorten sail or stand and fight.

He saw *Wakeful*'s jib and foresail hardening on the new tack, the canvas clean and pale in the early sunshine.

Chesshyre called, "We don't even know why we're here!"

Paice did not turn on him. He knew Chesshyre was afraid, and he needed him now as never before.

"D'you need a reason, then?"

Chesshyre thought of *Snapdragon*, the corpses bobbing around her like gutted fish.

Paice was right. In the end it would make no difference.

17

Ships Of War

BOLITHO mopped his streaming face for the hundredth time and watched *Wakeful*'s seamen sheeting the mainsail home, while others swarmed aloft in the freezing wind to execute the next command.

Yet again *Wakeful* had fought round in a tight arc to her original course, with the approaching corvette lying directly across the starboard bow. The enemy would have the wind-gage, but for *Wakeful*'s small guns it might be their only advantage.

"*Loose tops'l!*" Queely was everywhere, never more acutely aware of Kempthorne's loss.

Bolitho could see it, the gangling lieutenant swinging around, the gaping hole in his throat. Then nothing. He plucked the sodden shirt away from his skin, another reminder of the man who had stopped a ball which had been intended for him.

Queely came aft again, his chest heaving. "What now, sir?"

Bolitho pointed to the scarred jolly-boat. "Drop it outboard."

The boatswain glanced at Queely as if for confirmation. Queely nodded curtly. "Do it!"

Bolitho watched the spare hands hoisting the boat up and over the lee bulwark. Like all sailors they were reluctant, fearful even of letting go of their only boat. Bolitho knew from experience it would have been the same had there been ten times as many people in the company, and still only one boat. Always the last hope.

Queely understood although he lacked experience of it.

He was saying, "We'll have enough splinters flying about before too long, man!"

Bolitho waited for the boatswain to hurry away to tend to some frayed rigging. The choppy sea and freezing wind could play havoc with even the best cordage.

He glanced around the deck. "Have all the hammocks brought up and lashed around the after gratings. It will give the helmsmen some protection." He did not add that an unprotected deck could be swept into a bloody shambles by one well-aimed burst of grape. It gave every man something to do. After *Snapdragon*'s destruction they needed to be busy even in the face of the oncoming corvette.

La Revanche had seemingly vanished, tacking back and forth, each precious minute taking her away from the drifting smoke which still floated above the sea where *Snapdragon* had dived for the bottom.

They had not been able to see much of the encounter, but the broadside which had followed *Snapdragon*'s last futile shots had stunned all of them.

Bolitho saw Allday supervising the stacking and lashing of the tightly lashed hammocks. In battle, even a strip of canvas gave an impression of safety to those denied protection.

Allday crossed to his side and said, "She'll be up to us in twenty minutes, Cap'n." He sounded unusually desperate. "What can we hit her with?"

"*Telemachus* has run out her stuns'ls, sir!" Another voice muttered, "Gawd! Watch 'er go!"

Bolitho saw the other cutter surging across the diagonal ranks of angry white horses, her hull dominated by her sails, her stem and forecastle rising and dipping in great banks of bursting spray.

Bolitho took a telescope and rested it against Allday's shoulder. It took time to train it on *Telemachus* and as soon as he had found her he saw one empty gunport, like a missing tooth. Paice had forgotten none of the things Bolitho had brought to their small flotilla. He was at this moment man-handling his second carronade over to larboard so that both could be laid on the corvette.

The enemy fired again, but the ball fell outside his vision. It was strange that the corvette did not alter course just long enough to pour a full broadside on the approaching cutter. It was unlikely that such a compact man-of-war would mount stern-chasers, and she could not fail to miss as the range dwindled away between the two vessels.

Queely shouted, "She's coming for us, sir!"

Bolitho watched the corvette. She was almost bows-on now, her canvas tall above *Wakeful*'s starboard bow. He could see her flag whipping from the gaff, and was glad Brennier had at least been spared that.

"Shall I shorten, sir?" Queely was watching him, as if trying to shut out the menace of the oncoming enemy.

"No. Speed is all we have. Hold her on this tack, then put the helm up when we cross their path. We can luff, but only with speed in the sails!" He looked along the crouching gun crews. "I suggest you bring the men from the larboard battery." Their eyes met

337

and Bolitho added gently, "I fear we will take heavy losses if they manage to rake us. The weather bulwark will give them some cover at least."

A whistle shrilled and the men scampered across from the other battery. They ran half-crouching as if already under fire, their faces stiff and pinched, and suddenly aged.

Queely made himself turn and stare at the corvette. He said, "Why does she hold so straight a path?"

Bolitho thought he knew. In this icy north wind and after the snow and sleet it was likely that every piece of her rigging was packed solid. It was also possible that the corvette had spent most of the past months in harbour while the loyalty or otherwise of France's sea-officers was decided. Her company would be unused to this kind of work. *Wakeful*'s company was also new to it, but each and every hand was a prime seaman. It was pointless to mention his thoughts to Queely. It might offer a gleam of hope where there was none to be had. If the corvette was able to destroy or cripple the remaining cutters she could still chase and catch *La Revanche* before she reached a place of safety.

He hardened his heart. It was their sole reason for being here. To delay this enemy ship no matter what.

Bolitho raised the telescope again and saw *Telemachus*'s topsail yard brace round, her hull merge then vanish beyond the corvette. Above the sounds of sea and wind he heard the faint crackle of musket fire, the harder bang of a swivel.

Then there was a double explosion and for a moment longer Bolitho imagined that the corvette did after all carry stern-chasers, and had fired directly into the cutter as she veered wildly across her quarter.

Queely muttered thickly, "Hell, he's damned close!"

Bolitho saw smoke billow over the corvette's poop and knew Paice had fired both of his carronades into her stern. If one of those murderous balls managed to pierce the crowded gundeck it would keep them occupied until *Wakeful* was able to engage.

He heard the crack of Paice's six-pounders and saw a hole appear in the enemy's main topsail, some rigging part and stream out in the wind. But she was still coming, and Bolitho could see the details of her beakhead without the need of a glass, the white painted figure beneath it holding some sort of branch in one outthrust hand.

"Stand by on deck!" Queely swung round, his eyes angry as if searching for Kempthorne. He saw Bolitho watching him and gave a small shrug, but it said everything.

Then he drew his hanger and held it above his head. "We fire on the uproll, my lads!"

Bolitho saw their despairing faces. The way they pressed close together, friend with friend, waiting to fight and die.

The corvette was sliding across the starboard quarter, and marksmen were already firing from her forecastle, one insolently straddling a cathead with his legs to obtain a better aim.

A musket banged out from below the mast and Bolitho saw the Frenchman hurl his weapon into the sea below as if it had become red-hot, before toppling from the cathead and plunging down the side.

Allday muttered, "Good shot, matey!"

339

The tiller went over and as blocks squealed and the forecourse and topsail yards were hauled taut, *Wakeful* seemed to pivot round to windward when minutes before it had seemed she would be run down by the enemy.

"*Fire!*" The six-pounders cracked out in a ragged salvo, the double-shotted muzzles spitting their orange tongues as the trucks squealed inboard on their tackles.

Queely yelled, "*Stand fast!*" He waved down some of the gun crews who were about to sponge out and reload. "*Take cover!*" The hanger gleamed in the smoky sunshine as Queely signalled to the carronade crew. "*As you bear!*" The gun captain jerked his lanyard and the ugly, snub-nosed "smasher" lurched back on its slide, the heavy ball exploding against the corvette's gangway, blasting one of the nine-pounders from its port, and flinging splintered woodwork and ripped hammocks over the side.

Bolitho watched the corvette's exposed battery recoil. The two attacks had broken their timing, and the broadside was ragged, each one firing independently.

Bolitho tensed as a ball smacked through the mainsail and another parted some rigging and struck the sea far abeam. One gun had been loaded with grape and canister and Bolitho ducked as the charge exploded over the maindeck, hurling shattered planking into the air, and thudding into the opposite bulwark where the gun crews would otherwise have been crouching.

Queely shouted, "Reload!" He stared wildly at his men. Not one had been hit, although a splintered piece of wood had been hurled into the hammocks around the helmsmen with the accuracy of a spear.

And there was *Telemachus*. As *Wakeful* charged past the enemy's poop, they all saw the other cutter tacking around to follow the corvette on the same course.

It took longer to bring *Wakeful* about and under control again. With so much sail, it was like trying to slow a runaway team of horses. The corvette lay directly ahead of them, with the cutters using wind and rudder to hold station on either quarter as if they were escorting her rather than forcing another engagement.

The corvette's captain seemed unwilling to wear ship and confront them. But the cutters were unable to damage the enemy vessel without overhauling her. And the next time the French captain would be ready.

Bolitho watched Paice manoeuvring his cutter closer and closer, the occasional stab of musket fire exchanged between the ill-matched vessels. *Telemachus* had been badly mauled, and Bolitho had seen there was a hole punched through her hull, just a few feet above the waterline, before she had changed tack to continue her attack.

Sunlight flashed across the corvette's stern-windows and Bolitho raised his glass to read the name painted on her counter.

La Foi. So the girl's figurehead must be Faith. In the stained lens he saw heads moving on the corvette's poop, the flash of muskets, an officer pointing with his speaking trumpet. He also saw the massive scars on her lower hull where one of Paice's carronades had found its mark. A foot or so higher and—he stiffened

341

as two of the stern-windows shattered and pitched into the vessel's frothing wake.

For one more moment he thought a lucky shot had hit the stern, although reason told him that none of Paice's guns would yet bear.

Then he stared with sick realisation as another window was smashed out, and the black muzzle of a nine-pounder thrust into view.

"Signal *Telemachus* to stand away!" Bolitho had to seize Queely's arm to make him realise what was happening. "They'll blow him out of the water!"

But *Wakeful* was a good cable's length astern of Paice's cutter, and nobody aboard was bothering to look and see what she was doing. Paice had at last realised what was happening. Bolitho saw the yards coming round, the mainsail suddenly free and flapping wildly as Paice let her sway over while she took the wind across her beam.

Bolitho watched anxiously. Paice was doing what he thought was best. Lose the wind, but stand away from the onrushing *Wakeful* and so avoid a collision.

Bolitho snapped, "We'll engage to larboard!" He did not want to take his eyes from the two vessels ahead, but needed to watch the mast and bulging topsail. *Wakeful* was tearing through the waves; the mast must be curving forward under such a pressure and weight of canvas and spars.

He turned his head, and at that very moment *La Foi* fired her hastily-rigged stern-chaser.

Queely shouted, "More grape!" He wiped his eyes wildly. "She's still answering, sir!"

Telemachus was certainly under command, but her sails were pockmarked with holes, and, as he lifted his glass again, Bolitho saw bodies on her deck, a man

342

on his knees as if he was praying, before he too fell lifeless.

He wanted to look away but watched as two thin threads of scarlet ran from the washports to merge with the creaming sea alongside. Like seeing a ship bleeding to death, as if there was no human hand aboard.

Wakeful's men were staring over the bulwark, the gun crews from the opposite side hurrying to join their comrades for the next embrace.

Bolitho said, "It'll take time to load and train that gun with makeshift tackles." He looked at Queely, his gaze calm. "We must be up to her before she can use it on us."

They bore down on *Telemachus* and Bolitho saw men working like demons at halliards and braces, others clawing their way up broken ratlines to discard or repair damaged rigging.

He saw a lieutenant amongst some fallen rigging and knew it was Triscott. Then right aft near the tiller, Paice's tall figure, with one hand thrust inside his coat. He might have injured it, Bolitho thought, but it was somehow reassuring to see him there, in his place. As *Wakeful* swept past Bolitho saw Paice turn and look across the tumbling waves, then very slowly raise his hat. It was strangely moving, and some of *Wakeful*'s men raised a ragged cheer.

Allday stepped nearer, his cutlass over his shoulder while he watched the other ship's stern rise above the larboard bow. He had been a gun captain himself aboard the old *Resolution* before he had met up with Bolitho. But then Allday had turned his hand to most things.

He knew better than most that if they overhauled

the French ship they would be destroyed by her main battery. At close quarters like this, *Wakeful* would be pounded to fragments in minutes. Their only hope of delaying the corvette long enough to be worthwhile was to hit her with a carronade with no chance of a miss. For if they remained on the enemy's quarter, the improvised stern-chaser would finish them just as brutally.

He saw a musket fire from the French ship and heard a spent ball slap into the deck nearby. In minutes, each ball could be deadly, and he stood close to Bolitho, just so that he would know he was here when it happened.

Bolitho said, "I would that we were in *Tempest*, old friend." He spoke quietly, so that Allday could barely hear him above the chorus of wind and sea.

He added in the same unemotional voice, "I shall always remember her."

Allday watched him grimly. Who did he mean? *Tempest* or his lady, Viola?

He heard Queely shouting to his gun crews, saw a terrified ship's boy dash past with fresh charges for the six-pounders, and one of the seamen of the boatswain's party staring at the deck, his lips moving as though in prayer, or repeating someone's name.

He saw all and none of it. Bolitho had shared something with him, as he always did.

Allday lifted his chin and saw a movement in the corvette's stern-windows. It was almost over. He stared up at the sky. *Please God, let it be quick!*

Lieutenant Andrew Triscott tore his eyes from *Wakeful*'s straining sails and made himself turn inboard again. He had thought he was prepared for

344

this, had trained himself to accept the inevitable when it came. Instead he could only stare at the utter chaos on *Telemachus*'s deck, fallen rigging and scorched pieces of canvas, and worst of all the blood which ran unchecked into the scuppers. He had never believed there could be so much blood.

Faces he had come to know, some dead, others screwed up in agony, like strangers.

He heard Paice's strong voice forcing through the noise and confusion. "Clear those men from the guns!"

Triscott nodded, still unable to speak. He clung to Paice's strength like a drowning man groping for a piece of flotsam in the sea. He saw Chesshyre by the tiller, two helmsmen down, one gasping with pain as his companion tied a rough bandage around his arm to staunch the bleeding. Triscott retched helplessly. The second man was headless, and he saw some of his blood and bone spattered across Paice's breeches.

The boatswain swam into Triscott's blurred vision, his face smeared with powder smoke, his eyes like coals.

"You all right, sir?" He did not wait for an answer. "I'll muster some spare 'ands!"

Triscott stared round, half-expecting to find nobody alive, but Paice's powerful voice and the burly boatswain's angry gestures with a boarding axe brought them from cover, while others dragged themselves from beneath fallen sails and cordage. Obedient even in the face of death, from fear or from habit, or because they did not know how else to act.

Triscott lurched away from the bulwark and saw some of the bloodied corpses being dropped over the side. The wounded were taken to the main hatch or

345

aft to the companionway, their cries and screams ignored as they were hauled to some kind of safety.

Triscott had seen Paice raise his hat to the other cutter, and wondered how he could stand there, with the ship shaking herself apart around him.

Paice seemed to read his mind from half the deck's length away.

He shouted, "Stand to the guns again, Mr. Triscott! Point the carronades yourself!"

Triscott realised that he was still gripping his hanger, the one his father had given him when he had passed for lieutenant.

He saw the gunner's body being toppled over the side. A dour but dedicated man, who had helped Triscott many times when he had learned the ways of handling the cutter's weapons. Now he was drifting away from the hull, no longer a face at gun-drill, or yelling threats to his own special party of seamen. Triscott stuffed his fist into his mouth to prevent himself from crying out aloud.

Hawkins rejoined him and said harshly, "It's up to you, sir." He regarded him steadily and without sympathy. "We must engage again. *Wakeful*'s trying to close with the enemy. She'll never manage unsupported!"

Triscott stared aft, seeking the aid which had always been there.

Hawkins said flatly, "You'll get no 'elp there, Mr. Triscott. 'E's badly wounded." He watched his words sink in and added relentlessly, "The master's as scared as shite, 'e'll not be much use." He stood back, forcing himself to ignore the shouts and demands which came from every side. He had to make Triscott understand if only for a moment longer. *"You're* the lieutenant, *sir."*

Triscott stared at Paice who was gripping the compass box, one hand still thrust inside his coat. His eyes were tightly shut, his teeth bared as if to bite back the pain. Then he saw the blood which had soaked the left side of Paice's breeches, all the way from beneath his coat to the deck around him. He had been hit in the side.

Hawkins persisted, "Took a piece of iron the size of three fingers in his ribs. God dammit, I tried to get 'im to let me—" He watched the lieutenant, his voice suddenly desperate. "So act like *'im*, sir, even if you does feel like runnin' to yer mother!"

Triscott nodded jerkily. "Yes. Yes, thank you, Mr. Hawkins." He looked at the watching faces. "We shall follow *Wakeful*, and attack to—" He hesitated, thinking of the dead gunner. "To larboard. There's no time to transfer the carronades this time."

The boatswain frowned and then touched his arm. *"That's* more like it." He turned to the others nearby. "The lieutenant says we'll engage to larboard!" He brandished the axe. "So stand to, lads! Man the braces there!"

From aft Paice watched the sudden bustle, with even injured men limping to their stations, the sudden response as the punctured mainsail tugged at the long boom and filled reluctantly to the wind. He dragged himself to the tiller, the remaining helmsmen moving to give him room.

He gripped the well-worn tiller bar and felt his *Telemachus* answering him through the sea and rudder. His head dropped; he jerked up his chin, suddenly angry, and doubly determined.

God Almighty, what a bloody mess. He did not know or care if he had spoken aloud. A terrified lieutenant, and a third of his company killed or wounded. Two guns upended, and so many holes in the remaining sails they would be hard put to put about when the worst happened.

He closed his eyes and gasped while the agony lunged through him. Each time it was worse, each one like the thrust of a heated blade. He had bunched his waistcoat and shirt into a tight ball against the wound, and could feel his blood soaking his side and leg. It felt warm while the rest of his body was shaking and icy cold.

"Steady, men!" He peered forward but the compass seemed too misty to read. He said thickly, "Steer for the bugger's quarter!"

Chesshyre cried, "*Wakeful*'s nearly there!"

Paice leaned hard on the tiller and growled, "Get up on your feet, man! D'you want the people to see you cringing like a frightened cur?"

Chesshyre scrambled upright and stared at him wildly. *"God damn you!"*

"He most likely will!"

He heard Triscott yell, "All loaded, sir!" Paice hoped that nobody else had guessed just how terrified Triscott really was. But his was the true courage, he thought. More afraid of showing fear than of fear itself.

Hawkins hurried toward him, his gaze taking in the blood and Paice's ashen features.

He said, "*Wakeful*'s goin' to engage, sir! But I reckon the Frogs 'as got their chaser rigged again!"

Paice nodded, for a moment longer unable to

348

speak. Then he asked, "What can you see now, Mr. Hawkins?"

Hawkins turned away, his eyes burning. He had served with Paice longer than anyone. He respected him more than any other man, and to see him like this was worse than the stark death which had torn the decks open in a merciless bombardment. Now he could barely see. Hawkins said, "She's up to 'er starboard quarter!" He slammed his hands together and shouted, "The stern-chaser is runnin' out, sir!"

The explosions seemed joined as one, the stern-chaser's sharper note almost lost as *Wakeful*'s carronade belched fire at point-blank range even as her bowsprit outreached the enemy's quarter.

Paice asked, "*Well?* What's happened?"

Hawkins said, "Not sure, sir. *Wakeful*'s payin' off." He could not bear to look at Paice. "Their jib and fores'l are shot away."

"And the enemy—speak up, man!"

Hawkins watched the other vessel. The carronade had blasted away the stern windows and must have completely destroyed the makeshift stern-chaser. But otherwise she seemed intact, with only her foresail in disarray. Some of her hands were swarming aloft, and he saw the corvette begin to change course for the first time.

Then he said with chilled disbelief, "I think 'er steerin's gone, sir!"

Paice gripped his shoulder and shook him. *"Thank God!"* He peered along the torn and littered deck. "Ready there?"

Triscott called aft, "Aye, sir!"

Paice forced a grin. "We'll close with her now, before the buggers can rig new steering-gear!"

Hawkins asked urgently, "Will you let me fix a bandage?"

Their eyes met and Paice said, "You bloody fool. We both know the truth." Then he grimaced as the pain came back. "But I thank you, and I plead to my Maker that you see another dawn break, Mr. Hawkins!"

Hawkins swung away and waved his axe at some unemployed gun crews.

"To me, lads! Stand by to wear ship!"

He thought he heard faint cheering, and when he peered through the drifting smoke he saw *Wakeful* falling with the wind, temporarily out of control, her forecastle torn and splintered by that last charge of grapeshot.

He turned on his heel and shouted, "They'm cheerin' you, sir!" Then he waved his hat and yelled to his own men, *"Huzza, lads! A cheer for Wakeful!"*

They probably thought him mad, with death lurking so close. But it helped to save Hawkins's last reserve of strength. When he had turned aft he had seen that for Paice, victory, like defeat, was already out of reach.

Bolitho crouched on his hands and knees, his mind and ears cringing to the twin explosions. He had felt the massive charge of grapeshot smash into the bows, the screams and yells of men who had been scythed down even as the carronade had crashed inboard on its slide.

Then Allday's hand was beneath one armpit, lifting him to his feet, and he saw Queely offering him the old sword, which must have been cut from his belt by a single iron splinter. He felt his breeches, the jagged tear. The splinter had been that close.

Then he stared at the enemy's blackened stern. All windows demolished, the counter stove in like wet felt, the ornate taffrail high overhead splintered and unrecognisable.

Queely said hoarsely, "I think we got her steering, sir!" He looked at him with sudden desperation. "It's still not enough, is it?"

Bolitho watched the small figures swarming up the corvette's ratlines. Soon they would have a jury-rig, and be ready to face them once more. He shifted his glance to *Wakeful*'s foredeck. Six men dead, several more crawling to safety, or being carried to the hatchway. It was a miracle that anyone had survived.

It would take Queely's men an hour or more to re-rig the foresail and jib, and it was obvious that most of the forward rigging was rendered quite useless.

He watched the corvette turning very slowly, wind, and not rudder, carrying her off course. At this range she would use her broadside to bombard *Wakeful* until she followed *Snapdragon* to the seabed.

Allday exclaimed harshly, "Here comes *Telemachus*, Cap'n! By God, haven't they taken enough?"

Bolitho saw the other cutter bearing down on the drifting corvette for another attack, her sails in rags, her bulwark and forecastle looking as if they had been torn and gnawed by some nightmare monster.

He said quietly, "Give them a cheer, Mr. Queely. I'd not thought to see such valour this day."

The cheers echoed across the lively wave crests to the men on the other cutter, and probably to those working aloft aboard *La Foi* whose captain had ordered his stern-chaser to fire just seconds too late.

351

Men were running aft and shooting towards the oncoming cutter, but once under the corvette's quarter there was not a single nine-pounder which could be brought to bear.

The two carronades fired within seconds of one another. More debris burst from the stern and up through the deck beyond. The force of the explosion flung men from the gangways, while some even fell from the foresail yard to the deck below.

Bolitho stared until his eyes throbbed. Was it the constant strain, the agony of seeing men cut down, who had never known the savage demands of sea warfare? He seized Queely's arm. *"Is it going?"*

Queely nodded, unable to answer. The corvette's main mast was beginning to topple, held for a while by stays and shrouds until the weight of spars and wind-filled canvas took control. In those few seconds Bolitho saw some of the French sailors who had been sent aloft to free each frozen block by hand, stare down as they realised too late that there was no escape or survival.

Then, with rigging parting like pistol shots, the mast thundered over the side, to be snared by the remaining lines and dragged alongside to make any chance of steering impossible.

Bolitho watched the confusion, and knew that *Telemachus*'s last shots must have exploited the damage left by Queely's carronade.

Queely stared along the deck, his eyes wild, hungry for revenge. For Kempthorne and the others who lay dead and dying, for *Snapdragon*, and for his own command.

He said huskily, "We can still close with them, sir!

God damn them, they'll not be able to move before nightfall!"

The sailing master called anxiously, "*Telemachus* is standing away, sir!" He hesitated, as if he too shared Bolitho's mood. "She's dipped 'er Ensign, sir!"

Bolitho looked across the smoky water to where *Telemachus* was tacking very slowly away from her crippled adversary.

So Jonas Paice was dead. After all he had suffered, or perhaps because of it, he was now at peace.

Aloud he said firmly, "There's been enough killing. I'll not countenance cold-blooded murder and smear our name." His grey eyes lingered on the other battered cutter. No tall figure at her bulwark. He must have been dying then, even as he had doffed his hat in a last salute. "Or *his* especially. A worthy and honourable man."

Queely watched him dully, shoulders heaving from the madness of battle.

Bolitho looked at him and added, "We have saved Brennier and his treasure." He did not even glance at the drifting corvette which moments earlier had been ready to destroy them all. "Her captain will pay a more terrible price for his failure—so why fire on his men, who cannot defend themselves?"

He saw Allday watching him, his hands crossed over the hilt of his cutlass.

Bolitho said, "I'll board *Telemachus* as soon as we can work alongside. I shall take command and pass you a tow."

"You in command, sir?"

Bolitho smiled sadly. "Mine is the honour this time, Mr. Queely."

Later, as *Wakeful* tugged reluctantly at her towing

warp, Bolitho stood by *Telemachus*'s taffrail and looked at the damage, the bloodstains, the *hurt* of this vessel, where it had all begun for him.

Paice's body had been carried below and laid in the cabin. Hawkins the boatswain had asked about burying him at sea with the others. Bolitho had seen the boatswain's rough features soften as he had replied, "No, Mr. Hawkins. We'll lay him with his wife."

Allday heard and saw all of this, his mind dazed by the impossible shift of events.

The sky was even bluer than when he had looked up and offered his prayer. But his senses refused to accept any of it.

Only when Bolitho drew near him and said gently, "Look yonder, old friend. Tell me what you see."

Allday slowly raised his eyes, afraid of what might be there. Then in a small voice he murmured, "White cliffs, Cap'n."

Bolitho nodded, sharing the moment with him, and with Paice.

"I never thought to see them again."

Allday's face split into an unexpected grin.

"An' *that's* no error, Cap'n!"

At eight bells that evening, they saw the murky silhouette of Dover Castle.

The two little ships had come home.

Epilogue

ALLDAY glanced at the rigid marine sentry posted outside the frigate's stern cabin and after a brief hesitation thrust open the door. He had been surprised to discover that leaving England again had been so easy. There was no knowing what lay ahead, or what the war might mean to him and to his captain. But on the nine days' passage from Spithead aboard this frigate, the thirty-six-gun *Harvester*, it had felt more like a homecoming than some of the anxious moments they had shared in the past.

For a few seconds he stood by the screen door and saw Bolitho framed against the tall stern windows, with a sunlit panorama of sea and hazy coastline turning very slowly beyond as the frigate was laid on her final tack for the anchorage.

In the vivid light the Rock itself was a hint of land, rather than a solid reality; but just the sight of it made Allday tense with excitement, something else he found difficult to explain. Gibraltar was not merely the gateway to the Mediterranean this time. It opened for them a new life, another chance.

He nodded with slow approval. In his best uniform with the white lapels, and the newly adopted epaulettes gleaming on either shoulder, Bolitho was a far cry from the man in the shabby coat, facing the smugglers', then the corvette's, cannon fire with equal determination, and with a defiance which had never left him despite the setbacks, the suffering and the procession of disappointments which had taken them both to the Nore.

Bolitho turned and looked at him. "Well? What do you see?"

Allday had served with him for eleven years. Coxswain, friend, a right arm when need be. But Bolitho could still surprise him. Like now. The post-captain, a man envied not a little by *Harvester*'s young commanding officer; and yet he was anxious, even afraid, that he would fail, and betray all the hopes he had nursed since his return to duty.

"Like old times, Cap'n."

Bolitho turned and gazed at the glistening water below the counter. Nine days' passage. It had given him plenty of time to think and reflect. He thought of the frigate's young captain—not even posted yet, about his own age when he had been given *Phalarope*, when his and Allday's lives had crossed and been spliced together. It could not be easy to have him as a passenger, Bolitho thought. He had spent much of his time in these borrowed quarters, alone, and cherishing that precious moment when the orders had at last arrived for him.

"*To proceed with all despatch and upon receipt of these orders, to take upon you the charge and command of His Britannic Majesty's Ship* Hyperion."

He smiled wistfully. *The Old Hyperion*. Once something of a legend in the fleet. But what now after all those years, so many leagues sailed in the King's service?

Was he still disappointed that he had not been offered a frigate? He bit his lip and watched some

Spanish fishing boats idling above their images on the clear water.

It was not that. For Bolitho it was still too easy to recall the months of illness, then his daily pleading at the Admiralty for a command, any sort of ship they might condescend to provide. No, it was not that. Failure, then? The lurking fear of some weakness, or of the fever which had almost killed him with no less skill than an enemy ball or blade?

A muscle jumped in his cheek as the frigate's salute crashed across the bay, shaking the hull gun by gun like body blows. He heard the timed response from one of the Rock's batteries, and wondered why he was not even now on the quarterdeck seeking out his new command from the many vessels moored beneath the Rock's changeless protection.

He moved to a mirror which hung above one of his sea chests and studied his reflection, dispassionately, as he might a new subordinate. The uniform coat, with its broad white lapels and gilt buttons, the gold lace and epaulettes, should have offered immediate confidence. He knew from hard experience that no matter what kind of ship lay ahead, her company would be far more concerned about their new lord and master than he should be about them. But it failed to repel the uncertainty.

He thought of his last appointment and wondered still if the thankless task of recruiting at the Nore had been the true reason behind it. Had Lord Marcuard known even then that Bolitho was his choice for the other, deeper trust? Using his desperation for an appointment, a chance, no matter what, of returning to the one life he knew, and after losing Viola, needed more than ever. Perhaps he might never learn the complete truth.

He had found himself thinking of Paice very often. *That worthy man*, as he had described him in his despatch to the Admiralty. Many hundreds would die in this war, thousands, before it was ended in victory or defeat. Names and faces wiped away; and yet there were always the solitary men like Paice, whose memory never died.

He thought too of Vice-Amiral Brennier. He had received barely a mention in the newssheets, and Bolitho guessed that Marcuard's powerful hand was in that too. Perhaps Brennier would after all be involved in some counter-revolution.

The last gun thundered, and he heard voices calling commands as they were sponged out and prepared for the final cable or so of the frigate's entrance. Many eyes would be watching her. Letters from home— fresh orders—or simply the sight of a visitor from England to prove that Gibraltar was not entirely alone.

Allday crossed the cabin, the old sword held in his hands. "Ready, Cap'n?" He offered a grin. "They'll be expecting to see you on deck."

Bolitho extended his arms and heard Allday muttering to himself as he clipped on the sword.

"You needs a bit o' fattenin' up, Cap'n—"

"Damn your impertinence!"

Allday stood back and hid a smile. The fire was still there. It just needed coaxing out.

He ran his eyes over Bolitho's slim physique. Smart as paint. Only the cheekbones, and the deeper lines at his mouth betrayed the grief and the illness.

Bolitho picked up his hat and stared at it un-
seeingly.

It was very strange, he had often thought, that at
no time since the French treasure had been landed at
Dover and put under guard, had it ever been publicly
mentioned. Perhaps Marcuard, or even the prime
minister, Pitt, had their own ideas as to how it might
be used to better advantage?

How things had changed, just as he had known
they would; just as Hoblyn had so bitterly prophesied. Especially with Pitt, he thought. The man who
had cursed and condemned the smuggling gangs, who
had used dragoons and the gibbet to keep their
"trade" at bay if not under control, had now been
quoted as paying tribute to the very same scum.
"These men are my eyes, for without them I am blind
to intelligence of the enemy!" It was so incredible
that it was all the harder to believe, and to stomach.

As Queely had remarked dourly, "Had Delaval
stayed alive he might well have held a letter of marque
from the King!"

Queely: another face in memory. He had been
appointed to command a sturdy fourteen-gun brig at
Plymouth. Bolitho wondered if he would take all his
books with him to this different ship and different
war.

He turned to Allday. In his blue coat and flapping
white trousers, the tarred hat in one big fist, he would
stir the heart of any patriotic landsman, or woman.
Bolitho thought of the song he had heard when he
had boarded *Harvester* from Portsmouth. "Britons to
Arms". How poor Hoblyn would have laughed at
that.

He heard a yell from the quarterdeck, the instant

359

creak of the rudder as the wheel was put over. He could see it in his mind, as clearly as if he had been there on deck. The cluster of figures around the cathead ready to let go one anchor. The marines lined up on the poop in neat scarlet ranks. Captain Leach, anxious that everything should be right on this fair June morning, and justifiably proud of his fast passage from Spithead.

Bolitho shrugged and said quietly, "I can never find words to thank you, old friend." Their eyes met and he added, "Truly, heart of oak."

Then he walked through the screen door, nodding to the sentry before moving out into the sunlight, the expectant seamen who were waiting to furl every sail with only seconds between them when the anchor splashed down.

Leach turned to greet him, his expression wary.

Bolitho said, "You have a fine ship, Captain Leach. I envy you."

Leach watched him cross to the nettings, unable to conceal his astonishment. Surely Bolitho wanted for nothing? A post-captain of distinction who was almost certain to reach flag rank before this war showed signs of ending, unless he fell out of favour or was killed in battle . . .

"Ready, sir!"

Leach held up his arm. "Let go!"

Spray burst over the beakhead as the great anchor splashed down, but Bolitho did not see it.

I am a frigate captain.

And that gentle, remembered correction. *Were—a frigate captain.*

He ignored the voice in his memory and stared at

the large ships-of-war anchored astern of one which wore a vice-admiral's flag at the fore.

One of them is mine.

He looked at Allday and smiled freely for the first time.

"Not a lively frigate this time, old friend. We've much to discover!"

Allday nodded, satisfied. The smile gave light to the grey eyes once more. It was all there, he decided. Hope, determination, and a new strength which her death had once taken away.

He breathed out slowly.

The Old Hyperion. So be it then.

HARRY'S GAME
by Gerald Seymour
The Prime Minister himself was ordering a special agent to be sent into the dangerous world of the I.R.A. gunman. And Harry was the choice.

IN HONOUR BOUND
by Gerald Seymour
A thriller about the forgotten war of the 1980s in Afghanistan.

RED FOX
by Gerald Seymour
Two unconnected events make headlines. A British businessman is kidnapped and Italy's most wanted woman terrorist is captured.

ACCEPTABLE LOSSES
by Irwin Shaw
A strange voice in the dead of night full of menace and loathing shatters the confidence of Roger Damon, a respected literary agent.

CROSSINGS
by Danielle Steel

Armand de Villiers, the French Ambassador, was crossing the Atlantic, with his American wife, Liane, when they meet Nick and Hilary Burnham, The spark between Nick and Liane is instantaneous . . .

GOING HOME
by Danielle Steel

Gillian and Chris pledged their love for always, their happiness seemed complete. Until a moment's infidelity broke the bond they shared . . .

ONCE IN A LIFETIME
by Danielle Steel

To the doctors the woman in the ambulance was just another casualty—more beautiful than most . . .

THURSTON HOUSE
by Danielle Steel

At forty four, Jeremiah, a mining baron was marrying for the first time. Camille was a captivating eighteen-year-old girl. But can money buy happiness, a family . . . or love?

THE ADVENTURERS
by Vivian Stuart
The fifth in 'The Australians' series, opens in 1815 when two of its principal characters take part in the Battle of Waterloo.

THE COLONISTS
by Vivian Stuart
Sixth in 'The Australians' series, this novel opens in 1812 and covers the administration of General Sir Thomas Brisbane and General Ralph Darling.

THE EXPLORERS
by Vivian Stuart
The fourth novel in 'The Australians' series which continues the story of Australia from 1809 to 1813.

FIREFOX DOWN
by Craig Thomas
The stolen Firefox—Russia's most advanced and deadly aircraft is crippled, but Gant is determined not to abandon it.

SEA LEOPARD
by Craig Thomas
HMS 'Proteus', the latest British nuclear submarine, is lured to a sinister rendezvous in the Barents Sea.

THE DREAM TRADERS
by E. V. Thompson
This saga, is set against the background of intrigue, greed and misery surrounding the Chinese opium trade in the late 1830s.

THE RESTLESS SEA
by E. V. Thompson
A tale of love and adventure set against a panorama of Cornwall in the early 1800's.

SINGING SPEARS
by E. V. Thompson
Daniel Retallick, son of Josh and Miriam (from CHASE THE WIND) was growing up to manhood. This novel portrays his prime in Central Africa.

PAY ANY PRICE
by Ted Allbeury
After the Kennedy killings the heat was on—on the Mafia, the KGB, the Cubans, and the FBI. . .

MY SWEET AUDRINA
by Virginia Andrews
She wanted to be loved as much as the first Audrina, the sister who was perfect and beautiful—and dead.

PRIDE AND PREJUDICE
by Jane Austen
Mr. Bennet's five eligible daughters will never inherit their father's money. The family fortunes are destined to pass to a cousin. Should one of the daughters marry him?

CHINESE ALICE
by Pat Barr
The story of Alice Greenwood gives a complete picture of late 19th century China.

UNCUT JADE
by Pat Barr
In this sequel to CHINESE ALICE, Alice Greenwood finds herself widowed and alone in a turbulent China.

THE GRAND BABYLON HOTEL
by Arnold Bennett
A romantic thriller set in an exclusive London Hotel at the turn of the century.

A HERITAGE OF SHADOWS
by Madeleine Brent
This romantic novel, set in the 1890's, follows the fortunes of eighteen-year-old Hannah McLeod.

BARRINGTON'S WOMEN
by Steven Cade
In order to prevent Norway's gold reserves falling into German hands in 1940, Charles Barrington was forced to hide them in Borgas, a remote mountain village.

THE PLAGUE
by Albert Camus
The plague in question afflicted Oran in the 1940's.

THE RIDDLE OF THE SANDS
by Erskine Childers
First published in 1903 this thriller, deals with the discovery of a threatened invasion of England by a Continental power.

WHERE ARE THE CHILDREN?
by Mary Higgins Clark
A novel of suspense set in peaceful Cape Cod.

KING RAT
by James Clavell
Set in Changi, the most notorious Japanese POW camp in Asia.

THE BLACK VELVET GOWN
by Catherine Cookson
There would be times when Riah Millican would regret that her late miner husband had learned to read and then shared his knowledge with his family.

THE WHIP
by Catherine Cookson
Emma Molinero's dying father, a circus performer, sends her to live with an unknown English grandmother on a farm in Victorian Durham and to a life of misery.

SHANNON'S WAY
by A. J. Cronin
Robert Shannon, a devoted scientist had no time for anything outside his laboratory. But Jean Law had other plans for him.

THE JADE ALLIANCE
by Elizabeth Darrell
The story opens in 1905 in St. Petersburg with the Brusilov family swept up in the chaos of revolution.

BERLIN GAME
by Len Deighton
Bernard Samson had been behind a desk in Whitehall for five years when his bosses decided that he was the right man to slip into East Berlin.

HARD TIMES
by Charles Dickens
Conveys with realism the repulsive aspect of a Lancashire manufacturing town during the 1850s.

THE RICE DRAGON
by Emma Drummond
The story of Rupert Torrington and his bride Harriet, against a background of Hong Kong and Canton during the 1850s.

THE GLASS BLOWERS
by Daphne Du Maurier
A novel about the author's forebears, the Bussons, which gives an unusual glimpse of the events that led up to the French Revolution, and of the Revolution itself.

THE DOGS OF WAR
by Frederic Forsyth
The discovery of the existence of a mountain of platinum in a remote African republic causes Sir James Manson to hire an army of trained mercenaries to topple the government of Zangaro.

THE DAYS OF WINTER
by Cynthia Freeman
The story of a family caught between two world wars—a saga of pride and regret, of tears and joy.

REGENESIS
by Alexander Fullerton
It's 1990. The crew of the US submarine ARKANSAS appear to be the only survivors of a nuclear holocaust.

THE TORCHBEARERS
by Alexander Fullerton
1942: Captain Nicholas Everard has to escort a big, slow convoy . . . a sacrificial convoy. . .

DAUGHTER OF THE HOUSE
by Catherine Gaskin
An account of the destroying impact of love which is set among the tidal creeks and scattered cottages of the Essex Marshes.

FAMILY AFFAIRS
by Catherine Gaskin

Born in Ireland in the Great Depression, the illegitimate daughter of a servant, Kelly Anderson's birthright was poverty and shame.

THE SUMMER OF THE SPANISH WOMAN
by Catherine Gaskin

Clonmara—the wild, beautiful Irish estate in County Wicklow is a fitting home for the handsome, reckless Blodmore family.

THE TILSIT INHERITANCE
by Catherine Gaskin

Ginny Tilsit had been raised on an island paradise in the Caribbean. She knew nothing of her family's bitter inheritance half the world away.

THE FINAL DIAGNOSIS
by Arthur Hailey

Set in a busy American hospital, the story of a young pathologist and his efforts to restore the standards of a hospital controlled by an ageing, once brilliant doctor.

IN HIGH PLACES
by Arthur Hailey

The theme of this novel is a projected Act of Union between Canada and the United States in order that both should survive the effect of a possible nuclear war.

RED DRAGON
by Thomas Harris

A ritual murderer is on the loose. Only one man can get inside that twisted mind— forensic expert, Will Graham.

CATCH–22
by Joseph Heller

Anti-war novels are legion; this is a war novel that is anti-death, a comic savage tribute to those who aren't interested in dying.

THE SURVIVOR
by James Herbert

David is the only survivor from an accident whose aftermath leaves a lingering sense of evil and menace in the quiet countryside.

LOST HORIZON
by James Hilton

A small plane carrying four passengers crash-lands in the unexplored Tibetan wilderness.

THE TIME OF THE HUNTER'S MOON
by Victoria Holt
When Cordelia Grant accepts an appointment to a girls' school in Devon, she does not anticipate anyone from her past re-emerging in her new life.

THE FOUNDER OF THE HOUSE
by Naomi Jacob
The first volume of a family saga which begins in Vienna, and introduces Emmanuel Gollantz.

"THAT WILD LIE . . ."
by Naomi Jacob
The second volume in the Gollantz saga begun with THE FOUNDER OF THE HOUSE.

IN A FAR COUNTRY
by Adam Kennedy
Christine Wheatley knows she is going to marry Fred Deets, that is until she meets Roy Lavidge.

AUTUMN ALLEY
by Lena Kennedy
Against the background of London's East End from the turn of the Century to the 1830's a saga of three generations of ordinary, yet extraordinary people.